On Walking With Angels

SHEILA M. WATSON

Best wishes,
Sheila Watson

© Copyright 2004 Sheila M. Watson.
All rights reserved.

No part of this publication may be reproduced, stored in a retrieval system, or transmitted, in any form or by any means, electronic, mechanical, photocopying, recording, or otherwise, without the written prior permission of the author.

Note for Librarians: a cataloguing record for this book that includes Dewey Classification and US Library of Congress numbers is available from the National Library of Canada. The complete cataloguing record can be obtained from the National Library's online database at:
www.nlc-bnc.ca/amicus/index-e.html
ISBN 1-4120-3103-6

Printed in Victoria, BC, Canada

TRAFFORD

This book was published *on-demand* in cooperation with Trafford Publishing.
On-demand publishing is a unique process and service of making a book available for retail sale to the public taking advantage of on-demand manufacturing and Internet marketing. **On-demand publishing** includes promotions, retail sales, manufacturing, order fulfilment, accounting and collecting royalties on behalf of the author.

Suite 6E, 2333 Government St.,
Victoria, B.C. V8T 4P4, CANADA
Phone   250-383-6864
Toll-free   1-888-232-4444
Fax   250-383-6804
E-mail   sales@trafford.com
www.trafford.com/robots/04-0930.html

10   9   8   7   6   5   4   3

DEDICATION

To Noni and Al, whose teenage marriage has survived the test of time; and to Dean, whose courageous and victorious battle with cancer gave me the inspiration to write this book.

CHAPTER ONE

A light drizzle was falling that night as Duncan McCallum steered the old blue Desoto around the sharp corners of the twisty gravel road high above the lake. Beside him, his wife Florence, made small talk of the musical they had just seen in Harrison, and of the homemade bread and huckleberry jam they would have with their tea when they got home.

Above them on the hillside, three whitetail does made their way daintily down toward the road, intent on crossing to the narrow trail below the road that led down to their watering place on Fletcher Creek. Florence saw the blur of motion first and cried out a warning to her husband. She slammed her foot down on the non- existent brake pedal at her feet. The does bounded across the road in front of the car as Duncan swerved to avoid them. The first two made it across, but the third, mesmerized by the headlights, hesitated just long enough for the right fender to catch her hip. The car went into a spin as the doe flipped up onto the hood and crashed through the windshield. Florence put a hand over her eyes to protect them from the flying shards of glass. A flash of instinct told her that the little doe had died instantly. *Thank God*, she thought, but had no time left to say the words.

Duncan knew and saw nothing but

blackness as the Desoto slid backwards, smashed through the guardrail, and plummeted down the steep embankment. It bounced off jagged rocks and snapped trees for almost five hundred feet down before it landed nose first and crumpled with a sigh, like an old accordion wheezing out its last notes.

*   *   *   *   *   *

Despite the heat of the bonfire, Jodi felt a shudder run down her spine. Try as she might, she couldn't get the vision of her parent's accident out of her mind. They had been dead for three months now, but Jodi's grief was as sharp and painful as a newly opened wound. She squatted on her heels and turned the stick slowly over the coals. She had two marshmallows impaled on the end of the willow. She liked them cooked to a golden brown.

    Jodi's friend, Linda Shannon, sat on a beached log just behind her, chatting to Bob Schaumburg, her new boyfriend. Linda, who had short, sandy hair and a freckled face, lived just across the lane from Jodi. The girls had been best friends since the second grade when Jodi moved to Kelso from another small mining community in the Kokanee District.

    Jodi slipped the carefully roasted marshmallows off the end of the willow stick and ate them slowly. "You guys want a marshmallow?" she asked over her shoulder. Linda and Bob were holding hands and giggling, totally immersed in each other. Jodi shrugged and stuck another marshmallow on for herself. Now that Linda had a boyfriend, Jodi could sense that things had changed between them. The days of being little tomboys, hiking up the surrounding mountains, playing Cowboys and Indians, swimming in the cold lake, and doing their chores together were long gone.

    Jodi hadn't really wanted to come to the beach party, but it was somewhere to go to get away from the loneliness. Besides, it was a beautiful, warm, August night; the kind that made her feel restless and yearning.

    Jodi sat down on the sand with her back to the big log and pulled her knees up to her chin. Someone had brought down a transistor radio and she sang along softly with the hit tunes that were playing.

    Even before loss and loneliness had taken over her life Jodi had been quiet. She never pushed her opinion on anyone. Rather than do team sports or other group activities, she preferred riding bareback on Blossom, her black and white pinto pony.

    More kids arrived, hearing about the party and curious to see what was going on. Small groups stood around talking and laughing. Some had smokes in their hands, and Jodi could smell beer and maybe something stronger than cigarette smoke.

Suddenly, Jodi got a strange feeling and looked up across the fire into bright blue eyes partly hidden by unruly strands of straw blond hair. Brett Randall, a boy she had just met this afternoon, was staring at her. She smiled and raised her hand in greeting. He nodded back and in a few minutes excused himself from his friends and came over to her. He picked up a willow stick, put two marshmallows on the pointy end, and, squatting beside her, held them over a small flame at the edge of the fire.

"Hi, horse lady." He turned towards her and flashed her a dazzling smile. "I was hoping you'd be here tonight."

"Hi, home run hero." she replied.

A bunch of the gang had been playing softball that afternoon, and Jodi was riding by on Blossom just as Brett hit a whopper of a homerun. Now she felt a surge of excitement at his nearness and the fact that he had hoped to see her again.

As Brett knelt by the fire, slowly turning the willow stick in his hands, the dancing flames picked up the highlights in his blond hair, making it shine like burnished copper. His eyes were dark and half closed against the smoke and heat of the fire. He was wearing jeans, sneakers, and a red flannel shirt, with the sleeves rolled up halfway, exposing his muscular brown arms. His features were so even and perfect that Jodi couldn't't take her eyes off him. She thought he must look like a Norse God- Odin -or one of those Scandinavian mythological creatures."Your hair is pretty, hanging loose like that," Brett said, turning to glance at her. "At the game you had it in two braids." She blushed, and to cover it, Jodi put her hand to her face and brushed away a few wisps of long, dark, chestnut hair.

Standing up gracefully and turning towards her, Brett lowered the stick of marshmallows and asked, "Would you like one of these?"

"Sure. How did you know I like them cooked just like this?"

"I watched you cook the last ones, that's how".

"Really?" she asked, biting into the gooey mess. "How long have you been here?"

Brett laughed." Long enough to know that you're alone." He laid the stick on the log, and sat down close beside her, their backs against the rough driftwood log. Jodi hugged her knees and glanced at him quickly, almost in panic.

"I guess I was off in dreamy-dream land somewhere," she apologized. I didn't even see you there."

"And what were you dreaming about, if I may ask such a personal question?" Brett finished the marshmallow and licked his fingers.

Jodi glanced at him shyly. She didn't feel comfortable flirting, but something about Brett gave her confidence. "Well, it seems that today I met someone special, and he's been on my mind ever since."

Brett chuckled, then leaned close to her so that their bodies were touching lightly, and said, "That's funny, because today I met a pretty girl mounted on a beautiful horse. I think she may have come from the mists of the lake, because she rode up from the water with her long pigtails flying out behind her, and that pony skimmed across the ground like she had wings on her feet."

Now it was Jodi's turn to laugh. She giggled and looked into his eyes. "Ooo, you are such a terrible tease." She was starting to have fun. She dropped her hands down beside her, self consciously, sifting sand through her fingers, while staring at the fire. She felt giddy with excitement.

Brett seized the opportunity to take her hand. He snuggled closer to her and entwined his fingers with hers.

Now that Jodi and Brett understood and accepted that there was an attraction between them, they relaxed and began to enjoy each other's company. Much to her surprise, Jodi found him very easy to talk to. Their closeness did not go unnoticed. Jodi was aware of some nasty jealous looks from the older girls who had been tagging around with Brett and his cousin Rick earlier that day. She said, "I don't think your friends are very happy about you paying attention to me."

Brett shrugged. "Don't worry about it. They're not really friends. This may sound conceited, but girls flirt with me because I do pretty well at track and field, and I'm on the senior basketball team. Girls just hang around cause I'm sort of a sport jock. But I don't want to go out with any of them. I want a girlfriend who likes me for the person I am inside, not what I appear to be. I want someone I can talk to and just be myself. I like you."

Brett looked into her eyes for a long moment. Jodi thought he was going to kiss her, but he continued, " You're quiet, and down to earth; not phoney and loud like most of them. And besides, you've got really cool eyes - blue, with little brown and green flecks."

Jodi nodded and smiled. "Like the wild heather. That's what my mom always told me." She felt a stab of sorrow at the memory, but it couldn't destroy her elation over Brett's interest in her.

Getting to her feet, she pulled him up. "Come on, let's go get a hot dog." There was lots of food. Everybody had brought something; wieners, buns, chips, pop, squares, cookies, marshmallows, and under the tables and behind the logs there were stashes of beer.

They got themselves a couple of wieners to cook, and sat on the log side by side eating them. Jodi introduced Brett to Linda and Bob, and they all joked and laughed for a while. Brett said, "I'm going to get myself a beer. Anyone else want one?"

Bob and Linda said yes, they would have one. "Jodi?" Brett asked, eyebrows raised.

"No thanks," she replied, feeling somewhat embarrassed. At sixteen, she had never even tasted beer before.

Brett disappeared into the darkness and came back with three cold bottles. He sat on the log beside Jodi, took a long drink, and slipped his arm around her, holding her tight. Bob and Linda spread out a blanket by the fire to enjoy theirs.

To hide her embarrassment, Jodi tried to explain. "My parents never had any alcohol in the house, except maybe at Christmas time, when Dad got a bottle of sherry for visitors that dropped in." She felt a little annoyed and disappointed that Brett liked beer. She continued, "I know that most dads down a few beers when they get home from work in the mines, or sawmills. And I know that the guys that come in from the logging camps are pretty big drinkers, but my dad or my mom never touched the stuff."

Brett leaned close to her and whispered, "I heard about you losing your parents in that accident. I'm sorry." When Jodi didn't answer, he asked, "What did your dad do?"

"Oh", Jodi shrugged, "Dad was an Accountant. He did the books for some of the stores in town and for the two doctors. He was involved in lots of community stuff too, like the Scouts and church choir. I guess you could say he was a 'goody two shoes.'"

Brett grunted. "Well, nothing wrong with that. But just because you have a few drinks doesn't mean you're an outlaw or something. Here, have a little taste. It's not so bad."

Jodi almost said no, then changed her mind. She took the bottle and tipped it to her lips quickly, taking a small mouthful. She swallowed it, shuddered, and made a face. "Ugh! It's awful!"

He laughed. "It's an acquired taste, I guess. I got to like it last summer when I was out with a forestry crew planting seedlings. It sure hit the spot at the end of a long hot day. Don't get me wrong, though. I don't drink very much. I enjoy a beer once in a while, that's all."

Jodi was relieved to hear this, and when he offered it to her again, took the bottle for another taste. They ended up sharing it back and forth, and Jodi got a little buzz from it. She felt light hearted and slightly giggly, totally relaxed and happy.

The party was starting to swing. The music was blaring, and some couples tried to dance on the sand. It worked okay for the slow ones, as long as they didn't mind sand in their shoes, but trying to jive in the sand was hilarious.

By eleven p.m. a half moon had risen above the mountains over the lake. The air was still warm. Brett took Jodi's hand in his and kissed her fingers. "Let's get away from this noise, and go for a walk," he suggested.

CHAPTER TWO

Hand in hand, Jodi and Brett headed down the beach toward the water's edge. It seemed very dark at first, but Jodi knew the way. She was familiar with every log and rock on that part of the beach, and holding Brett's hand, guided him around the dangers. Soon their eyes adjusted to the lack of firelight as they walked along the shore. The waves lapped gently on the shingle, and the moon sent a silvery, shimmering beam dancing across the water. " How old are you Jodi? Sixteen? Seventeen?" Brett asked.

"I'll be seventeen in February."

"So," he paused, "Sweet sixteen and never been kissed, right?"

"Right," she replied honestly.

Brett stopped and turned her towards him, slipping his arms around her.

Pulling her to him, he said softly, "I could change that, if you wanted me to."

"Okay," Jodi whispered.

Brett laid his cheek against hers and stroked her silky hair. At seventeen, he had kissed a lot of girls. He had done a little exploring too, but had managed to keep himself under control so far.

Jodi relaxed against him and tentatively moved her hands up and down his back, marvelling at the feel of his muscles under his shirt. She reached up and put her arms around his neck. He kissed her lightly on both cheeks, and then on the mouth. His lips were full and sensuous, and Jodi was thrilled at the feeling the kisses created.

Jodi didn't want to just be kissed. She kissed him back with all the passion and feeling she could muster. She pressed against him and felt the desire there. She played with the hair on his neck. She loved the way it curled around her fingers. They kissed twice more, and breathing heavily, Jodi reluctantly pushed herself away from him.

Holding hands, but lost in their own thoughts, they walked along the beach a ways. Jodi was surprised and elated at how exciting it was to be kissed by Brett. Her body was alive and tingling with the feel of his hands on her.

They could see fairly well now, and coming to a log, Brett sat and pulled her down beside him. The stars sparkled overhead in glorious profusion. They always filled Jodi with wonder and lately, with great sadness. They made her think of her lost mom and dad. She wondered where they were; if they were up in those vast heavens somewhere; if they could see how happy she was tonight.

Without warning, the tears started to slide down her cheeks. In the moonlight, Brett saw the tears and was immediately concerned. He encircled her in his arms.

"Hey, what is it?" he asked gently. "Did I scare you back there? Did I come on too strong?"

Jodi cried harder, both hands over her face, elbows resting on her knees, which shook with her sobs.

"Oh God, Jodi - don't. I'm really sorry if I hurt you in some way."

She managed to shake her head and blurt out, "It's not you! It's just that I can't go home and tell my mom what a wonderful guy I just met." She sobbed into her hands, her shoulders shaking. Her long hair hung over her face and muffled the sound of her crying.

Brett was both relieved that Jodi wasn't upset with him and taken aback at her pain and sorrow. He lifted her hair off her face with a gentle touch of his fingers. At his touch she threw her arms around him, burying her face in his chest. He held her close and rocked her until her crying ceased. "Would you like to tell me about it?" he asked gently.

Jodi sat up and fished around in her overalls pocket for a tissue. She wiped her eyes and blew her nose, and nodded. "There isn't much to tell, I guess. It was three months ago, on a Saturday, May the 16th. Mom and Dad had gone to Harrison for the day to do some grocery shopping, and Dad had an appointment with a chiropractor. He had an old hip injury from his mining days and it was bothering him. They used to go down there about every two or three months, kind of like a date or something. They'd go out for dinner and maybe a show or a play or something.

They usually got back around midnight."

Brett held her hands in his, and said, "Go on, I'm listening."

Jodi swallowed, took a deep breath and continued. "I was in bed. My sister Carol and her boyfriend Len had come back from the show and were downstairs. I woke up some time later when I heard voices. I looked at my clock and it was almost two in the morning. I tried to make out who was down there, but I couldn't recognize the voices. I had a terrible feeling that something was wrong."

Brett wiped away two tears that trickled down her cheeks and held her hands tightly. "Go on," he said.

"I pulled on some jeans and a shirt and went down. A policeman was there, and Linda's dad, and our Minister. I knew by their faces that Mom and Dad had been in an accident. Carol was crying, and she ran over and grabbed me. Len held on to me too, and they told me that the car had gone over the cliff at Fletcher Bluffs, and they had both been killed. The cop said they could tell by the skid marks that Dad had tried to avoid hitting a deer. You know what the road is like there, twisty, with steep drop offs." Jodi shivered. "Mom always hated that piece of road. Maybe she had a premonition that she would die there someday. They were such good people. I don't understand why they had to die."

Brett took a deep breath and let it

out slowly. "I don't know why these things happen either. I'm so sorry Jodi." He hugged her again.

She held on to him too. "Just don't ever say you hate your parents. I've heard kids say that when they don't get their own way, and I feel like telling them what it's like not to have any parents around."

"I'll remember that," he said softly.

Jodi slid off the log backwards and lay down on the still-warm sand with her arm under her head. She gazed up at the stars, sprinkled like a million jewels overhead. Brett hesitated for just a few seconds, and then dropped down beside her. They lay close with their heads touching. Brett took her hand while Jodi continued. "Marnie and Rob, that's my sister and her husband from Vancouver, came up for the funeral, and stayed a few days making the arrangements. They took care of the bills and things. They wanted us to go back with them, but I refused. I couldn't leave my animals. They still want us to come. I think Carol wants to go, but I don't for sure." Brett detected a note of defiance in her voice. She sounded stronger now.

"Anyway, Carol and I are doing okay. The house is paid for, and there was a little insurance money that we'll keep to pay the taxes and utilities. Carol's wages at the bakery provide us with grocery money. We don't need much. We grow all our own vegetables and fruit, and we have milk, eggs, and some meat from the chickens and goats. We get our wood off the beach. Blossom eats grass for eight months of the year, and I work at any job I can get to pay for her winter feed."

Brett kissed her on the cheek. "So, you're independent." he said. "I like that."

"Yeah, I know what I want." Reaching out for him, she whispered, "I want you." She undid the snaps on his flannel shirt, running her fingers over his chest and back. His bare skin was like velvet under her exploring fingers. His hand slipped under her shirt and undid her bra. Then he was kissing her throat, her shoulders, and her breasts. She pulled his shirt off.

"Jodi! We have to stop," Brett gasped. "I can't take any more of this. Things are just moving too fast."

Jodi didn't answer, but continued to stroke his bare back, slowly and sensuously. "God, Jodi, don't!" Brett pulled away and took her hands, holding them tightly. He was breathing hard.

"I don't think you understand," she said. "I want to make love with you."

Brett stared at her for a moment, unbelieving, then got to his feet, brushing sand off his jeans. "Come on," he said, "we'd better get back."

Jodi stood up too, but slipped off her overalls and underwear. Laying them on the sand, she put her arms around Brett's waist and laid her head on his bare chest. He couldn't resist running his hands down her naked body. They kissed again, deeply. There was nothing amateurish in the way Jodi kissed him now. She had learned fast.

Brett was so full of desire he could barely speak, but he asked one more time. "Are you sure you want to do this?"

"Yes. Absolutely." She popped the snap on his fly, and un-did the zipper. He sighed, gave in to the inevitable, and pulled off his jeans.

Moments later, Jodi and Brett lay together kissing and touching. They had been so hot before, but now, as the sweat dried on their naked bodies, the air felt cold. Jodi shivered, even though Brett's body mostly covered her. He lifted himself off her onto his knees, and then stood up, pulling her up too.

"Come on," he said, "Let's get dressed. I'll take you home."

Jodi shook sand out of her hair and brushed it off her body. Without a word, the lovers dressed in the semi-dark, then sat on the log and dumped sand out of their shoes. Holding hands, they made their way up through the willows to the road, through the park, and on up to Jodi's house. They walked quietly, neither one knowing how to express the thoughts and emotions that whirled around in their minds. Jodi felt strangely elated. Never in her wildest dreams would she have done what she did tonight. It was entirely out of character for her to be the leader in anything, especially a sexual encounter. She knew she had played with fire and that it was extremely dangerous, but she felt no guilt or remorse. In fact, she could hardly contain her happiness.

Jodi and Brett came up the back alley in the dark and entered the yard by the back gate. The house was in darkness. Scamp, Jodi's little black Cocker Spaniel, barked at their approach and she quickly shushed him, bending over to pet his wriggling little body.

Brett took Jodi in his arms and held her tight. She snuggled her head under his chin and hugged him. She hated to let him go or see the evening end. Brett's voice was husky as he whispered against her ear, "I don't know what to think about tonight. It was wonderful, but also scary. I don't know where we go from here." He paused, unsure of what to say. "Are you sorry?"

Jodi raised her head, and looked at him. "No, I'm not. I'm happy, but I'm also in a state of disbelief. I have never done anything like that before - never wanted anything so badly before."

"Not even Blossom?" he asked, grinning.

"Well, maybe Blossom, but that was a little girl's dream come true. This was different. Yeah, it was special. I think we have lots to think about; lots of feelings to sort out".

"Yeah, I guess." Brett agreed. "I don't

know when I can see you again. I don't have a car, and it will be difficult to get up here, but I'll phone you, okay? What's your number?"

"It's 99-X. You can call me collect if you want."

"I might have to do that if my parents get too suspicious." He sighed. "I should get going. It seems pretty strange to say thanks for a wonderful evening."

She laughed. "It was an *enchanted* evening! I think we were under a fairy spell. *They* made us do it."

Brett kissed her several times, pushing himself away reluctantly.

"That will have to last us for a long time," he said, holding her hands in his. "So long, Princess."

"Goodnight, Prince Charming." she giggled.

Brett disappeared into the darkness. Jodi stood still for a moment, listening to his footsteps receding across the lawn, and then she and the little black dog entered the quiet dark house.

Brett made his way back through the darkened yard, out the back gate, and down the alley. His footsteps made no noise on the soft dirt track as he passed the sleeping campers in the park. He worried as he walked. He liked Jodi a lot, and sure he had wanted to make love with her, but he felt it was too soon. They didn't know each other well enough. They hadn't followed the rules, and it bothered him. Still, she fascinated him and he was thrilled with the experience they'd just had. It was just like he'd always hoped it would be, like being on a roller coaster that you couldn't stop; fast, wild and exciting.

Nearing the beach, Brett could see a small, red light through the willows. Somebody was still at the fire. He stood in the shadows for a moment, and then approached quietly out of the darkness. Rick and Diane Peters were cuddled up on a blanket near the fire with their backs to a big log. A few more couples sat around drinking beer.

"Well, well, well! Look who's back! Where the hell have you been, man?" A chorus of suggestive catcalls and whistles greeted him. He heard the word 'score' mentioned and was glad of the darkness. Brett was sure he was blushing. He sat on the bench of the picnic table, facing the fire and when the noise subsided, said: "Jodi and I went for a walk on the beach...then I took her home. That's all." He heard some more snide comments such as 'hell of a long walk' and 'how convenient - nobody home' but he ignored them.

Rick piped up, "You must be tired from all that walking. Check the cooler, there might be a beer left."

Gratefully, Brett got up and rummaged in the cooler. He found a beer, popped the cap, and took a long swig. His mind was full of the images of Jodi. He didn't want to hang around here and listen to these jokers. He sat and sipped his beer in silence.

When the last two beers were gone, the party ground to a standstill. The girls gathered up the bottles and garbage, while the boys carried water up from the lake and doused the fire. They carried the stuff up to Rick's truck and boisterously piled into the back. Rick, Diane, and Brett climbed into the cab. Rick drove slowly. He'd had a little too much to drink, and besides, he liked having Diane pressed up against his side with her hand resting on his thigh. He took the girls home, waiting while their dates said goodnight and hopped back into the truck. Finally it was his turn with Diane. Brett waited in the cab while Rick walked her to her door and kissed her goodnight. It didn't take long. He could see her tomorrow and every day when school started. Brett missed Jodi already. He would be going back to Harrison with his mom in the morning, so there wouldn't be a chance to see her again.

Rick got back in and headed the truck for home. "Well, how did it go tonight?" he asked, giving Brett a searching glance. "You seem pretty quiet."

Brett didn't answer right away. He wasn't sure how much to tell his cousin. He let out a deep breath. "I like her a lot. We hit it off really well...we had a great time together...it's going to be tough to see her again though." Then, changing the subject, he asked, "Are we going to be in trouble at home?"

Rick shook his head. "I don't think so. They knew this was our summer-end bash before school starts. They probably won't be up." He was right. The porch light was on for them, but the house was dark. Rick parked the truck, and the two slightly tipsy boys tiptoed up the stairs to bed.

CHAPTER THREE

Jodi swam up from the depths of sleep, still dreaming of a golden-haired boy on a golden horse. She opened her eyes to see her own familiar room, the walls covered with horse pictures. *Had last night been a dream too?* She turned over and saw her overalls and shirt on the floor where she had dropped them before climbing into bed. There were still traces of sand on her clothes, and she could feel it in her hair too. She smiled to herself, and ran her hands over her body, then curled up tight and hugged herself. It was true! It had happened! She - Jodi McCallum - had made love!

She yawned and stretched then, got up, went downstairs, started the fire in the kitchen stove, and was showered, dressed, and cooking breakfast when Carol came down.

"Coffee?" Jodi asked.

Carol nodded. She had come in even later than Jodi last night and was still sleepy. Her dark brown shoulder length hair was still rolled around the fat curlers she used to make her hair full and bouncy, and her eyes, which were the same shade as Jodi's, were distant and dreamy as she remembered how tender and loving Len had been with her just hours before.

"How was your date with Len?" Jodi asked, as she scrambled the eggs.

"Oh, the usual," said Carol, trying to

be vague. " We went to the show - that western that's playing - then we went for burgers, then a drive up the lake. We parked at Bennett's Point for a while. The moon was beautiful on the lake last night. Did you notice?"

    Jodi said she had and proceeded to tell Carol about the beach party, leaving out her encounter with Brett. She didn't dare tell Carol the truth. She might never see him again, and the whole evening would fade into a beautiful dream. She decided to keep her secret locked up for now.

A week remained before school started and much work needed to be done. Because of Carol's job at the Bayside Bakery, most of it fell to Jodi. There was a huge garden to harvest. The corn and beans had to be picked and processed. The onions must be tied in bunches and hung to dry from the porch ceiling. Pickles from the cucumbers and beets had to be made, and later on the potatoes, carrots, and turnips needed to be dug and stored in crates in the basement. The squash, zucchini, and pumpkins had to be cured in the sun and covered at night in case of frost. As well as the vegetables, there were bushels of fruit to pick. Cherries, plums and apricots were already canned, but now the apples and pears had to be stored in boxes, bins, and barrels in the porch. It was a big job, and Jodi worked diligently in all her spare time to get it done.

There was also the endless job of bringing wood up from the beach. For this task, Blossom was indispensable. Jodi rigged a makeshift harness for her out of gunnysacks, an old cinch, and some soft, cotton rope. With this device, the pony, with Jodi leading her, pulled whole logs up to the yard. Len was a great help, bringing his chainsaw to buck up the wood, while Jodi and Carol stacked it in the woodshed.

Jodi also devised another way to bring up the small pieces of driftwood that they used in the kitchen stove and for starting the fires. She spread out a large canvas tarp on the sand and threw the wood into the center. Then, gathering up the edges by a rope passed through the eyelets, she pulled it into a large bundle. With the rope tied in a quick-release knot to the makeshift harness, Blossom obligingly pulled the load home. Often Jodi would bring a load for the Shannons too. It was much more efficient than carrying two burlap sacks up by yourself, which is how Linda had to do it.

Jodi's days were full. She worked cheerfully and hard on the outside jobs, but she hated the long hours working over the hot stove, canning and preserving the jars of food that they must have for the winter months. Only the memory of Brett kept her going. He was in her thoughts constantly. She re-lived over and over every look, word, and touch that they had shared. She longed to see him again. Falling into bed exhausted every night she prayed that he would come back into her life somehow. But she did not hear from him.

September came, and Jodi enrolled in grade eleven. She went through the motions of going to her new classes and pretending to have fun. She walked to school with Linda and listened to her prattle on about Bob. She listened as Linda told how they held hands and kissed on dates, and that he phoned her every night. Linda stopped asking if she had heard from Brett. Jodi didn't talk about him. She was heart-broken and convinced that he had dropped her.
    Jodi was so busy with her schoolwork, chores, getting the garden and wood in, and making supper for herself and Carol every night, that she hardly noticed the season changing. The days were still hot with clear blue skies; but by afternoon, a chill was in the air, and some nights the ground was covered with frost. The maples and chestnuts that lined the streets were ablaze with glorious colours; but, for once, they didn't interest Jodi.

One night, in the third week of September, Jodi lay in bed trying to read. Tears slid down her cheeks. Her mind drifted off constantly to Brett, and she couldn't concentrate on the story. She kept reading the same page over and over, not comprehending what the words meant.

Jodi glanced at the calendar on her bedside table. It would be a month tomorrow since she and Brett had met and made love on the beach. Suddenly, her heart beat faster, and the blood rushed to her cheeks. Jeez! She was late. Oh, dear God, she was overdue! Jodi frantically flipped the calendar back to August. Then, counting to today's date, she counted thirty-one days. Her period usually came on the 27th or 28th day. Jodi took a pen and circled August 23, then drew an arrow through it.

Closing the book as a lost cause, and turning out the light, Jodi told herself not to panic; her period could still come. She'd been working too hard, that's all. She pretended to be asleep when Carol came up to bed, but sleep evaded her. The more she tried to relax, and not think about her period, the more tense she became. She stared, wide-eyed at the black ceiling, feeling numb with fear. Her head began to ache.

Finally, unable to sleep, Jodi crept out of bed and went downstairs. Quietly she lifted the lid on the kitchen range and dropped some wood onto the coals. Putting the kettle on to heat, she pulled a chair up to the stove and opened the oven door, resting and warming her feet on it. When the water was steaming, she made herself a drink of hot milk and swallowed two aspirins from the medicine cabinet. She sat by the fire in a daze, sipping the warm drink, until she was drowsy enough to crawl into bed and sleep.

The next few days at school were hard. Jodi forced herself to pay attention long enough to get the gist of her lessons and to do her homework, but she had trouble keeping her mind focused on the work and had to be sharply reprimanded several times.

    Finally, late in September, on a Sunday afternoon, one month and three days after the beach party, the longed for, now unexpected phone-call came. Jodi had the record player turned up loud in the living room, so she could hear it in the kitchen as she made pickled beets. She didn't hear the phone ringing at first.

    Then, all of a sudden, between songs on the Peter, Paul, and Mary album, she heard it. She was completely stunned when she answered and the operator asked if she would accept a collect call from Brett Randall. "Yes!" she almost shouted, competing with the noise. "But just a minute please." She rushed over and lifted the arm off the record, and shut the machine off. Heart racing, she picked up the phone and said, "Hello?"

    "Hi Princess," came the deep voice over the wire, and Jodi almost collapsed with joy at hearing him again. Her tinkly little laugh spilled over. "I don't look like a Princess today. I'm up to my elbows in beet juice, and I smell like vinegar and cloves. I'm making pickles."

"Mmm...sounds good," Brett answered. "You're so different, aren't you? I don't know any other girls who make pickles."

"Well, I kind of have to use up all this garden produce. I used to help Mom do it, but this is the first time I've done it by myself." Jodi went on to tell him how busy she had been getting wood up from the beach with Blossom's help, digging and storing vegetables, and picking apples. They talked about school, and Brett told her about his basketball and track teams. They chatted happily as if they'd never been apart. Then he said, "Jodi, I want to apologize for not calling you." When Jodi didn't answer, Brett went on. "I tried to forget you. I was confused and scared... about things...and I thought it might be best if we didn't see each other again." He paused, and still she waited. "But, damn it all, I can't stop thinking about you, and I miss you!" She listened, too overcome with emotion to speak. "Jodi?" She could hear the uncertainty in his voice. "Do you still like me?

"Of course," came her soft reply. "But, if I hadn't had so much work to keep me busy, I might have died from a broken heart. It's going to need some T.L.C. to mend it".

Brett chuckled. "It will have to be long-distance T.L.C. because I have no way to come up and see you. And phoning you as much as I would like to will get expensive, especially if we talk as long as we have today."

"We could write to each other," she suggested

"Yeah, I'd like that, even if it's just a few lines to know what you're doing and thinking." They exchanged addresses, and reluctantly ended their visit. Jodi was ecstatic as she hung up the phone. She was happier than she had been for weeks and went back to the kitchen to tackle pickle making with much more enthusiasm than before.

September slid quietly into October, and when Jodi's period didn't come she knew she was indeed pregnant. She felt none of the initial panic; instead, a sense of joy and wonder came over her as the realization dawned that she was going to have Brett's child. Now that he was keeping in touch with her by phone and by letter, Jodi did not feel so alone and hopeless. Still, she was afraid to tell him. She didn't want to lose him, or even go through another month of silence while he sorted out his feelings.

Jodi began to notice her body changing, but still she kept it to herself. The first thing was the increased hunger.

Then, sometimes when she was working hard, she felt dizzy and had to sit down for a while. When she rode Blossom she had no desire to gallop wildly as she used to do. She rode quietly, bundled up against the chill of approaching winter, lost in thought.

Just after Halloween, Marnie phoned to invite the girls for Christmas and to encourage her sisters once again to move down to West Vancouver and stay with them. They had a large house and could easily accommodate them. Carol was quite interested in pursuing a business career and was keen to go. She was tired of her job at the bakery and wanted to do something with her life. Jodi knew she was the one holding her sister back and she felt guilty for it. They had talked of the move many times, and Jodi argued that she could look after herself if Carol wanted to go. But both older sisters felt responsible for Jodi and wouldn't hear of her living alone.

The issue had not yet been resolved when, in early November, Jodi made an appointment at the Health Clinic in Harrison. She didn't want to go to either of the two doctors in Kelso, for fear her secret would get out.

Stuart Saunders, who drove the old green van he called ' Stuey's Stage,' made the trip into Harrison on Monday, Wednesday, and Friday mornings at nine and returned in the afternoon. Jodi carefully arranged the details for a midweek trip, when Carol would be at work. She somehow couldn't bring herself to tell her sister yet, although she knew she would have to soon. She told her teachers that she had to go to Harrison on some business about her parent's estate, and they didn't question her about it. She desperately wanted to see Brett in Harrison, and she thought long and hard about telling him she was coming down. She knew what the verdict would be at the clinic, and she wasn't sure if she was ready to tell him. Besides, where could they go to be alone? She'd have to tell him in a coffee shop or something, and she didn't want that. He'd have to get out of school too, and she didn't want him to get in trouble.

    At the clinic, she dutifully gave a urine sample and endured the embarrassing physical exam. The results were positive, and the very serious older doctor gave her a lecture on birth control and tried to talk her into a therapeutic abortion. She declined both his advice and his request for the father's name. What she really wanted was information on pregnancies and care of babies. He gave her some booklets that looked pretty interesting and informative. She told him the exact conception date, August 23rd, and he calculated her due date as May 16-18. With a jolt, Jodi realized that the birth would coincide with the anniversary of the car accident. A profound sense of wonder came over her, as she contemplated the fact that this child was no mistake - it was a gift of life, given to heal the loneliness and loss she had suffered. She knew it in her inner being. It was a truth she believed and would hold onto, through the stormy days ahead.

Two more weeks went by, and Jodi knew she had to tell Brett soon. Her waist thickened, causing her jeans to feel too tight. She began to wear sweat pants, telling Carol they were warmer than jeans for winter. She felt ravenous throughout the day and had to take a snack to school for recess, or else she felt faint and dizzy. After lunch, she was overcome with a deep exhaustion and had to force herself to stay awake, even in English, her favourite class. At night, she went to bed early, and slept heavily. She and Brett exchanged letters once a week. He still called her his 'Princess' and always ended his letter with a line about missing her and wanting to see her. When he phoned the next Sunday, Jodi had a plan.

"How about if I get Rick to invite you up for the day? Do you think your parents will let you borrow the car to spend a Sunday with your cousin?"

"It might work. Let's try it." he agreed enthusiastically.

"Okay, I'll ask Rick to phone you. I really need to see you. There are some things I have to talk to you about." Although he was curious, he sensed her seriousness, and didn't press her for details. Besides, he wanted to see her too. It had been far too long. There were lots of cute girls at school, and a few of them were definitely interested in him, but he could only think of Jodi.

The next day at school, Jodi stopped Rick and told him the plan. "So", he said, his blue eyes twinkling mischievously, "You two still like each other, eh? I guess absence does make the heart grow fonder. Sure, I'll call him tonight." He laughed as he hurried away to catch up to Diane. Jodi gave him her best smile and hugged her books to her. *I hope this works*, she thought.

That night, Brett got a phone call from Rick. He and some friends were going on a bike ride to Moose Lake on Sunday and would like Brett to come with them. He put the question to his mom and dad, and after a few moments discussion, they said yes. Brett thanked Rick, and said quietly into the phone, "You know what's going on, right?"

"Yep", said Rick. "You do your own thing when you get here. I'm only the go-between."

"Thanks again, Rick. See you Sunday." Brett almost whooped with joy when he hung up the phone but managed to control himself and say 'yes, Dad' several times, as he listened to a talk on responsible driving and care of the car.

CHAPTER FOUR

Brett stood hesitantly in the old porch for a minute. He hadn't seen Jodi since their strange, brief, passionate encounter on the beach nearly three months ago. He was nervous, but excited at seeing her again. There was something about her that intrigued him, and he really wanted to get to know her better. The way she responded so strongly last time had left him in a whirlwind of confusion and excitement. It had been his first sexual experience, and he was definitely eager to try it again. He wondered if there would be an opportunity. Just in case, he had two condoms in his jeans pocket. He had worried for weeks about the unprotected sex they had. Next time, he was going to be careful.

    Brett wished they didn't live so far apart. School, a job, and an eighty mile round trip over bad roads between them, didn't exactly make courting a girl easy. He took a deep breath, opened the screen door, and cranked the old bell ringer twice. He hoped that Carol wasn't home.

    Jodi was waiting, as nervous as he, and almost ran to the door. Her navy blue sweat pants and long, loose, football sweatshirt hid her secret as she opened the door. Brett's big smile and his deep blue eyes immediately dazzled her. She felt her heart pound, and her insides go mushy as he grinned at her and said, "Hi! It's good to see you."

Regaining a tiny bit of composure, she replied, "You too, come on in."

Brett's athletic body was clad in tight blue jeans and a dark blue sweatshirt, which picked up the blue of his eyes. He held a denim jacket by one finger over his right shoulder. Leaning forward without touching her, he kissed her lightly on the cheek. Savouring the moment, Jodi closed her eyes, breathing in the scent of wood smoke and fresh air. After the kiss, their eyes held each other; questioning, wondering, wanting; then she looked away and asked, "Have you been burning leaves? Your clothes smell smoky."

"Oh, sorry, yeah" he said. I helped Rick rake and burn some leaves for a while. I had to make at least a token visit there before coming over."

"Oh, it's a wonderful smell. I love it!" *And I love you too,* she was thinking, but she didn't dare say it.

It was the third weekend of November. The day was blustery, with a hint of snow in the air. Misty clouds moved quickly across the slate-grey sky, pushed by a brisk wind. Jodi had lit a fire in the fireplace, which gave off a cozy warmth and glow.

"Where's Carol?" Brett asked, as he gracefully sank onto the tired old couch that Jodi had pulled up to the fire.

Jodi plopped onto the other end

nonchalantly and said, "Oh, she's at work until six, and then she's going to Len Morrison's for supper. They're going steady, you know."

"I didn't know," he replied. "How long have they been dating?"

"Um, they've been going out for about a year now. Pretty serious, huh?"

"Yeah, I guess." Brett grinned. "They have the advantage of seeing each other every day, not like us 'long distance lovers.' At the mention of the word 'lovers', they both blushed a little and there was an awkward silence. Jodi counted nine ticks of the mantle clock before Brett cleared his throat, kicked off his shoes, and asked, "You wanted to talk to me about a couple of things. What's on your mind?"

Jodi nodded and pulled her knees up to her chin, encircling them with her arms. Her long, shiny, chestnut brown hair fell in cascades over her shoulders and reached almost to her ankles in this position. She felt as if she was cradling and protecting her secret for the last time. She was about to share it with him, and she was terribly afraid of his reaction.

Brett desperately wanted to reach out and touch that beautiful hair, but she looked distant and dreamy, and he didn't want to intrude. Gently he asked; "Is it something bad?"

Jodi felt a lump rising in her throat and tears spring to her eyes. Hugging herself tighter and forcing herself to breathe deeply, she said in a small, quavery voice, "One sad thing, and one happy thing."

"Well, I'm glad to hear it's not all bad then." He gave a little laugh, moved closer, and took her hand in his. " What do you want to talk about?" She looked at him, her eyes soft with sorrow.

"I have to go away." she said simply. "My sister down in Vancouver wants Carol and me to come for Christmas."

"That's great." he said, feigning joy. "It will be nice for you sisters to be together at Christmas." Jodi saw the relief on his face as he gave her a reassuring smile. "It won't be so bad, you'll have fun."

A tear rolled down Jodi's cheek. "You don't understand. They want me to stay and go to school down there. Carol is going to enroll in Business School, and they won't let me stay here alone". Her voice rising in intensity, Jodi went on. "Everybody's trying to run my life. I don't want to live in Vancouver! I love it here with my chickens, goats, dog, and cat, and Blossom, and this old house, and my friends, and..and..you." Her voice broke as she looked at him in despair. Then, her anger spent, the tears spilled over and she laid her head on her knees, sobs shaking her body.

Brett put his arm around her and pulled her to him, finally stroking that silky head of hair as she buried her face in his chest and wept.

"It's okay," he said gently. "I feel like crying too. I know you're still hurting from the loss of your parents. I know you don't want to leave everything you love behind. What's the meaning of our relationship if it has to end so soon?"

Brett held her in his arms and whispered against her ear. " I love the feel of you. I love your soft curves, and the warmth and weight of your body against mine. I love your silky hair, and you smell nice, like roses or something. You are arousing the most incredible feelings in me. I feel tender and fierce, all at once. I want to kiss you and make love with you.

Jodi managed to push herself away from him and smile a little."No, you don't. I'm all red, wet, and sticky. I'm sorry", she mumbled. "I've only seen you twice, and both times I've blubbered all over you. You must think I'm a big cry-baby." She rose and went over to the coffee table in the corner of the living room, pulled a tissue from the box, wiped her eyes, and blew her nose. She knew she must look awful, but what did it matter now?

The fire had burned down, and the room was becoming dark as the short wintry afternoon came to an end. The mantel clock chimed four times as Jodi threw some more wood on the fire. She pulled a string on the red swag lamp that hung over the easy chair in the corner. The old white cat, Samantha, looked up and gave a soft, throaty, questioning sound, somewhere between a purr and a meow. Then she tucked her head back under her paws. A soft glow from the light and from the revived fire brightened up the room. Jodi turned back to the couch and Brett.

Brett held out his hands to her and pulled her down beside him. Looking into her eyes, he said softly, "I'm sorry Jodi. You're not a crybaby. You have a lot to deal with right now, and it's tough. I don't want to lose you either."

Their eyes held, as they moved closer. Jodi slipped her arms around his neck and his went around her waist as their lips and bodies touched in a tentative embrace. Surprised by the depth of feeling there, and the immediate arousal in them both, they separated quickly. Then, wanting more, they kissed again, and again, each one longer, deeper and more passionate than the last. *This isn't fair!* thought Jodi, as she pushed him away. *I've got to tell him.*

"Wow! You sure turn me on," Brett said with a wicked grin, "but I guess we should slow down. We've got to figure out a way for you to stay here. I can part with you for a little while so you can have Christmas with your family, but I sure want you to come back. By the way," he added, "you haven't told me what the other thing is."

Oh God! Here it was! Time for her to drop the bomb and see him disappear. They really didn't have a hope in hell of seeing the pregnancy through together, getting married and living happily ever after. Everything was against them: their ages, the distance between them, family pressures, and finances.

Brett was still holding her hands in both of his, and waited expectantly for what she was going to tell him. Jodi took a deep breath, let it out, and said with a little smile, "I'm going to have a baby."

"Holy Jesus!" he exclaimed softly, as his eyes grew wide in disbelief. The colour drained from his face, as he dropped her hands and sprang to his feet.

"Are you positive?" he asked, as he backed away towards the door. Jodi sat still, hands folded on her lap, feeling quite serene now that she had told him.

"Yes, I've missed two periods, and I've been to a doctor in Harrison, and it's for sure. Already my jeans are too tight, and my breasts are bigger, and well, kind of tingly." Jodi dared not look at him and fully expected to hear the door open and close as he made his escape. She heard nothing. The room was silent except for the ticking of the clock and the occasional sigh of the driftwood as the fire consumed it. Stealing a glance behind her, she saw him standing at the window, his back towards her, staring out into the gathering darkness.

"Brett, are you okay? Are you angry with me?"

Turning, he walked over and stood with his hands on the back of the couch, just behind her. "Is it mine?" he asked in a whisper. His eyes were misty, and his voice trembled.

Jodi spun around into a kneeling position and faced him over the back of the couch. "Of course it is! I was only ever with you, and only that one time. Do you think I would screw around with other guys? I've never even had a date before!" She was getting angry. "You know it was a first for both of us. We talked about it that night, remember? We just didn't seem to have any control over what happened. It was like it was meant to be, destiny, or something." Jodi looked up at him, her eyes pleading, her voice softening.

"Jesus!" Brett said, as he turned away and paced back and forth across the room. "Don't give me that destiny crap! It was a stupid mistake!"

Brett looked as if he had been punched in the stomach and could scarcely breathe. He looked scared. Jodi could just imagine how shocked he felt, as he confronted the chain of events he had set in motion. He turned to face her. "What can I tell my parents?" His hands came up in a helpless gesture. "My dad's gonna kill me!"

Jodi said, "What about your mom? Will she be understanding?"

Brett shook his head. "Mom will probably cry and tell me how much I've disappointed them. I know they expect more responsibility from me" He resumed his pacing then turned and faced her with his arms folded across his chest.

"Jodi...look, I'm sorry. I really like you, but I can't quit school, get a job and marry you, if that's what you want. What could I do to support a family without even a high school education? I mean... we hardly even know each other. You'll have to get rid of it! Nobody can know about this!"

Jodi felt herself recoil against his words, and she hugged herself tighter. This was not what she wanted to hear. "I can't do that." she said.

Brett came back to the couch and sat down on the edge. Leaning his elbows on his knees, he buried his face in his hands and groaned.

"I feel so guilty for what I've done to you. I'm a year older, and more experienced. I should have made sure it didn't go that far." He reached out and took her hand in his. He looked into her troubled eyes, begging her to understand. He sighed, and a little bit of the tension left his body. He moved closer and took her other hand in his.

"That night was so wonderful, so soft and warm, with the moonlight on the lake, and you crying in my arms and wanting me. I couldn't resist you." He kissed her lightly, and then shook his head. "You are such a sweet kid. I might be falling in love with you, but marriage and babies are the furthest thing from my mind. I think it would be best if you got rid of it. I've got some money saved up. I was going to buy a car, but I'll give it to you. You go to a clinic in Vancouver and get an abortion, okay?

"No," Jodi said, shaking her head. "I told you I can't do that. It's not just like cutting off an infected toe or something! This is a real human being, growing inside of me. Its part of you and part of me, and well," she faltered, "I mean, I think that this was meant to happen." Seeing the look of scepticism on his face, she continued. "Okay, this sounds really weird, but I think you were sent by God to give me a special gift; a gift of life, a child. I think this baby is a replacement for my parents, something special to love and nurture, and someone to fill the terrible loneliness in my life."

"Oh God Jodi, don't give me that spiritual rubbish. I don't believe it. We were careless and stupid. I accept the blame and I'm willing to help you get out of it."

Jodi gripped his hands tighter. "It's not your fault. We did it together. We both wanted to make love that night. But *I'm* the one that was pushy. I know you would have stopped if I had wanted you to, but I didn't."

Brett sighed and leaned back, still having trouble accepting the fact that Jodi was pregnant. "Yeah, it was wonderful. But now what? You really want to keep it?"

"Yes." Jodi said. "Of course I do. I could never destroy something that you and I created and that I feel is a gift from God."

"Well then, how about adoption? Why not give it up to someone who can take care of it? There must be lots of couples who want a healthy baby."

"Adoption would be even worse. I couldn't part with that baby after carrying it so long in my body, and then holding it in my arms. You just don't give family away. The only thing to do is keep the baby, and let it be a blessing in our lives."

"In *our* lives?" he asked, eyebrows raised and questioning. "Where do I fit in?"

"Wherever you can," she smiled. "I know it will be difficult, but you are the father, and I hope you can be around as much as possible."

Brett shrugged. "Well, you know as well as I do that the shit will hit the fan when my parents find out. I don't know how much support I can be after that."

They sat in silence. The reality of their predicament was beginning to sink in. Brett slid off the couch onto the rug, threw some more wood on the fire, and stretched out on his back in front of the blaze. Jodi knew he was bewildered at the turn of events. "Come here," he said quietly, patting the space beside him.

Jodi grabbed two cushions off the couch and slid to the floor. Lifting his head, she placed one under his tawny mop of hair and placed one for herself. Then she lay down beside him with her back to the warm fire. They put their arms around each other and snuggled close. Brett kissed her on the lips gently. He smoothed back her hair and spoke softly. " I think you're crazy, but if you want to keep the baby, I'll do everything I can to help you. I can't promise any more than that."

Jodi hugged him tight. "Thanks," she whispered. "It's more than I expected. I thought you'd freak out and run away. I sure wouldn't blame you. This is a pretty scary thing."

"Yeah, you're not kidding'" he replied, as he returned the hug. She giggled in his arms, and he raised his head to look at her and say, "Now what do you find funny in this situation?"

"Not kidding?" she asked with a grin. "I certainly will be 'kidding' along about mid-May."

"Oh, I get it." he laughed. "I guess that was the wrong thing to say to a goat-lady." They smiled into each other's eyes, and then became serious again. "No matter what happens," Brett promised, "I'll be there for you."

"I love you Brett, so, so, much. When I was sitting on Blossom that day at the ballgame, and you came up to me and looked into my eyes, and took my hand, I almost fainted. That's the instant I fell in love with you. Do you remember that your arm brushed against my leg when you reached for my hand?"

Brett shook his head, "No."

"Well, it did, and I got shivers up and down my spine, and I felt all hot and giddy. I had a strong feeling then, that you were going to be someone special in my life."

Brett sighed deeply. "For me," he said, "that special moment was when I saw you coming up from the beach, galloping Blossom so wild and free, with your hair streaming out in the wind. I was so excited I think that's why I hit that ball out so far. I just couldn't stop thinking about you. I wanted to meet you, and after I did, I wanted to see you again. I was so happy when I saw you at the beach party."

"I almost didn't go. I don't like parties much, but I was hoping I might see you there too. It's the only reason I went. So you see, it must have been destiny that brought us together."

"Well, I don't know about destiny, but there's just something about you...."

Brett and Jodi lay close, happy for the moment, and tried not to think of all the troubles that lay ahead for them. They grew drowsy in the warmth of the fire and, in a few minutes, drifted off to sleep with their arms around each other.

CHAPTER FIVE

The chiming of the mantel clock disturbed Jodi's sleep. She thought she counted five bongs. She sat up and looked at the clock. They had slept for an hour. It was pitch dark outside, and all that remained of the fire were a few red coals. Brett's arm was draped over her. He stirred as she lifted it and slipped out of his embrace. Her hip hurt from lying on the hard floor, and she was ravenously hungry.

"Where're you going?" Brett mumbled, still half asleep.

"Gotta pee," she whispered, and stood up. She went out through the dining room into the kitchen, turning on lights as she went. Samantha, who had been curled up in the big chair with a paw over her eyes, yawned, stretched, jumped down, and shook herself awake. She followed Jodi into the kitchen.

Jodi went to the bathroom, washed her face and hands, and brushed her hair. Looking at her reflection in the mirror, she said to herself, "Hello little mommy." She was so hungry, she felt faint.

Returning to the kitchen, she took out the butter, peanut butter, and bread, and made herself a sandwich. She had to have something before she collapsed. She was surprised that the tiny creature inside her could have such an effect on her already. She munched on the sandwich and concentrated on getting the fire going in the wood stove.

The uneven kitchen floor creaked as Brett came in, still looking sleepy, his golden hair tousled. He came up behind her as she was putting kindling into the still hot coals and slipped his arms around her waist, holding her tight. He nuzzled her neck and said, "I got lonely when you didn't come back."

Jodi smiled and said teasingly, "Someone has to do the work around here. Can't always be lying around sleeping. Besides, I was so hungry I had to get a snack. I can't believe what this little one does to my body. It's weird."

"You do weird things to my body too," he replied in a husky voice, kissing her on the ear.

"I know, I can feel it", Jodi said as she took his hands and unlocked herself from his arms. They would deal with this later. Right now she wanted food, and her animals needed tending to.

"Can you stay for supper, or do you have to go?"

"I should get going, but I'm pretty hungry. What are you making?" He picked up the cat and sat down on the chair she had been occupying.

"I've got lots of eggs."

"That'll be fine," he said, stroking Sam's ears and scratching her under the chin. Samantha purred loudly, turned around a couple of times on Brett's knees, and settled down on his legs. Her eyes narrowed to slits as she went for a little catnap.

The kindling was crackling. Jodi lifted the lid to add a couple of chunks of driftwood and some coal. *I'll have to call the coal guy soon,* she thought. Then with a sudden start, she remembered that she probably wouldn't be here for the winter.

Jodi sighed, went to the refrigerator and brought out bacon, eggs, milk, and cheese. She took the cast iron frying pan down from a hook on the wall and placed it on the stove. She filled up the kettle and set it to boil. It felt good to have something to do, even a simple task such as preparing a meal. Keeping busy helped to keep her mind off parting with the good-looking young man who now sat in her kitchen, watching her every move.

She had thought about him constantly; day dreaming, night dreaming, reliving over and over their night at the beach party back in August. Now, he was here, and he didn't seem to be in a hurry to leave. His eyes and his actions told her that he liked her, but she still had trouble believing it. *I don't even know him,* she thought, *and I'm going to have his child!*

Jodi sliced the bacon, and tossed it in the frying pan where it sizzled and smoked, sending out a delicious aroma immediately. Cracking five eggs into a bowl, she began to beat them vigorously with a fork.

"Can I help?" Brett asked. "I feel kind of guilty sitting here watching you work."

"Sure, thanks. Could you bring in some more wood from the porch please? And I think Scamp is outside. He'd probably like to come in. I have to go out and shut the chickens in, and feed Blossom and the goats, but we can do that after supper."

"Okay," Brett agreed, brushing cat hairs off his sweatshirt. "Glad to help."

As Jodi added milk to the beaten eggs and got out the grater for the cheese, Brett came back with a huge armful of wood and a very excited little black dog. Scamp leaped and wiggled his whole body in delight at finally being invited in. Jodi felt sorry for ignoring him all afternoon. Now that she was alone so much, he was her closest companion. She made a big fuss of him; then as his excitement faded, and he flopped down on the braided rug with a big sigh of contentment, she went back to grating the block of cheese.

"You could get a couple of plates and cups out of the cupboard over there, and cutlery is in there", Jodi pointed. She quickly drained the bacon fat into a tin, poured the egg mixture over the cooked bacon, sprinkled the grated cheese over it all, popped a lid on it, and pulled the pan to a cooler part of the stove. The kettle was starting to steam.

"Sure, but I should wash up first." he agreed.

"Bathroom's right over there," she indicated with a nod. "You passed it on your way out for wood."

"Yep." he replied. When he came back, she busied herself making the toast and watching the eggs while he set two places at either end of the small table. Then, donning oven mitts, Jodi carried the cast iron frying pan over to the table and set it down in the middle on a hot mat. Going back to the oven for the toast, she told him, "Go ahead and sit down. Everything's ready."

The omelette had puffed up beautifully. It was a golden brown on the bottom and a bright yellow on top. She wished she'd had a few chives to sprinkle on top, but the garden was finished.

Jodi cut the omelette into eight wedges, and slid four of them along with two pieces of toast onto Brett's plate. "Dig in." she invited.

He did just that while she took two pieces for herself and some toast.

"Mmm"...Brett said. "This is good. You're a good cook. I'll have to teach my mom how to make this."

"The fresh eggs help," Jodi replied. "They give it the nice colour and flavour."

"I think Mom would draw the line at having chickens in the back yard." he said with a grin.

Ooh! Those beautiful, even white teeth and flashing blue eyes made Jodi's heart beat faster. She laughed to cover her sudden embarrassment and asked, "Would you like a glass of milk? It's goat's". She picked up the jar and poured herself a glass.

"You first," he said. "I've never tried it."

"Oh, it's good," Jodi said, and took a drink. "I doubt if you could tell the difference."

"Really? I always thought that goat's milk was strong tasting."

"There are a lot of misconceptions about goats," Jodi said. "They don't eat tin cans or the laundry off the line either."

Brett laughed, and said, "Okay, just a little, to try it." She poured him a half glass of milk and went on eating, but watching his reaction. He paused a moment, looking puzzled, then held out his glass for more. "You're right. No difference."

"Uh-huh," she said, "And it's better for you than cow's milk too."

"Oh? How so?" he said as he took a bite of toast.

"Well," Jodi said, " goat's milk is already naturally homogenized. That is, the fat globules are evenly distributed throughout the milk. It doesn't separate easily like fresh cow's milk. That makes it easier to digest. It's why some babies and small children with allergies or eczema often can tolerate it better than cow's milk."

There it was again - that 'baby' word! Jodi noticed that the word jolted Brett, and a look flashed between them before they quickly looked away and resumed eating. "Well," he recovered, "I learned something about goats today."

In the awkward moment that followed, Samantha came to their rescue. She had been very polite, sitting on the empty chair between them, watching the meal progress. Now, she narrowed her eyes, stared at Jodi, and put a paw tentatively on the table. She uttered a little questioning "meow?"

Jodi smiled. "Would you like some Sam?" She took a tiny bit of omelette and put it in front of the cat. Up came the little paw again, deftly hooking the morsel of food, drawing it over the edge of the table and onto the chair, where she daintily chewed it up. The tension gone, they both watched in amusement as Sam's head came up again, her big, green eyes demanding more. Brett obliged this time, and the performance was repeated. Offered a third bit, she sniffed it, refused politely with a little shake of her head, and settled down again, tucking her paws carefully under her. She was content.

"Well, her ladyship doesn't want anymore. How about you?"

"No, thank you," he replied, holding up his hands. "You gave me twice as much as you ate."

"I had a sandwich before supper," she reminded him, "so we're about even." Jodi stood up and began to gather up the dishes.

"Here, I'll do that," Brett offered. "Bev and I have to do the dishes at home."

"Just put them in the sink for now, and I'll put the food away, okay? I should get out and feed the animals."

At the mention of the word 'out', Scamp was on his feet looking excited, his stubby tail wagging. He wiggled around Jodi's feet as she put on her shoes and took an old coat off the hook by the back door. Brett went for his shoes and jacket that he had left in the living room, then the three of them headed out the back door. Jodi took the kerosene lantern down from a shelf in the porch, lit it, and picked up an ice cream bucket. They pushed open the outside door and went out into the darkness. The night was cold, *close to freezing,* Jodi thought. They would have snow soon. She could smell it in the air. She raised the lantern, and said, "This way."

Brett followed her along the path beside the dormant garden to a group of small wooden sheds. "That's the woodshed," she pointed with the light. "This middle one is sort of a garden shed. Here's the hen house. Watch your head," Jodi instructed as they ducked through a dark doorway. She shone the light over the roosting chickens, counting out loud.

They blinked and gawked stupidly, as the light moved over them.

"All present and accounted for," Jodi said. "They run free in the daytime, and once in a while a hawk gets one so I always check to see if they're all here." She shone the light into the nests and picked up eleven eggs. "Not bad for fifteen hens at this time of year." she said, with a hint of pride and concern in her voice.

Closing and latching the door behind them, they made their way in the dark towards the other animals. Scamp dashed ahead, nose to the ground. Blossom heard them coming and whinnied a greeting. Then she stamped her feet with impatience, and snorted loudly. Jodi laughed, "She's giving me heck for being late."

The goats too, began to blat and natter, excited at the prospect of being fed. "Leave the bucket out here," said Jodi, "or you'll be mobbed, and the eggs will be scrambled."

"Good thinking," Brett agreed, and set the bucket down by the gate. Jodi pushed the animals back with one hand, and held the gate open just enough for him to slide through. The pony nickered and tossed her head up and down. Jodi encircled her neck with her arms and hugged her, while Blossom blew gently into her hair and neck. "Sorry I'm late, little one," she said to the mare. "It's all his fault," she said teasingly, turning to Brett and taking his hand.

Brett had never been around livestock much, although he had often thought he would like to have a horse someday. He stepped closer and stroked the pony's soft, fuzzy neck. Blossom turned her head and sniffed him, lipped his hair, and then took hold of the collar of his coat in her teeth and gave it a tug.

"Hey! Easy girl!" he cried, just a little alarmed.

Jodi laughed. "She's just checking you out. I think she's jealous."

"Well, that makes two of us," Brett replied, patting her gingerly. "We'll have to work on our relationship."

The goats were also crowding around for attention. "This is Annie, the nanny," Jodi said, stroking a pretty black and white Alpine goat. "These are her kids, Fritz and Fanny."

As Brett bent down to pet the friendly goats, he said, "I haven't been surrounded by animals like this since I was a little boy in kindergarten when the teacher took our class to a farm."

Jodi and Brett made their way across the paddock to another old shed, followed closely by the animals. The shed was actually an old house that Jodi's dad had moved onto the property about ten years ago. They called it 'the green shed' because its now faded cedar shingles had once been painted green. There was a full length porch with the windows long boarded up, and the floor boards had been removed. This served as a run-in shelter for the animals. At the far end, Jodi had built a small pen for the three goats, with a hay manger, feed box, and milking stand in the corner.

Jodi hung the lantern on a nail on the inside wall where it cast a soft yellow light and long dark shadows. She stepped up onto a block of wood that served as a step into the little house. "I keep the feed in here," she said, pushing the door open. "Are you coming in? You have to be quick, or else the goats will barge in too."

Brett stepped up behind her, grabbing her hand as they slipped through and closed the door in the goats' faces. The smell of sweet green hay assailed their senses. "I think you should hold small children by the hand," he said. "I can't see."

Jodi was beginning to recognize when he was teasing her, and she bantered back, "If I have to stand here and hold your hand, I'll never get these hungry animals fed." Although it was still dark inside the old house, Jodi knew her way around perfectly. She left him standing by the door and moved over to the square bales that were stacked against the wall. She had built mangers for the pony and the goats just under the old window openings of the house, so all she had to do was drop a couple of flakes through these spaces. She had to go into the back room to fill the goat mangers. Brett's eyes had adjusted to the dark now, and he watched with interest as she moved quickly and efficiently at her chores. He heard the clang of a metal lid being lifted off and immediately inhaled a sweet sticky smell.

"That smells yummy. What is it?" he asked.

"It's sweet feed," she replied. "It's the molasses you smell." She scooped out a small coffee can of the sticky stuff and poured it into Blossom's feed box. She disappeared into the back room again, shaking the can and calling the goats. "Annie! Fritzie! Fanny! Come on!" They immediately left off trying to climb into Blossom's feed box and ran to their pen, greedily shoving their heads into their own grain, butting each other as they ate.

"There, all done," said Jodi as she tossed the can back in the barrel and closed the lid. "I just have to kick the two kids out and lock Annie in so I can milk her in the morning."

"That sounds like fun," he joked.

"What?" she asked, with a little laugh. "Kicking them out, or milking?"

"Both", he answered. "It's neat, watching you work around your animals. You obviously enjoy them a lot."

"I do. It's not work to me. I just like being with them. Animals are not nearly as difficult to deal with as people are."

"Oh-oh, I think I have some tough competition here," Brett sighed.

Jodi didn't answer. As soon as the goats had finished their grain, she went into the pen and grabbed Fritz by the horns. Dragging him out the gate, she deftly flipped it shut with her foot. Then, re-entering, she cornered Fanny. Fanny didn't have horns, so by putting one hand around her neck and grasping her tail with the other hand, Jodi manoeuvred the unwilling animal out the gate as Brett held it open and then slammed it shut.

"There. They can eat hay with Blossom now." Taking the lantern off the nail, she called, "Goodnight, you critters."

Jodi was thankful for the diversion that dealing with the animals had created. Brett was pretty quiet, and she knew he was desperately trying to come to grips with the realization that two months before his eighteenth birthday, he was going to be a father. It was a staggering thought.

CHAPTER SIX

Brett picked up the bucket of eggs outside the gate, and followed Jodi, Scamp, and the light back to the house. "I guess I should be going now," he said, "while I've got my coat and shoes on." But when they entered the porch, he just couldn't bring himself to say goodbye. He looked at his watch -quarter to eight - early yet. He really did not want to leave Jodi. He knew it would have to be soon, but not yet.

    Jodi hung up her coat on the hook beside the door and put her shoes on the rubber mat. Brett kicked his off onto the mat too and draped his coat over the back of a kitchen chair. Scamp went to his spot on the rug.

    "Phew! It's hot in here", Brett said, pulling off his sweatshirt as well, laying it over his coat.

    "Yeah, it's quite a contrast from outside," she agreed, as she put the eggs on the counter. "Want to wash your hands?" She couldn't help but admire his upper torso, with his broad shoulders and heavily muscled bare arms. He looked good in a T-shirt.

    Jodi ran the water, and he joined her at the sink, using a squirt of dishwashing soap to get the animal smell off their hands. They shared a towel, standing close, looking into each other's eyes. He was just going to take her in his arms and kiss her, when she took his hand and said,

"Come on, I'll show you the rest of the house."

"Okay," he agreed. She pulled him a few steps into the next room, flipping on the light.

"We call this the back bedroom," she said. It was a fairly small room with bunk beds along the south wall, a dresser, and a potbelly stove surrounded by a freestanding screen. "Whenever we were sick, we would stay here so Mom could nurse us back to health. It's sort of an extra bedroom."

Moving along to the next room, Jodi told him quietly, "This was my parents' room." Brett could hear the pain in her voice, and he slipped his arm around her waist, giving her a squeeze. The room faced onto the street. It had one window, with the blind pulled right down. The double bed took up most of the room, with a large closet filling up one corner. Right across from the bed, with only about a foot of space between, was an antique dresser with an oval mirror in the center. There were brushes and a few ornaments there. A small bedside table stood on the opposite side of the bed, and beyond that, a door led out to the living room.

"You can go around in a circle on the ground floor," Jodi said, sounding brighter. "It used to be hilarious when Mom would chase us with the wooden spoon, and we'd just run around in circles until she got tired and gave up."

Brett squeezed her again. I can't imagine you being bad," he said.

"Yeah, well, I admit to being stubborn sometimes." Changing the subject, she said, " Carol and I have to get busy and pack up all Mom and Dad's things. We haven't got around to doing that yet."

"That will be hard for you." he said. Jodi nodded, acknowledging the sympathy in his voice.

"Then," she went on, " I would like to make the little room into a nursery for the baby. I'll move down here, so I can be close by. I want to haul the bunk beds out to the green shed, get a nice crib put in, and maybe wallpaper the walls with something cute. It's so dingy in here."

"I'd like to help you with that," he offered. " We could have fun doing it together."

"Yeah, thanks. But I'm such a dreamer. I probably won't even be here when the baby's born. I know I'll be under a lot of pressure to stay in Vancouver after Christmas. And when Marnie finds out I'm expecting, she'll never let me come back here. If she doesn't make me give the baby up, she'll likely want to keep it and raise it along with her three kids." She sighed. "Come on, I'll show you the upstairs."

Still holding hands, Jodi led Brett back through the kitchen. A doorway between the kitchen and dining room opened onto a set of steep wooden stairs.

Jodi flipped on the light. Halfway up, she stopped and said, "See this little hole here? I used to sit here and eavesdrop when Mom had friends over for tea. I always knew what was going on in town."

"You little brat." Brett teased. I'd wallop you with a wooden spoon too, if I could catch you."

At the top of the stairs, Jodi said, "This is my room. I guess you can tell I'm sort of horse crazy." The walls were plastered with horse pictures, some drawn, some from old calendars, and some cut out from magazines. Straight ahead of them was a small desk with a fold-down tray and several drawers on the right. "This is where I used to do my homework, but I mostly work at the dining room table now."

Jodi's bed was tucked under the sloping attic roof, next to her desk. It was an old iron bedstead with saggy springs, but there was a good thick mattress, and the bed was neatly made and covered with a patchwork quilt. It looked cozy. Next to the bed was a little night table, with a clock on it, and a couple of horse magazines. The brick chimney from below took up the next two feet of space, and next to that was a table with a partially completed thousand-piece puzzle on it.

Brett walked over and took a look. "Might have known it would be horsy," he grinned, as he picked up a piece and put it right where it belonged. It was a western scene of cowboys trying to rope a beautiful wild, palomino horse. "Next time I come, I'll help you work on it. I like jigsaw puzzles too."

Jodi liked the sound of that 'next time'. A surge of happiness flowed through her. He was coming back!

"Here's my horse collection," she said, pointing to a five shelf open bookcase in the opposite corner, also under a sloping roof.

"Holy sheep-dip!" he exclaimed. "What a lot of horses!"

"Yep," she replied proudly. "Over one hundred, and they're all named too."

"No way," he protested. "You couldn't possibly remember all those names."

"Sure I can." she said, sounding a bit indignant. Picking up a blood bay, she told him, "This one is Cimarron, the first one I ever got. This pinto here is Prince, and that palomino lying down is Honeycomb. This tiny little family is Tumbleweed, Trinket, and Tan. That black there in the rearing position is Fury, and this family of bays is Bonfire, Firefly, and Flicka."

"All right, already!" he laughed. "I believe you! They *are* all named. I'm impressed."

"Well, you'd better be. She laughed with him. "They all hold a special memory for me."

Brett looked around the room and said, "I like your bedroom. It's a cool place. I can see you enjoy spending time here." He nodded towards Carol's room." What's the other one like?"

"Oh, it's kind of a mess, but you can look." They walked over to the doorway between the two rooms. Jodi stepped in and turned on the light. It was a large room and very untidy. Books, shoes, and clothes lay everywhere. The double bed against the wall was unmade. Records covered the table. More were stacked haphazardly on the floor. Jars of makeup, curlers, brushes, a comb and a hand mirror were all in a jumble on the dresser. Across from where they were standing was a large window overlooking a huge apple tree and the yard below.

"I love falling asleep up here in the spring when the tree is in blossom and the scent drifts in the open window", said Jodi.

"Sure is an interesting old house," Brett remarked, looking around.

"Yep, I think it's over eighty years old."

Brett leaned his back against the doorjamb and reached for Jodi, pulling her close. His hands went around her waist and then moved down over her hips, as he kissed her lightly.

Jodi leaned against him. She could feel his heartbeat and was also very aware of that other feeling; his growing urgency pressing against her.

"Jodi," he whispered hoarsely. "You know I have to leave soon, and I don't know when I'll see you again." She knew what he was asking, and in answer, reached up and stroked his hair and lifted her face to accept his loving kiss. They moved over to her bed, and Jodi gave a little gasp as Brett slid his hands under her shirt, unhooked her bra, and slid everything off over her head. He sat on the edge of the bed and drew her to him, so that she stood, trembling between his knees. Shivers of excitement shot through her body, and her nipples stood up hard and erect. He was staring at them too, as he gently ran his hands up her back. He cupped a breast in each hand, running his thumbs over the nipples. His eyes devoured her as the most delicious sensations rippled through her body.

"They're just perfect," he whispered. "Just the right size to fit in a man's hand."

Jodi felt hot and weak. Somewhere way down deep in her middle, she felt a desperate need. Brett stood up quickly, shed his jeans, underwear and socks, and fell back on the bed with a groan, pulling her on top of him. They kissed frantically while he tugged at her sweatpants and underwear, sliding them down. She helped him by kicking them off. They lay for a moment, touching each other all over. Jodi had never seen a naked man before. Shyly, she cast a glance down the length of

Brett's body, her eyes registering surprise. When she raised them to meet his, he grinned while she blushed and stammered, " I just didn't get to see it. It was dark." Her hands travelled over his body, delighting in the feel of his smooth muscles, and the texture of his skin. There was no fat on him. He was lean, hard and fit, and beautiful to look at.

Brett kissed her throat, then lowered his head and took a nipple into his mouth. He nibbled gently, before letting go and doing the same with the other one. It was as if an electric shock went through Jodi. Her back arched, and she cried out, digging her fingernails into his neck as the sensations washed over her.

"Hey, you didn't even wait for me," he teased. He entered her, moaning with pleasure. She wrapped her legs around his hips and encouraged him. He wouldn't take long. He had been ready to burst for the last ten minutes, but he had wanted to prolong it as long as possible.

Jodi lightly ran her fingers down his back, which was glistening with sweat, as he quickly neared his climax. Then he shuddered, and letting his breath out, buried his face in her long hair. He lay for a moment, spent by his effort, and then rolled off her onto his back, flinging his arm across her belly. She took his hand, raised it to her lips, and kissed his fingers one by one. They were blissfully happy.

Brett turned towards her, leaned on his elbow, and said, "This is the part in the movies when the guy lights up a cigarette, blows smoke in the chicks' face and says, was it good for you, baby?"

She giggled in response. "That's so dumb. You shouldn't have to ask. And I'm very glad you don't smoke. It's so disgusting."

"Yeah," he agreed, resting his hand on her stomach. "I hope I didn't disturb the little one." He tried to visualize the tiny bit of humanity that lay in there.

"Oh, I think he's okay," she said, putting her hand over his.

"He?" Brett asked, with raised eyebrows. "Do you think it's a boy?"

"I have a strong feeling it is," Jodi said. She had a faraway, dreamy look on her face.

"You're probably right," Brett grinned at her. "Women's intuition, or something like that." Then, looking serious, he said, "Jodi, you know it probably wouldn't work if we got married right now. I mean, my parents wouldn't allow it anyway, and I don't know about your family. They'll probably hate my guts when they find out. I'd like to graduate and get a good job, and we need to see if our relationship is going to last. Right now, I just couldn't do it. What do you think?"

Jodi's fingers wandered through Brett's silky golden hair, as he laid his head on her shoulder and held her tight. With a sigh, she said, "I think you're right. As much as I'd love to have you live with me, getting married wouldn't work. I don't want to just jump into it, and make a mess of everything. Apart from the great sex, we hardly know each other. We need time to sort things out and let our families adjust to us having this baby. Besides," she continued...then she was still, listening... She sat up suddenly, pushing him away. "Oh jeez! I think Carol's home! I heard a car door slam!"

"Oh shit!" Brett swore, as he leaped up, grabbing for his clothes. He hopped on one foot as he pulled on his underwear, jeans, and T-shirt. Jodi scrambled around, picking her sweatpants and shirt up off the floor and getting them on in a flash. Her bra and panties lay on the floor too. She kicked them under the bed, and quickly smoothed out the covers and pillows.

"Get over there, and make like you're doing the puzzle." she instructed. "Have you got a comb?" He shook his head. She raced into Carol's room and grabbed a brush off the cluttered dresser, brushing her long tangled hair as she came back to her room. Spying Brett's socks on the floor, she kicked them over to him, as they heard Carol's voice call, "Jodi? Where are you?"

She tossed Brett the brush, sat at her desk, and answered, "Hi! We're up here, working on the puzzle."

Brett frantically yanked on his socks, gave his hair a few swipes, and hid the brush under the puzzle lid as Carol came up the stairs.

"Hi Carol, I'd like you to meet Brett Randall," Jodi said, getting up from the desk chair and looking towards Brett.

The two girls had a strong family resemblance except that Carol liked to use the Avon cosmetics she sold as a sideline to her Bakery job. Her bluish-green eyes were accented with eye shadow, her lashes were thickened with black goo, and she wore blush and lipstick. The result was an attractive nineteen year old with a face that, at that moment, was a study in astonishment, as she was confronted with the fact that her younger plainer sister was entertaining a boy in her bedroom! Recovering her shock, Carol stood staring at Brett, and said, "Hello, where did you come from?" At the same time, she shot Jodi a questioning look that said many things - who is he, what the hell is he doing here, and what are you up to?

Brett stood up, walked across the room, shook her hand, gave her his dazzling smile, and said politely, "Hi Carol, it's great to meet you. I live in Harrison, and I'm just up for the day visiting my cousins, so I came over to see Jodi. We've known each other for a couple of months."

"Oh, I see," said Carol. Her eyes that were so much like Jodi's glanced around the room, flicked over the bed, checking things out. Jodi cringed inwardly, fearful that Carol suspected something. She watched her sister carefully and noticed that she was immediately taken with Brett's good looks, manners, and charm. Brett had himself under control now and was chatting easily with Carol about her evening out.

"Uh...we were just going to come down and make some tea," Jodi said nervously. "Brett has to leave pretty soon. He has to drive back to Harrison tonight. Is Len here?"

"Yes, he's downstairs, stoking up the fire," Carol answered, turning to go. As Carol disappeared down the stairs, Jodi gave Brett the 'thumbs up' sign and breathed a huge sigh of relief. Brett retrieved the brush and met her in the middle of the room with a hug. "Let's never be that careless again," he whispered.

"Seems like we've been careless twice in a row," she whispered back. "It could get to be a habit with us."

Brett gave her butt a playful light smack with the brush, and said; "Now that's for being careless and naughty. Don't do that again."

Laughing, Jodi took the brush and returned it to Carol's room. Brett started down the stairs, and she followed him.

CHAPTER SEVEN

Down in the kitchen, Carol was making the tea and setting out mugs, cream and sugar. Jodi said to the young man sitting at the kitchen table, "Hello Len, I'd like you to meet my friend, Brett Randall." Len's dark brown eyes registered shocked surprise as he stood and shook Brett's hand.

"Pleased to meet you." he said. "Morrison is the last name. Haven't I seen you around before?"

"I was here in August," Brett said, looking at Jodi. "My mom has a brother here, Dan Taylor. He works for Hydro. Rick, Janet and little Ronnie are my cousins. I don't get up from Harrison too often."

"So, you're courting the kid, eh?" Len said, winking at Jodi.

"Len," Carol said, a warning in her voice.

"Oh, don't mind me. I just want to tell him to treat her decent. She's a good kid." Jodi looked at the floor in embarrassment, as Brett blushed slightly and sipped his tea.

Len was all right. He meant well, but was a little rough around the edges. He was six foot something and well built, with dark, curly hair and a moustache that matched his brown eyes. He worked in the sawmill up the lake and liked to hunt and fish in his spare time. He loved Carol and wanted to marry her; but she resisted, partly because she felt responsible for Jodi, but mostly, she wanted to get out of this small town.

How she and Len were going to resolve this conflict was a mystery to Jodi. Carol had worked at the bakery ever since graduation two years ago. She had also dated just about all the boys in her age group and found them all boring. She was pretty and smart, with a flair for writing, fashion and design, and she wanted more out of life than this place had to offer.

Jodi couldn't blame Carol for wanting adventure in the big city, but for her, leaving would be torture. It wasn't fair that Carol wanted to go so badly that she would leave Len behind, while Jodi wanted so much to stay near Brett. Jodi knew she would be forced to go once they found out about the baby.

"How come you're so quiet?" asked Carol, looking intently at Jodi.

She *knows*, thought Jodi. "Um...I was just thinking. Did you happen to bring anything good home from the bakery?"

"Thought you'd never ask," Carol smiled, producing a bag of donuts from the fridge. "Here you go."

They helped themselves, and were soon licking sugar and chocolate from their sticky fingers. They made small talk for a few more minutes, and then Brett said, "It's getting late. I'd better hit the road. Thanks for the tea and donuts Carol.

It was nice to meet you. You too Len."

"Good to meet you too," Len replied, and Carol added, "Take care going home."

"I will, goodnight."

Jodi followed him out through the dining room, into the living room, and to the front door. The room was dark except for one small lamp in the corner. He stopped by the door and held out his arms. She flung herself at him, not shy with him anymore. They held each other tightly, not wanting to say goodbye. She willed herself not to cry, but already she missed him.

"Gotta go," Brett whispered against her ear. "I'll call you in a couple of days, okay?" He took her face in his hands and kissed her gently. She didn't trust herself to speak. They hugged again, and then he opened the door and eased through, still holding one hand.

"Bye", Jodi said sadly, hating to let him go. He kissed her hand, let it go with a squeeze, and closed the door.

She watched from the window as he got into the car and started it. With a little toot of the horn and red lights disappearing into the dark, he was gone.

Jodi sighed and went back to the kitchen. She knew she would be in for some teasing, so she started cleaning up the tea things and washing the supper dishes.

"Nice catch Jodi!" Len grinned.

"Cute too," added Carol. "Wish I'd found him first." She winked at Len, and tousled his curly hair. "Of course, you're not bad looking either."

"You're lucky you said that. You just redeemed yourself." They teased each other, alternating insults and compliments. Jodi ignored them, her mind on Brett and all the feelings he had aroused in her.

She finished washing the dishes, and leaving them to drip, went into the bathroom to get ready for bed.

Carol and Len had disappeared into the living room. Jodi wondered if they were going to make love before he left. She was fairly certain that they were intimate, but Carol had never offered to tell her, and Jodi didn't like to pry. It suddenly occurred to her that maybe it was Carol's way of paying him for the help he gave the girls around the place, fixing things up, getting wood up from the beach and chopping it, picking fruit, and anything else they needed help with. *Yeah,* she thought; *he wouldn't be around all the time, if he wasn't getting something.*

Jodi took her nightgown off the hook on the bathroom door, slung it over her shoulder, opened the door, spoke to Scamp and Samantha, and called "Goodnight!" in the direction of the living room.

"Goodnight Jodi, sweet dreams" called Len, and Carol added, "See you in the morning."

Jodi went up the stairs, followed by the dog and cat, and for the second time in two hours, shed her clothes. She pulled her nightie on. Retrieving her underwear from under the bed, she hung her clothes over the back of the chair. These would do for after school tomorrow. She'd have to wear something clean in the morning. She groaned inwardly and thought, *Oh no, P.E. tomorrow! I'll have to run that damn cross-country course. I don't want the girls to see me in the change room because somebody's going to notice pretty soon. And I'll probably faint running that course. I know I won't feel like it!*

Jodi switched off the light and crawled under the covers, resolving to talk to Mr. Evans tomorrow. She heard the phone ring three times downstairs, and Carol's muffled voice as she answered it. *Probably one of her friends,* she thought.

Samantha jumped on the bed, and walked up the length of Jodi's leg. She sat on Jodi's chest, waiting. Then as Jodi turned on her side, the cat settled on the pillow, purring loudly. Jodi knew that once she stopped moving around, Sam would crawl under the covers beside her. She would circle two or three times, then curl up in a ball against her body with Jodi's hand on her head. It was a nightly ritual and a comforting one for both of them.

Scamp stretched out on the rug beside the bed and began to snore softly.

Jodi wondered where Brett was now on the road. *Almost eleven. He should be home soon. Wonder what he's thinking.* "Goodnight Dream boy," she whispered. "Sleep well."

After she hung up the phone, Carol came back to the couch where she had been cuddling with Len. They had built up the fire and the room was warm and cozy, just lit with the flickering firelight.

"Who was that?" Len inquired, reaching out for her.

"It was Rick," she replied, slipping back into his arms, and laying her head on his shoulder. "He was looking for Brett." Carol sounded concerned. "Apparently, his mother thought he was at the Taylor's. I don't think they knew he spent the day with Jodi. What do you think is going on?"

Len squeezed her shoulders gently and kissed her, before he looked right into her eyes and said, "I think he's bonking her."

Carol sat up with a start. "What? Jodi? She wouldn't!"

Len said seriously. "I think you'd better have a talk with her. The way they looked at each other tonight makes me wonder just how innocent they are. There are some pretty strong feelings between them." Len wondered how much he should say here. It really wasn't his business, but he wanted to be honest with Carol, and she had asked his opinion. He plunged in with a sigh. "Haven't you noticed that she's putting on weight, and that she's been wearing baggy clothes lately?"

"I hadn't noticed, but you're right. Oh God, Len, are you saying that you think she's pregnant?" Len didn't answer. Carol moaned and covered her face with her hands. "I've been blind! I've been so busy with work, and with you, I've been ignoring her. I didn't even know she had a boyfriend. I didn't even think she was interested in boys!"

"I can't blame her for flipping out on that guy," Len laughed. He's mighty attractive!"

"Len! This isn't funny! What if she is pregnant? What should I do?" Carol started to cry softly.

"Hey, don't cry sweetie." He hugged her. "If she is, we'll just have to think of something." He took Carol's hands in his and kissed them. "You know I love you. I'd marry you and adopt the kid if that would help. I want to make an honest woman out of you, but you won't let me."

"I know Len," she sniffed, " and I'm sorry. And thanks for that offer. I just don't feel ready for marriage yet. There are things I want to do first, like travel, and take some courses that I can't get here. I've been thinking seriously about going to Vancouver for a year or two."

Len let go of her and stood up. He was hurt and just a little angry. This was the second time he had suggested marriage. He reached for his coat and said grimly, "Maybe you should just go and get Jodi out of here, whether she's pregnant or not. If she is, she's going to take all kinds of shit and abuse from this town. It would be quite a scandal. And maybe you need to get this 'big city thing' out of your system. But it will be the end for us if you go away." He shrugged into his coat. "Goodnight."

Carol jumped up and wrapped her arms around him. "Len," she whispered, "Please don't go. I need you." She removed his open coat, kissed him, and began to touch him in all the places he liked. She took his hand and led him to the front bedroom. He tried to resist, but he was crazy about her. He wanted her so much. They sank onto the big bed and began to make love.

CHAPTER EIGHT

Brett drove slowly out of town and headed south on the winding road back to Harrison. He checked his watch. Jeez. After ten. He should have got going sooner. He'd probably get a lecture when he got home. He pressed the Chev into a little more speed, watching carefully for deer on the road.

He felt a sense of urgency to get home, yet dared not drive too fast. The gravel road was twisty along the lake, and there was forty-two miles of it. Well, he certainly had lots to think about! *When, and how should he tell his family?* He wanted so much to see Jodi again, especially if she was going to be leaving for Vancouver soon. *What could he do to help her get through this?* He still felt a sense of shock at becoming a father. *What kind of father can I be under the circumstances?* The thought of having a real live baby in his life seemed impossible. He'd never had anything to do with them. He didn't relish the thought of dirty diapers, the crying, the teething. Yikes! *How long before a baby got control of itself, and became even remotely human?*

Brett knew intuitively that Jodi would bear most of the unpleasantness regarding the child, and he felt sorry for her. "Oh Jodi, I'm crazy about you. Sleep well, my

Angel," he spoke aloud. He envisioned her curled up in her bed and longed to be there with her, holding her in his arms all night. He re-lived in his mind their kisses, their caresses, and their coming together for only the second time. He wouldn't want to do it with just anyone, but with her, it was wonderful. He wondered when she would tell Carol and how Carol would react.

Just past the tiny sleeping community of Kit's Hill, Brett pulled the car over and got out for a pee. The night was clear, and still, and cold. Millions of stars glittered overhead in the night sky. He looked up at the heavens and marvelled at the beauty. *Jodi believes that this is all a part of God's plan,* he mused. He hadn't prayed since he was a little kid in Sunday School, but he said now, "God, I'm scared. If you're out there, and you're in control please help me to be strong and stick with Jodi through this thing." Then, feeling a bit foolish, he got back in the car and eased out onto the dark and lonely road.

Brett pulled up to his home at eleven-twenty p.m. The Randalls lived in a quiet subdivision in upper Harrison, in an area of older, well-kept homes. The street was in darkness. Everyone had school or work in the morning. The porch light was on, as well as one in the living room. Brett knew his mom would be waiting, and he felt mildly irritated. He didn't feel like talking to her or giving explanations tonight.

"Hi Mom, sorry I'm so late." he apologized, coming in quietly.

Carmen Randall closed the book she had been reading. The lamplight shone on her thick light brown hair, which was now streaked with grey, and her soft blue eyes rested lovingly on her son. "I was getting worried when you weren't home by ten, so I called Taylor's. Rick said you had just left."

Oh cripes! thought Brett. *Good thing Rick answered the phone.* He'd have to be more careful.

"Did you have a good time? What did you do all day?"

"Oh, just hung around; raked and burned some leaves. Went for a long bike ride up to Moose Lake."

 What did you have for supper?"

Jesus! Why couldn't she lay off? Why the third degree?

"Oh some kind of omelette. It was good. Thanks for letting me use the car Mom. I'd better get to bed. G'night." He made his escape into the bathroom and waited until he heard her go down the hall and close her bedroom door. *Coward,* he said to himself as he brushed his teeth. The truth would have to be told soon enough. He got along well with his mom, and was close to her. He could usually talk to her, if things were bothering him. This thing was *so* big, though. He didn't know how to approach it.

Brett passed Bev's open bedroom door on the way to his room. He glanced in at the sleeping form on the bed. As he gazed in at his sister, with her golden hair spread on the pillow, he felt a surge of remorse. Bev was just a little younger than Jodi, and Brett couldn't imagine his sister having a child.

Entering his room, he remembered the package of two safes still in his jeans pocket. He'd bought them yesterday in case he might need them. He removed them from his pocket and sat on his bed thinking, *fat lot of good these are now. I should have had them back in August. But then, who knew?* He tucked the package under his socks and underwear in the top drawer of his dresser, dropped his clothes on the floor, and slipped into bed, naked. He lay for a long time, unable to sleep, overwhelmed by the events of the day.

CHAPTER NINE

Jodi awoke a few minutes before her alarm went off. She could hear Carol in the kitchen below, getting breakfast. The heat from the kitchen stove came up through an open grate in her floor, warming the room nicely. She hadn't even heard Carol come to bed last night, or get up this morning. Jodi wondered if she'd come up at all. Maybe she slept with Len downstairs in the front room. She didn't remember hearing his car leave either. Oh well, she'd find out sooner or later. It seemed that they both had secrets to tell each other.

As soon as she was standing up, she had to go to the bathroom in the worst way, and hunger pangs gnawed at her belly. As she put on her dad's bulky old housecoat and ran down the stairs, she realized that the tiny blob inside her was already making demands on her body that she didn't appreciate.

She called out "good morning" to Carol, as she disappeared into the bathroom. Thank God she wasn't sick. It would be pretty embarrassing if Carol could hear her throwing up in there.

Carol had decided to wait a bit before confronting Jodi with her suspicions. She hoped that Jodi would tell her if anything was wrong. She called out as Jodi emerged from the bathroom, "Would you like scrambled eggs this morning?"

"No thanks," Jodi said. "Brett and I had eggs for supper last night. I'll just have some toast." She loved saying Brett's name. It brought him close to her. Jodi slid into a kitchen chair and reached for the toast. "Who phoned last night, after I went to bed?" she asked.

"It was Rick. He said that Brett's mom had called, wondering where he was, so Rick told her that he had left. He called here to tell Brett to get going."

"Oh-oh." Jodi said. "I hope he's not in trouble for staying so long." She bit into a thick slice of toast spread with huckleberry jam. "He was supposed to be at the Taylor's, not over here."

"You mean, his parents didn't know he was coming up to see you?" Carol asked with a mischievous grin.

"No," Jodi grinned back. "It was the only way they would lend him the car for the day. They don't exactly know about me yet. His dad's pretty strict. He wouldn't let him come up here to see a girl."

Carol brought her scrambled eggs over to the table along with more toast and a pot of tea. "He's gorgeous, Jodi! How did you meet him? And why didn't you tell me about him before?" Without waiting for an answer, she continued. "He really likes you too. I can tell by the way he looks at you."

Jodi blushed and said, "I met him back in August. Remember that beach party I went to with Linda? He was there with Rick that night. I'd actually met him that afternoon when I was riding Blossom in the park. A bunch of guys were playing ball, and Brett hit a home run out to the field. I was just coming up from the beach at a gallop, and they yelled at me to get the ball. I got it for them, and then I hung around to watch. I guess I impressed him with my riding ability or something. After the game, I was just sitting on Blossom talking to my friends. Brett came over and introduced himself. The girls were just hanging on him, flirting, and trying to get his attention. It was disgusting."

Jodi made a face, took another bite of toast, and washed it down with a swallow of hot tea. " Anyway, he admired Blossom, and then he shook my hand, looked right into my eyes, and smiled that fabulous smile. I felt so weak, I almost fell off!" Jodi sighed.

"Go on," Carol said, fascinated. "What happened at the beach party?"

Jodi glanced at the kitchen clock. She didn't have time to tell Carol everything right now. "Well," she said, "We spent some time together, and then he walked me home."

"Why didn't you tell me about him?" Carol asked again, looking hurt.

"I'm sorry. I should have. It was just that it was so romantic. I didn't want to share it with anyone...and I really didn't think I would ever see him again. You know he could have any girl he wants. They're all crazy about him."

"Yeah, I can see why," Carol smiled. "He could be a movie star with those looks and that body."

A vision of Brett's naked body joined to hers flashed through Jodi's mind. She quickly stood up and took her dishes to the sink. "I'd better hurry, or I'll be late for school." she said.

She left Carol sitting at the table with her cup of tea and ran up the stairs to get dressed. She selected her brown cords with the stretchy elastic waistband, and a loose-fitting sweater. She hurried through her chores and was just changing her barn coat for her school one when Linda came to call on her. They always walked to school together.

"Hi Linda. Bye Carol." Jodi called. "See you tonight. I'll make supper."

"Okay, thanks. See you guys." Carol called back as the girls went out the back door.

"So!" Linda babbled excitedly. "Tell me about yesterday. And don't leave out any juicy details! It was all I could do not to come over, knowing he was here." Her brown eyes, sparkling with anticipation, bored into Jodi and her freckled face was alight with excitement. "Come on, how'd it go?" she pressed.

"Linda," Jodi protested. "You *have* a boyfriend. Why are you so interested in mine?"

"Jeez, Jodi! It's just that you've never even been out with a boy, and all of a sudden you've landed the cutest, most popular guy in the county! *Everybody* in town is going to be interested in this romance!"

"*Everybody*?" Jodi asked, laughing.

"Well, all the girls, anyway. When they find out you're dating him, they're going to be awfully jealous of you."

Jodi felt a twinge of sadness. "There won't be much dating, I guess. He doesn't have a car, and it's pretty hard to get up here without one. He was late getting home last night, so I don't know if his parents will let him use their car very often. He probably has lots of girls in Harrison after him. I doubt if he'll stay interested in me."

Linda snorted. "Don't give me that! I took a walk past at nine thirty last night, and his car was still there. The only light on was upstairs, in *your* bedroom!"

Jodi blushed hotly. "Dammit Linda!" she exclaimed. "My best friend was spying on me! I can't believe you'd be so nosy." They walked in silence for a minute. "We were working on my jigsaw puzzle, okay?"

"Okay, okay, sorry," Linda apologized.

"Look," Jodi said. "I know he's a handsome hunk. I can't understand why he likes me, but I don't really care. I *know* I'm in love with him. I haven't been able to think of anyone or anything else since I met him. He's nice, he's polite, he's fun, and he's incredibly sexy. When he touches me, I could melt into a pool of butter."

"What's it like to kiss him?" Linda asked.

"Oh," Jodi sighed. "It's wonderful, like being on cloud nine, wherever that is." They both giggled. "And," she continued, "he just doesn't keep still while he's kissing. His hands are in my hair, down my back, on my hips.... He turns me to jelly." Linda's eyes were wide, her breathing quick. This was more like it. This was the stuff she wanted to hear.

"God, Jodi.... Do you think he's a virgin?"

"No, I know for a fact that he isn't."

The next question was just burning on Linda's lips when two other girls in the schoolyard joined them. The bell rang, and they entered the building to begin their day's work.

Jodi enjoyed her morning classes in Language Arts and Social Studies, but by third period as she headed over to the gym for P.E. she felt light-headed and hungry again. She would go home for lunch, but first she had to run the cross-country course. Her class had been training for over two months, and normally she was a fast strong runner. Linda and she had been running for years over the beaches and through the woods with their imaginative games and adventures. Jodi loved to run. She had never liked team sports like volleyball, basketball, or baseball, and she'd never been popular because of her lack of team spirit. But running was different. You had to reach into your own inner strength to go the distance. It was a test of your own worth and stamina. She wanted to do well. Linda came jogging out. They would run together, but each one would be individually timed. The course was two miles long, and contained a couple of tough hills.

Miss Somers blew the whistle and clicked the stopwatch as Jodi, Linda, and the rest of the class crossed the start line. The sprinters tore off, setting a fast pace; but the two girls jogged easily, somewhere in the middle of the pack. After half a mile, Jodi felt strange, but she willed herself to run, stretching her legs out to keep up with Linda. Soon, she started to fall behind, gasping for breath.

"What's wrong?" Linda called back over her shoulder. "Too much kissing make you weak?" She laughed and tossed her hair out of her eyes. "Come on, pokey! Let's start to move it!"

Jodi slowed to a walk. She felt terrible, on the point of collapse. "You go on. I don't feel good," she called to Linda. She felt cold all of a sudden, even though she was hot from running. Shivers ran up and down her spine. She heard Linda call something back, but she couldn't make it out. She dropped to her knees, senses reeling, and retched into the grass. Then she rolled away from the spot, and lay on her back, eyes closed. She just wanted to sleep.

"Jodi! What happened?" It was Linda. She had run on a bit, but turning and seeing Jodi go down on her knees, had come back to help her friend.

"Go on, I'm okay," she muttered. "Don't mess up your running time. I just need a rest, and then I'll walk back."

"Jodi, what's wrong?" Linda kneeled beside her and stared at her with concern. "I'm not going to leave you like this. I saw you puke over there. Come on, I'll help you up and we'll walk back together."

Jodi sat up and watched the last of the runners disappear up the road. She tried to be brave as she accepted defeat, but big tears filled her eyes, and spilled down her face. She knew the time had come to tell Linda her secret.

Linda put her arm around her friend and helped her up. Jodi was grateful for the support and caring. She saw the concern in Linda's eyes and knew she could trust her.

"Linda, can you keep a big secret for just a little while?" she asked, still snivelling.

"Of course," she answered, stopping to look at Jodi. "You've been acting weird for quite a while, and well, I've been wondering, what's going on?" They walked back towards the school.

"Pinkie swear you won't tell anyone until I say so?" Jodi pleaded. I need to talk to some other people, but I'll tell you first if you'll keep it to yourself.

"Yes." Linda said solemnly, as they locked their little fingers together. "I swear."

"Okay then." Jodi took a deep breath, and let it out again. "I'm pregnant."

Linda stopped and stared at her. Her dark eyes flew to Jodi's stomach then back to her face. "Oh no! Wow!" They walked again.

"Brett?" she asked. Jodi nodded, starting to cry again.

"Beach party?" Linda asked softly. Jodi nodded again.

"Jeez, I never suspected you guys did *that* when you went for a walk. We should have gone with you".

"It just happened. We didn't plan it or anything."

"I don't think so, Jodi. You should have been more careful. That guy is a mover and a shaker. He took advantage of you and your inexperience." Linda was rallying to her friend's defence and was getting mad. "Those cute guys with all the charm just think they can do whatever they want, and you were probably so star struck, you just let him!"

"No! It wasn't like that!" protested Jodi. "*I* wanted it. He would have stopped, but I wanted to do it. I was pretty shocked when I realized I was pregnant, but I'm really happy about it."

"How come you're crying then? You seem pretty upset to me."

"Well, I'm just feeling emotional about all the changes. I have to go away. We're going to Marnie's for Christmas, and once they find out about the baby, I probably won't be back for quite a while. I want to keep the baby, but my sisters might make me give it up for adoption."

The girls were just about back to the starting line in the big field. Miss Somers was glaring at them. She was busy for a few minutes, clocking in some runners, and then she turned to them. She was just about to erupt into a tirade when she saw Jodi's tear-stained face.

"Miss Somers," Linda explained, "Jodi got sick and couldn't run, so I stayed with her and walked her back."

Miss Somers eyed Jodi critically. "And how do you feel now, Jodi?"

"Kind of weak and tired," Jodi replied. "I'm sorry Linda missed her run. I tried to get her to keep going, but she came back when I threw up."

"You threw up? " Jodi nodded.

"Can you walk home?" Miss Somers asked her, looking a bit more sympathetic. She was tough and not overly kind when kids tried to skip out of P.E. However, she was somewhat concerned at Jodi's pale colour and the fact that she had thrown up. She spoke to Linda. "Can you make sure that she gets home all right then, Linda?"

Linda slipped her arm around Jodi. "Sure, Miss Somers. I can do my run after school, if that's okay."

"All right. I'll be here." She turned her attention to more runners coming in, while the girls made their escape and headed home.

"So anyways," said Linda, continuing their conversation from before, "What does Brett have to say about it?"

"I just told him yesterday, and he took it pretty well. He was upset at first, and I thought he'd run out on me, but he didn't. He was very sweet and supportive. He's a good decent guy. He's scared, but he said he'd stick by me through this as best he could."

The school was situated up on a high bench overlooking the lower part of town, which jutted out into the lake. Towering, steep mountains surrounded it like soldiers guarding a precious gem. The scenery rivalled that of Switzerland, but in 1973, Kelso was still an undiscovered paradise; a quiet little backwater of a town.

Various trails led down through the wooded hillside as well as a short, curved, gravel road that led to the long trestle bridge that connected the upper and lower town sites. Jodi and Linda took the Camel Trail, their favourite, so-called because of the hillocks and humps on it. Running it was fun, but today they walked. Their relationship would never be the same again because of Jodi's pregnancy.

Jodi once again asked Linda to keep quiet about her news until she talked to Carol and the rest of her family. Linda promised, and they parted at Jodi's back gate.

"Are you going back this aft?" inquired Linda.

"Oh yes," Jodi said. "I'll be okay after I have something to eat. I want to talk to Mr. Evans."

"See you in a little while then."

"Yeah, bye, and thanks for helping me Linda."

"What are friends for?" Linda flashed her a smile, and waved goodbye.

Jodi greeted Scamp as he came running to meet her, and she gave Blossom a pat on her way through the paddock to the house.

Jodi and Carol had a two-burner hot plate that they used when they didn't have time for the wood stove to heat up. Jodi opened a can of spaghetti and plopped it into a pan to heat on one of the elements. She poured herself a large glass of goat's milk and drank half of it immediately. She was starving! She grabbed a spoon, stirred the spaghetti once or twice, and clicked off the burner. Taking it to the table, she sat down and ate right out of the pot. No use dirtying extra dishes.

Samantha sat on her chair, watching Jodi, but spaghetti wasn't her favourite, so she didn't ask for any.

Her hunger satisfied, Jodi took the pot and glass to the sink and rinsed them out. She was looking through the leftovers in the fridge, trying to decide what to make for supper, when the phone rang in the dining room. *Probably Linda,* she thought. *Wonder what she wants.* She lifted the receiver on the third ring, said "Hello?" and heard an operator say, "One moment please." She caught her breath, and her knees felt weak. She waited, listening, as coins were dropped into the pay phone. She pulled up a dining room chair and sat down, as Brett's deep voice came on the line.

"Hi Jodi, how are you doing?"

"Oh fine," she blurted out. "I didn't expect to hear from you so soon. Where are you?"

"At a pay phone, about a block from school. I've been thinking about you so much; I just wanted to see how you are."

"Well, I was sick before lunch in P.E. We had to run the marathon, and I couldn't do it. I had to stop and throw up."

"I'm sorry. That was awful for you. You shouldn't be running any distance like that."

"Yeah, I know. Linda stopped and helped me back, so I told her what was the matter. She was pretty shocked." There was a silence on the other end. "Brett? Are you there?"

"Yes, I'm here. I guess I'm kind of in shock too. I couldn't sleep last night. It all hit me pretty hard. We have some tough times ahead of us, but mostly I'm concerned for you. You have to deal with a lot of stuff, both emotional and physical. I'm feeling very guilty. I should have been more responsible."

"Don't torture yourself, please. There's no use in looking back. We'll deal with it one day at a time."

The operator broke in and said, "Deposit another fifty cents, please sir." Jodi waited while the coins were deposited.

"Did you get heck last night for being late? You know your mom phoned Rick?

"Yeah, Mom was waiting up. She was more worried than mad. Dad gave me a good lecture this morning though. He was fairly ticked off at me for getting home so late. I'm grounded for being late. I can't come up for a while."

"Well," Jodi's little laugh bubbled over. "Seeing you was worth it. You made me so happy yesterday. I loved being with you, and I just feel so lucky that you care about me and didn't cop out on me. I know now that I can rely on you when things get tough."

"Yes. I promised you that, and I mean what I said. I want to see you again, but I'm not sure how I can swing it."

"We'll find a way." Jodi looked at her watch. "I guess we'd better get back to school now."

"Yep, I'd better hustle here too. I'll call you on Sunday, okay?"

"Sure, but call me collect. The pay phone is a nuisance, having to have the right change, and the operator interrupting."

"I don't want you to have to pay for my calls, Jodi." He sounded a bit offended.

"Don't be silly." she replied. "It's a small price to pay for having a visit with you."

"Okay then," he agreed. " Got to go. Have a good week."

"Bye-bye. Thanks for phoning." She hung up, feeling a mixture of sadness and elation. She went into the kitchen and yanked open the freezer section of the fridge and pulled out a package of ground beef. Tossing it into the sink to thaw, she grabbed her coat and ran out the door. Linda was waiting at the gate.

CHAPTER TEN

Jodi made it to school ten minutes before her math class started. She went into the small office and approached Mrs. Zalinski, the school secretary. The students affectionately called her "Mrs. Zee". Edna Zalinski had worked in the school office for many years so she knew everyone from kindergarten to grade twelve. She stopped typing as Jodi came in and said, "Hello Jodi. Can I help you?"

Jodi was nervous. "I'd like to see Mr. Evans this afternoon, please".

"What about?" Mrs. Zalinski asked bluntly, pencil poised over a notepad.

"Umm...Jodi shifted her books, and looked at the floor. "It's kind of a private matter."

Mrs. Zalinski looked at her sharply "You're not in some kind of trouble, are you? "Whatever it is, I can handle it. Mr. Evans doesn't like to be bothered with trivial matters." She waited, expectant, tapping the pencil.

"I'd still like to talk to him", Jodi insisted. "Will he be here after school?"

Mrs. Zalinski sighed and shook her head, looking annoyed "He has to rush off to a board meeting in Harrison. I'll give you a note and you can come fifteen minutes before your last class ends. What do you have?"

"Band", she replied, "Mr. Cross."

The older lady scribbled out the appointment note and handed it over. Jodi smiled, gratefully. "Thanks Mrs. Zee". She got a small grudging smile back.

At three o'clock Jodi put her flute away and excused herself from band practice. She had already showed Mr. Cross the note. She slipped past Mrs. Zalinski, who gave her a slight nod, and knocked on Mr. Evans' open door.

"Come in, Jodi" he called heartily. "And what can I do for you today?"

Jodi came in, her heart pounding, and closed the door behind her. She slid into the big chair facing him and tried a tentative smile. Mr. Evans sat resting his chin on folded hands, waiting for her to speak. Jodi looked into his kindly face, noticed his receding hairline, the thin moustache and wire-rimmed glasses perched on his nose.

She came right out with it. "I need to leave the school system Sir, and I was wondering if I could get my lessons by correspondence and work at home."

Mr. Evans looked at her in stunned silence, not understanding. "Leave school?" he asked. She nodded. "Have you got a job, or something?" he asked, fiddling with papers on his desk.

"No, I'm three months pregnant." His face almost fell apart as his jaw dropped and his eyebrows shot up somewhere in the vicinity of his forehead.

"My God! How did that happen?"

Jodi blushed and looked at the floor.

"I mean," he stammered, getting up and stroking his moustache, "It's just...well...I didn't expect that from *you!*" Poor man. He was so embarrassed. He had two daughters himself, and Jodi felt a little sorry for him.

"Who's the father?" he asked, getting control of himself and sitting again.

Jodi looked at the floor again, studying the worn dark patterns in the wood. "It's nobody from here."

"Is he going to marry you?"

"No, we don't think that would be best right now. Maybe in a year or so, when we're out of school."

"I see", he said, not looking convinced. "Is there...ummm... He cleared his throat and tried again. "Is it too late to terminate it?"

Jodi looked him right in the eye, fiercely protecting her unborn.

"I'm a Christian. I don't believe in taking an innocent life."

Mr. Evans interrupted her, equally stern. "I'm a Christian too, Jodi, and I don't believe in young girls experimenting with a relationship that belongs in a marriage bed."

Well, that stung. She blushed and dropped her eyes.

The bell rang, and there was an immediate flurry in the hallway outside. Mr. Evans said, "I have to leave for a meeting. We'll talk again. I'll order the correspondence courses for you in the morning. They'll be here in about a week. They have to come from Victoria."

"Yes Sir, thank-you." She stood up. "Oh, and one more thing. Could I drop out of P.E.? I'm finding it too hard to keep up."

"Yes, I'll speak to Miss Somers tomorrow." He stood up, dismissing her.

Jodi eased out into the hall and headed for her locker. She heard her name called out. Looking around, she saw Dave Paulson heading her way. He fell in step beside her and asked, "Are you in trouble with Mr. Evans? I saw you come out of his office."

She smiled at him. "Nope! Everything's fine." She knew Dave liked her. He had asked her to the Halloween Dance a couple of weeks ago, but she declined. He stopped at her locker and asked, "Could I walk you home today?" He looked so innocent; so hopeful.

"Sorry, Dave. I promised Linda I'd wait for her. She's running the cross-country after school."

"Aw...shucks." Dave looked down and shuffled his feet awkwardly. "Would you go out with me Jodi? To a show, or something?"

Jodi put her math books and flute in her locker and picked out her L.A. and Socials books for homework. Shutting the door with a bang, she turned to him.

"Dave, I really like you, but I've got something going on in my life right now, and I can't go out with you. I'm sorry. Can we just be friends for now?" She smiled at him again.

He looked disappointed. "I guess so, although you've crushed me to the quick." He grimaced, clutching his heart with both hands.

"Clown." she teased. "You'll get over it! See you tomorrow in English class."

"If I don't die tonight of a broken heart." he laughed, walking away.

Jodi went out and sat on the front steps to wait for Linda. The stones were cold and hard. A few snowflakes were beginning to drift down from an already darkening sky. She stuck out her tongue and caught some. The lake was a dark, slate blue, lying at rest. Remembering the time she and Linda had gone out on a raft and had been carried out by big strong waves, she knew it could be a real demon. She shuddered to think what might have happened if those two brave ladies hadn't swum out and rescued them. She had a lot more respect for the lake now.

Jodi hugged herself to keep warm. She wished she hadn't agreed to wait for Linda. But then, she'd have had no excuse but to let Dave walk her home. They had been friends since first grade, and she didn't want to hurt him. He'd know soon enough why she wasn't encouraging him.

She got up and stamped her feet and walked around to avoid going out to the field and confronting Miss Somers. Let Mr. Evans tell her. She had to tell Carol tonight, because by tomorrow, the whole town would be buzzing with the news.

Finally, Linda came, eyes sparkling, cheeks red from running in the cold.

"Sorry I'm late! You should have just gone ahead without me." Linda said, as she put her arm around her friend. They went home arm in arm, sharing the events of the afternoon. Linda confided that Miss Somers had asked a lot of nosy questions about Jodi, like whether or not she had a boyfriend, and if she had noticed anything unusual about Jodi's behaviour lately. "I think she suspects, but I swear, I didn't tell her anything."

Linda listened breathlessly, as Jodi told her of Brett's phone call and how he had called her 'sugar' and promised to keep in close touch with her. Linda apologized for bad mouthing Brett earlier on. They talked of Linda's boyfriend, Bob Schaumburg, who was taking her to the show on Friday night. Jodi asked how the run went, and told of her interview with the principal, and that she didn't have to take P.E. anymore. There was no shortage of things to talk about, even though they had only been apart for not quite three hours.

The girls parted at the back gate. Although Jodi was hungry again, she started right in feeding the animals. It was almost dark, and she didn't want to have to come out later. Scamp ran to meet her as soon as he heard the girls approach, and he joyfully bounded around her.

Thick snowflakes were falling in earnest now, and the ground was beginning to turn white. It was November 20th, *less than five weeks to Christmas!* Jodi thought with a start. "Where will I be?" she said to Scamp. She always talked to the little dog as if he was a person; and, indeed, he seemed to understand everything she said. He was quick to match his mood to hers; happy if she was happy and immediately droopy and sad eyed if she was melancholy. If she cried, he would sidle up to her, whimpering in sympathy, and offer a paw to shake, his way of holding her hand. He recognized the few bad words she used when she was angry; and at these times, he cringed in shame, but with his tail wagging to show he understood her frustration. When she left for school, he knew he had to stay home; but he sat for hours looking up the road, watching for her return. Jodi wondered sadly what she would do with him if she had to stay in Vancouver. She knew she had to get things hashed out with Carol tonight.

Chores finished, Jodi headed into the house. She set the eggs down in the porch and picked up a load of wood. The house was cold. Samantha came to greet her, purring loudly, curling herself around Jodi's legs. "Look out, you goofy cat!" she exclaimed. "I know you're cold. I'll have the fire going in a minute." She picked up the cat and stroked her head and back. She held her over her left shoulder with one hand, while she lifted the lid on the kitchen range and stuffed paper and kindling in. Sam hung on with her claws, as her tail flicked back and forth across Jodi's face. Setting Sam on the wood-box, Jodi lit the paper, watching while the cedar kindling caught and flared. She adjusted the damper.

"Now for a snack," Jodi said to the cat. She selected a jar of homemade apricots. She turned on the radio and sat down to eat. The cat and dog looked at her adoringly, happy to have her home. Jodi chatted to them as she ate.

When her hunger was sated, she added wood to the stove and checked the thawing meat in the sink. She asked Scamp, "What should I make with this? spaghetti sauce, or chili?" Scamp wagged his stubby tail enthusiastically for both, but Jodi decided on chili. "Chili it is then. Thank you Sir." Scamp grinned stupidly and wiggled in pleasure.

Jodi had no trouble cooking a meal. Her mom had been a good cook of simple plain food, and the girls had been expected to help with meals. She crumbled the meat into a large pot and added chopped garlic cloves and an onion.

She browned the meat, stirring it and breaking up the chunks, then drained the fat into the grease tin. Jodi sang along with the radio as she worked. Next, she opened a jar of preserved tomatoes, added them to the meat, and went to the cupboard for a can of kidney beans. She added a liberal dose of salt and pepper, some oregano, parsley flakes, and a few chili piquins. She didn't want the sauce too spicy. She had noticed already that some foods gave her heartburn.

With supper simmering and the place warming up, Jodi turned her attention to the heater in the dining room. She cleaned out the ashes first and took the bucket out, then carried several armfuls of wood in for the evening. She fetched in the eggs, more wood for the kitchen stove, and then brought her schoolbooks in and dumped them on the dining room table. She might as well do homework for an hour. She got out the National Geographic she had borrowed from the Library and began to write her report for Social Studies on the culture, geography, and people of Japan.

At the Bayside Bakery, Carol was busy taking the trays of sweets to the cooler in the back, washing the tables, and tidying up before closing time. A few customers stopped in to buy bread or something for dessert. She was somewhat surprised to see Miss Somers come in. She definitely wasn't a regular.

"Hello Carol," she smiled. "Could I get a cup of that coffee before you dump it out?"

"Sure thing, Miss Somers. How are you?"

"Oh, same as usual. Things haven't changed all that much since you were in my Phys. Ed. class." Carol grinned and brought the coffee and some fresh cream over to the table.

"Have you got a minute to join me? I'd like to talk to you about Jodi." Miss Somers stirred her coffee, watching the spoon go round and round.

Carol's heart skipped a beat, as she glanced at the clock and slipped into the chair across from her former teacher. There were no other customers in the store. It was five to six.

"Sure, we're as good as closed anyway" she said, feeling nervous.

Miss Somers could be blunt, and she came right to the point. "Jodi couldn't complete the cross-country run today. She collapsed, and vomited, and her friend Linda had to bring her back." She paused, sipping her coffee.

Carol caught her breath and managed to squeak out, "Oh no! Is she okay?"

Miss Somers nodded. "I think so. She came back for her afternoon classes. I was just wondering..." She hesitated, looking directly at Carol.."If there's any chance that she might be pregnant?"

Carol let out her breath in a big sigh and leaned her elbows on the table, propping up her head in her hands. She looked exhausted.

"I don't honestly know. Len asked me the same thing last night. I honest to God hadn't noticed, but I'm going to find out tonight when I get home."

Miss Somers nodded sympathetically. "I've never seen her hang around with boys."

"Me neither." Carol thought about telling Miss Somers about Brett, but decided to keep quiet about him until she knew the truth.

"If she's in trouble, let me know if I can help. You know...if you need money or anything...I'll do what I can." Miss Somers looked a little embarrassed, as she stood up to leave.

"Thanks." Carol smiled warmly at her. "I'll keep it in mind. Good night Miss Somers."

Carol let her out the front door, and flipped the sign around so that the 'Closed, Come Again' faced outwards. She put the empty coffee cup in the sink, took the cash and cheques out of the till, and put them into a cloth bag. She turned out the lights, and looking around, went out through a swinging door to the kitchen and on through the back hall to a stairway.

She went up and delivered the money to the owner, Fritz Kriegle.

Fritz and his wife Anna had come to Kelso twenty years ago, looking for a new start in life, and fell in love with the lake and mountains. It reminded them of their native Austria. They loved the beauty, the peace, and the friendly people. Fritz worked at the old hotel as a dishwasher and a cook while Anna had cleaned rooms and waited on tables. After many years of hard work, they had saved enough to start up the small bakery.

"Zank-you Carol!" he said, in his heavy European accent. "How was every leetle ting this afternoon?"

"Just fine, Mr. Kriegle," she replied, anxious to get going. "Did you have a good rest?"

"Ya, ya, very goot, zank-you." He always slept and rested in the afternoon since his workday began at three a.m. "You be sure, take some bread home and a treat for your leetle sister."

"I will. Thank you very much. Goodnight."

"Gute nacht, my dear," he said, closing the door.

Carol went downstairs, into the kitchen. Putting a loaf of whole wheat bread and two butter horns into a bag, she slipped into her coat and stepped out the back door into the snowy night. She checked the door to make sure it was locked, and started home, her mind full of questions.

CHAPTER ELEVEN

At ten after six, Jodi set the table and cut several thick slices of Mr. Kriegle's light rye bread. The chili was ready, simmering on the back of the stove. She was jittery, thinking of what to say to her sister. She was making the tea when Carol came in, shaking the snow out of her hair. She looked tired.

"Hi!" Jodi called cheerily. "How was your day?"

"A lot better than yours, evidently," Carol replied tersely, hanging up her coat. Jodi set the chili and the pot of tea on the table. "What do you mean?" she asked, sitting down at the table.

"Miss Somers was in today, and she...."

"Oh that! Jodi interrupted. "I'm fine now." Carol took a critical look at Jodi.

"Stand up!" she commanded.

"What for?"

"Because I want to look at you!" Carol shouted. Jodi sighed and stood up slowly. Her face grew hot and she felt faint. Carol stared at Jodi's thickened waist and slightly protruding belly under the baggy sweater.

"You *are* pregnant, aren't you? How could I have been so blind?

Jodi nodded and sank back into her chair, her eyes filling with tears. Carol also sat down heavily and began to cry too.

"Damn it Jodi!" she sputtered through her tears. "How could you be so stupid?" You know the facts of life." She covered her face with her hands. "And why didn't you tell me? Why am I the last to know? When I get my hands on that little punk he won't look so handsome with his face re-arranged! I should get Len to go down and punch his lights out. Damn guy has his brains located directly below his belt buckle! And you! You ought to get a damn good licking too!" Carol jumped up and got a tissue from the bathroom, blowing her nose loudly.

"Don't blame Brett for this." Jodi sniffed "It wasn't his fault. I'm absolutely, crazily, head over heels in love with him, and I'm *very* happy about having his baby!"

Carol exploded. "That's bullshit!" Then, looking more hurt than angry, added, "Why didn't you tell me?"

"Because," Jodi answered, tears still glistening on her cheeks, "You are the closest to me and the hardest to tell. I just told Brett yesterday and today I told Linda because she helped me when I got sick trying to run the marathon. I told Mr. Evans this afternoon. Miss Somers must have guessed. I knew I couldn't hide it anymore. I was going to tell you after supper. Speaking of supper, let's eat this stuff while it's hot. I'm hungry." She ladled some chili into her bowl and took a bite of bread and butter. Carol helped herself and they ate in silence for a while.

Carol asked," How far along are you?"

"Three months and two days, exactly."

"You should have told me. We could have got rid of it. It's probably too late now."

Jodi said, "I know. That's why I didn't tell anybody. I didn't want anyone to force to me have an abortion. I want to keep it. I think that it's a special gift, coming to fill a huge hole in my life - that big, empty space that Mom and Dad left. The baby's due on the anniversary date of their death. Isn't that weird?"

Carol looked surprised, but sceptical. "That's crazy, Jodi. So, you're trying to tell me that Brett was sent to you as an angel with a pecker instead of having wings; you had a religious experience with him, and now you're pregnant?"

Jodi grinned. "Yeah, something like that...except that he's no spirit. He's all man." She sighed dreamily, fiddling with her food. "He feels guilty too, and he's scared, but he's kind and caring, and responsible, and he promised to help me all he can. His parents will be very angry and will probably make things difficult for us. He hasn't told them yet.

"If you're three months along now, this must have happened back at the beach party, right?"

"Right."

"Jodi, I'm ashamed of you. You only met him that afternoon, didn't you?"

"Yes."

"And you slept with him that night?"

Not slept with him; made love," Jodi corrected, "On the beach."

Carol shook her head in dismay. "I can't believe you did something like that. I thought you hadn't even looked at boys yet. I never worried about you, because you were so square. It's so unlike you!"

"I know," Jodi agreed, "I can't believe it myself. But we're crazy about each other."

When the chili was finished, the sisters started on the butter horns and drank their tea.

"You don't know anything about babies." Carol continued seriously. "You've never even liked baby-sitting. You've always preferred to work with animals, rather than kids."

It was true. To earn extra money, Jodi had done jobs like shovelling snow, stacking wood, weeding gardens, cutting lawns, or feeding animals. She had always avoided looking after children. Nevertheless, she was looking forward to this child. She didn't see the baby so much as a son or daughter as yet, but more like a playmate, a companion.

Carol broached the dreaded subject. "You know I'll have to let Marnie and Rob know. They'll be so shocked. They'll want you to have the baby down there, and I'm sure they will want to help you look after it."

Jodi steeled herself and said stubbornly, "I'll go for Christmas, but I want to come back. You know how much I love this place. Even if Brett and I can't be together, we can see each other once in a while. He should have the chance to see his baby when it's born. He loves us."

Carol snorted. "Jodi, he's too young and immature to give you any lasting commitment. He'll get over it once you're far away. You'd be better off to come down to the city and let your family help you raise the baby. We can give you so much more support than he can. A little one is such a lot of work. They're extremely demanding of your time and energy. And not just when they're babies. You're looking at twenty years of your life and more that has to be dedicated to this project. It's a huge job. If you try to do it alone, you'll fail."

Jodi knew that Carol was trying to help, and what she said made a lot of sense, but still, every fibre of her being rejected the idea of moving away from her beloved home.

"Do you want me to phone Marnie, or do you want to do it? Carol asked.

Jodi was quiet for a moment, thinking. "I'd like to write to her; try to explain how I feel. I'm better at expressing myself in writing than having to talk.

Besides, it will give them time for the shock to wear off before she talks to me."

"Well, you had better do it right away," Carol advised. "It's only a bit more than a month to Christmas already."

"I know, I'll do it tonight," Jodi said with a heavy heart. She knew that Marnie would call as soon as she got the news and insist that they move down there. She felt trapped.

Changing the subject, she asked Carol, "Do you love Len?" Her sister started to gather up the dishes, looking at her busy hands. "Well?" Jodi prompted. Carol set the plates down again.

"I'm very fond of him, but I don't love him enough to marry him, and stay in this town." There. She had said it. She had never really admitted it to herself or to him, but she suddenly knew it was the truth.

"Do you think he'll get over *you* when you're far away?" Jodi asked. It was a dig, and she knew it.

Carol chose to ignore it, knowing Jodi's feelings were raw. "I guess he will, in time. I'm sorry for him, but I can't stay here. I want to leave. And I'm sorry for you too. I know how badly you want to stay, but it just isn't possible. You can't support yourself here alone." She sighed. "Go on and write your letter. I'll do the dishes."

Jodi jumped up from the table,

fighting back tears of rage and frustration. She shouted at Carol, "It's not fair that you would give up the love of a good man for a life in the city! And it's not fair that you're forcing me to go either. What about Scamp and Sam? What about Blossom? Who's going to milk Annie? And what are we going to do with all the food we worked so hard to store for the winter? We can't just leave it here to freeze! And how about the house? With no heat the water pipes will burst. Vandals will bust in and wreck it when they find out it's empty. I can't go away and leave all this!"

Carol let Jodi rant and rave while she cleared the table and started the dishes. Then she said calmly, "Okay, you tell me how you would manage here on your own."

Jodi thought a moment and sat down again at the table. With tears glistening on her cheeks and in a halting voice, she said, "Maybe I could have your job at the bakery. Or instead of supporting me down there, Marnie and Rob could send me some money. I wouldn't need much. Friends and neighbours would help me, and Brett would too."

Jodi, get realistic!" Carol said with some exasperation. "You couldn't stand on your feet eight hours a day at a job, look after animals, chop wood, keep the fires going, do the yard and garden, *and* look after a baby! The loneliness and drudgery would drive you crazy." Carol spoke with her back to Jodi, hands immersed in the sink.

"We can get temporary homes for the animals, until we know what we're doing. We could rent the house out, or Shannon's could have the food and wood in exchange for looking after it. And we might not be gone forever. I might want to come back, start a business or something, maybe even settle down and get married. But for now, I can't see any way out except to go to Vancouver for a year or so. And now that you're pregnant, you'll just have to go along with moving so we can look after you. Be reasonable Jodi. It's for the best."

But Jodi wasn't listening. She stomped up the stairs and flung herself on her bed, sobbing hysterically. The whole day had been tough emotionally and she was exhausted. After some time, her sobs subsided, and she fell into a restless sleep.

Carol left her alone, and when she came up to bed, she tucked a heavy quilt around her sleeping sister. She tiptoed into her own room for what turned out to be a sleepless night for her. She had to face a confrontation with Len, deal with Jodi's pain, tell Mr. Kriegle that she was leaving, and make all the arrangements for the move to Vancouver.

CHAPTER TWELVE

The next morning, Jodi awoke feeling tired, crabby, and depressed. She decided not to go to school. She and Carol were not saying much to each other. Carol was tired too, and did not know what to say to console Jodi, or Len for that matter. They ate cereal and toast in silence; then Jodi went out to feed the animals and milk Annie.

Jodi leaned her head against the goat's silky side as she wearily squeezed the milk into the bucket. Tears slid down her cheeks. She listened to Blossom banging her feed bucket around as the pony enjoyed her morning oats and then the small ripping and chewing sounds as she started on her hay. *Oh, my beloved creatures, how can I leave you?* She thought. *And my golden boy. How can I survive with you so far away?*

Jodi's feet were slow and leaden as she went back into the house. Carol had left for work. She phoned Linda and asked her to bring her any homework. She strained the milk and cleaned up the kitchen. Then she sat down at the dining room table, and, with great difficulty, composed a letter to her sister Marnie.

At mid-morning, Mr. Evans phoned to see if she was all right. He informed her that he had called a staff meeting for after school during which he would tell the teachers about her condition. He wanted to emphasize that Jodi would be welcome to attend such classes as she was able to but he could not promise that the students would treat her kindly. Mr. Evans cautioned Jodi that she might be in for some teasing and rude comments. She was to come to see him if the teasing got too hard to handle. Jodi thanked him, and hung up.

 In the afternoon she bridled Blossom and rode up to the Post Office with her letter. She got a few 'why aren't you in school looks' but she ignored them. Her letter deposited, she rode slowly down to the beach, and along the sand where she and Brett had walked. The mountains were almost obscured by low hanging misty clouds. Jodi knew there would be fresh snow gracing their peaks when the clouds lifted. The lake was almost black, it was so dark and the surface looked dull and somber. A swirl of light snow filled the air and stuck to Blossom's long mane and forelock. It was very still and quiet. Softly Jodi sang, "The earth in solemn stillness lay, to hear the angels sing." *What had made her think of that line from some old Christmas carol?* It had just popped into her head. Then, as Jesus had cried out on the cross, she said out loud, "My God, why have you forsaken me?"

 Scamp chased some sandpipers off that were bobbing and dipping along the shore for food. He ran back to Jodi with his long ears flapping, eyes and body alive with excitement. Jodi had to smile at him and tell him he was a clever dog.

Jodi stopped Blossom at the log where she and Brett had sat talking and looking at the stars. She remembered the feel of Brett's arms around her as she cried against his chest. She stared at the spot where they had lain to conceive the child she was now carrying. Hot tears spilled over and ran down her cheeks. She wiped them away fiercely before they could freeze on her face.

Blossom stamped impatiently, tossing her head. She wanted to get going. With a sigh, Jodi released the reins and spoke to her, turning for home.

As Jodi rode, several Biblical passages swirled through her mind. *Fear not! For lo, I am with you always.* She thought with surprise, *where did that come from?* Then, a few minutes later as she slipped off of Blossom's warm back, she heard, *The Lord is thy strength and thy redeemer.* Jodi felt a little spooky. She watched Blossom drop down on her knees, and plop onto her side with a sigh. Then the pony rolled over and over in the snow, kicking her legs wildly in the air. Getting to her feet with a heave, Blossom shook herself, sending snow flying. In spite of her sadness, Jodi laughed at her. Leaning on the fence, watching the pony's antics, she heard, *The Lord is thy shepherd,* and from another direction, *If God is for us, who can be against us?* And then, from behind her, *trust and obey! Jodi* whirled around. There was no one there! *Am I going crazy* she thought, *or have I just been visited by a legion of angels?* Jodi felt a great joy bubbling up from deep inside her and she knew her prayer of anguish had truly been answered. She was *not* forsaken! She was *not* alone!

With a renewed sense of peace and purpose she went into the house and began to prepare a meal for Carol and herself. She took chicken pieces out of the freezer section of the fridge, laid them on a baking sheet, and sprinkled them with salt and pepper, tarragon, and onion slices, before popping them into the oven. She peeled potatoes, turnips, and carrots, and put them in their pans ready to cook. She made a cobbler with canned cherries, brown sugar, flour, and spices.

In a short time, delicious aromas were coming from the kitchen. Jodi brought her books into the kitchen and did a little homework while keeping the fire hot and tending to the cooking.

She realized that things were almost as difficult for Carol as they were for her and she resolved to co-operate and go along with the move. She would go, but she would be back.

Carol had been dreading coming home to a night of tears and quarrelling with Jodi so she was very surprised to find a lovely meal ready and a pleasant helpful sister bustling around looking after her. After supper they talked and made plans for the care of the animals in their absence and for the house. Closer than they'd been for years, they shared the pain of leaving their girlfriends, Carol's job, Jodi's animals, and especially, their lovers.

Carol said wistfully, "If it's meant to be, they'll still be here if we come back."

"*When* we come back" corrected Jodi. "This is my home."

CHAPTER THIRTEEN

When Jodi showed up at school the next morning, she felt like a complete stranger. Teachers and students alike stared at her as if they didn't know her. Jodi felt, rather than heard, the whispered comments as she passed. Linda stuck by her, talking and walking with her as though nothing had changed, but it was a strain for both of them to act naturally.

In English class Jodi caught Dave Paulsen's eye and smiled at him, but he looked away in embarrassment, and hurried out at the end of class without speaking to her.

Nothing stayed secret in Kelso for long. Everyone knew everyone else's business, and discussed that business openly. There was little else to discuss except small talk and gossip. Not all of it was nasty, by any means, but an individual's business was of personal interest and concern. When that personal business was the least bit spicy, the gossip exchange perked up considerably. The whole town was a-buzz with the news of Jodi's pregnancy. There hadn't been anything this exciting to talk about since Olie Rennard had shot and killed his wife in a drunken rage, three or four years ago.

Rick was stunned at the news. The circle of friends that had been at the beach party was discussing Jodi's condition when he joined them in the cafe after school.

He knew that if it was true, then his cousin Brett was responsible. No wonder Jodi had needed to see him and had asked for his help in arranging a visit. He was determined to keep as quiet as possible about it to protect his cousin and when asked point blank if Brett was the father, he shrugged his shoulders and said he didn't know. *Keep 'em guessing,* he thought grimly. *None of their business anyway.*

A few days later, Rick's dad asked him what he knew about the affair, and again, he refused to divulge what he knew. *If Brett is involved,* thought Dan Taylor, *I wonder if his parents know?* He decided to give them a phone call to find out.

The phone rang about nine-thirty that night in the Randall house, as Brett and Bev sat at opposite ends of the dining room table finishing up their homework. Their parents were watching T.V. in the adjoining living room.

Bev answered and when Brett realized that it was Uncle Dan she was talking to, he went hot and cold at the same time. He had a dreadful feeling that his world was about to come crashing down. Bev exchanged pleasantries with her uncle and assured him that everything was fine. Then she called her mom to the phone.

As Bev sat down again at the table, Brett closed his books and said to his sister, "It's been nice knowing you sis. I think I'm about to get kicked out of the house."

Bev looked at him in surprise. "What do you mean? What's wrong? You look like you've just seen a ghost." Brett didn't answer; he just stared at his closed books, listening to the conversation coming from the kitchen.

Carmen was saying, "Well...I don't know. He didn't get home til almost eleven thirty...He wasn't? I see." A long pause ensued. Then Carmen said, "No, I've never heard of her...I certainly will. I'll talk to him. Thanks Dan. Goodbye."

Carmen hung up the phone; shock and disbelief washing over her as she sat in the dark for a long minute. Then, coming into the dining room, she slipped into a chair and gave her son a long look. She was pale and her dark blue eyes registered hurt disillusionment.

Bruce Randall glanced over at the silent trio, turned the sound down on the T.V., and asked, "Is something wrong, Mother?"

Carmen nodded, still mute, then finding her voice, said quietly, "I think you'd better come over here."

Bev asked timidly, "What's going on?"

Carmen Randall took a deep breath and looked straight at her son as Bruce strode to the table.

Carmen asked, "Do you know a girl

by the name of Jodi McCallum?"

"Yes. I met her last August." Brett kept his eyes downcast, studying the pattern on his math textbook.

"Were you with her the night of the beach party?"

"Yes." Brett's face was white; his big, blue eyes open wide.

"Did you spend the day with her last Sunday, instead of with Rick?"

"Yes."

"So, you know she's pregnant...and she's only sixteen?"

"Yes."

"Did you get her pregnant?"

"Yes." The word came out in a whisper. Brett bowed his head, and then looked desperately at his mom. "I'm sorry, Mom...Dad...I wanted to tell you, but I just couldn't find the right words. I...."

"You're sorry?" Bruce shouted. "Sorry? You got a sixteen year old girl pregnant, and you're *sorry?* Christ! Were you drunk?"

"No, I wasn't drinking that night. It was..." Again his dad interrupted.

"You've brought shame to this family! You've acted in an irresponsible manner; you've breached the trust we had in you; you lied to us about your whereabouts!"

Bruce's face was contorted with rage as he grabbed Brett by the collar and lifted him to his feet. His blue eyes were blazing; his face red with anger. He hadn't spanked either of his kids for a very long time, but by God, he was angry enough to strike out now. He smacked Brett across the side of his face with his open hand and quickly backhanded him again across his mouth.

Brett was caught off guard by the blows, which caused him to twist and fall back across the side of the armchair. He let out a blood-curdling yell as Bruce yanked him up by the hair and rained blows on his back and shoulders with his fists.

At the first slap, Carmen jumped up and grabbed at her husband, begging him to stop. Bev ran around the table to her brother, screaming, "Daddy! Stop it! Don't hit him!"

Carmen got hold of Bruce's arms, and implored him to stop. She and Bev were crying.

Brett staggered up, and stood spread-legged, breathing heavily. His left ear was a bright red from the stinging slap and his bottom lip was split and bleeding where Bruce's wedding ring had cut into it. His eyes blazed with defiance and it was all he could do not to launch himself at his father and punch him out.

Bev saw the look and desire and put a hand on his arm. "Brett, don't!" she warned.

Bruce backed off and sat on a dining room chair, panting with exertion. He spit words out with disgust. "I talked to you about treating girls with respect. I talked to you about staying in a group and not pairing off. I talked to you about getting an education and a good job before getting serious about anyone. I warned you over and over again to be careful because girls will chase you and tease you. Didn't any of it penetrate your thick skull?"

Bruce didn't expect the boy to answer. He ran a hand over his tight, blond curls, and muttered, "Ungrateful brat. We trusted you to behave in a responsible manner, and this is how you repay us!"

Carmen put a steadying hand on her husband's shoulder and asked Brett, " Is she going to put the baby up for adoption?"

"I don't think so," Brett muttered. "She wants to keep it. But she's going away soon to Vancouver to stay with her sister, and it will be born down there."

"Good!" said Bruce emphatically. "Little slut. I hope she never comes back. You can forget her, and put this mess behind you, and get on with your life."

Brett's jaw and hands tightened again in anger. It was no use trying to explain things to him. "I can't do that," he said tersely, "I love her".

"The hell you do!" shouted his father, jumping up again. "I don't want any teenage marriages in this family! Forget it!" Brett backed away, fearing another attack.

"And remember," his father

continued, "You're grounded until further notice. Now get to bed - the pair of you! " He dismissed them with a wave of his hand.

Bev ran from the room, still in tears. She disappeared into the bathroom. Brett backed away slowly, holding his sore jaw, and went down to his room. He didn't even turn the light on. He sat on the edge of his bed, holding his head in his hands. Then with a groan, he rolled over into a ball in the middle of his bed. He stared at the black wall. His whole body started to shake. He clasped his hands together between his drawn up knees, as the tears, unbidden, welled up and spilled over.

Brett had expected a scene, but nothing this violent. He was shaken that his dad had attacked him physically like that. He felt a deep revulsion for him and knew that in that first slap he had stopped loving and respecting him. He remembered Jodi's words - *don't ever say you hate your parents.* Okay, he wouldn't say it, but he sure felt it.

Brett lay like that for a long time, fully clothed, cold and shaky and unable to sleep. He tasted salty tears, and blood from his cut lip. His ear still stung, and his shoulders ached. He heard his parents go to bed; their voices still sounding angry and upset.

After a while, Brett heard his bedroom door open and close softly. He stilled his body, listening.

"Brett?" came a whisper in the dark. It was Bev. She felt her way over to the bed, reached out, and touched his face, feeling the wetness there.

"What do you want?" he whispered fiercely. "Go to bed, and leave me alone!"

Bev ignored the outburst, as she reached out again and touched him. "God, you're freezing!" She retreated a few steps in the dark, groped around in his closet and pulled a thick quilt down from the shelf. Coming back to the bed, she threw it over him, then lifted a corner and crawled in alongside him. She laid her head against his back and put her arm around his waist, finding her brother's cold hands and holding them tight.

"I'm sorry Dad beat you up. He shouldn't have done that. Tell me about Jodi," she said.

The warmth from Bev's body and the quilt felt good. Brett took a deep breath and stretched his legs out. He was stiff and sore already. He turned onto his back and in whispers told his sister everything that had transpired over the past few months.

When they were small, Bev had sometimes crawled into bed with Brett when she had a bad dream. Brett would cuddle and comfort her until she fell asleep. It was strange and wonderful to discover that the bond was still there, only this time; Bev was giving the comfort and understanding. They talked far into the night until finally, warm and drowsy, Brett suggested that Bev get back to her own bed before they both fell asleep.

Brett got up too, and went into the bathroom. His lip was puffy and caked with dried blood. His jaw and shoulders were sore. He washed the blood off, and rinsed his mouth out. His teeth hurt too. "Son of a bitch." he muttered, surveying the damage. He wasn't going to be in great shape for basketball practice tomorrow. Oh well, he didn't imagine his dad was going to have a great day at work either. Brett went back to bed and fell into a dreamless sleep.

CHAPTER FOURTEEN

On Sunday, Brett called Jodi and told her what had happened when his dad found out. Jodi was sorry and sympathized with him but she begged him not to hate his father for the beating. She encouraged him to try to understand Bruce's feelings and forgive him his bad temper. Brett assured her he would try but just now they weren't speaking to each other. Their relationship had been damaged and Brett felt responsible. He felt guilty about disappointing his parents with his behaviour. Jodi was equally sorry that she had caused this conflict and pain for him. She was glad that Bev had stepped in and given him comfort and support. She was going to be a good friend and ally.

Jodi related to him how their affair had rocked the town. Everyone was talking about them. She had experienced everything from snide looks and comments and tight-lipped scorn to outright cruel and nasty accusations and jealousy on the part of the girls that had been chasing Brett, and genuine sympathy and concern from her few close friends. She heard the words 'slut,' 'whore', and 'easy lay', but none of the boys in town approached her. They knew it was unlikely that you could get sexual favours from Jodi McCallum.

Jodi and Brett agreed that it would be best if he were not seen in Kelso for a while. It was not likely to happen anyway, since he was grounded, and the time was fast approaching when Jodi and Carol would leave for Vancouver.

In a day or two it was Jodi's turn to face the consequences of *her* family's shock. Marnie phoned as soon as she received Jodi's letter. She cried, scolded and pleaded with Jodi to let her arrange an abortion, but Jodi steadfastly refused.

Finally Marnie gave up and insisted that she get down there as soon as possible. Jodi said she would come on a trial basis, and see how it worked out. They agreed on a date, December 15th, a Friday. Carol and Jodi would go with Stuey down to Harrison in the morning and catch the bus for Vancouver at four-fifteen p.m. The sisters would arrive in the city on Saturday morning.

Now that plans were made Jodi felt calm and resigned. With an air of detachment she made arrangements to leave school and said goodbye to her teachers. Her correspondence courses had arrived. Apart from band, she could now keep up in all her main subjects.

On Friday at school Jodi asked Linda if she would help her get some good pictures of herself on Blossom to give to Brett for Christmas. Linda agreed, so the girls stopped in at the drugstore after school to buy a new film.

Jodi told Linda, " Brett says that the instant he fell in love with me was when he saw me galloping Blossom in the park, with my hair flying out behind me. I want to try to capture that 'free-spirit' look for him. I want you to take a whole roll, and I'll get the best one or two enlarged."

Jodi had never used her dad's camera, but it was a good one. Duncan had taken many beautiful slides of Kokanee Lake and the surrounding mountains and had recorded numerous family celebrations and gatherings.

Jodi and Carol had boxes and boxes of pictures. The family had often enjoyed picture nights. Sometimes after evening church, Duncan would do a slide show for friends and neighbours. Florence would bake scones and serve tea and afterwards there would be a singsong around the piano. A wave of nostalgia washed over Jodi as she remembered the good times they used to have when her parents were alive.

Saturday was a beautiful sunny day. The girls hurried through their chores and by mid-morning were off, riding double, down through the park towards the beach.

Linda had the camera slung over her shoulder by the leather strap. Last night they had studied the booklet about the operation of the camera and they now felt competent about changing the light settings, adjusting the focus, and how to take good colour prints.

Blossom's hoof beats made a series of muffled 'plops' in the soft powdery snow. She arched her pretty neck and snorted rollers through her nose at the prospect of a run. Jodi hadn't been riding her much lately. Darkness came early, and with schoolwork, chores, and supper to make, there just wasn't time.

Time! It was running out fast. This was the last opportunity for Linda and Jodi to be together before she went away. Neither girl knew when they would see each other again and both knew that things would never again be the same between them. Next time they saw each other, Jodi would have a baby. That was too weird to even imagine!

As they rode Jodi filled Linda in on all the arrangements they had made for the care of the house and the animals. Old Mrs. Elliot, the one who always sang loudly and off key in church, had just lost her aged cat, so she wanted to take Samantha. She lived on a quiet street in an old house that was surrounded by a large unkempt jungle of a garden. Jodi went to see her and was satisfied that Sam would like it there. When Jodi told her about Scamp, Mrs. Elliot agreed to look after him too. She promised to take him for walks and give both animals plenty of attention. The Shannons had also offered to look after Scamp but Jodi wasn't too happy about accepting. Linda already had a dog that wasn't allowed in the house and with their large family, Scamp wouldn't get much attention. Jodi knew that her little lonely dog would sit sadly, looking up the road all day. So when Mrs. Elliot offered him a home Jodi accepted with thanks.

Clarence White was happy to have the extra hens and Carol had arranged for Blossom and the goats to live at Len's grandfather's farm. He had two grandchildren who would enjoy riding the pony on their visits to the farm, but most of Blossom's days would be spent in leisure in a large pasture with two milk cows. Since Mr. Morrison milked the two cows anyway, he didn't mind milking Annie as well.

Len suggested to Jodi that she draw up a lease agreement so that there would be no argument as to who owned the pony when she wanted her back. Jodi had the papers ready. She was going to ride Blossom the six miles out to the farm on Wednesday, two days before they left. Mr. Morrison had promised to give her a ride home.

The Shannons were going to look after the house. Jodi and Carol were to move all their personal effects upstairs so that if a suitable renter could be found they could have the ground floor.

The last few days Jodi was busy packing and sorting in their parents' room, cleaning out the kitchen cupboards, and packing up the books, records, pictures and non-perishable food items into boxes and hauling them up the stairs for storage.

Arriving at the water's edge, Linda slipped off over Blossom's wide rear end. "Okay," Jodi said, "I'll just take her for a canter to warm her up. Then you can start shooting. There's a big log down the beach a ways. Maybe you could get one of Blossom jumping over it."

"Are you sure you should be cantering and jumping?" Linda asked, concern knitting her sandy eyebrows.

"Sure, I'll be fine, Jodi reassured her. "I'm as safe up here as I would be on a pair of skis, zooming down a mountain, or jumping out of a plane with a parachute."

Linda laughed, and waved her off. As Jodi turned the pony and nudged her into a canter, Linda opened the lens cover on the camera and adjusted the light settings. The sun was behind her in the southwest and as Jodi turned at the point and came galloping back along the shoreline, Linda snapped several pictures in quick succession.

Jodi had left her toque with Linda so that her long, dark chestnut hair could fly out free behind her. She wore a red wool sweater trimmed with white over grey sweat pants. The red added a splash of colour to an otherwise drab landscape. Blossom's fuzzy winter coat was a mixture of black and white patches; the somber looking lake was dark blue, and the mountains were snow-covered, with fingers of brown and grey where the trees and rocky cliffs showed through.

Linda took another picture of Jodi, sitting on Blossom at the water's edge. Blossom had her neck arched in mock fright as she pretended to spook at the little waves coming in. Then the threesome moved off down the beach to find the log that Jodi had mentioned. This wasn't the one that she and Brett had sat on that fateful night. It was a much larger one, a huge hemlock that had drifted in with last years' spring flood. The tree had an immense root system. The base of the tree was about six feet across, tapering to two feet at the top end. The immense log was going to make a lot of firewood for someone, probably the Shannon family.

Linda leaned into the roots at the large end, positioning her elbows firmly in the tangled fibres. She could hold the camera very steady like this as she looked down the length of the big log. "Okay, let's try some action shots. I'm ready!"

Jodi circled the pony and calculated just where she would jump the log. She decided to come at it from the lakeside. She would be jumping slightly uphill towards the camera, as the log lay on a gentle slope. This turned out to be the best choice. The shot was pretty with the lake and mountains in the background, and was also the safest.

Jodi cantered Blossom towards a

spot about two feet high and the pony cleared it easily. As she sailed over the log, Blossom's front feet curled gracefully, her back feet tucked up neatly, and her ears pricked forward with interest and excitement. Despite being three and a half months pregnant, Jodi still rode with grace and style. With her body leaning forward for the jump, and Blossom's long mane streaming back, it was hard to tell that she was expecting. Jodi's face was animated and flushed with the cold air and the thrill of jumping and her mouth was slightly open as she encouraged Blossom up and over the log. Linda snapped the shutter at what she hoped was the right moment, just a fraction of a second before horse and rider filled up the whole frame.

"Got it!" she yelled triumphantly. "Better do a couple more though, just to make sure." Jodi gave her the 'thumbs up' sign and rode off a little distance to get a run at it again. After several more jumps Jodi rode alongside the log so that Linda could get on behind her. She put her hat back on and they rode at a walk so Blossom could catch her breath. Jodi didn't want to get her too hot and sweaty in the cold air.

The pony and her two riders wandered along the beach, and up through the park. The branches of the willows and poplars were completely covered with hoarfrost. Each individual twig and leaf was clothed in sparkling crystal-like forms.

The weak winter sun shone on each object, causing it to sparkle like diamonds. Jodi looked around her, and marvelled at the wondrous beauty of her surroundings. She would keep this memory in her heart forever.

Coming across the ball diamond, the snow was at least two feet deep, and was completely undisturbed. "How about a picture of you dashing through this snow?" Linda suggested.

"All right, let's do it," Jodi said. Linda slipped off again and readied the camera. She had five shots left.

Jodi rode away towards the sun and came back at a fast trot through the fresh powder. Blossom's feet churned up the snow into a fine white spray and Jodi laughed with delight as little snowballs bombarded her face. Linda took two more of the pair cantering and trotting through the snow.

"Okay, I've got two left," she called. "Do you want me to finish up the roll?"

"Let's save them, and get somebody to take a couple of us together," Jodi suggested.

"My mom could do that. Let's go over to my place. We can have some hot chocolate too. I'm getting cold."

"Okay, that's a good idea. You should try riding. It keeps you warm."

"Well, let's go over to that park bench, so I can get on." Linda said.

At the house, Linda went in and got

her mom to come out and take two pictures of the girls. Linda held Blossom by the bridle while Jodi stood behind her with her arms leaning over the pony's back. Then for the last one the girls stood with their arms around each other's shoulders, trying to look happy, even though they were filled with sorrow at the circumstances that were forcing them apart.

Jodi thanked Mrs. Shannon, led Blossom home across the alley, and let her go in the paddock. She watched while the pony went through the ritual of rolling and shaking off the feel of her riders. Then she went back into her neighbour's warm, spicy-smelling kitchen for hot chocolate and cinnamon buns.

After the rest and snack, Jodi felt like falling asleep. The morning activities in the fresh air combined with the heat of the kitchen made her drowsy. However, she wanted to take the roll of film up to Mr. Bowman's photography shop. She had to have them developed right away if she was to give some to Brett for Christmas.

Excusing herself and thanking Mrs. Shannon again for the delicious buns and cocoa, she walked the three blocks uptown to see Mr. Bowman. He had a little shop on Front Street where he processed film in his basement darkroom. Jodi explained the need for urgency in the developing and printing of her pictures, and to her surprise, the photographer agreed to do them while she waited. Jodi chose the two best ones for enlargement; the first shot of her jumping the log, and one of her trotting Blossom through the deep snow. She asked to have the rest of them printed as well. She would give some to Linda for Christmas. Jodi chose two 5" x 7" black frames from Mr. Bowman's glass case, and slipped the two photos in to see what they looked like. She was pleased with the results. She happily paid Mr. Bowman, wished him a Merry Christmas, and went home.

After showing the pictures to Carol, who admired them greatly, Jodi took some newspaper and went up to her room. She wrapped the pictures carefully, taping the newspaper around them. Then she chose some bright red Christmas paper for the final look. She would have to look for the right card to go with it; something sweet and sentimental, but not too mushy.

Feeling satisfied with her efforts, Jodi called Samantha to her, pulled her quilt up around her, and snuggled into her bed for a snooze.

The next day being Sunday, Jodi waited impatiently for Brett's collect call from the pay phone several blocks from his house. There wasn't too much to talk about. They were both sad that she had to leave. Christmas didn't hold much excitement for them this year, since they couldn't be together.

"All we have to do", Jodi told him, "is pack our clothes, and clean the house. Mr. White is coming for the chickens today. I'll take Blossom to her new home on Wednesday and Len is going to give me a ride to Mrs. Elliot's place to deliver Samantha and Scamp on Thursday. We're invited to Linda's for supper on Thursday night."

"Sounds as if you're all organized to go then," he replied. "I'll skip last period on Friday so I can spend some time with you, okay? I'd take the whole day off, but we're in the middle of exams. I have a Math mid-term in the morning, and Biology after lunch. I should be able to get away as soon as I finish writing my exam."

"Okay," Jodi replied. "I guess it's our only chance to see each other before I go. It's going to be hard to say goodbye."

"Yeah, I know...You will write to me, won't you? I'm going to get a box number at the Post Office, so my dad won't see any letters coming from you."

Jodi assured him she would write faithfully, and he promised the same. After a little more small talk they reluctantly said goodbye. There was nothing more to be said. Events beyond their control had been set in motion and they, like dust in the wind, or bits of flotsam in the water, were swept along in the flood.

CHAPTER FIFTEEN

On Friday afternoon Jodi and Carol were in Harrison waiting for the bus that would take them to Vancouver. Carol had experienced a stormy break-up with Len the night before. Her nerves were raw and she hadn't slept all night. Jodi was trying to keep a lid on her emotions too. She was watching eagerly for Brett. He was coming to see them off at the station. They would have less than two hours together before they would have to part. She tried not to think about that, only about being together. He had been forbidden to see her since his parents found out about the baby and they did not know he was coming here today.

Jodi saw Brett through the window just before he came through the door and looked around. Brett's lively blue eyes lit up when he saw the girls and his handsome face broke into a big smile showing his even white teeth. Jodi's heart did a flip-flop and even Carol murmured, "Wow, he's *so* cute!" Her attitude had softened towards him over the past month as it became apparent that he and Jodi were in love.

Brett looked fabulous in his tight jeans, red sweater, and long black coat that hung open. A white silk scarf was draped around his neck. Under his left arm he carried a large parcel wrapped in brown paper and tied with string.

Putting the parcel down, he said, "Hi", and held out his hands to her. Jodi caught them, and he pulled her up, enfolding her in a big bear hug. Brett winked at Carol over Jodi's shoulder. Then, releasing her, he said, "Come on. Let's get out of here for a while. Oh, can you check this parcel through with your luggage? It's your Christmas present, Jodi."

"It is?" Jodi looked surprised and interested. "What is it, a horse blanket?"

"Nope." he grinned. "Nothing horsy. No peeking until Christmas!"

"Here," offered Carol, picking up the parcel. "I'll check it through with our other things."

"Thank-you," said Jodi softly, both to Brett and Carol, as she took her lover's hand.

The three of them went out into the frosty air and walked down the street to the large new mall. Brett walked between them holding hands with both girls. The snow crunched under their feet while small light snowflakes tickled their noses.

"Would you like a drink or a snack, or something?" asked Brett. "There's a little coffee shop down here."

"Sure," Carol answered. "How about you, Jodi?"

"Okay." Jodi didn't care what they did. She was so happy, just being with Brett. But there was an ache just under the surface, knowing their time together was so short.

They removed their coats and slid into a booth. The girls ordered hot chocolate and muffins; Brett asked for fries and a coke. Jodi and Brett sat close together, holding hands until their food came. As soon as the snacks were finished, Carol suggested that Jodi and Brett go off by themselves for a while. She said she had a little private shopping to do, but Jodi knew that Carol was giving them a chance to be alone. She gave her sister a grateful look.

"Just be at the bus station at a quarter to four," warned Carol. "Don't do anything stupid like running off together."

"We won't " Jodi promised. "We'll be there."

Jodi and Brett strolled down the mall, fingers laced together. Brett spotted a passport booth and steered her into it yanking the curtain shut behind them. His hands moved inside Jodi's open coat, pulling her close. He kissed her passionately, once, twice, three times, and then another long slow kiss while his hands moved sensuously up and down her spine. Jodi felt like she was on fire. She was hot and breathing fast. Her eyes were bright and her cheeks flushed a rosy pink. Jodi could tell that Brett felt the same.

Brett stroked her silky hair and murmured in her ear, "You're so beautiful, my Princess. I love you!"

"And I love you too." Jodi's eyes searched his. " Will you wait for me?"

"Yes. We'll find a way to be together, the three of us." He smiled, patting her stomach. "We'll just have to be patient for now." He kissed her lightly again and let her go.

Brett said, "Let's get our pictures taken while we're here." He opened the curtain and read the directions. He dropped some quarters into the slot, re-entered the cubicle, grabbed Jodi's hand, and pulled her down on the little bench beside him.

"Okay, kiss me quick!" Their lips met, and Jodi jumped a little when the flash popped. "Now, look straight ahead, and give 'em your best smile." The camera clicked again. Brett put his arm around her shoulders, and laid his cheek against hers. 'Click' again. "One more," he said. "Look at me." They looked into each other's eyes, almost nose to nose, smiling as the camera clicked and flashed for the last one. "That's it."

In a couple of minutes, the strip of four pictures emerged from a slot. Jodi picked them up, exclaiming, "Hey, these aren't too bad."

Brett took them and folded the sheet in half. Then carefully, he ripped along the fold, leaving two pictures in each half. "I'll keep two, and you can have two. Which ones do you want?"

Jodi chose the first two and slipped them into her bag, while Brett put the others into his wallet.

"Well," he said wistfully, touching her face with the back of his hand, "we'd better get out of this booth before someone calls Security."

They emerged laughing, and wandered arm in arm to the end of the mall, down one side and up the other. The place was crowded with shoppers, all intent on getting those perfect gifts. Christmas carols floated around them. The store windows were gaily decorated with fake frost, scenes of elves, reindeer, and jovial Santas. The two young lovers hardly noticed the trappings of Christmas around them. Jodi and Brett had eyes only for each other, and both were painfully aware of the great loneliness that would stretch between them, once they were apart.

Reluctantly, and with time running out, they stepped out into the cold and headed back to the bus station. Carol was waiting and seemed relieved to see them. Jodi, Brett, and Carol were all quiet. There was nothing left to say. They sat like three bumps on a log, Jodi and Brett holding hands tightly.

Shortly, their bus was announced. Carol stood up and said gently to Jodi, "Come on, it's time to go. Thanks for coming Brett. I think she would have gone crazy if you hadn't been here to say goodbye."

Brett forced a smile, gave her a hug, and said, "Have a good Christmas, and good luck with your business courses.

Take care of her for me, won't you?" Carol nodded, and moved into the line of people getting on the bus.

Brett turned to Jodi and held her tight. Unwanted tears spilled over and ran down her cheeks. Brett's eyes were soft and misty as he gripped her shoulders and said, "It's not forever...don't cry."

Jodi looked into the face she loved and brushed back a golden strand of hair that had fallen over Brett's eyes. "I know...but it doesn't make it any easier." She sniffed; reached into the woven shoulder bag she carried, and produced a small package. "Merry Christmas." she said, putting it into his hand. "Be careful - it's breakable." She reached up and kissed him, then turned and stepped up into the bus.

Brett lifted a hand in farewell as she disappeared down the aisle. Jodi waved back,and then was lost from view as she took a seat beside Carol on the opposite side of the bus.

Brett stood on the sidewalk, holding the gift in his hand, watching forlornly as the bus disappeared into the gathering darkness and the swirling snow.

CHAPTER SIXTEEN

The bus trip was long and tedious. Jodi's legs and feet cramped spasmodically throughout the night from lack of circulation. She had to endure the pain and discomfort in silence. She cried for long periods of time out of frustration, loneliness, and pain; letting the tears run down her face silently.

Carol tried once or twice to comfort her, taking her hand and squeezing it saying, "It's for the best," or some such useless phrase. Her own emotions were mixed up. Along with a great sense of freedom, she felt Jodi's loss and pain deeply, and her own separation from Len which had been far from friendly.

As the bus rolled through the fertile green Fraser Valley early the next morning, Jodi felt her spirits start to rise a little. She had always loved the valley with it's wide green pastures hemmed in on both sides by great towering mountains and cut by the mysterious dark winding river. Jodi was fascinated by the many dairy farms. She tried to imagine what it would be like living in one of the big farm houses; getting up while the mists still hung over the valley to milk the black and white Holstein cows that dotted the landscape.

The whole Delaney family was there to meet them when the bus arrived at the Vancouver Depot. There were hugs and tears all around and excited chatter from the children. Jodi hadn't seen them for two years. The little girls, Lisa and Lori were now five and four; the baby, John Kelly (or Jake as they called him) was five months old.

Jodi's body was stiff and sore and she was desperately tired but she followed dutifully as the noisy group walked the two blocks to The Pancake House for breakfast. She looked across the table at her sister Marnie and smiled through her tiredness.

Sixteen years older than Jodi, and twelve years older than Carol, Marnie was not as tall as her younger sisters but the family resemblance was striking. Brown curls framed her face and lively green-blue eyes. An odd but completely natural white streak ran through the front of her hair. When she was younger, friends thought she had dyed it, and liked the effect.

Marnie was a gifted pianist, and had won top honors in B.C. for Highland Dancing when she was Jodi's age. She had taught elementary school before her girls were born, and she was looking forward to helping Jodi with her studies. Marnie was a deep thinker, somewhat of a philosopher, a wise and loving mom, a good cook and a very capable homemaker. She had a strong faith and an interest in pursuing the Ministry someday. Jodi knew she should feel lucky to be going home to live with Marnie and Rob.

Jodi's siblings were not meant to be so spread out in age. There had been two more born and lost to Duncan and Florence McCallum. A little boy had been born between Marnie and Carol and had been a part of the family for three precious years. He passed away after complications during a red measles epidemic. Then, when Carol was two and a half, another girl was born; full-term, but tragically, stillborn. Jodi didn't really know why that baby died, but now, looking around the table at these beautiful lively children, and carrying her own, she suddenly understood the heavy sorrow her parents carried from the loss of those two little ones. Her father never spoke of it. If her mother ever did, her eyes filled with tears and she would be sad and quiet for a long time.

Jodi couldn't stop staring at the children. The little girls were adorable with their big blue eyes, long dark lashes, and pert little turned up noses. Lisa and Lori were so close in age and looks; they could almost pass for twins. Their dark blond hair was straight and framed their little faces in identical pixie cuts. Jodi had only seen pictures of Jake as a newborn. Now, he didn't look anything at all like that little bundle wrapped in blankets. He was trying hard to sit up in a highchair and was vocalizing happily. He had the same huge deep blue eyes and long dark, curving lashes as his sisters. Jodi looked at the kids with renewed interest. These were going to be the little cousins that her baby would grow up with.

After breakfast, they all piled into the old grey station wagon and headed for West Vancouver. Jodi stole a glance at Uncle Rob. A somewhat moody and quiet man, he looked slightly harassed as he expertly wove in and out of the city traffic. At forty-five, Rob was head Math teacher at a large North Shore high school. He had been in the war, the Merchant Marines. *That experience was probably enough to make you a little odd,* Jodi thought. He was a fusser and a procrastinator, an avid gardener, a chocoholic; an artistic and sensitive man. Looking at him from her kitty-corner spot in the back seat Jodi mused, *the kids certainly inherited their deep blue eyes from him.* She wondered just what he thought about taking a pregnant teenager into his home. No matter what Rob thought, he would be too polite to say anything to Jodi. For her sister's sake, Jodi promised herself not to cause any trouble or get in his way. She knew the marriage was rocky at times and she did not want to be the cause of any arguments.

Jodi had not seen their new home in West Vancouver. When she had been here two years ago, the family lived in Coquitlam in an area of new bungalows in a subdivision. A year ago, Rob had bought the rambling run-down Tudor home overlooking Caulfield Cove for twenty thousand dollars. Thirty years later it would be prime real estate with a value of over a million dollars!

    As the family traveled along a twisty scenic road skirting the ocean, and entered the narrow winding lanes bordered by wild blackberry bushes to where the great house stood poised on its rocky half acre, Jodi felt a sense of wonder and delight. Huge dripping cedar trees lined the stone walkway to the house. Despite being December, green grass poked up in little patches between the rockeries and a great profusion of shrubs, trees, and foliage that Jodi had never seen before grew in the garden. She took deep breaths of the fragrant air. She could smell the sea, only a short distance away down at the bottom of the steep hill. The pungent, spicy aroma of the cedars mingled with the damp earthy smell of the garden. This was a paradise! She thought, *I might even like it here!*

    Once inside, with an excited little girl pulling on each of their hands, Jodi and Carol were shown the wonders of the old English mansion. The elegant entranceway with the plum-coloured tile floor and great sweeping wooden stairs led up to the tower room with a pink brick fireplace; the playroom, which had a fabulous view of the cove; a small bathroom, and the tiny bedroom which was going to be renovated for Lisa.

The main floor consisted of a dark awkward kitchen, which would also undergo many changes and improvements and a huge open dining area and living room. The mossy green carpets throughout and the dark wooden beams made it appear like an extension of the beautiful grounds outside. Glass doors led out to a huge patio. There were two more doorways leading off the living room. Double sliding glass doors led out to the entrance hallway, bathroom, dressing room, (which was a temporary nursery for Jake) and then up three carpeted stairs to the master bedroom. It was a beautiful room - all carpeted in mossy green and lined with big windows. The cedar trees were so close outside it felt like being in a forest glade. This room had the ocean view too.

An enormous picture window faced out to the ocean in the living room, and coming back through, Jodi paused to look at the view. The house overlooked the cove and Burrard Inlet, where all the ships came into Vancouver Harbour. There was a constant stream of vessels going by; tugs pulling barges, pleasure craft, sailboats, passenger liners, and freighters. It was fascinating. Jodi would have loved to sit out on the patio and watch the ships, but the girls were urging them on.

"Come on, Auntie Jodi! We'll show you your room!" Jodi and Carol were led back through the kitchen and down a flight of narrow stairs to the bottom floor. Three doors opened off the hallway. The first room was a little study lined with books. A door beside it led out to the garden. The middle room contained the huge furnace, hot water heater, washer, dryer and freezer.

"Hurry Jodi!" cried Lisa excitedly, running ahead. "This is your room." Jodi pushed open the door to see a quaint little room with a four-poster bed nestled under a double window that looked out over the garden. She could just see a little stone bridge arched gracefully over a narrow pond filled with lily pads and rushes. In one corner of the room there was a dark wooden antique dresser. A small desk stood between the closet door and another door, which upon investigating, led to an adjoining bathroom. Shelves filled with books lined the walls. "Oh," she sighed, feeling choked up with emotion. "It's perfect. It's so peaceful and pretty. Thank-you!" She gathered the girls into her arms and hugged them.

Carol was going to stay upstairs in the little room until after Christmas. She had enrolled in some Secretarial Courses and Interior Design at Langara College. She hoped to find shared accommodation or rent a room closer to the college when the new term started in January.

Past Jodi's room there was still more of the house. The hallway finally ended in a large room lined with bookshelves. The room must have been the old library. A red brick fireplace graced one wall. Large windows faced the greenery and tangled growth spilling down the slope to the neighbour's house almost invisible below them. *What a wonderful, intriguing, old place!* thought Jodi. *No wonder they loved it so much.*

But for Jodi to adopt a new home and family would take time. She hoped they would understand that. She had survived a good many partings so far losing mother, father, lover, home, friends, and pets. She needed time to grieve her losses, but she would survive.

CHAPTER SEVENTEEN

The days before Christmas passed in a whirlwind of baking, decorating, shopping and housecleaning. Jodi hardly had time to be lonely or homesick. Only at night, her thoughts turned to all she had left behind, as she cried into her pillow.

The big day began while it was still dark, with the excitement of what Santa had brought. There was a huge Christmas breakfast, phone calls from friends, and the preparation of the turkey and vegetables for dinner. Everyone went for a walk in the afternoon and came back to the tantalizing aroma of the cooking turkey and the cozy fire. Guests arrived for dinner and Jodi went down to her room for a rest. Brett's gift to her had been a cuddle-wrap; a soft, fleecy garment that could be worn as a robe, or unzipped, used as a blanket. Jodi wrapped it around her and lay down, re-reading the letter she had received from Brett yesterday.

My Darling Girl,   *Dec.20/73*

Every jolly jingly Christmas song I hear on the radio makes me ache with longing for you. I want so much for us to be together. It doesn't seem possible that you are so far away. I have only to think of that bus disappearing into the snow and mist taking you away from me to know it is a reality. I went to the Christmas Dance a couple of nights ago partly to keep up appearances at home that I am functioning normally, and partly to hold some pretty girls in my arms and pretend they were you. It didn't help. I can't get excited over any of them. I miss you so much.

We have a pile of new snow, about 18 inches. It looks so pretty. A winter wonderland, but empty without you. I hope you like the gift. I know how you're always cold when you sit around in the evenings, so I thought it would keep you cozy. I wish I could snuggle up with you by the fire like we did the night you shared your secret with me. I love you.

Brett

Jodi sighed and closed her eyes. *If only he could be here,* she thought, *Christmas would be perfect.*

Later on in the evening family and friends sat around in comfort by the fire with an eggnog, coffee, or glass of wine. Marnie played the piano for the carol singing and several people brought guitars and an accordion. It was a wonderful time of music and fellowship. The reflection of the huge pine tree in the picture window made a double image of beauty as the lights on the tree winked and glowed. The kids, dropping from exhaustion, were carried up to bed with new dollies and stuffed toys tucked under their arms.

Jodi was sitting on the raised

fireplace hearth staring into the flames, lost in dreams, when somebody called her from the kitchen. "Jodi! Phone!" With a jolt of excitement, she realized, *I don't know anyone here - it's got to be him!* It was!

"Hi Princess. I've only got a few minutes. Dad's downstairs playing pool with Uncle Dan and Rick. I told Mom I was going to call you and she didn't say anything."

Jodi felt so happy, she could burst. She thanked him for the gift, and told him how she had already had a snooze cuddled up in it. Brett said something about wishing he could cuddle with her too. He told her that he hadn't waited until Christmas to open her present. The night Jodi had left he opened the pictures in his room. He had sat for a long time, holding them in his hands. Then he put them on his dresser where he could see her as soon as he opened his eyes each morning.

Jodi and Brett talked a little more; then, reluctantly, he had to go.

"Thank-you so much for calling me," Jodi said. "It made an already wonderful day special. I was just looking into the fire, wishing I could talk to you, and my dream came true."

"Well, I've been thinking of you all day too, and waiting for a chance to call you...I guess I'd better go. Uncle Dan is yelling at me to come and play."

Jodi laughed, lightly and happily.

"Okay, go and beat the pants off them. Goodnight, Dream-Boy"

"Dream-Boy?" Brett asked sounding amused. "Hmph! That's a new one."

"Yeah, you're the one I dream about, day and night, so it's appropriate."

"Okay...whatever...Goodnight my Princess. I love you."

"Love you too. Write soon."

"I will. Bye-bye."

"Bye"...click. Jodi hung up and sat staring at the now silent phone. Music, chatter, and laughter floated around her but she was scarcely aware of it. Carol came into the kitchen with John, one of the guys that had brought his guitar. They seemed to be getting along famously. Carol re-filled their wine glasses and slightly tipsy, they toasted each other.

"Was that your angel, Jodi?" she asked, grinning.

Jodi smiled back. "Yep. What would Christmas be without a special angel?"

John looked puzzled but Carol put an arm around Jodi and hugged her. The three of them went back into the living room to celebrate what was left of Christmas.

CHAPTER EIGHTEEN

The New Year was celebrated with a seafood fondue in front of the blazing fire. Jodi had thought that their Christmas feast was sumptuous but this was also a bountiful meal. In Kelso, Jodi and Carol simply did not get fresh seafood like the giant prawns, crabmeat, and scallops the family was enjoying here. Jodi felt thoroughly spoiled with such beautiful surroundings, and so much good food.

At last all the celebrating was over. The Christmas tree was undressed and taken out; all the cards and decorations were put away. Rob went back to the classroom. Carol started her courses at Langara. She had moved in with two other girls in a basement suite on West 12th, near the college. The household settled into a routine.

Every morning Jodi helped with breakfast and general cleanup. She helped the kids get dressed and make their beds. She learned how to change Jake's diapers and she was a good help with the piles of laundry. She looked after Lori and Jake while Marnie took Lisa to Playschool twice a week. Jodi was no stranger to work and Marnie was grateful for the extra help.

About ten o'clock, Jodi went downstairs to her desk to work on correspondence courses. She worked till noon, and again for two hours after lunch, only coming up to ask Marnie for help once in a while.

In the afternoons while Jake had his nap, Jodi often took the little girls down to the beach or for walks along the beach trails. They played in the tidal pools where they caught tiny crabs and minnows. The girls collected seashells and sand dollars and sometimes brought home pretty purple starfish in a bucket of seawater. Jodi, Lisa and Lori made pretend ice-cream cones out of the sea kelp and built playhouses on the beach out of the junk that floated ashore. The girls were in awe of Jodi having a pony back home, so they pretended they had ponies too, galloping them over the rough beach trails and jumping logs.

Jodi didn't feel much like running these days. Although the constant walking and climbing over the rocks kept her fit, by mid-February, she was getting heavy and awkward. For a month or more now, she had been aware of the baby moving within her. It was such a weird feeling but it always made her smile.

Marnie took her to the library and they got some wonderful books that showed the month-by-month development of the fetus and what to expect at birth. Jodi questioned her sister and other mothers closely about the birth process.

Jodi was getting a real education about babies. Many young families lived in the neighbourhood and she was much in demand for babysitting. She was becoming an expert in cleaning up messes, wiping noses and bottoms, settling fights, and calming fears and tears. Jodi realized she was being trained for motherhood and that without this experience she would have been totally unprepared for the demands of caring for a child. Carol was right. It was a tough job being a mom.

On Valentines Day, a large fancy heart-shaped box of chocolates arrived from a 'Secret Admirer' for Jodi. Two weeks later, when she turned seventeen, another parcel arrived from the interior. It was a beautifully illustrated book on the history and breeds of horses. Jodi was now writing to Brett at the box number he had rented for their private correspondence. In these letters they poured out their frustrations, loneliness, dreams, and plans - things they could not speak of to their families. Brett never mentioned her at home, except to Bev in private. He kept his sister up to date on all the news from the coast.

March came in like a lamb instead of a lion. Many flowers were in bloom already as it had been a mild winter. Brett wrote that they still had two feet of snow in Harrison, and that he missed her terribly. He was trying to figure out how he could come down to see her when their baby was born. Jodi wrote back that Marnie and Rob did not hate him, and that he would be welcome to come for a visit. *That* got the wheels going around.

Easter break arrived. The Randalls had gone up to Kelso for Easter dinner with Carmen's brother Dan and family. Rick and Brett went for a walk to be alone and catch up on the news. Walking past Jodi's empty silent house, Brett was almost sick with longing for her. He had to see her.

Back in Harrison, Brett went down to the bus depot the next day, and bought a return ticket to Vancouver. He would leave tomorrow morning. He confided to Bev what he was going to do.

Eyes wide and looking shocked, she cried, "Oh no, don't go, please! Dad will be so angry! He'll have a fit when he finds out. I'd hate to be you when you get back." She threw her arms around him, hugging him tight. "I don't want you to get beat up again. Please, don't go!"

Brett held her away and looked into her eyes, which were mirror images of his own. "He won't touch me. I'm strong, and I'm fit, and he won't catch me off guard again. If he tries anything, I'll let him have it, right back!"

Bev sighed. "You really *do* love Jodi, don't you?"

"Uh-huh, and there ain't no cure for love," Brett grinned. "I need to go and see her."

That night, Brett packed his rucksack carefully. Early the next morning while the family was still sleeping, he stepped out into the frosty morning and walked resolutely downtown to the bus station.

CHAPTER NINETEEN

On Tuesday morning Jodi was just cleaning up the breakfast mess when the phone rang. Lisa answered it, and holding out the phone said with a giggle, "Jodi, it's for you. It's a man!"

Jodi's heart leaped. She thought Brett would have called her for Easter, but he hadn't. It had to be him! She closed her eyes and let out her breath as she heard his voice. "Hi Jodi. How are you?"

"Just fine. How 'bout you? How was your Easter?"

"Pretty good. We were up at Kelso on Saturday. I walked past your place. Sure seems quiet and lonely."

Jodi felt a stab of homesickness for the old place. They talked a bit more, and then he said, "So where is this Rosedale Lane you live on? I'm coming to see you. How do I get there?"

There was a stunned silence, then, finding her voice, she asked, "You mean...you're here...in Vancouver?"

A delighted chuckle came over the line. "Oh, didn't I mention that? I got in late last night on the bus. I didn't want to disturb you so I stayed here at the 'Y' last night. Do you know where that is?"

"Yes!" Shivers went up and down Jodi's spine. "Oh my God." she breathed. "If I wasn't sitting down, I'd fall down. What a surprise! I can't wait to see you!"

"Me neither." "How do I get there?"

"Hang on a minute. Let me check the bus schedule." Jodi opened the cupboard by the phone where the West-Van. schedule was taped to the inside. Running a finger down the timetable she quickly made some calculations. It was just after nine now. There was a bus leaving Horseshoe Bay at ten. She could catch it at ten-fifteen. The bus coming the other way left Vancouver at the same time. They could meet halfway, at Park Royal.

She was explaining to him where to catch the bus and where to get off when Marnie came into the kitchen. She had been listening to the conversation and signalled for Jodi's attention. "Just a sec, Brett" she said. "Marnie wants to tell me something." She covered the receiver with her hand, and looked at her sister.

"I just wanted to say, bring him home for supper, and he can stay here if he doesn't have a place to go."

Jodi flashed her sister a huge smile of thanks, and relayed the invitation to Brett.

"Well, sure, if it's not too much trouble. Tell her thanks!"

"Okay, I will. See you about ten-thirty at Park Royal. Oh, by the way, I...um...I look a lot different than when you last saw me. Don't be too shocked."

"Okay, see you soon. Bye!"

Jodi went down to her room in a happy daze. She washed her face, brushed her teeth, and discarded her grubby T-shirt for a turquoise maternity smock with white trim on the collar. She shook out her braids and brushed her hair straight back, then tied a light blue nylon scarf around her hair just behind her ears. She applied lipstick and blush lightly - just a little for colour. She didn't really need it. Her cheeks were flushed and her eyes sparked with excitement.

An hour later the bus slowed to a stop at the Park Royal Shopping Centre. Jodi had spotted Brett's blond head while the bus was still half a block away and immediately her heartbeat quickened and she felt faint. She took a couple of deep breaths to steady herself and stepped down from the bus.

    Jodi and Brett stared at each other, almost unbelieving, for a moment. Then he held out his hands and she slowly reached out and grasped them. He held her at arms length, letting his gaze roam over her face, and then down to her swollen belly. Moving close and laying his cheek against hers, he said into her hair, "Wow! You sure do look different. But you're even more beautiful." Brett looked into Jodi's eyes again, and spoke softly, "Sometimes when I'm so far away, it seems as if it's not really happening. But seeing you...there's no doubt...is there?"

    Jodi smiled and said, "Being pregnant is always a reality to me. Every waking minute and even in my dreams it's a part of me, and of you. I feel blessed. I am at peace to know that even if we can't be together, I'm never alone. I always have part of you with me."

He nodded in understanding. Taking Jodi's face into his hands, Brett gently kissed her on the lips and hugged her tight. People had to move around them on the sidewalk, as they stood in each other's arms, oblivious of their surroundings. Jodi broke away first and said, "Come on. Let's go in to the restaurant. They have the best cheesecake you've ever tasted!"

Brett was mesmerized by her. Sitting across from Jodi in the booth, he couldn't take his eyes off her. He wanted to touch her so much. There was something different about her now. He sensed a new maturity. She radiated a new beauty, and a new confidence. She was changed with the responsibility of carrying the life within her. Brett slid one sneakered foot around under the table, finding her feet. In a sudden movement, he caught her legs in his, and squeezed lightly. Jodi's eyebrows shot up in surprise, and then she laughed. "You don't have to trap me; I'm not going to run away."

"I know. I just need to feel you to make sure you're real." He grinned back.

When their cheesecake and coffee was finished and paid for, Brett shouldered his pack and Jodi led him out into the spring sunshine. They walked hand in hand along to Ambleside Park. Two teams of young boys were playing soccer on the grass. Their uniforms of bright red and yellow made a splash of colour against the green playing field. A young family was flying a kite. Walkers, joggers, and bike riders were out enjoying the day.

    Brett and Jodi sat on a bench facing out to the sea. He put his arm around her and kissed her several times. He nuzzled her neck and her ear, and kissed her again. He whispered to her, "I wish we could be alone somewhere for a little while." His hand lay on her thigh, but was not idle. His fingers squeezed gently sending little shivers up and down her body. With his male closeness, his kisses, and touching her there, she felt the delicious sensations of desire building, and she knew he felt the same.

    Jodi looked at him, eyes wide, incredulous that he could still want her in that way, despite her advanced pregnancy. She placed her hand over his and detached his busy fingers. She gripped them firmly. "Don't, please. We can't do this here."

    "Where then?" Brett whispered against her cheek. "I want you."

    "Even when I'm this fat and awkward?" Jodi asked with a grin. She stole a glance at the bulge in his jeans, and knew the answer.

    "Yeah, I want to...Oh, come here!" Brett took her by the shoulders then and kissed her hard. Loneliness and longing fused into a solid bolt of desire. She clung to him, trembling in his arms. His hand slid inside her coat collar, resting on her neck, and tangled hair. He touched the pulse in her throat. It was hammering. So was his.

A sudden gust of wind swirled around them fluttering the leaves of the Japanese Cherry tree overhead and sending twigs and leaves scattering along the walk. It was enough to divert their attention and break the spell.

Brett stood up and said, "Let's walk. If we don't get moving, I'll have you down on the grass in front of all these people."

Jodi giggled. "I wonder if anyone would really stop us?"

"I don't know. I'm too shy to find out." Brett took hold of the third finger of her left hand and gave it a little squeeze. "Someday, I'm going to put a ring on this finger, and no one's going to take you away from me again." He added thoughtfully, "That is, if you'll have me."

"*If* I'll have you?" she repeated with amusement. "I do believe I've already *had* you, several times."

"Oh, be serious!" Brett chided, swinging her around to face him. "That was a proposal."

"Oh," she smiled. "In that case, I accept." They looked deep into each other's eyes, searching for any doubts or misgivings. Finding none, Jodi reached up and pushed a long, blond strand of hair aside just before their lips met in a long, lingering kiss. They parted, breathless, and walked on. "Sealed with a kiss." Brett said.

"We'll have to bide our time, and be careful," Jodi said. "And no hanky-panky at my sister's house."

Later on in the afternoon when the introductions had been made and the initial shyness had worn off, Brett became a great hit with the kids. He wrestled with the girls after supper and gave them horse rides on his back. Even Jake screeched with excitement. Marnie liked him right away. She was impressed with his good looks, nice manners, and his obvious love and concern for Jodi. He kept his distance physically from her while in their presence, but his eyes betrayed his feelings, and it did not go un-noticed.

Over the next few days, Brett and Jodi took the little girls with them everywhere they went, 'as chaperones,' Brett kidded. Jodi and the girls showed him the beach and the trails. They spent a day up on Grouse Mountain with a picnic and a ride on the gondola. On Friday, Jodi, Brett, and the girls took the bus to Capilano Canyon. They walked the thickly wooded trails, and had tea in the Teahouse. Even Jodi felt woozy crossing the suspension bridge.

The girls were scared to death, and had to be led by the hands across the undulating, wavering expanse of boards. Far below, the Capilano River went cascading and boiling over the boulders, sending up plumes of misty spray.

The evenings were spent cleaning up the dishes after supper, reading bedtime stories to the kids, and watching T.V. Marnie talked to them both about their hopes, dreams, and plans, encouraging them to put off marriage until they were older and financially secure. She assured him that she and Rob would support Jodi and the baby until such time as they could support themselves. Encouraged by their acceptance of him, Brett sat close to Jodi on the couch, holding her hand. He even kissed her goodnight in front of them, and got no reaction, other than a smile. It was a small victory for them.

    Brett's return ticket was for Sunday afternoon. Saturday morning arrived cloaked in rain; a steady drizzle that dampened everyone's spirits as well as everything outside. Brett was restless. He was beginning to think about the consequences he faced upon his arrival at home. Jodi was feeling depressed and frustrated at the weather and the lack of privacy for herself and Brett. Thoughts of their impending separation tomorrow weighed heavily on her mind.

    The kids were noisy, argumentative,

and demanding. Jodi felt a twinge of irritation as they begged Brett to play Hide and Seek with them. He let himself be dragged away, rolling his eyes heavenward in good-natured desperation. Brett was very good with kids. He was going to be a great father. Jodi smiled in spite of her annoyance and tried to concentrate on her book.

CHAPTER TWENTY

After lunch, the rain eased off and Brett suggested they go for a walk. He hadn't been alone with Jodi since the day he arrived. Someone was always around. Not that he minded the kids; they were great fun and he enjoyed having them along. The evenings were hard. The sexual tension between them was strong, yet all he could do was hold her hand once in a while or give her a kiss on the cheek. It wasn't enough and it was driving him crazy. He had almost sneaked down to Jodi's room last night, but was afraid that he might be found out. Jodi had said 'no hanky-panky', and he was trying hard to behave.

Taking his empty backpack, Jodi and Brett walked the beach trail along to Hampton Park, to the small grocery store. Brett wanted to pick up a few things for Marnie in thanks for his stay with them. He selected milk, bread, a roast of beef, and some candy.

As they walked back, the rain quit, and a weak sun broke through the mist. Droplets of water hung like crystals from the leaves and branches of the bushes that lined the muddy paths. The earth smelled of humus, dank and sweet. The air was fresh and clean with the tang of salt from the seashore. Gulls wheeled and cried overhead, scavenging, now that the rain had stopped.

"Where are you going to have the baby?" Brett asked. They hadn't even had a chance to discuss the fast approaching birth. Jodi was due a month from today.

"Lion's Gate Hospital." she said. "It's in North Van. Not too far away."

"That's good." Brett replied. " I wish I could be with you. I don't know if I can come down again at that time. Our school track meet is in mid-May. I'm running the 1500 meter race. I'm doing shot-put and high-jump too."

"Oh," Jodi said, somewhat dismayed. She hadn't thought it through carefully, or even talked to him about it, but she had just assumed Brett would come when the baby was born. "I guess having your first child born isn't as important as those things."

"Hey, don't be like that!" Brett looked at her sharply. " I'll come if I can. I want to be here, but I may not be able to, okay?"

Jodi shrugged and sniffed. "How do I let you know, anyway? I can't phone you, and if I write, your baby will be a week old before you even know he's born."

"Yeah, I know," Brett said. "It's the pits. I guess when it gets nearer the time I'll call you every day to see what's happening. I'll have to call collect."

Jodi said, "That's okay. We'll keep it short until something's happening."

Brett ran a hand through his hair, pushing golden strands out of his eyes.

"Oh Jeez!" he said. "It's going to be so hard at home when I get the big news, and I can't even say anything."

Jodi turned to him. "Won't they *want* to know that they're grandparents? Can't you tell them?" She just couldn't understand why Bruce and Carmen wouldn't even want to know about the birth.

"I don't know," he sighed. " Maybe I will. After all, they'll know I've been down here seeing you all this week."

"What's going to happen when you get home?" Jodi asked. "Is your dad going to be very angry with you?"

"Uh-huh, although maybe he'll have cooled down by now. I imagine he was pretty mad when he found out I had just gone."

"I'm sorry. It's such a mess, isn't it? It's tough for both of us."

They stopped for a rest on a rocky promontory crowned by a huge Arbutus tree. Brett lowered the loaded backpack to the ground and put his arms around Jodi. She leaned against him, her head tucked under his chin, while he smoothed out her rain-dampened hair.

"It doesn't matter how much trouble I'm in at home", he said quietly. "What matters is that we love each other and are willing to wait out the bad times until we can be together."

"You know what I really want to do?"

Jodi looked up at Brett's rugged handsome face.

"What?" He looked curious.

"Go back with you tomorrow. I can't stand the thought of being so far apart again."

Brett held her at arms length, giving her a quizzical look. "Are you serious?" His big blue eyes were wide, twinkling with amusement.

"Of course I'm serious! I've been thinking about it a lot. I know I could manage on my own, if Marnie and Rob would send me a little money."

"Don't be crazy," Brett smiled, looking into her eyes. "I think that would be very foolish. You're surrounded by a family that loves you and cares for you. You've got wonderful medical facilities here. And it's easier for me to know that you are comfortable and happy instead of struggling on your own. You have a beautiful home and all this fabulous scenery. It would be stupid to leave now."

Jodi's eyes filled with tears. "But I'm homesick. I miss my animals. And I want to be with you!"

Brett sighed and pulled her close again, tightening his arms around her. "I know, Doll. There's nothing I'd like more than to have you near too. But for a while, I think it's best for you and the baby if you stay here." He lifted her chin with a finger and kissed her lightly. "I love you. Come on, let's go." He shouldered the backpack again, and took her hand to steady her over the rocky pathway up to the road.

"I just wish everyone wouldn't be so damn practical!" Jodi said, annoyed. She had expected support from him. She angrily kicked a stone out of her way, and fell silent.

As they walked, the silence stretched between them. Just before they turned into the yard, Brett asked, "How would you like to go out on a date tonight? I'll take you out for supper, or we could go to a show or concert. There's a lot going on over town. Let's go look in the paper."

Jodi brightened considerably. "That would be great." Then, she apologized, "Sorry I was bitchy. I guess I'm upset about you leaving tomorrow."

Brett gave her a big smile. "I know. It's okay. Forget it."

Marnie was surprised and pleased to receive the groceries. She liked Brett very much and appreciated his thoughtfulness. She had been baking while they were out. The kitchen smelled wonderfully spicy. She sat them down at the kitchen table to tea and butter tart squares. Jodi got the entertainment section of the paper and they perused the movie and restaurant choices while they ate.

To Jodi's surprise, Marnie offered Brett the use of the car for the evening. He was equally surprised, accepting with thanks, and assurance that he would drive carefully.

At seven that evening Jodi appeared, looking lovely in a long blue print wrap-a-round skirt and a white peasant blouse. She wore sandals on her feet, a plain gold chain around her neck, and a jade bracelet. Her eyes and cheeks were already bright, but she had accented them with a little make-up. As on the day Brett had arrived, her hair was tied back with a blue silk scarf.

Brett had donned a striped shirt and tie and clean jeans. He looked great in anything he wore and Jodi told him so. He blushed and kissed her cheek, complimenting her on her appearance too. As they went out the door, Jodi called, "Bye! Oh, do I have a curfew?"

"No, I don't think so," came the reply. "Just go, and have a good time. Don't stay out too late though, or we'll get worried."

"Okay, thanks."

In the end, after much discussion, Jodi and Brett decided to go to the steakhouse in Horseshoe Bay. Brett wasn't too confident about driving the car downtown on a Saturday night. Besides, the Bay was close by and the restaurant had excellent food. Afterwards they went to a little coffeehouse to listen to local entertainment. It was Jamboree Night;

anyone could get up and perform. They sipped their non-alcoholic drinks, sitting close in the dark, and enjoyed most of the music.

Along about midnight, Jodi was feeling tired out. The smoke and noise was bothering her. It had been fun, but it was time to go. In the car she cuddled up to Brett, leaning her head on his shoulder and resting her hand lightly on his thigh. The warmth from her fingers radiated into his groin. He took her hand and raising it to his lips, nibbled each finger in turn. She felt jolts of pleasure surge through her, beginning in her spine, and spreading over her belly.

"Turn right, here." she directed, at the top of the hill. "It goes to Whytecliff Park. It's just a little way. We could see what the moon looks like over the water."

Brett gave her a quick glance and obediently swung the car onto the winding narrow road to the park. He pulled up in the parking lot, turned off the ignition, and reached for her. "To hell with the moon," he whispered, "I'd rather look at you." He slipped a warm hand under her skirt and followed the curve of her calf, knee and thigh up to the large uncomfortable lump that was their baby.

Jodi untwined her fingers from the unruly blond hair on his neck and let her hands wander down over his back and over his body.

He gasped and groaned, "Oh God,

Jodi. Can we"-- he stopped as the headlights of an approaching car swept over them and pulled up alongside them.

"Shit!" Brett exclaimed. "Cops!"

They separated quickly and sat up. An officer came over and shone a flashlight into the station wagon as Brett rolled down the window. "Everything all right here?" asked the cop, shining the light around the interior of the car.

"Yes Sir." Brett replied. " Just watching the moon rise over the water."

"Yeah, right." said the cop, sarcastically. "You'll have to move along. There's no parking here after eleven p.m."

"Oh, sorry," Brett said. " We didn't know. Didn't see a sign. Thank you, Sir." He turned the key, and started the car. The Officer watched as he slowly backed up and drove away.

"Lousy bastard!" Brett grumbled. Jodi's laugh bubbled over.

"Aren't you glad we didn't get caught with our pants down?" she giggled.

Back at Rosedale, Brett and Jodi entered the kitchen quietly and Jodi said, "Will you come and tuck me in?"

"Now that's an invitation I can't refuse," he said, hugging her. Their desire had barely been dampened. It lay, just below the surface like a coiled spring waiting to be released.

Leaving the hall light on, they entered Jodi's room in the dark. A sliver of moonlight peeped through the window as they lay down on Jodi's bed. She felt a little dizzy, and very tired, but she wanted to finish what they had started.

Brett cupped her breast and she felt her nipple harden under his touch. She laid one hand over his heart and rested the other on his hip, where her fingers made little circles. Between kisses, she said, " Thanks for taking me out tonight. I had a wonderful time."

"Mmm..." he said, lips against hers. "It was a pleasure, but I think the best is yet to come."

She kissed him hard then, and clung to him, but an instant later, they froze. Someone was coming down the hall! The would-be lovers sprang apart and sat up on the bed with some distance between them.

"Jodi?" they heard Marnie whisper. "Are you here?"

"Yes, we're just sitting in the dark, talking." Jodi switched on the lamp, beside the bed.

Marnie came in, wearing a housecoat and slippers. She said, "I thought I heard something, but I couldn't see if the car was home, so I thought I'd check to see if you were here." She looked a little embarrassed.

Jodi and Brett couldn't be accused of anything. They were still fully clothed and the bed covers had not been disturbed. Jodi yawned and stretched. "Yep, we had a really nice time. We had steak and lobster at the restaurant and there was some good entertainment at The Attic. But I'm really tired now. I need to go to bed."

"We were just saying goodnight", Brett added. "Thanks for the use of the car."

Marnie gave them a smile, and backed out. "You're welcome. Goodnight then."

"Goodnight," they both chimed.

Brett sighed in exasperation. "Why can't people just leave us alone on our last night together!"

"I don't know. I guess it isn't meant to be," she answered softly. "I'm sorry... she'll be waiting to hear you go upstairs now. You'd better go.

"Yeah, I guess."

"Night, Dream-Boy. I love you."

"Night Princess, I love you too." They kissed quickly, and then he was gone.

CHAPTER TWENTY-ONE

Jodi couldn't believe her luck! Brett was catching the bus at four in the afternoon to return to Harrison. She had begged off going to church with the family so she could spend a few more hours with him, and her sister had agreed. Jodi never thought that Marnie would leave them alone in the house.

"As soon as he gets up,"Jodi told Marnie, "we're going to spend the day at Stanley Park. I'll see him off, and be home in time to help you make supper." She helped the kids get into their coats, and sighed with relief as they all trooped out to the car.

Jodi was wearing her clean soft-brushed denim jeans this morning, with the sewn in elastic front panel that stretched over her enlarged belly. The nursing bra she wore was a hand-me-down from Marnie; two sizes larger than she used to wear. It lifted up her swollen breasts, and they looked great under her loose-fitting, fawn coloured T-shirt with the horse head on it that served as a maternity smock. She had showered earlier that morning, and her long dark tresses were still slightly damp and curly.

She re-boiled the hot water in the kettle and made a pot of tea. Too anxious to wait for it to brew, she stirred the tea bags vigorously, and poured the steaming liquid into two mugs already fixed with cream and sugar. Then, her cheeks coloured with excitement, she carried the hot drinks carefully up the broad wooden stairs to Lisa's room where Brett slept.

Shifting the mugs into her right hand at the top of the stairs, she turned the glass knob of his door with her left. Entering the tiny room in silence, she set the tea on the low pink dresser that occupied the space in front of a large window. She was aware of Brett's even breathing in the single bed to her right, which was built right in under the eaves of the sloping roof.

In front of her the roof pitched downward over the kitchen, and below that was the crab apple tree, just starting to bloom, and the stone walk leading down to the garden and out to the road. To her left, across the short width of the room, was a little desk with a small stain glass window above it and a miniature closet to the left of that. It was an adorable little room - just right for a little girl.

With a smile, Jodi turned towards the bed. A pair of half-opened sleepy soft blue eyes met her gaze. Brett's lashes were like dark honey; almost touching his cheeks. His untidy blond hair spilled over the pillow, gleaming in the shaft of sunlight that peeped in through the window.

Jodi caught her breath, and, picking up a mug of tea, dropped carefully to her knees by the bed, looking right into his eyes. Her heart beat faster, and she felt a flush creep into her cheeks.

"Good morning, Dream Boy," she whispered. "I've brought you some tea."

The blankets fell away from his muscular arm and shoulder as Brett reached out and touched her hair. He leaned over the edge of the bed and kissed her lips, whispering back with a smile, "thanks."

He took the mug and sipped his tea, lying on his side, while Jodi retrieved her cup and sat on the edge of the bed. They talked about how well they had slept and other trivial matters, both painfully aware that only a few hours of togetherness remained. Brett casually mentioned that the house was very quiet and Jodi just as nonchalantly informed him that the family had gone to church. The knowledge that they had the house to themselves crept upon them like a ship coming into its home harbour; relief and exaltation all at once.

Handing Jodi the empty cup, Brett asked Jodi if she would close her eyes for a moment, so that he could get up and go to the bathroom.

"Why?" she asked, with an impish grin. "I've seen you naked before."

"Because," he implored, "it's been a long time, and I'm shy."

"Oh, all right." she laughed. She stood up and put the cups on the dresser, turning her back politely to him as she did so. Brett quickly slipped out of bed, stark naked, and made a run for the little bathroom off the hallway.

When he came back, Jodi was still standing with her back to him, gazing out the window. Brett encircled her in his arms, burying his face in her hair. He smelled of toothpaste and deodorant; clean and fresh. Jodi turned in his arms, and ran her hands down his bare back and over his buttocks. Their lips met in deep and sensuous kisses.

Jodi stepped back, breathing heavily and as he watched in anticipation, she dropped her clothes to the floor. As Brett moved to the bed, holding out his arms to her, she came to him and straddled him quickly. Her hair cascaded over onto his face and chest as their bodies melted together in a frenzy of lovemaking.

In a very short time, it was over. Jodi, with her legs cramping, slid off and lay in the narrow space between him and the wall. Brett had to shift onto his side to make room for her protruding belly. They hugged, kissed, and touched each other, not wanting the intimacy to end. Finally they lay still, letting their breathing return to normal.

Brett spoke first. "That was *so* great! So unexpected... I didn't know you could...didn't think you'd want to...you know...I thought it might be too uncomfortable for you."

"Umm..."she sighed, lips against his

throat. "I may be awkward and clumsy, but I can still ride. It doesn't hurt the baby so don't worry about that. He's well protected."

As if in answer, a sudden movement rippled over Jodi's belly, followed by a couple of quick kicks right under where Brett's hand lay. His eyes grew wide in amazement, and Jodi laughed with him as they both felt their child move.

In that joyously shared moment, Jodi suddenly knew what she would do. She would go back with him. She lay quietly, letting the realization sink in, asking herself if she was sure. *Yes! She was ready to go home!* She wasn't sure how she would manage, but she knew somehow she would survive. She felt a pang of remorse that she wouldn't have a chance to say goodbye to her sisters and the kids. Maybe it was better this way. If they knew she was leaving with Brett, there would be a big nasty scene.

Suddenly filled with a sense of urgency, she swung her leg over Brett's torso and sat up on his stomach. "What's this?" he laughed. "Do you want another ride?" He held her breasts in his hands, and started to move his hips under her.

"I do, but there isn't time. We have to hurry!" She caught his roving hands and held them tight. "Brett, I'm going with you today."

He looked into her eyes and said slowly, "Yes, to Stanley Park to see the animals, and then to the bus station..." he trailed off, not really comprehending what she had meant.

Jodi repeated it, as much as for herself, as for him. "I'm going with you today, *on* the bus. I'm going home! That is, if you don't mind."

Brett sat up and hugged her. "I'd *love* to have you come with me," he said with a smile, "but I don't think you should." Then, realizing that she was serious, and not likely to be convinced otherwise, he added, "It's just that I don't want to get blamed for spiriting you away from here and your family's care. You know we discussed this yesterday, and I really think you're better off here, at least for a while."

Jodi gave him a kiss and said, "Don't worry. I'll write a note, telling them it was my idea. They like you, and they know I can be a stubborn little wretch." She grinned at him, and slid off, picking up her clothes. She went to the bathroom to wash and dress. He was up immediately, following her.

"Have I got time for a shower?"

"Yes, if you're quick. I have to run down and pack my things. I just want to wash first."

Brett draped his arm around her, and pulled her close. "Come and have a shower with me. I'll wash you." He kissed her neck, and her lips.

"Brett, don't!" she cried fiercely,

pulling away. "We can't be here when they get back. We have to hurry!"

"Sorry," he mumbled. "I get carried away when I'm in a small space with a naked woman!"

"Get in there!" Jodi commanded in mock sternness, as she turned on the shower for him. "I'll see you downstairs."

"Yes ma'am." He stepped in and drew the plastic curtain shut.

Jodi filled the sink with warm water, then washed and dressed quickly. Leaving the bathroom she grabbed clean sheets out of the hall closet and changed Brett's bed. Then, picking up the bedding and the two mugs, she went downstairs. Jodi literally flew around the kitchen loading the dishwasher with the breakfast dishes and wiping the counters clean. Picking up the dirty sheets where she had dropped them at the head of the basement stairs, she ran down, threw them into he laundry hamper, and entered her bedroom.

She had already made her bed, but there was no time to change it anyway. She flung open her closet and rummaged around in the back until she found her dad's old brown canvas backpack with the wide leather straps. She didn't have much. The pack would easily hold it all.

First, she took the blanket sleeper that Brett had given her for Christmas and folded it into the bottom of the pack. Then she threw in her underwear, socks, T-shirts, stretch jeans, and her brown and red wool sweater. Next, she gathered up her schoolbooks and stuffed them in, along with her runners. She would wear her hiking boots. There. That should be everything. She was about to lace up the flaps, but, re-considering, pulled out the warm sweater. She might need that later. Jodi removed her wallet, gum, and chap stick from her purse, and stuffed it down into the pack. She had a three-pouch fanny pack, and into this she placed the articles from her purse, plus her toothbrush and toothpaste. She buckled it around her, looked around, and checked under the bed and in the tiny bathroom.

Satisfied that she had everything, she picked up a jar of money from the dresser and emptied the change into the fanny pack. There were a lot of quarters and fifty-cent pieces. She didn't have time to count it, but thought there was around fifty dollars in there. Then she sat down at the desk and took a sheet of paper. With a rising lump in her throat, and tears threatening to spill over, she wrote:

Dear Family: It is with regret that I have decided to leave today with Brett. I am going home, where I belong. Although I love you all very much, there are things, places, and people I hold even dearer to my heart. Thank you all for what you have done, and would still do for me. I know you will be disappointed to miss out on the birth of my baby, but I want so much to be near Brett when he is born, and to have him with me if at all possible. Please don't blame Brett for my leaving. It is entirely my decision. He tried to talk me into staying, but I feel very strongly that the time is right to leave. Please try not to worry about me. The Lord is my Shepherd, and I am never alone.

Love, Jodi

Letter in hand, she hoisted the bulky pack as Brett came down the hall and into her room. He was dressed in clean brown cords and an open-necked white shirt, over which he wore a navy blue hooded sweatshirt.

He caught the look of uncertainty on her face, and gently took the packsack from her. "I'll carry that". Jodi nodded. "Could I read your note?" he asked cautiously. She nodded again, not trusting herself to speak, and handed it to him. Brett read it quickly, gave her a look of approval, and said, "It's good. Short and sweet. Do you mind if I add a note of my own?"

"Sure." He set the pack down, sat at the little desk, and wrote:

Thanks very much for your great hospitality this week, and your understanding and acceptance of me despite the trouble I have caused. Jodi is determined to go with me and although I am delighted, I am sorry for the heartache it will cause you. I love her very much, and although we can't be together yet, I will help her as much as I possibly can. She is very capable, and has good friends in her church and community. I just wanted you to know that I did not encourage her to come back. She made up her own mind, and I can only respect that and help her to do what she feels is right. So long. See you again, I hope!

Brett.

Jodi sat on her bed while Brett quickly added his message to hers. He turned and handed it to her and picked up the big pack again. "Do you think that's okay?"

Scanning the note, she nodded and said, "Yes, it's fine." Thanks for doing that. They'll appreciate you more for trying to explain things, rather than just walking out the door."

"I hope it helps," Brett replied. " How much time do we have?" Jodi checked her watch for what seemed like the hundredth time in the last hour.

"It's ten to twelve now. There's a bus leaves Horseshoe Bay at noon. It takes about ten minutes to get to the Rosedale stop, so we'd better get moving.

"All right then." Brett grinned. "We're off on our adventure!"

CHAPTER TWENTY-TWO

Brett went ahead down the hall and up the narrow basement stairs carrying her pack in front of him by the leather straps. Jodi put the note on the table where it would easily be seen and sat down to put her boots on. It was becoming difficult to bend down to tie them. Her face coloured as she strained to reach the laces over her large belly. She could barely see them, let alone tie them up.

Brett, watching with amusement from the open door, came back in and kneeled in front of her. "Do you require assistance, Madam?" he asked politely, in a put-on English Butler accent.

"Yes, please, Jeeves" she answered, playing the game. "I can't seem to find my own feet today."

As Brett tied the laces his carefully groomed hair flopped down over his forehead and he tossed it back like an impatient stallion. The hair didn't stay. Jodi ran her fingers through it lovingly, and gave it a playful tug.

"Your hair is getting pretty long. Are you trying to catch up to me?" He looked into her eyes, hands on her knees.

"Nope. It's in defiance of my dad, for hitting me. He's always after me to get a haircut, but I refuse. Come on, let's move it." He pulled her up, and put his little blue backpack on her shoulders. "Here, you carry this one. It's not nearly as heavy as yours."

"Thanks". He set Jodi's pack on the ledge above the back porch stairs and wriggled into the straps. They picked up their coats, Jodi's dark navy one with the carved deer antler buttons, and Brett's denim jacket. Jodi locked the door. The family would have to use the spare key that was hidden under a certain rock in the garden.

Jodi was very quiet walking up the familiar lane to where the bus stopped on the lower highway. It was about half a mile. The smell of blossoms from the forsythia, lilacs, and Japanese cherry trees perfumed the air as they walked along the narrow lane. Brett held her hand, but didn't bother trying to talk. He knew her emotions were raw and that she was torn by guilt and indecision.

They got up to the highway with five minutes to spare and Jodi began to get change out of her fanny pack. Brett caught her, and said, "Don't worry, I'll get the bus fare. How much is it?"

"I've got lots of change right here," Jodi said. "It will be $2.50 each right to the depot. We might as well go there, and put our bags in a locker. Then we can go eat. There's a restaurant just near the terminal. Sorry you didn't get any breakfast this morning." She grinned and winked at him.

"Oh, that's all right. I got a sweet treat that was even better than breakfast!"

Brett flashed her a beautiful smile, which she returned.

In a few minutes, the blue and silver bus came over the hill and screeched to a stop for them. *This is it!* Jodi thought as she stepped onto the bus and took a seat on the ocean side near the front. Brett paid the fare, and lurched into the seat beside her as the driver eased the big bus out into the Sunday afternoon traffic.

    Jodi grew melancholy again watching the familiar scenery passing before her. The sunlight sparked on the water and a fresh spring breeze rippled the surface into tiny wrinkles like the skin on an elephant. Several large cargo ships lay at anchor waiting for harbour space to load up their exports for strange and exotic lands. Jodi tried to identify some of the flags, but other than one from Japan, she wasn't sure of the countries of origin.

    It was Brett's first trip to Vancouver and he was impressed with the beauty of the city and all the ocean-going traffic. The narrow road wound through little business sections called Dundarave, Ambleside, and Park Royal. He was intrigued with the beautiful expensive looking homes perched on rock faces, jutting out over the ocean, and clinging to the cliff sides up the mountains.

    Soon, they were traveling over the Lion's Gate Bridge and into the Stanley Park Causeway. Brett wished they had time to visit the park and walk along the seawall. He would love to come back sometime. There was much to see and explore.

Ten minutes later, the bus crawled through the downtown section, passing huge buildings that housed the big department stores, the Bay, Eaton's, and Sears. They passed a large stone church and the Birks Building that had a gigantic clock built into the facade. It was a popular meeting place, Jodi told Brett.

The bus entered a more drab part of town and pulled into the main terminal. They got their bags and Brett steered Jodi through the crowded station towards a bench.

Brett said, "Stay here for a sec and watch the packs and I'll go and check the bus time and see when we can get on."

Jodi nodded in agreement as he moved off towards the ticket booth. Brett already had his return ticket so he bought Jodi a one-way ticket to Harrison and confirmed the bus arrival time. He stuffed the ticket in his jacket pocket, closing the snap decisively. There was no turning back. They were going home!

Jodi and Brett found the lockers and shoved the packsacks inside as well as Jodi's big coat. She didn't want to pack that around with her. Jodi produced more quarters from her fanny pack and dropped them into the slot.

"Where did you get all the quarters?"

Brett asked.

"It's my baby-sitting money. It's been my only source of income for the past four months, and I've taken every job that came my way. I've been saving for my bus fare home."

"You've been planning this all along, then?" he asked, taking her hand and heading for the main doors.

"Yes, kind of, but I wasn't sure how I would pull it off. With you here, it just made it a whole lot easier." Jodi gave his hand a squeeze. "I just needed a big hunk to carry my backpack."

"At your service, Ma'am" he quipped. "Always pleased to help a lady in need."

Hand in hand, they walked the two blocks to the restaurant. Though it was very busy, the couple was shown to a small table for two near the back. Since Brett hadn't had breakfast, he ordered pancakes, eggs, and sausages. Jodi opted for a mushroom burger, fries, and a salad. They were very hungry, tucking into the food with enthusiasm. Talk could wait.

When the plates had been taken away and they sat regarding each other over coffee, Brett asked, "How are you off for money, Jodi?" She squirmed. It was a touchy subject. She really didn't know how she was going to manage. She had very little, and wasn't sure if she could get some sort of job, being eight months pregnant. She had to keep up her schoolwork too, and just keeping the fires going, planting a large garden, and caring for the animals would demand most of her time. Once the baby came, she would be busy day and night.

Jodi looked into her coffee cup, not daring to meet his eyes, and said, "I don't have much, but I'll get by." Blinking rapidly, she fought back hot tears.

Brett reached across the table and covered her hand with his. "I bought your ticket. That's a present from me." She looked at him with gratitude as he continued. "I only work Friday nights and Saturdays, and I have to buy my own school supplies and clothes. I'm saving for a car, so I can get up to see you, but it's going to cost a lot for insurance, maintenance, and gas".

She got up her courage to meet his eyes. What was he getting at?

"I want to send you some money every month," he said slowly, as if he was figuring something out, "but it may vary. Right now, I want you to have this." He reached for his wallet, and took out five twenty- dollar bills. Jodi's eyes grew wide.

"Oh, I couldn't! It's too much!" she protested. He took her hand, and putting the bills into it, closed her fingers around them.

"Take it. You'll need it."

"Thank-you," she said simply, as she put the money away in her fanny pack. "Can I at least buy lunch?"

"Sure, it's a deal."

Jodi and Brett finished their coffee and made use of the washrooms, where Jodi braided her hair into one long plait over her shoulder. They paid the bill, and walked out into the weak April sunshine. It was mild, but not really warm, and Jodi was glad she had her big sweater on.

With arms around each other, they wandered down the city sidewalks towards Chinatown. They had about two hours to wait, not enough time to go to Stanley Park as they had hoped.

"Someday," Brett promised her, "we'll come back here for our honeymoon, and we'll do all the things we didn't have time for. We'll walk on the sea-wall, and along the beach, we'll go to the zoo and watch the whale show, and" --

Jodi interrupted him with a giggle, "And we'll leave the kid with my sister while we do all this, right?"

"Right!"

Young and in love, Jodi and Brett wandered through the streets and shops of Chinatown and Gastown, marvelling in the smells and sights and sounds of the big city. Whole plucked chickens and strange vegetables hung in shop windows. The aroma of teas and spices from foreign lands assailed their senses. Bamboo and rattan furniture stores were everywhere; tiny coffee shops and trendy little jewellery boutiques were wedged like dainty sandwiches between the larger establishments.

The people fascinated Jodi. There were resident Chinese, street people in rags, drunks sitting in doorways, or on benches with a brown bag in hand, hippies in jeans and bare feet wearing colourful fringes and beads, street musicians, and visitors like themselves. It was an interesting melting pot of cultures and races.

Brett went into a small grocery store with only Chinese lettering out front and bought some kind of candy made with sesame seeds and honey. He and Jodi sat on a bench and munched it before heading back up to the bus station.

Jodi was weary. It was tiring walking around with all the weight she was carrying. Her back ached, and her feet were hot in her hiking boots. She almost looked forward to getting on the bus, though she knew it was a long time to sit and that she would be very uncomfortable by morning. Her main concern right now as they entered the terminal and found a bench to wait on, was that Marnie or Rob would be there to prevent her from leaving. She looked around nervously while Brett went to get the bags and check them through. So far - so good! She didn't see anyone she knew. They had half an hour to wait.

The station was busy; people moving constantly, loudspeakers announcing arrivals and departures, kids crying. Jodi leaned against Brett and closed her eyes. He draped an arm around her protectively.

Brett was lost in his thoughts and not really looking at anything, when he suddenly realized there was someone standing in front of them. He jolted upright, startling Jodi, whose eyes flew open to see Carol standing there.

She went pale, and managed to stammer, "Hi Carol. Have you come to stop me from leaving?"

Carol smiled, amused at their shocked expressions. She motioned for Jodi to move over, and sat down beside her.

"Listen, you two. Marnie called me, and read me your note. We can see there's no use trying to force you to stay." Looking at Brett, she said, "We know you care for her Brett, and we know you'll do everything you can to help her. But she's stubborn and independent. She won't ask for help."

Brett looked at Jodi fondly. "I know. I'll help her as much as I can; as much as she'll let me."

Carol reached into her purse and took out fifty dollars. "Being Sunday, this is all I could scrape up for now." She thrust it at Jodi. "We'll send you some more, as soon as we can."

Jodi's eyes were misty as she mumbled, "Thanks Carol, for everything." She stuffed the bills in her fanny pack. Then, she was overcome with emotion.

Tears spilled over as she hugged her sister tightly.

Carol's eyes were misty too. She said, "Take good care of yourself, and do what the Doc says. Call us collect, anytime. I'll phone you tomorrow night to see how things are."

The bus departure was announced. Carol hugged Brett too and he said softly, "Thanks for letting her go."

Carol nodded, and stepped back. Brett took Jodi's hand, and they moved towards the waiting bus.

CHAPTER TWENTY-THREE

Jodi and Brett chose a double seat at the back of the bus. With the increased pressure on her bladder, Jodi needed to be near the washroom. Also, she knew her legs and feet would cramp from the long hours of sitting and if she could just stand up at the back to relieve the pressure and let the blood flow, she would be more comfortable.

The driver got on and explained that they would be stopping for a supper break at Hope in two hours. After that there would only be short stops for passenger pickups and drop-offs.

Jodi was feeling strange, like it almost wasn't real that she was back on the bus after only four months, heading back home to a very different situation. She wondered if she had been too hasty. Had she made the wrong decision? No matter, she was on her way, and was not going to turn back now.

Brett took her hand and gave it a squeeze. "Are you all right, Sugar?" She nodded, but could not find the words to express her emotions. She leaned against Brett's shoulder, drawing strength from his body. He felt solid and comforting. Everything would be all right.

At supper, when they had finished their pizza, Jodi took a napkin and poured a measure of salt into it. Folding it up carefully, she tucked it into her pants pocket.

"What's that for?" Brett asked, looking puzzled.

Jodi explained, "I get really bad cramps in my feet when I sit for long periods of time. I don't know how or why licking salt helps, but it gets rid of the spasms almost immediately. I didn't have any salt on the way down, and I sure suffered from leg cramps...one of the joys of pregnancy, you know."

Back on the bus it was soon pitch dark outside. The lovers cuddled close together with Jodi's big coat draped over them. For a while, the baby was very active, causing Jodi to smile and grunt occasionally when he kicked hard. She drew Brett's hand under her coat and placed it on her belly as it rippled and undulated with the baby's stretching and kicking. Brett laughed with her. He felt a tremendous surge of pride and love for Jodi and his unborn child. He watched her face in the dim light and saw it glow with happiness as they tenderly focused on the activity of their baby.

"What should we call him, or her?" he asked in a whisper. Jodi answered very quietly too. This was a private conversation and not for the ears of anyone else on the bus.

Jodi said, "I'd like to name him something from the Bible. What do you think?"

"I don't know. Anything but 'Bruce'

though. I don't want him named after my father. Give me some suggestions"

"Okay, how about Matthew, or Mark? Or Luke, or John?"

"Tell me some more Bible names."

"Umm...there's the Old Testament names like Abraham" -

"No."

"Benjamin?"

"Uh...Ben's not too bad."

"Aaron? Levi? They were Priests."

"Nah"

They were quiet for a while, both thinking. Brett let out a long sigh and turned to her. "Don't you think we should have a girl's name ready too, just in case?"

Jodi sighed. "Well, maybe...but I've sort of known all along that it will be a boy."

"Humph!" Brett said. " I don't know how you can be so sure. What will the last name be, anyway?"

"I asked Marnie about that. The baby will have my name now, then if we get married, we can easily change it when I take your name."

"Oh, I see. What do you mean *if* we get married?" Their heads were close together so they could speak in whispers. Jodi kissed his cheek. "I'm sorry, I mean *when* we get married."

He kissed her back. "That's better. Let's not lose sight of our goals. I want us to be together as soon as we can manage it."

"Yeah, me too." Jodi agreed. After a pause, she said, "Do you like Peter, Paul, James or Timothy? They're all New Testament names." Brett considered for a moment.

"Mm-hmn. I like all of those names, but I was thinking, how about 'Christopher'? It's got Christ in it, and if it's a girl we can call her Christine or Christie."

Jodi sat up and stretched. She said the names out loud, trying them out. "Christopher McCallum...Christopher Randall. That sounds nice, either way. I like it. You're a genius."

She shifted her bulk onto her left side so that she was facing Brett. Sliding an arm around his chest, she snuggled against him and planted little kisses along the line of his jaw from ear to chin.

He shivered and giggled, "That tickles, but it sure feels nice." He kissed her then, so long she could hardly breathe. They would have to be careful. They were so attracted to each other, but there was nothing they could do about it, crammed into a narrow seat and surrounded by strangers.

Jodi broke from the long kiss and laid her head on his shoulder. "There's something else I want to talk to you about."

"Yeah? What's that?" he asked, rubbing her shoulders lightly.

"Well, I have this awful fear and

dislike of hospitals. I'm really dreading going in to have this baby...I'm afraid of the big E's."

"What are they?" he asked.

Jodi lifted her head and looked at him in the semi dark, then said slowly, "When you are in labour they make you have an enema and then just before the baby's head pops out they cut you so that you don't tear. It's called an episiotomy. I don't want either of those things."

"Can't you tell them not to?"

Jodi gave a little snort of derision. "Do you think they'd listen to me? I'm just a dumb kid!"

Brett sighed. "Well if it's hospital procedure, I guess you'll just have to go along with it. Hospital's the best place to be."

Brett was getting to know her pretty well, and he could detect a note of stubbornness in her voice when she answered, "I don't think so. They probably won't let you near me in hospital, because we're not married. I want to have my baby at home and I'd really like you to be there. I need you to be my coach...you know, help me through it."

Brett stared at her in disbelief. "Cripes! I don't know anything about it. I can't help you. Hospital staff is trained in these things."

"Maybe so," Jodi replied. But the nurses can't make any decisions without the Doctor's say-so. And the Doctor in

Kelso is a drunk. Everyone knows it. He's had his license lifted several times."

"No kidding?" Brett sounded genuinely surprised, and somewhat concerned. "That's terrible. I don't want you under his care either. Jodi, you're a stubborn little brat! You should have stayed in Vancouver where you'd get proper care. You can be so exasperating!"

"I know. I'm sorry, but I feel very strongly about this." The two of them sat in silence for a moment. The bus was passing through a small town. A few lights winked by and then the driver picked up speed and they were plunged into the dark roadway again.

Jodi said, "I have a really good book that explains everything. It has colour pictures of the whole delivery process and tells you everything you need to do. You could study up on it and then come and help me. Think what a rush that would be, delivering your own baby."

Brett removed his arm from around her shoulders and sat up. *What would she throw at him next? This was bizarre!* He rubbed his hands over his face and ran his fingers through his hair. He excused himself as he rose and went into the washroom.

Jodi stood up too and stretched her legs, then sat, staring out the window into the darkness.

Brett came back and sat down beside her, taking her hand. "Don't ask me to do this Jodi," he said quietly. "I'm no doctor, and if anything happened to you or the baby, I'd never forgive myself. It's too risky. I love you too much to take chances like that."

Jodi's eyes filled with tears and ran down her face. She turned to Brett and threw her arms around him. Crying quietly, she whispered, "Women have been having babies by themselves for thousands of years. It's a natural thing. I'm strong and healthy, and we know the baby is too. There should be no problem."

Brett patted her shoulder and rubbed her back. "Even so, I don't want to be responsible if there *is* a problem. I mean...things go wrong sometimes... babies come backwards and get stuck, or they can get the cord wrapped around their neck and suffocate."

"So, you'd put me in the care of a drunk before you'd deal with a birth yourself?" she asked.

Brett felt some exasperation as he said, "I didn't know the Kelso doctor had a drinking problem. Remember, it was your choice to come back now. You had good care down in Vancouver."

She sniffed and spoke haltingly. "I know, but I didn't want to go to the hospital there, either. I thought if I came home, you and I could run away together to have the baby."

"You're crazy! Where would we go?"

Jodi didn't answer; just heaved a big

sigh, and laid her head against his chest.

Brett sighed too, and kissed her wet cheek. "I'll think about it, okay? No promises. Now, let's try to get some sleep."

They snuggled up, getting as comfortable as possible in the confined space and managed to doze off, lulled by the swaying of the bus and the dull throb of the diesel engine.

Jodi was up at least three times to the bathroom and was bothered several times by severe cramps in her feet. The salt came in handy. She used it each time to alleviate the pain. She stood up in the small space between the seat and the washroom for a half hour or so in the pre-dawn hours, just letting the blood circulate. She looked down with affection on Brett's sleeping form. Even in the poor light, his golden hair was a bright contrast with the dark coat he laid against.

She put her hand gently on his head, as if in blessing. "I love you," she whispered. He stirred, but did not waken. Jodi dropped her awkward bulk into the seat beside him and pulled part of the coat over her. She leaned against his solid body and tried to sleep.

They arrived in Harrison about eight a.m. The small interior city was just beginning to come to life. There was still snow on the ground, but it was dirty and soft. Spring was definitely making its' presence known with the crocuses and daffodils that poked up from window boxes lining Front Street.

Jodi ordered breakfast at the Shamrock Grill while Brett phoned home. When he came back to the table he looked happy. His mom had answered and was very relieved to hear he was home. She and Bruce were afraid he wasn't coming back. Brett had asked her to phone the school to tell them that he wasn't coming in today; he had some things to attend to. By the time he went home, and got his books, he'd be late anyway. Besides, Jodi couldn't leave until four, when Stuey's Stage returned to Kelso and he wanted to spend the day with her. Carmen was beginning to realize that her son had a secret life of his own and that they could lose him entirely if they didn't give him a little rein. Convincing Bruce of this though, was going to be an on-going battle.

Stuey was surprised to see Jodi and shook her hand warmly. "Welcome back, Miss McCallum!" he grinned. " Coming home to have your wee one, are you? And is this your young man?" he asked, as Brett lifted her heavy pack into the back of his van.

"Yes," she beamed. "This is Brett Randall." Stuey and Brett shook hands; the youth looking into the seasoned, weather-beaten old face with interest.

"We'll see you later Stuey,"Jodi said.

"Right-O, Miss McCallum! I leave at four on the dot.

Jodi wanted to go shopping. She had nothing at all for the baby and she wanted to get to work on that back bedroom. She wanted paint and wallpaper, something bright and cute.

She was delighted that Brett was going with her. She had thought he would be going right to school, and she would be alone for the day. Hand in hand, they walked down to the mall. Jodi spotted a pay phone and called Mrs. Shannon in Kelso to let her know that she would be home tonight. Linda's mom was very surprised and somewhat concerned that Jodi would be on her own, but she assured her that they would get the fires burning and she was to come over for supper.

Jodi also wanted to go to Social Services. She had to have financial support if she was to survive. She could not burden Brett with their needs right now. She knew he would help, as would her family, but it would be easier on everyone if she could just go on welfare for a while. She looked up the number and address, called, and made an appointment for two p.m. that afternoon.

It didn't seem real that just four months ago, Jodi and Brett had walked down the same mall, miserable at the prospect of being parted. Now, they bantered lightly, teased each other, and laughed a lot. They were like kids in a candy store, shopping for their baby. Jodi bought a few newborn outfits, a rainbow coloured blanket, and some diapers. She knew people would give her lots of hand-me-downs once they knew the sex of the baby. Marnie had boxes of Jake's baby clothes to give her.

    At Sears Jodi chose white latex paint, some Robin's Egg blue paint for trim, and wallpaper with a Disney design. The little characters from Bambi were on the paper, Flower the wide-eyed skunk, the wise old owl, Thumper and the other bunnies and of course, Bambi himself.

After lunch, Jodi steeled herself for the interview at Social Services. She was embarrassed to go on 'relief' as her parents had called it. They always regarded people on welfare as somewhat inferior, and lazy. Jodi knew she was neither. She was just someone who needed help until she could sort her life out.

    Brett went to a nearby park to wait. It wouldn't do to be seen with her, when Jodi was going to have to tell some little white lies about being abandoned by her boyfriend and family. She was surprised how easy the interview and application went. Jodi was assigned a caseworker, not that she wanted one, but someone had to check that her situation was as she had described it. She was quoted an amount, and the date on which the cheque would arrive. She was advised that her caseworker would be paying her a visit next week, and that was that. It was over. Jodi stepped out into the April sunshine, vastly relieved that she would be able to manage after all.

    She and Brett spent the last hour in the cafe sharing ice-cream sundaes and coffee. They were relaxed and happy even though they would be parted soon. Brett told her he would try to come up on the following Sunday. He was going to start looking for a cheap car, but he'd have to rely on hitchhiking until he found one he could afford.

    Back up at the bus depot Brett kissed Jodi goodbye and helped her up into the front seat of Stuey's van. There were no other passengers today and Stuey had asked her to sit up front so he could 'catch her up' on the news from home. She smiled and gave Brett a 'thumbs up' sign as the van headed out of the depot and down to the mall to pick up her purchases before heading up the lake road to home.

Brett picked up his backpack from the depot locker and turned for home. He would have a lot of explaining to do.

CHAPTER TWENTY-FOUR

Jodi was in her glory being home. She brought down the record player and the records from upstairs and listened to music as she puttered around getting the house liveable again. She tired easily and found many things tedious and awkward such as carrying the wood in. Her tummy was so big there was nowhere to carry the load so she had to take many trips back and forth with a few pieces at a time.

Jodi had gone up to Mrs. Elliot's house to get Scamp and Sam the day after she arrived home. She had tea with the lonely old widow and felt almost guilty taking the animals away. The cat and dog had been happy here and well cared for.

Samantha gave Jodi a cursory sniff and then chose to ignore her, but Scamp went wild with excitement when he saw her. He kept bounding back to her on the walk home, leaping and barking exuberantly. For days he would not leave Jodi's side, for fear of being left again. Sam growled and cried piteously in the box while Jodi carried her home, but once in familiar territory, she checked everything out, and resumed her Superintendent duties as if she'd never been away.

Jodi decided to leave Blossom with Len's grandfather until after the baby was born. There was no way she could ride her that far right now.

On Sunday, Brett caught a ride all the way to Kelso, arriving about noon. He had not told his parents that Jodi was back, or where he was going. Bruce had been so angry with Brett for going to Vancouver that he could not bring himself to talk to his son. Unfortunately, father and son were completely estranged now and were extremely hostile towards each other. Carmen suspected that Brett might be seeing Jodi again, but she was waiting for an opportunity to talk to him about it. Her heart ached for both of her men; for she loved them both. She knew that they were hurting, but neither would give an inch to start the healing process.

 The two young lovers were lying in bed in the front room, propped up on pillows, looking at Jodi's book on the birth process. At last, there had been no one to interrupt them and they had made love, somewhat awkwardly. Jodi loved Brett's kisses and the way he touched her body, but found the rest not very comfortable or exciting. She was glad he didn't take very long. He was very sweet and gentle with her and she loved him all the more for it. She leaned her back up against his chest, with the book opened on her knees. Brett's right arm lay around her with one full, warm breast resting on his forearm. From time to time, he kissed her on the ear, or brushed her neck with his lips.

 Jodi turned to him and looked into his soft deep-blue eyes. "Will you go away with me, and help me give birth to our baby?" Brett shifted his weight, and tried to look away.

Jodi took his face in her hands and made him look at her. "Will you please? I want it to be just us. If you study this book carefully, you can do it. We can do it together." She implored him with her eyes.

Brett protested, "But what if something goes wrong? That's what I'm afraid of." He put his hand behind her head and gently pulled it down onto his shoulder. His arms went around Jodi's bulk and held her tight.

Jodi said, "Nobody wants this baby more than I do, and I'm willing to take that chance. I know that God has blessed us with this gift, and He won't take it away."

"I wish I had your faith, Jodi," he said. " I need to think about it some more."

The book fell to the floor as he slid down in the bed, pulling her with him. He ran his lips eagerly over her face and neck, and then buried his face in the cleft between her swollen breasts. He rubbed the small of her back gently as she closed her eyes and clung to him. She could have fallen asleep then, but she wouldn't have deprived him of his pleasure for the world. She heaved her bulk up and rolled on top of him, letting his pent up passion flow between them until they lay spent and wordless in each other's arms. They lay tangled in drowsiness for a while and then

Jodi stirred and gave him a playful smack on his behind.

"Are you going to sleep all day, or are you going to get busy on that room?"

"Hmph" he grunted, as Jodi got up, gathered her clothes, and headed for the bathroom.

Linda had offered to help carry the bunk beds out to the green shed. She would be here soon.

Jodi quickly made a couple of sandwiches and a pot of tea. As soon as they had finished eating, she got the supplies ready for painting and wallpapering the baby's room. She tied her hair back, and donned an old shirt of her dad's.

Linda arrived and kept looking at Brett as if he were a movie star or something. She was thrilled to be working alongside him. He was so lithe and graceful, oozing sexuality in his tight jeans, with his muscles bulging out of his T-shirt as he stretched and bent to hang the paper.

As she painted the windowsill, baseboards, and trim, Jodi enjoyed watching Linda and Brett; secure in the knowledge that one was her lover, and both were good friends.

Linda had broken up with Bob a month ago and was feeling rather lost and lonely. The good-natured joking and teasing between the three of them made the work go quickly and was actually fun.

By five o'clock, the room was transformed with Disney wallpaper on two sides and a fresh coat of white paint with blue trim on the rest.

While Brett and Linda cleaned up the mess, Jodi made a salad and spaghetti. She invited Linda to stay and was pulled aside for a quick, whispered conversation.

Linda asked,"Are you sure, Jodi? Don't you want to be alone with him? I don't want to be in the way."

Jodi grinned at her friend. "Relax, would you? We've already had our jollies. You're welcome to stay."

Linda's sandy eyebrows shot up at this revelation and her freckled face blushed hotly. Her hand went up to her mouth to stifle a giggle as she accepted with thanks.

After supper, Brett said he had to get going if he hoped to hitch a ride home before dark. Again, Linda squirmed in embarrassment as Brett took Jodi in his arms and kissed her passionately.

"S'cuse us, Linda," he said with a wink. "This has to last us a week, so we have to make it good." They walked to the door, and kissed some more before he left her.

"Safe home, sweetie," Jodi whispered. "Thanks for all your help today. I hope you get a ride right away."

"Bye, Princess", he said. "See you soon. Maybe I'll have a car by next weekend."

"Yeah, I hope so. We haven't got much time." Jodi said.

The next few days were spectacular. Tiny wisps of white cloud punctuated brilliant blue skies. Spring had sprung like a slinky toy bouncing down the stairs. The cottonwood trees came to life with the increased heat. Tassels of golden pollen burst from sticky buds and the sweet smell of new grass, warm earth, and lilacs permeated the air.

Jodi was struggling to turn over the earth in the garden, when, warned by Scamp's sharp bark, she looked up to see Len approaching.

"Hi kid!" he said with a grin. "Heard you were back." He gave her an awkward hug. "Wow! You're close, eh?"

"Yes," Jodi said, leaning on the spade. " I'm due in two weeks, more or less."

Len took the shovel from her and started digging. "You shouldn't be doing this heavy work. Where's that man of yours?"

Jodi flashed him a look of gratitude. "He's in school. He was here on the weekend. We painted and papered the back bedroom for the baby."

"Oh, so he's still on the scene?" Len asked. Jodi thought that he sounded a little disappointed and the thought flashed through her mind that Len might be interested in her. She filled him in on all the developments since she and Carol had left Kelso last December. They chatted like old friends, as Len turned over the rich dark soil.

"Actually," Len said, wiping sweat from his face as he paused for a moment leaning on the shovel, "I came by to see if you would like to take a drive with me out to Grandpa's. I thought you'd like to see your old pony."

Jodi's face lit up. "Oh! I'd love to! I've talked to Carl on the phone, but I had no way of getting out there to see her. You know I'm going to leave her there until after the baby's born."

Len nodded, as he bent to work again. "Tell you what. Why don't you go in and make me a sandwich and a big cool drink? I'll finish this, and then we'll go."

"It's a deal!" Jodi said.

Soon they were driving out along the beautiful but rough lakeside road towards the cluster of small farms that dotted the bench-lands on the hillsides above the lake.

A few miles out of town, Len asked her how Carol was doing. He tried to be nonchalant but Jodi sensed the pain in his guarded questions, and realized that he still loved her. Jodi told him all she could about Carol's courses at Langara, where she lived, and with whom, and no, she did not have a boyfriend as far as she knew. She saw Len visibly relax, and he turned to her with a smile.

"If there's anything you need, Jodi, just let me know. I'd like to help."

"Thanks, Len, you're a good friend." They rode in silence for a while, and then Jodi had an idea.

"Len, there is something you could do for me," she said, tentatively.

"Sure, what is it?" He looked interested, glancing between her and the twisty road.

"Umm...does your friend still have that hunting cabin up on Lake Leviathon?"

"Paul? Yeah, we were up there, ice fishing in February."

"Do you think he would let me use it for a couple of days? What's it like, anyways?"

Len gave her a quizzical look. "Well, it's small, and rustic. It has a wood stove, a table, and some shelves; lots of dishes and pots and pans. There are two double bunks along each side behind the kitchen and a couple of apple crates for clothes and such. There's a front porch and a couple of lawn chairs. There's an outhouse out back. Scalp Creek runs just behind the cabin and empties into the lake. Lots of trout in the lake."

Jodi was quiet, thinking. Len pulled into the Morrison farm and parked the truck.

"Want me to get you the key?" Len asked, studying her face.

"Could you?" Jodi came out of her

reverie and stared at Len.

"Sure, but you haven't told me what for." He looked at her expectantly.

"Tell you on the way home." she said. "Here comes your Grandpa."

They had a great visit, beginning and ending with a trip to Blossom's pasture. The pony came up to Jodi and shoved her head up against her chest. Jodi's arms went around Blossom's arched neck in a big hug. They exchanged several big kisses and then Blossom moved off in search of new green shoots. Her long winter coat was almost all shed off. She looked fat and healthy. Jodi was pleased to see the pony looking so good.

Two very pregnant goats appeared out of a shed and Jodi laughed as the animals came over to investigate the visitors.

"Well girls." cried Jodi. "Who's going to kid first? Looks like you're both due about the same time as I am."

"Yep." grinned old Carl Morrison. "They were with the billy in January, so they're both due pretty soon. Maybe the young feller could take them home for you in the truck. I sure don't need the milk. I've got my Bessie cow."

Len said, "Sure, might as well. I might not be around for a while."

After tea and a visit with Len's grandmother, Len, Carl, and Jodi went back out to load the goats. Carl tied a soft, cotton rope around each of their necks, knotting it so it wouldn't tighten. He then instructed 'the young feller' to lift the nannies up into the back of the truck, whereupon he tied them first to each other, and then with another rope to each side of the truck.

It was hard to believe that little Fanny was going to be a mother too. Jodi felt a twinge of pity for her twin, Fritz, who having the misfortune of being born a male, was now in the freezer in brown paper packages.

Back at her house, Jodi turned the goats into Blossom's paddock. Without the pony there was plenty of fresh sweet grass to nibble on. Jodi and Len hung over the wooden fence watching them. Jodi knew he was waiting for an answer about the cabin, so she tried to explain.

"Len," she began... "about the cabin...I just thought it would be nice if Brett and I could go somewhere when the baby's born, just to be alone together. His parents don't want him to have anything to do with me, so the less people in town see, the better for us. It would even be for the best if you didn't know where we were."

Len gave her a sly, mischievous grin. "Well, I'm going to be working out in the bush on a logging contract for the next month, so if I'm not around, I can't know anything about it, right?"

Jodi, nodded, smiling.

"I'm leaving tomorrow, so I'll go and see Paul tonight. I'll bring the key around later, if it's all right with him."

Jodi gave him an awkward hug. "Thanks, Len. You're a good guy."

The next Sunday, Jodi had breakfasted, showered, tidied up the house, and baked a carrot cake with cream cheese icing, when she heard a car horn blowing outside. Curious, she went to the living room and looked out the window. A strange, dark green car with the motor running was parked in front of the house. As Jodi stepped out onto the front porch, the passenger door swung open and she could see Brett, leaning across the driver's seat, beckoning her closer.

"Hi Honey, hop in!" He grinned like the proverbial Cheshire Cat. "What do you think of my new wheels?"

Jodi slid into the seat, threw her arms around him, and hugged him tight. "This is yours? It's great! It's really nice. What is it?"

"1968 Pontiac; one owner, low mileage, good condition", he said proudly. "I got a good deal on it."

"How much?" Jodi asked, as Brett put the car into gear and headed through town and out to the lake road.

"Seven hundred and fifty bucks. It's a little more than I wanted to pay, but it's a good solid family car. It should do us for a long time." He reached for her hand and gave it a squeeze. His blue eyes danced with happiness. "It's for all of us."

Jodi turned to him with a smile. "Wow! I'm impressed. I thought you'd get some old junker, you know, like a Volkswagon Beetle, or something. This is really very nice. Thank you for thinking of all of us."

Brett pulled into a campground that was still closed for the season, and parked in one of the tenting spaces. He slid over and pulled Jodi close, kissing her firmly on the lips while running his hands through her hair and over her body. "These nice, wide seats," he whispered against her throat, "are very conducive to love making."

She laughed and pushed him away. "Not when you're nine months pregnant, though."

"Mm...maybe not. How have you been this week?"

"Oh," she said, "tired and crabby. My back aches a lot, and I'm so clumsy. I'm getting very weary of being like this. The waiting is hard. I wish it were over. I don't want to be pregnant again for a very, very long time." Her eyes filled with tears and threatened to spill over; her lower lip stuck out just a little, in a bit of a pout. Realizing that now was not the time to be amorous, Brett removed his arm from around her shoulders and started the car.

Heading back to town, Jodi told him

about the cabin, watching overtly for his reaction. To her surprise, he seemed quite interested and excited. He had been reading the book on childbirth, and he had to agree with Jodi. To deliver your own child together would be a fantastic thing. As long as it was a normal birth, he knew he could help her. But God help them both if anything went wrong.

They drove for a while without speaking. Brett took Jodi's hand in his and kissed the inside of her palm. That erotic touch always sent shivers down her spine. In turn, she moved closer, and laid her hand on his thigh. He looked at her, his blue eyes twinkling with mischief.

"I'll do it, if that's what you really want. Are you sure you want to take the risk?"

"Yes." Jodi said. Her jaw was set in a stubborn line. Brett felt a wave of excitement and fear wash over him. He couldn't believe what he had just agreed to.

They sat quietly in the car in front of the house, discussing the details and making a plan. Brett said, "Okay, I'll give you my phone numbers at home, at work, and at school. You get all the supplies packed and ready to go down to the boat. I'll call you every day, but if there's an emergency, you get hold of me, and I can be here in just over an hour. The only day I can't possibly come is the 15th. I *have* to be there for the track meet. "

Jodi nodded, looking pale. They went in and spent a quiet day together. Brett had brought his schoolwork and they did some studying at the dining room table. In the afternoon, Brett jogged a couple of miles to keep in shape for the upcoming track meet, while Jodi walked along the beach. He did not approach her for sex, and she did not offer. There was an unspoken understanding between them because of Jodi's size and discomfort. They would wait.

CHAPTER TWENTY-FIVE

Jodi's sisters phoned her on the l6th of May, the anniversary of their parents' accident. The girls shared a few tears together and Jodi lit candles and said prayers for her parents and for her unborn baby. She found she could not dwell on the loss for long with the baby's birth being so close.

    Brett did well at the Interprovincial track meet the day before, winning his 1500 meter race and placing well in the high jump and shot-put. Jodi wanted to go down to watch him but was afraid she would be a worry to him, and jeopardize his chances of success. She might have gone into labour at any time and she didn't want to chance it.

Jodi thought she would go crazy if this child wasn't born soon. She felt crabby, weepy, and so restless. She was very tired but couldn't sit or relax. Her back had been aching for days and when Brett called on Sunday afternoon to see how she was, she realized with a start, that she had a low burning pain in her pelvis. She knew the baby must be down in position and ready to come. "I think you'd better come up," she told him. "I'm ready to pop."

    When he arrived, Jodi had everything ready by the front door; blankets, towels, food, clothes, medical and baby supplies. She had revised her lists over and over so as not to forget anything important. She had been taking small loads down to the boat all week. The cabin key was on a leather thong around her neck.

As Brett loaded the supplies into the car, Jodi left a note for Linda saying she had gone away for a few days and to please look after the animals. She wanted so much to take Scamp but there just wasn't room in the boat. "Sorry, little fella," she said, hugging him, as his mournful eyes pleaded to be taken along, "you stay here and look after things."

It was dusk when they set off across the lake. No one had seen them leave. The lake was calm as Brett headed the heavily laden craft in the direction of Walton Creek, a mile and a half up the far side of Kokanee Lake. Words could not be heard above the roar of the outboard motor, but each was lost in their own hopes and fears of the adventure they had embarked upon, foolhardy as it was.

The lake crossing was uneventful. Brett steered the boat into the little bay and pulled it up high on the sandy beach. Using Jodi's big brown canvas packsack that she'd had in Vancouver, he loaded it with supplies and started up the half-mile trail in the dark, aided by a flashlight. Jodi took a smaller load and started up at her own slow pace. As she climbed, the baby stretched and rolled, leaving her breathless; unable to move at times. Brett passed her coming down, and again on the way up, carrying supplies at a furious pace; driven by the need to get everything into the cabin in time for the birth.

With the last load deposited on the porch, he turned and jogged back down the trail to find Jodi leaning against a tree in the dark, clutching at the bulge of her abdomen. The whole thing had clenched hard in a massive contraction; every fibre responding to the abstract, yet intimate touch of the little person within.

"God, Jodi! Are you all right? Is it coming?" She heard the fear in his voice.

"No, I'm all right...I think" She took a deep breath and screamed silently. "*No, not now! I am not in labour!*"

Brett took her pack and hoisted it onto his shoulders. He encircled her waist with a strong supporting arm and she leaned on him as he helped her up the remaining steep path to the cabin.

While Brett bustled around lighting the lanterns and getting a fire going in the old wood stove, Jodi sat in a lawn chair on the deck of the little cabin, wrapped in a blanket. Apart from the sounds coming from within, the silence was awesome. Dusk dissolved into inky blackness and in the sky, a canopy of twinkling stars winked from horizon to horizon. Every detail of the forest stood out in stark relief as a nearly full moon rose, casting a silvery beam across the lake, far below.

Inside, by lantern light, Brett took

stock of the 15'x20' one-roomed cabin. Thankfully, the last occupants had left a good supply of wood and he soon had a fire crackling, chasing away the chill of the evening. He rummaged in a bag and found a couple of cans of soup. An array of pots and pans hung from nails on the log wall. Selecting one, he wiped it out with a dishcloth and put the soup on to heat. Taking the kettle and a large pot, he went out to the porch.

"Are you okay, Princess?" he asked.

"Yes, I'm fine," Jodi answered. "Nothing's happening."

"Good. Can you come with me then and hold the lantern so I can get some water at the creek?"

Jodi felt a surge of annoyance at having to get up and move, then immediately felt guilty sitting there while Brett did all the work.

"Sure," she sighed, and got clumsily to her feet.

On their return to the cabin, Jodi sat at the small wooden table and rested while Brett put the water on to heat. He then turned his attention to the beds. Two double bunks were positioned along the back wall of the room. Together, Jodi and Brett lifted a top bunk down and pushed it up against its' mate. Jodi found the groundsheet she had brought and spread it over her single mattress before Brett made up the now double bed with clean sheets and warm quilts.

As Jodi stirred the soup and put out bread and butter, Brett found and laid out the extra towels and medical supplies they had brought. He hoped they hadn't forgotten anything essential.

They ate their meal quietly, both very aware of the drama that would unfold very soon. The cabin took on a cozy warmth and the lantern cast a warm glow and a long shadow against the rough log walls.

A little after nine p.m. there was nothing left to do; so by mutual consent, Jodi and Brett agreed they might as well go to bed. Jodi dropped a loose cotton shift over her bulk. Brett always slept naked. Having never spent a night together and feeling just a little strange, they got into the bed.

Brett had positioned the lantern on a wooden apple crate beside the bed and he leaned over Jodi to turn it out. His hand caressed her as he snuggled against her back. He smoothed back her long hair, and kissed her cheek, then rested his arm around her middle. Jodi covered his hand with hers and held it tight, laying her arm over his. Both could feel the baby squirming and bumping inside his own little world.

"He wants out," Jodi whispered.

"Yeah, it won't be long now," Brett answered. Their breathing slowed as they became drowsy. Jodi turned a little towards him and said, "It doesn't seem real that I've only known you for nine months. It seems as if we've been together for a very long time."

"Mmph," came the muffled reply against her neck. "We've been through so much together...it just seems like a long time."

"I love you, Dream Boy."

"I love you too." Their lips met in a sweet kiss before the two young lovers dozed off into a fitful sleep.

About an hour later, Jodi awoke with a start. Something wet was running down her legs. Moonlight was filtering in through the cabin window. Jodi could see her way without a light as she slid her legs over the edge of the bed and made her way out to the porch. Another gush of warm fluid trickled down her legs and she grabbed the porch railing for support as a severe pain gripped her insides. As it passed, she straightened up to find Brett at her side, his tousled hair silver in the moonlight. He had thrown on his jeans, but his feet and his chest were bare. He took her in his arms gently.

"Has it started then?"

"Yes," she answered, leaning her head on his chest. "My water broke."

"Oh wow! What should I do?"

"Nothing yet. Just stay with me."

"Okay, come on in. You're shivering."

For the next couple of hours, Brett kept a lonely vigil as Jodi suffered the pangs of labour. He walked with her when she wanted to walk and lay down with her when she wanted to rest. He bathed her face with cool water and rubbed her back and heaving abdomen, all the time whispering encouragement and sweet nothings to her. Her moods swung from excitement and joy at the impending arrival, to crying and cursing against the horrible pain of the contractions. The pains were coming close together now, less than a minute apart.

Jodi was tired out. She was soaked with perspiration, and felt desperate to be rid of her burden. She couldn't concentrate, and felt herself slipping away into blackness.

Jodi felt Brett's hands taking hold of hers as she lay propped against the pillows and heard his voice calling her back.

"Jodi! Stay with me now. Come on, you have to stay focused. It's time to push."

Brett had lifted her shift up to have a look and was surprised to see the end of the baby's head appear and then disappear as her muscles contracted and then relaxed. He kneeled then and held on to Jodi's hands as he encouraged her through the toughest stage of the birth.

Three, four times, he saw the head emerge only to disappear as the spasms subsided. Jodi groaned and pushed, her face becoming dark red with effort.

Brett put her hands on her raised knees and instructed, "When the next one comes, hold on and push hard!"

It came almost immediately. With teeth clenched, and her back curling off the pillows, Jodi felt as if her pelvic bones were being split apart. Brett eased his fingers around the tiny head and applied gentle pressure. With an audible 'pop' the head was out! It was 6:05 a.m.

"Come on, Princess," he encouraged, "Push him out! You're almost done! "

With the next push, the baby slid out easily in a whoosh of blood and fluid. Brett gazed in awe at the slippery red baby boy he held in his hands. He reached for a clean towel and wiped away the mucous from the mouth, eyes, and nose. The baby started to sputter, making little outbursts of angry sounds, while his tiny fists punched at the air. "It's a boy!" Brett cried jubilantly.

Jodi nodded weakly. "Is he all right?"

As Brett wrapped the towel around his son, he replied, "Yes, he's just fine." He placed the bundle on Jodi's now flattened stomach as her hands reached out to receive him. A moment later the afterbirth came away and Brett cut the cord, tied it off, and disinfected it as he had learned to do from the book. The baby howled in protest.

Jodi cuddled him up against her neck and made soothing noises to him.

Christopher stopped hollering and made little grunts and sucking sounds instead. Jodi tried him at her breast where he immediately latched on to a nipple and sucked vigorously. She laughed in surprise. "You've got some tough competition here, honey."

She was exhausted, but happy. Her eyes shone with love and pride for her little son, and for Brett who had done such a great job of coaching.

While Jodi rested, Brett took the bloody towels out to soak in the creek and then busied himself stoking up the fire and making some tea and toast.

They were both hungry and thirsty after their night's work. Brett sat on the apple crate beside the bed as he and Jodi shared their simple meal together; staring in wonder first at each other, and then at their little son, who was also enjoying his breakfast.

Jodi felt stronger once she had eaten and she gave Brett the baby to hold while she got up to wash. She stood on a towel by the old wood stove and cleaned the dried blood and sweat off her body, then dressed in sweat pants and an old flannel shirt. She wanted to be comfortable, not glamorous. As she dressed, she said, "I guess we should wash him too; he's still got blood and guck on him". Brett nodded in agreement.

"Here, I'll take that water out, and dump it," he offered, handing her the baby and taking the basin from her. You'd better hop back into bed."

"Yes sir, Doctor" she obeyed. "I need to lie down, before I fall down. I feel a little woozy."

Brett brought fresh warm water, soap, and a cloth. Laying the infant on the bed, Jodi unwrapped the towel to look at his perfect little body. Brett began to wash him gently. The newborn resented the loss of his warm covering and immediately started to cry lustily.

"At least we know his lungs are okay," Brett yelled over the din. "My God, can he ever holler."

When the bath was finished, Brett fumbled with a diaper and a tiny sleeper while his son screamed and kicked in protest. Jodi looked on with amusement as Brett finished his task and handed the baby back to her with relief.

"Here, stick him on a booby and shut him up." he grinned. The crying decreased to a few sniffles as the baby snuggled into Jodi's bosom and sought comfort there.

Brett took the water out and dumped it over the railing of the porch. The morning air was fresh and clear with the scent of pine drifting through his senses. The tiny lake, which was no more than a small depression left by the last ice age, lay shimmering like a jewel just ten feet from the cabin door. As Brett watched, trout leaped, flashing like silver boomerangs in the early morning light, leaving ever widening circles on the glassy surface. The sun was just beginning to send its warmth over the high peaks to the east. The sky was turning from pearly grey to glorious shades of pink, blue, and gold. Up high in the pines and spruce a cacophony of bird sounds erupted to greet the day with a chorus of songs.

Holding on to the railing with both hands, Brett bowed his head as tears trickled down his face. He couldn't express or understand the emotions that overwhelmed him but he felt close to God at that moment and he mumbled his thanks for Jodi and the child. Taking a deep breath, he popped his head in the doorway, and called softly. "Jodi, can you come out here? You have to see this."

Carrying the baby, she padded quietly out to the porch. She was momentarily alarmed when she saw his face, wet with tears, but he smiled and pulled his little family into his embrace.

"It's just so beautiful out here. I wanted to share it with you," he said. Jodi shook her long hair back and lifted her face to the morning sun. She took deep breaths of the pristine, mountain air.

"Oh, what a paradise this is," she said. "It's wonderful to be here with you. And I haven't even thanked you for the great job you did as my coach. I think you should consider a career as a doctor. I love your bedside manner." She laid a hand on his cheek and wiped away the remnant of a tear. They gazed into each other's eyes; his deep blue, and hers a reflection of the blues and greens of nature around them. He bent and kissed her and then, being careful not to crush the baby, pulled her closer and covered her face and neck with passionate kisses. The love that they had declared had grown deeper with the birth experience they had just shared. Jodi broke away, somewhat breathless and dizzy.

"Come on." Jodi smiled. "Let's have a Naming Ceremony." She turned from him and with eyes closed, held the baby out at arm's length, toward the sun.

Brett stood back; somewhat unsure of what she was doing. As if sensing his confusion, she turned and gave him a radiant smile. "Will you stand with me to bless him?" she asked.

"Sure, what do you want me to do?"

"Just stand close here, and help me hold him up. Yeah, like that." She nodded as Brett moved close to her side and put his hands under the infant. Together they lifted him up again towards the sun and then in a circle that encompassed the lake, the mountains, and the cabin.

"Heavenly Father," Jodi began in a quiet voice, "Mom and Dad..."her voice faltered, then began again. "We present our son, Christopher Duncan McCallum Randall. May he enter the circle of life and be a part of all that is good and kind, and loving in your kingdom. We give thanks for the safe delivery of this child, and ask for your blessing upon him."

She brought her arms down and put the baby into Brett's arms. Christopher was awake, and watched them with solemn deep blue eyes, so much like his father's.

"Christopher," Jodi said as she laid a hand gently on his little bald head, "May the Lord bless thee and keep thee. May the Lord make his face shine upon thee and be gracious unto thee. The Lord lift up his countenance upon thee, and give thee peace. Amen."

As they stood there, a whitetail doe made her way delicately down to the water's edge. Sensing human presence, she remained motionless for a long moment, staring in their direction before lowering her head to drink. Then, with a springy bound, she disappeared from view.

The spell broken, Jodi leaned on Brett as he slipped a strong arm around her. "That was beautiful," he said, "and so was the blessing you did. Do you know a lot of scripture?"

"Not as much as I would like. But verses that I learned in Sunday School come back to me when I need them.

"Hm...maybe you'll be a minister some day."

"Yeah. And maybe you'll be a doctor some day. Who knows? Let's go get some sleep"

"Good idea. It's been a long and

exciting night."
 With Christopher between them, Jodi and Brett lay down and pulled the quilt over them. They wrapped their arms around each other and drifted off to sleep.

CHAPTER TWENTY- SIX

The rest of that day and most of the next two were spent lazily. Jodi slept, ate, and looked after Christopher's needs while Brett chopped wood, caught fish for their supper, and worked on his homework assignments. They were blissfully happy with each other and with their little son but each knew the bubble would burst and they'd have to face reality soon.

That reality materialized Wednesday afternoon as Jodi sat in a lawn chair on the porch nursing Christopher. Brett was inside, doing schoolwork. Jodi had been watching a cabin cruiser coming across the lake down below and when it turned in towards Walton Creek, she called to Brett, "Looks like we're going to have company. I guess we've been found."

Brett came to stand beside her and dropped a hand onto her shoulder. She turned and kissed it, then reached up and covered his hand with her own.

"Whatever happens now," he said softly, "I'm glad we had this time together." He sat in a lawn chair beside her to wait.

"Me too," she agreed with a smile.

In a little while, an R.C.M.P. officer came puffing up the trail and headed towards the cabin.

"Afternoon," Brett smiled at him. "Nice day for a hike."

The Mountie ignored the comment, and said, "Are you Brett Randall?"

Brett stood up. "I am," he said, "and this is Jodi McCallum and our son Christopher. Are we being arrested for something?"

"Not exactly," the officer replied. "But you must realize that your families are frantic about your disappearances." He looked at Brett. "Your parents are in Kelso. They filed a Missing Person's bulletin two days ago, when you didn't show up at school. And your sisters have been calling from Vancouver," he said to Jodi. "They're worried about you and the baby. When was he born?"

"Early Monday morning," Jodi answered proudly. "Brett delivered him." She opened the blanket to show off her son. "He's just fine." she added.

The officer leaned over to look and then smiled and leaned back against the railing of the porch. He tried to look stern but a small smile tugged at the corners of his mouth. "You know you're both damn crazy fools to pull a dangerous stunt like this."

"Yes Sir, we know," answered Brett. "But we decided to take the risk, so we could be together. If Jodi had gone to a hospital, they wouldn't have let me near her. Even if we are in big trouble at home, it was worth it."

The Mountie sighed, understanding in his eyes. "Well, I'm Corporal Brown, from the Kelso Detachment. I'm instructed to escort you home."

Jodi piped up, "Yes, we figured on that. We watched your boat coming across the lake. Have a seat here and I'll get you a drink of water. We'll get packed up."

The two men carried their belongings down to the beach and stowed them into the larger R.C.M.P. boat. Jodi's little scow was tied on behind and towed back to the Marina. From there, the young family was taken to the Police Station for questioning, and for reports to be filled out. Corporal Brown called the Taylors, and let Brett's parents know that he had been found. Within five minutes Bruce Randall's voice was heard out in the front office and Jodi and Brett knew they were being torn apart again.

Brett cupped the sleeping infant's head in his hand and kissed his cheek. Then he took Jodi in his arms and gave her a thoroughly satisfying kiss. She felt all a-tingle inside, warm and glowing with life. There was no falseness in the love they felt for each other. It was genuine and fierce. Her eyes were misty with held-back tears as she whispered, "I love you."

A dark form in the doorway interrupted them. A young Officer said, "Ahem, Your father's here, Brett."

Brett answered, "I know, I'm coming." He picked up his packsack containing his clothes and books and disappeared out the door. Jodi overheard him ask his father if he would care to see his grandson and cringed when she heard the curt angry reply, "No. Let's go!"

Outside, Brett was instructed to get into the family car. His mom was waiting in the front seat. Carmen knew better than to speak when Bruce was in this kind of a mood.

"But I have to get my car!" Brett protested.

"You won't be needing it!" came the angry reply. "You're grounded! Get in!"

Brett tossed his stuff into the back seat and slid in after it. "Mom," he pleaded, "I need to pick up my car. It's down at the park." His blue eyes smouldered and his jaw was set.

"Your mother can drive it then," barked Bruce. "You're riding with me, in case you try some other dumb ass escapade!"

Trapped in the car, Brett endured a scathing lecture for the next twenty miles or so. He tried to explain his actions, and tell his dad how much he loved Jodi and the baby, but Bruce was too angry to listen. When both vehicles arrived home, he confiscated the keys to Brett's car, and forbade him to leave town. Brett was furious, but he knew it was useless to argue right now. He would give it some time, and things would cool down.

Meanwhile, Jodi was only half listening to the scolding she was getting up at the hospital. She was forced to submit to an examination and despite her pleadings that she was fine, the crabby doctor ordered her admitted for a day or two 'for observation'. Christopher was weighed and measured, and had his birth recorded. Then he was whisked off to the nursery.

Jodi put in a collect call to Marnie, and told her everything that had transpired. Again she was chastised for her stubborn foolishness, but the relief and love flooded through in Marnie's excitement about the baby. She promised to bring the three kids up to see their new little cousin as soon as school was finished.

That night, Jodi lay in the strange hard hospital bed, feeling desperately lonely and unhappy. She missed Brett so much; missed the muscled feel of his lean hard body and the lingering scent of his skin. She wanted Christopher to cuddle but the nurse wouldn't let him stay with Jodi despite the fact that she had cradled him in her arms the last two nights, and intended to do so again, when she got him home.

Jodi had slept with Samantha for many years and was used to a live body snuggled against her. She knew there was no chance of crushing or suffocating the baby. It was the most natural thing in the world to have Christopher beside her and to put him to her breast when he wakened, hungry.

The Royal Victorian was a very small hospital; an old, turn of the century mansion that a now deceased widow had donated to the town. The small maternity ward was upstairs. Jodi was the only occupant in the large four-bed unit and the nursery was down the hall across from the Nurses' Station.

Around three a.m. Jodi lay rigid, tears streaming down her face. Christopher had been crying for at least half an hour. *Why didn't that damn nurse pick him up? Why couldn't she comfort her own baby when he was screaming like that?* Finally she could stand it no longer. She got up and padded down the hall towards the increased wailing. The Night Nurse, a thin lipped grim looking middle aged woman with short greying hair was sitting at the desk, reading a book. Jodi's fists clenched in anger and she flushed hotly. *That callous bitch! How could she just sit there ignoring those desperate cries?* She approached with trepidation.

"Yes?" Pat Olsen, R.N. looked up from her book. "What is it?"
What is it? thought Jodi in disgust. *Jeez! Was she ever dumb! Couldn't she hear the baby screaming his head off?* She choked her anger back and said, "My baby...he's been crying for a long time. Can I have him, please?"

Nurse Olsen looked at her watch and frowned. "But he's not due for feeding for another half an hour."

"I know, "Jodi said patiently, "but I've been listening to him cry for a long time and I know he's scared and hungry. Being all alone is frightening for him. He slept with me the first two nights and he didn't cry at all."

Ms. Olsen gave a snort of contempt. "Hmph! It's good for them to cry. Strengthens their lungs. And you should never have the baby in bed with you. It not only spoils him, but you might roll on him, or suffocate him with the blankets."

Jodi thought fleetingly of all the baby animals she'd seen; puppies, kittens, foals, and her goats, and how sensible the animals were. The young were constantly with the mother and were fed and comforted on demand, not on some dumb schedule that made the youngsters angry and frightened.

She took a deep breath, let it out, and tried again. "Please, Ms. Olsen. Just let me hold him and walk him. He'll stop that crying."

"Well," came the reluctant reply. "I suppose so. You go on back to bed and I'll bring him after I change his diaper."

"Couldn't I change it?" asked Jodi.

"Sorry, you're not allowed in the nursery."

Jodi wondered *why not?* But rather than start another useless argument she nodded agreement and went back to her room to wait.

When Ms. Olsen brought the baby to Jodi, he was still upset. His little face was red and sticky from the exertion of crying. He nursed greedily making sounds that Jodi hadn't heard before; whimpers and grunts of distress, while his tiny hands clutched desperately at her breast, as if he couldn't get enough of her.

"Poor little fellow", Jodi crooned, as she rocked and cuddled him. "I'll get you out of here just as soon as possible. There's no need for us to be here."

Unfortunately, with the new day, came more torture for Christopher. Without Jodi's knowledge or permission, he was circumcised that morning and once again she agonized as she heard his desperate screams down the hall. With the day staff on and the doctor somewhere around she dared not go down to see what was wrong.

Finally the nurse brought him to Jodi and told her about the little operation and how to care for it. Jodi was furious as she put the baby to her breast, but knew there wasn't a thing she could do about it now, and the less said, the better.

They were discharged at noon, much to Jodi's relief. Her hatred and fear of hospitals had just intensified, and she couldn't wait to get home. She called the R.C.M.P. office to see if they would bring her belongings over from the Marina. The Constable agreed to do that and to drive her home. She would get Linda to go with her one day after school to pick up the boat.

Christopher was fussy all the rest of that day and during the night too. Jodi made a little bed for him in the wicker laundry basket and she did put him down at times; but mostly, she carried him, trying to comfort the pain and indignation he had suffered.

Over the next few days as his wound healed and his every need was catered to, Christopher calmed down and became the contented happy baby Jodi knew he was. She talked and sang to him constantly when he was awake. She introduced him to Scamp, Samantha, and the goats, and showed him the garden. While she worked, Jodi told her baby all about his wonderful father and how they would all be together some day. Talking about Brett helped to bring him closer and made Jodi feel less lonesome for him.

Jodi told Christopher what a special baby he was; how he was a treasure sent from heaven and she told him what special people her mother and father had been. She talked to him about his aunts; Marnie, Carol, and Beverly, about Uncle Rob, and about his cousins that he would play with some day. Christopher's big, blue eyes followed her, looking so wise and thoughtful.

Brett managed to call her collect from a pay phone outside the I.G.A. on Saturday, after his shift. "Things are very tense at home", he said. I'm sorry, but I won't be able to come up for quite a while. Dad has threatened to kick me out for good if I dare go up to Kelso to see you."

As much as he resented the restriction, he had to go along with it. They both griped about the unfairness of it and Brett asked Jodi to be patient. He was studying for final exams and had applied for a summer job tree planting with the B.C. Forest Service. If he could get on a crew in the valleys around Kelso, he could possibly see Jodi and the baby on weekends. She resigned herself to waiting, and hoped that they would be able to see each other in a couple of weeks. Of course, he asked about Christopher, and was happy to hear how good and contented he was. Jodi was mildly annoyed with him for not being more sympathetic when she told him about the circumcision.

Brett laughed and said, "Who else do you know that's circumcised?"

Jodi felt herself flush, and stammered, " Well, you are. I haven't exactly looked at anyone else's privates."

He chuckled again. "It didn't traumatize me for the rest of my life. He'll get over it."

"I know, he already has, but boy, was he ever mad! You wouldn't believe how he screamed. It was scary!"

"Well," Brett softened, "I'm sorry I couldn't have been there with you. We both know you're the one that has to deal with the dirty stuff, for now, anyways."

"Yeah, I sure miss you...especially at night. This old house seems so empty." Jodi said.

Brett's voice took on a lower, more intimate tone. "You should see what you've done to me."

"What?" she asked innocently.

"Well...we were talking about a certain body part and then you said you missed me."

Now it was Jodi's turn to laugh. "It's probably just as well that we're separated for a while. You'd be ravishing my poor, battered body if you were here and I'm not ready for that yet."

"How long?" he asked, serious now.

"Oh, depends on the healing. About six weeks, I think."

"That's perfect. School will be finished, and I'll have my car back. I'll have a lot more freedom then." After a pause, Brett asked, "Are you going to go on the pill?"

"Do you think I should?"

"Well, yeah. You wouldn't want another baby right now, would you?"

"No, of course not, but I want to know if you'll be around enough to justify me taking the pill." Jodi felt a prickle of guilt, putting pressure on him this way and immediately felt sorry for saying so.

Brett sounded somewhat surprised and hurt, when he replied, "You know I'll be there as often as I can be. I'm not going to walk out on you. I've told you that before."

"I know," Jodi said softly, somewhat chastened. "I just wanted to hear you say it again. Yes, I'm going on the pill, and whenever you come, I'll be waiting and ready. I love you."

"Love you too, Princess. I guess I'd better go. Dad will be here in a minute to pick me up and I don't want him to see me using the phone."

They said their good-byes and Jodi promised to send some pictures of Christopher to their secret box number as soon as she got them developed.

CHAPTER TWENTY-SEVEN

May melted into June. The cherry, apple, pear, plum, and apricot blossoms burst into fragrant glory. Gardens planted in early May showed promise of a bountiful harvest. Already, Jodi had staked the peas and put the poles and strings in place for the scarlet runner beans.

She got her hens back from Clarence White and one of her bantams, the one she called 'Feather Feet', hatched out a brood of tiny brown and yellow chicks. The two nannies kidded within days of each other. Annie produced two black and white bucks; Fanny had a brown buck and a multi-coloured doe kid. The males would be meat for the winter and there was plenty of fresh sweet milk every day. Jodi gladly gave the extra to the Shannons.

Mrs. Shannon was a wonderful help to Jodi with advice and care of Christopher. She often kept him so the girls could go out for a coke or for a ride on Blossom. Linda went with Jodi to get Blossom and they took turns riding her the six miles home.

Being young, strong, and active, Jodi healed quickly from the rigors of giving birth. With the hard work she did she was soon back to her regular size. She went barefoot most of the time and with her hair in braids and her lithe figure clad in cut-off jeans and T-shirts, she looked even younger than her seventeen years.

On Sundays Jodi put on shoes, nylons, and a dress to go to the little United Church three blocks away. She felt strange coming back at first but soon she was accepted into the church family. She felt blessed and happy to be involved in the life of the church again. There was never a shortage of loving arms to hold Christopher when she went up to sing in the choir, help take the offering, or read the scripture.

The church ladies held a baby shower for her, and Christopher now had everything he needed and more in the way of clothing and blankets. Jodi had a crib on loan, a change table, and a stroller. Her favourite gift though, was a snugly. Jodi loved having Christopher with her and with his little body safely tucked into the pouch and secured to her front or back, she could take him with her to the garden, to milk the goats, and even for slow rides on Blossom.

Jodi studied for and wrote her grade eleven exams up at the school, passing with high marks. Brett too had done well on his finals. He attended his graduation ceremonies, the dance, and the all night party, but he wished Jodi could have been there with him. He didn't dare ask her to be his date because of Bruce's hostile attitude towards her.

The Saturday after grad, he was excited when he phoned to tell Jodi that he got the tree-planting job for the summer.

Brett had asked to get on a crew nearest Kelso, but he wasn't sure yet where his base camp would be.

Everything was perfect, except that she and Brett were not together. Jodi tried to be patient. She knew it would be at least a year before they could get married. She trusted in God to remove the obstacles that stood in their paths. She prayed for reconciliation between Brett and his dad and hoped that the Randalls would come to accept her and the baby in time. Jodi knew that God's timing was not always the same as human expectation and trusted that things would eventually work out for the best. Even so, it was hard waiting for him; missing his touch, his kisses, and his beautiful smile.

When Brett was finally free of his enforced exile and ready to leave home for the summer, his built up longings and passions were running high.

As he packed the work gear for his summer job, Brett told his family that he was leaving a day early so he could see Jodi and his son. Bruce took the news with a grim faced shrug before he went down to his workshop in the basement without saying goodbye. Carmen and Beverly hugged him with tears in their eyes and begged him to keep in touch and come home when he could. Brett had shown his mom and sister the pictures Jodi had sent and they were secretly thrilled about the beautiful baby. Carmen had tried to reason with Bruce, but always came up against a wall of stubborn sullen silence.

On the day of Brett's arrival, Jodi filled the house with flowers and set the table in the dining room with the good silver and china. She placed two new candles in her mother's old brass candlesticks and set them in the center of the table. A ham was baking in the oven and in the fridge was a dessert made with angel food cake, frozen raspberries, and whipped cream.

    Jodi bathed and washed her hair and dressed in a red and navy wrap-a-round skirt that flared when she turned, showing off her shapely tanned, bare legs. Her top was a white peasant blouse with a low-cut neckline edged with red roses. She brushed her thick silky hair until it shone and applied a little blush and lip-gloss. She prayed Christopher wouldn't be too fussy tonight. He was sleeping now, and with any luck would stay that way until she'd had some time to properly welcome her lover.

    Jodi saw the green Pontiac coming down the road as she stood at the kitchen sink, peeling potatoes. With "wild thing, you make my heart sing" repeating over and over in her head, she dried her hands and went to meet him.

    Brett came striding in without knocking, full of happy anticipation. He wore blue jeans, and the tanned muscles of his upper torso bulged from a black tank top. Jodi bounced to meet him, her lips parting in a welcoming smile. For a second, she was stabbed by his blue eyes that smoldered like sapphires, before she flung herself into his arms.

    He held her tight and breathed into her hair, "Oh Princess, you look fabulous!"

    Jodi blushed and with a little laugh, pushed herself away from him, just a little so that she could look into his eyes. Her long lashes closed slowly as Brett kissed her. Her hands clung to his neck, tightening suddenly, almost fiercely, as his lips touched hers again. Then cheek-to-cheek and deeply stirred, they hung on to each other for a long moment.

    "Where's the kid?" he asked, his voice husky with pent-up emotion and longing.

    "He's asleep," answered Jodi, dreamily, cuddled against him. "Do you want to come and see him?"

    "Yes, I sure do. Has he grown a lot?" Reluctant to let go, they broke their embrace and walked hand in hand toward the baby's room.

    Jodi answered, "Oh yes, he's gained almost two pounds already. He's a little piggy."

    They entered the bedroom quietly and approached the crib. Christopher was lying on his tummy under a light blue knitted blanket. His lashes lay like a fringe of gold against his ivory cheeks. His head, bald at birth, was now covered in a soft, golden down. He looked like a little cherub, all fat and rosy with sleep.

Brett looked a long minute, then stepped back behind Jodi, pulling her against his body. "He's beautiful," he whispered, "just like you."

Jodi leaned her head back against his shoulder and whispered back, "When I was carrying him, I thought I understood what it was to love him. But from the very first time I held him, it was so much more." She turned in his arms and nuzzled his neck. "I love him so much and I love you for giving him to me".

"You're welcome." Brett grinned. "It was my pleasure." His arms tightened around her. Jodi felt the hot sweet rush of his breath on her face. His hands moved restlessly over her hips and waist. His voice was hoarse and rough with need as he muttered into her ear. "I want you."

Jodi whispered, "I know...let's go upstairs, so we don't wake him."

Jodi led him up to Carol's room. She had cleaned up all the mess that used to mar the attractiveness of the odd-shaped room. A soft summer breeze wafted in from the open window, where the huge Beatonheimer apple tree was in full bloom just outside.

"Come here," Jodi invited. "Smell the blossoms. I told you the last time we were up here how heavenly it is to drift off to sleep here, with that scent in the air."

"It's heavenly, just being here with you," he said, taking her in his arms again. He turned her towards the oval mirror on the dresser beside the window and asked softly, "Have you ever watched two people making love?" She shook her head, 'no'. Standing behind her, he tugged her blouse out of the skirt band and lifted it over her head. Moving her long hair aside, he kissed her, starting at the nape of her neck and following down her spine. His busy hands released the hooks on her bra and as it fell away he cupped her breasts tenderly in his hands.

Trying not to rush the wonder of it, he pulled his own shirt over his head and dropped his jeans to the floor. Stepping out of them, he reached for her again, and undid the tie on her skirt. As he unwound the cloth, she turned and melted into his arms. Their hungry deepening of kisses and the pressure of her full breasts on his bare chest had an electrifying effect on them both. The inviting push of her hips against him was more than he could bear, and with a cry, Brett gathered her into his arms and carried her over to the bed.

He was rough and urgent then, not able to prolong the play any longer and for a short time they were lost in the joy and wonderment of their communion.

As soon as Brett could speak, he rolled off her and stared at the ceiling. "I'm sorry," he mumbled apologetically.

Jodi cuddled against him, still awed by the wild passion that had swept over them. "Sorry? Whatever for?" She raised her head and regarded him seriously with her soft aquamarine eyes.

Brett looked embarrassed, almost uncomfortable. He stammered..."I didn't want to be so rough. I lost control. I hope I didn't hurt you." He tenderly pushed back a strand of long hair that had fallen over her face. She sighed and laid her head on his chest.

"You didn't hurt me. I'm fine. You're an amazing lover."

He visibly relaxed then, and they lay entwined in the afterglow of love until the cries of the baby waking up disturbed them.

"Let me go," said Brett eagerly. "I'll bring him up."

"All right then," Jodi smiled. And can you check the ham in the oven and put some more wood on the fire?"

"Sure thing. Be back in a jiffy."

Coming back with the squalling baby, Brett slid back into bed and passed the angry kicking little body to Jodi. "He's not impressed with me," he said, grinning. "I don't have what he's looking for"

Jodi took the baby, and lying on her right side, put him to her breast. The crying diminished to grunts and sucking sounds as little Christopher began his meal. Brett snuggled in behind Jodi, looking over her shoulder and touching his son gently with his fingers. Christopher grasped Brett's finger with a tiny fist and held on tight while he worked away at the nipple.

At first the baby ignored Brett, being intent on eating, but as his hunger was satisfied, he began to cast furtive curious glances at the strange face looking down at him. His little brow furrowed in concentration, and his dark blue eyes gazed in curiosity at his father.

"I think he's trying to figure out if he knows you," Jodi whispered. "He's thinking hard about this."

"Yeah, you're right. He looks puzzled, like he's wondering, where have you been since I was two days old?"

Jodi sat up and offered the baby her other breast. He took just enough to take the pressure off, but now he was interested in looking at his dad. As Brett talked to him, Christopher's eyes brightened and he gurgled with delight, waving his hands and smiling happily.

Jodi got out of bed and dressed. She said, "You boys come down when you're ready. I'm going to get supper ready. How did the ham look?"

"Oh, I think it's done", Brett said, as he bounced the baby gently. " I took it out. Those yummy smells are making me hungry!"

Jodi had the vegetables cooking when he came down a short time later. Christopher had become worried that she was gone and was now fussing. Brett felt kind of helpless as he handed the baby over to her.

"Don't worry," Jodi assured him with a smile, "He'll be a momma's boy for about four years, then he'll want to be with his dad all the time. That's when we'll need another baby, so I won't feel left out."

"Sounds like a good plan," he said catching her in a quick hug before she disappeared into the bedroom to change him.

Supper was delicious, but not too romantic with the baby being passed back and forth throughout the meal.

Christopher cried when he was put down and Jodi agreed he was spoiled from being held all the time. "But," as she defended, "it's just him and me most of the time and he's used to having my undivided attention. It'll get better as he gets older."

In the evening, Brett carried his son in the snugly while Jodi put the goats in their pen and shut the hens in for the night. Then she rode Blossom and Brett walked, carrying the baby along the shoreline of the lake in the soft summer night. They returned home as the sun gradually dropped behind the jagged mountains in the west, leaving a rosy glow.

Christopher's active and fussy time was from suppertime to eleven or twelve at night. Jodi and Brett came in about nine o'clock and the baby showed his young parents no mercy in his demands for attention. He was carried and rocked and cuddled till both were frustrated and tired. Jodi usually had loads of patience but tonight she would have liked some time with Brett alone and she felt some irritation towards the baby. They hardly had a moment's peace to talk with the constant interruptions of wet diapers, squawking, fussing, feeding, and spitting up.

At last Christopher nursed for the last time, making contented sucking and gurgling noises at Jodi's breast. She had put her cuddle wrap on which was perfect for nursing and settled herself into the big easy chair in the corner of the living room.

The night had turned cool with showers threatening and Brett had built a fire in the fireplace. All was peaceful at last.

Brett lay on the couch, looking over at his little family. He had gained a new respect for motherhood. It was a tough job looking after a baby.

Jodi's long dark hair cascaded down over Christopher's head as she leaned over him, humming softly. Her eyes were downcast; the shadows and lights from the fire flickered over her face as she focused on the child. It was like they were one creature, connected by flesh and blood; bonded by need.

Brett felt a little jab of jealously, watching them, and a faint stirring of desire. *God! She was beautiful!* "What does it feel like?" he asked, staring.

Jodi lifted her head and gave him a dreamy smile. "It feels good. Kind of erotic, like he's pulling me down into him." She blushed, and looked down quickly. *That look he was giving her. He was so devastatingly handsome. Those azure blue eyes, that golden hair, and those nobly chiselled features took her breath away.* "Come over here," she invited.

Brett rolled off the couch, coming to kneel in front of her, hands and arms resting on her thighs. "Watch this," she said. She put her little finger into the corner of Christopher's mouth, breaking the suction. All at once, a stream of thin, bluish milk spurted out in an arc, spraying Brett's shirt. Jodi quickly put the baby back before he could howl in protest. Then reaching out, she stroked the silken strands of Brett's hair. Jodi slipped her hand behind his head and pulled him towards her. "God didn't give me two of these for nothing," she smiled, her eyes dancing with mischief. "I've plenty for two."

Brett's eyes met hers for an instant as understanding flashed between them. Pushing the garment off her shoulder, he exposed the other heavy, full breast. As his lips closed around the nipple, pinpricks of flavour exploded on his tongue. Brett's senses reeled with the closeness of her body; the sweet smell and texture of her flesh. Jodi closed her eyes and gave herself up to the sensations of pleasure that were building up in her. Her fingers tightened in Brett's hair and with eyes shut tight, and an exhalation of breath, she sighed deeply as the delightful spasms rippled over her.

After a moment, Jodi pushed Brett away and put the baby into his arms. "He's asleep. Can you put him in his crib?" Brett stood up with the sleeping infant. Christopher seemed heavy and dense for such a small body. On tiptoe, Brett carefully put the now angelic child into his bed and with a sigh of relief tucked the blanket up over his little shoulders.

Jodi appeared in the darkened room on her way back from the bathroom. Wordlessly taking his hand, she led Brett to her bed. They shed their clothes silently and moved into each other's arms. Brett's hands knew her body again; moved over every crest and curve of it; his lips knew the taste and touch of her skin; and once again, his body rocked with the rhythm of hers before they fell exhausted into blessed sleep.

CHAPTER TWENTY-EIGHT

The summer flew by far too fast for Jodi. Brett was stationed with his crew up at the Yutica Mine, a remote rough camp away up the Kokanee Glacier road between Kelso and Somerville. The work was brutal, trudging up steep burn-scarred slopes in all kinds of weather with a huge pack full of spruce, pine and larch seedlings over each shoulder. The crew worked on a quota system. The more planted, the more money the boys made. Brett was one of their best planters. Being lean and fit from his track training helped him cope with the tough challenges of the mountains. But often he arrived late at night at Jodi's, utterly exhausted, filthy dirty, and smelling of sweat and pitch. Sometimes he just slept most of the weekend, but Jodi didn't care. If he was too tired to make love, she was happy just to cuddle up to him in bed and hold him in her arms.

  They celebrated Brett's eighteenth birthday in mid-July with a party on the beach. Rick had also graduated in June and was working for West Kokanee Power for the summer. He and Diane were going steady. Brett hadn't been allowed to come up for his cousin's graduation, so the boys welcomed the chance to get together and party. Linda came with her new boyfriend, John Landon, and a few other friends showed up.

Jodi was happy to have her sisters arrive in July too, with the three little cousins. Everyone was crazy about Christopher. The girls had wonderful adventures riding double on Blossom and playing with the goat kids. Long, lazy afternoons were spent down at the beach; swimming, building sand castles, and picnicking.

When Brett arrived on the two weekends that Marnie and Carol were there, no questions were asked or eyebrows raised about he and Jodi sleeping together. Brett was treated with respect and admiration and included naturally as one of the family. He felt more at ease with Carol and Marnie than he did with his own family, at least at this point in life. Marnie made Jodi promise to come for Christmas and much to Jodi's delight, Brett was invited too.

The fruit ripened on the trees, demanding Jodi's attention picking and processing it. She gave away loads of it, having far too much for her own needs. She had scaled down the vegetable garden considerably to a manageable size, but still there was plenty of work to do to look after it all.

All too soon, the summer was gone. The maples, chestnuts, and oaks changed into their autumn coats of brilliant reds, oranges, and yellows. Jodi enrolled in grade twelve correspondence. She had no wish to go back to school full time, preferring to be with Christopher and her animals. She went up to the school twice a week for band practice while Mrs. Shannon looked after Christopher. Jodi enjoyed playing her flute and wanted to keep it up. She bought a second-hand guitar and was learning to play and accompany herself while singing all her favorite folksongs.

Brett's summer job with the Forestry ended. He insisted on giving Jodi a portion of his hard-earned summer wages and since she was doing all right financially she started a savings account for Christopher. Her Social Services caseworker came up once a month and seemed satisfied that Jodi was doing a good job of caring for her baby.
    With Uncle Dan 'pulling a few strings' Brett was put on the construction crew that cleared brush, installed power poles, and strung transmission lines to remote communities in the Kokanee District. It was the kind of work Brett liked; physically challenging, outdoor labour. The men usually slept in camps at night, but if they were near a town they would go to the bars in the evenings. The local girls were always on the lookout for young handsome men like Brett and Rick. They were out for action and fun and it didn't matter to these girls that Brett was as good as married. In fact, they didn't believe that he already was the father of a

baby. They teased him unmercifully. At times he was tempted to have a fling, but he kept himself under control, only having a few drinks, and dancing with them.

When the winter snows came in November and ended their outdoor work, Brett was hired on as an Apprentice Electrical Technician with Kokanee Power. It was a four-year program that involved taking courses at the community college in Harrison, as well as working out of that town on contract jobs. So, when Brett was able to come to Kelso once or twice a month, the re-unions between he and Jodi were always desperate and sweet.

    He was amazed at how much Christopher grew and changed in his absences. Now, at six months, the baby weighed sixteen and a half pounds and was attempting to crawl by pushing himself with one foot. He could sit up unassisted and loved bouncing to music in the jolly jumper. Jodi exposed their son to a wide variety of music including Classical, Broadway shows, Rock and Roll, and Folk. A real little boy, Christopher already liked cars and trucks, as well as balloons and pretty colored toys.

    Even though there were long gaps between Brett's visits, Christopher always knew him; his little face lighting up in recognition, full of smiles and laughter. He was a beautiful baby, and a contented one. The fussiness of the first few months had disappeared, and he now slept very well at night in his own crib. Jodi usually did her schoolwork when he went for his afternoon nap. It was the best time for uninterrupted study.

As Christmas neared, Jodi and Brett made plans to fly down to Vancouver. Marnie and Carol had paid for their tickets as a Christmas gift and the young couple was happy to accept. It meant they would be together, surrounded by love, laughter, and family, instead of enduring stolen moments amidst the friction of Bruce Randall's animosity.

Jodi and Christopher went down to Harrison on Stuey's bus the Friday before Christmas. Brett met them and the little family boarded the bus for the airport at Castle River. The drive took over an hour and in less than that time again, they stepped off the DC 10 in Vancouver, where the excited kids and happy sisters surrounded them.

Christmas was wonderful. Full of magic and excitement, wonderful food, great music, the celebration of Jesus' birth in worship and song, and for Jodi and Brett, the joy and peace of being in each others' arms every night with their child beside them.

When it was over, they faced the long winter separated once again by treacherous roads and obstacles of obligations and commitments placed in their paths by Brett's work and family.

In late March, an incident happened that almost got Brett barred from his position on the Community College All Star Basketball team. The Jr. Girls from Harrison High were also on the bus and both teams arrived in Kelso for a double game with the home teams. Jodi had never seen Brett play, so she hired Linda's younger sister Elaine to baby-sit. Jodi had Christopher bathed and in his sleepers when Elaine arrived, and she quickly explained when to give him his bottle and put him to bed. Christopher knew and liked the young teenager, so Jodi didn't expect any problems there.

Jodi and Linda walked up to the school full of anticipation and excitement. Linda's boyfriend John would be playing against Brett tonight and both girls were going to be cheering for their men.

Jodi didn't particularly like basketball or other team sports, but it was a thrill to watch Brett play. His eyes sought her out as soon as he jogged onto the court and he gave her a tremendous smile and a wink, as if to say, 'watch me! I'm playing for you!'

Brett was an aggressive player - leaping, checking, harassing his opponent - warding off the other players fiercely when he had the ball, and scoring several good points for his team. Jodi was mesmerized watching him; it was a side of him she had never seen and it fascinated her. Linda was screaming for her team beside her but Jodi had eyes only for her own love. It was a hotly contested game, with the Harrison Chiefs out-scoring the Kelso Eagles by two points.

Jodi had thought that Brett might come and sit with her to watch the Jr. Girls play, once he had showered and changed. She was surprised then, when Rick's sister Jan, who was on the Jr. Team, passed her a note when they came out to warm up. It read: *Go home. I'll be there in 10 minutes.* With eyebrows raised, Jodi showed it to Linda and said with a giggle, "Time for a quickie I guess. See ya."

Linda grinned and moved aside so she could get out. "Yeah. See you. Have fun!"

Jodi jogged down the Camel Trail, feeling excited but alarmed. *They hadn't planned this! What if he got caught?* She knew the penalty for leaving a college function could be pretty severe. She gave Elaine a dollar and practically pushed her out the door, such was her haste. Elaine had just put Christopher to bed and he was still vocalizing, talking to his stuffed animals and trying out new sounds. Jodi went in and kissed him, so he'd know she was there, and then tiptoed out, closing his door.

She met Brett a few minutes later at the front door. Hugging him tight, she laid a finger over his lips. "Shhh..." she whispered. "If Christopher knows you're here, he'll want up, and I've a feeling you didn't come to play with the baby."

"You're right," he whispered back, running his hands down her back and over her buttocks. "As much as I'd like to see him, I'm horny as hell. It's been too long."

Silently they moved to the bedroom, shed their clothes quickly, and climbed into bed, reaching for each other immediately. The early spring evening was chilly, but the heat and passion generated beneath the quilt soon had them gasping for breath. Jodi's nostrils filled with the male scent of him; a lusty, sweaty smell, since he hadn't taken the time to shower after the game. She opened her body to his desperate need and let herself be carried away by the sensations he was creating in and over her.

They tried not to express their passion vocally in case Christopher heard them. Afterwards, they kissed and cuddled and spoke in whispers while they talked about the game and got caught up on other news. Then the thing happened which Brett said must not. They dozed off, only to be awakened with a jolt by the phone ringing.

Jodi leaped out of bed to answer it. Already Brett was cussing and frantically pulling on his jeans and sweatshirt. As he pulled his runners on and bent to tie the laces, Jodi said; "It was your friend, Earl. He said the bus is ready to go, and the coach is furious. Earl said to be at the City

Hall in five minutes. They'll pick you up there."

Straightening up, Brett enfolded Jodi's naked body in a quick hug.

"I'm so sorry, Honey," she whispered.

"Yeah, me too. I'm going to be in big trouble for this." A quick peck on the cheek, and he was gone, running to meet the bus.

It came slowly around the corner as Brett crossed the road to the old City Hall and stood by the lamppost, breathing fast. Coach Johansen clumped down the steps and motioned for the driver to close the doors. Then he proceeded to tear a strip off Brett; yelling about school rules, irresponsibility, and being kicked off the team.

Brett stood and took it, mumbling "Yes Sir," at the appropriate times and trying to say he was sorry. Just before they boarded the bus, Brett pleaded, "Please Sir, don't call my parents."

The coach looked at him hard, still angry, and replied, "Be in my office at eight o'clock in the morning. We'll discuss it then!"

Brett was waiting when Coach Johansen showed up at five after eight, slammed a load of books onto his desk, and sank into his swivel chair with a sigh. "Okay, Randall, what's the story? Where did you go, and who were you with? " He fixed Brett with a steady gaze, waiting.

Brett flinched under the stare, and dropped his eyes.

"I'd rather not say, Sir."

"Look here!" The coach said, getting annoyed. "I'm giving you a chance to explain your actions. You know darn well I can have you suspended. And I haven't called your parents yet, but I will if you don't co-operate." He leaned back in his chair, hands behind his head, regarding Brett quizzically. *What was the kid trying to protect?* "What would happen if they knew you went AWOL last night?"

Brett squirmed in his seat and shot the coach a bitter look. "My dad would beat me up and ground me for the rest of my life."

Coach leaned forward and said, "No kidding? Has it happened before?"

Brett nodded miserably, "Yeah," he said, in a quiet voice. "We don't get along. We're at loggerheads over a certain issue, and he'd kill me if he found out what I did."

The Coach said, "But you must have thought the risk was worth it, or you wouldn't have done it"

He got a small smile then. "Oh, it was worth it! I just thought I could sneak away while the girls played and be back before anybody missed me."

Coach was getting very curious now. He needed to get to the bottom of this. "Was there any booze or drugs involved, Randall?"

Brett shook his head. "No Sir, nothing like that."

"What then? Tell me the truth."

Brett knew he was trapped. If he didn't tell what he was up to, he could say goodbye to his team and school right now. He flushed slightly, and looked at the floor.

"Okay...I'm involved with someone in Kelso, and I went for a visit."

"And what went wrong then. Why were you so late?"

"We fell asleep."

Understanding dawned on the coach's face as he smiled behind his hand. *This was not just his Granny he was visiting*, the Coach thought. "Mind if I ask you a personal question, Randall?"

"Sir, we're getting pretty personal now."

"It won't go beyond me, I promise you." Coach fiddled with a pencil, making small doodles on a scrap of paper. "Are you...uh...gay?"

Brett's blue eyes opened wide in surprise and regarded the coach solemnly before his face crinkled into a smile. "Why do you ask? Are there rumors going around?"

Now it was the Coach's turn to look embarrassed. "No...well,...it would explain this thing - you know - your reluctance to talk about it; your dad's anger. And...er...some of the staff here, and students too I would think, wonder why a good looking athletic jock like yourself doesn't even have a girlfriend. It's strange, don't you think?"

"Yeah, I guess," Brett grinned. "But I assure you, I'm very normal in that regard." It was time to share his secret. He reached for his wallet, took two pictures out and laid them on the desk in front of Coach Johansen. Leaning over, and pointing, he said, "That's my girlfriend, Jodi. I've known her...uh...you might say intimately for a year and a half. And this is our son, Christopher." He paused, watching the shock register on the coach's face. "He's ten months old now. He's a great kid! My dad is totally against our relationship. My parents have never even seen the baby. But the more he tries to keep us apart, the more determined we are to see each other. We hope to get married this summer, even if we have to elope."

He was babbling on now, but he didn't care. It was good to finally share it with someone, another male.

Coach Johansen sat upright. "Good God, Randall, this is amazing! You've kept this a secret all this time?"

"Yes Sir." Brett picked up the photos and tucked them back in his wallet. The bell rang for the first period.

"You'd better get along to your class, Randall." Coach stood up and offered Brett his hand. As they shook, their eyes met and held in understanding.

"In my book," said the Coach, "it's not a crime to love a woman and child. You're excused. Just be more careful in future."

"Yes Sir. Thank you Sir."

Brett couldn't believe his good luck. He'd had a sleepless night worrying about being kicked out of the Apprenticeship Program and facing the wrath of his father again.

He called Jodi at noon and gave her the good news. She laughed with relief, and then chided him gently. "Next time you'd better think of the consequences before you act so impulsively."

"Look who's talking!" he teased back. "It was your impulsiveness that got us started on this whole thing."

"True enough," Jodi agreed, "but I'm not complaining. Are you?"

"Yes." Brett answered seriously. "I don't get to see you enough. I'm tired of having to sneak off for a few stolen moments with you. One or two days a month just isn't enough. And I'm missing out on so much of what Christopher is up to. He changes so fast now, a week or two makes a whole lot of difference. I feel guilty that I didn't see him last night; there just wasn't time."

"I know, it's hard for me too." Jodi agreed. "It's been a tough winter with so much snow and the roads in such poor shape. I'd rather you be home safe than risking your life driving over them to see us. Anyway, spring is almost here and we should be able to get together more often now."

"Yeah, I sure hope so. I love you Doll. I gotta go now."

"Bye Sweetie. Love you too. It was great to see you last night."

They made kissing noises over the phone, returning reluctantly to the demands of the day.

CHAPTER TWENTY-NINE

Brett drove up to Kelso for Easter and risking the wrath of his father, stayed five days. He and Jodi had fun hiding jellybeans and chocolate eggs all over the garden and then watching with delight as Christopher, walking with support on each side, found the hidden treasures. He caught on to the game quickly, pointing and shrieking with excitement when they came upon another stash.

At the tiny church on Easter Sunday, whispers and nudges went around about that lucky Jodi and the handsome young man she had captured. Everyone knew of Brett's existence but few had really had a chance to stare at him as they did that day. Little Christopher with his riot of blond curls, impish blue eyes, and his pert little nose was a carbon copy of his father.

Much to their surprise, Rick's mom invited Jodi and Brett over for Easter dinner. Carmen and Bruce were not coming, knowing that Brett was 'shacked up' as they called it, with Jodi. Roberta Taylor did not want to be a part of the family conflict that excluded Jodi and Christopher from their lives. She knew Brett was often in Kelso, but he did not come to see them, and she was hoping to change that by including the young couple in their family's Easter celebrations. Roberta knew from town gossip that Jodi was a hard worker, an excellent mother to

Christopher, and that she possessed a forgiving nature; never criticizing or bad-mouthing Bruce Randall for his actions.

Everyone in town had pretty well got used to the idea of Jodi living alone, having a baby, and entertaining her lover on weekends and holidays. The young couple were accepted and included in most of the parties and activities that the teens had and they didn't mind that Christopher came too. Everyone wanted to hold him when he was being cute and happy, but he was returned to Jodi quickly if he cried or messed his diaper.

In fact, Christopher was kind of a controlling factor - a catalyst for the teens. Some of them that were considering having sex were a lot more careful, seeing the results so close at hand.

A few of the girls still tried to make a play for Brett and he would flirt with them outrageously, making Jodi seethe with anger inside. Then, when he knew he had gone far enough with the joking and teasing, he would come and hug Jodi, or kiss her so passionately that everyone would squirm with embarrassment.

The two of them were increasingly frustrated by their lack of time together. They talked incessantly of how and when they could manage to get married and end the constant separations that troubled them. Brett only got a small wage as an electrical apprentice, out of which he had to pay for his college courses and books.

Jodi and Brett still hoped that Bruce would give his permission and blessing for their marriage. They wondered how to resolve the conflict between Brett and his dad.

One night in May, Jodi had an idea. It came to her while she was lying with Brett on the couch. The night was hot and she was clad only in a long T-shirt and underwear. Brett had his jeans on but his chest was bare. With one bare foot he was stroking the backs of Jodi's legs with his toes. They weren't in a hurry. Both were enjoying the delicious semi-aroused state their closeness and touching was causing.

    Besides, Christopher wasn't in bed. His room was hot and he couldn't get to sleep, so Jodi had brought him out to the living room. He was playing happily on the floor with a stacking toy, putting the coloured rings on in the correct order of largest to smallest, then dumping them off and starting again. Sometimes on purpose he would put the wrong one on. Then he'd say, "Oh-oh," shake his head, and put the right one on.

    Brett's eyes were closed, enjoying the feel of Jodi's body stretched out on his, her nuzzling little kisses, and her fingers playing with his hair. But Jodi was watching Christopher, all the time thinking.

    Suddenly, she said,"Christopher's our answer, Hon." Brett's dreamy blue eyes popped open.

"What?" he asked sleepily, looking confused.

Jodi said, "Christopher's almost a year old and your parents haven't even seen him. Don't you think it's time we met?"

Brett shifted his weight under her. "Well, sure I do. I know Mom wants to see him, but it's Dad we have to convince."

"I know. We can't do that...but Christopher can."

The baby, hearing his name, stood up and looked over at them. Christopher was on the verge of walking but hadn't quite taken the first steps yet. He dropped down again and sidled over to the couch, pulling himself upright against it. A pudgy finger reached out and touched Brett's face. "Dada!" he said clearly.

He was learning new words every day. His favourite pastime was to point to an object and say, "Whazzat?" Jodi knew he was storing the answers away in his mind. She often stood outside his bedroom door listening with interest and amusement as he tried out new words and sounds before he went to sleep.

Brett put his arm around Christopher and pulled him up onto his chest beside Jodi. She had to shift over to make room for him.

Jodi said softly, "Lie down and go to sleep on Daddy, okay?" Brett rubbed his little tousled blond head gently and stroked his hot little back. Jodi sang an old lullaby to him that her mother had sung to her, long ago.

"Sweetest little fellow, anybody knows,
Don't know what to call him, but he's mighty like a rose.
Looking at his mommy, with eyes of bonny blue,
Makes you think that heaven is looking back at you".

As Christopher relaxed and drifted off to sleep, Jodi continued to develop the idea of letting the baby bridge the gap for them.

She continued, "If your dad just sees him, I know Christopher will melt his heart. A man would have to be made of glacier ice not to like this little guy. He doesn't have to like me, but he needs to know his grandson."

"Yeah, you're right." Brett said. "Hopefully, he'll come to like you too, but jeez, it will take a lot of courage to face him. Can you do it?"

"Can you?" Jodi asked, looking into Brett's gorgeous blue eyes. " I know you're afraid of him."

Brett sighed and kissed her. "Yes. Together we can do it. We *have* to do it!"

Jodi extracted herself from the warm bodies on the couch and carried the limp sleeping toddler to his bed. She came back and sat cross-legged on the floor beside the couch where she could look into Brett's face. He rolled onto his side and draped an arm around Jodi's shoulder as they discussed their strategy. Before they went to bed and continued what they had begun on the couch they had a plan for the following week.

CHAPTER THIRTY

The rain came in a steady drizzle all that day. At three in the afternoon, with the gloomy weather matching her apprehensive mood, Jodi approached the Randall's stucco house. Brett was going to get off work early, but would not be there when Jodi just 'dropped in'. She would have Brett's support later when Bruce arrived home. With her heart thudding in her chest and a prayer on her lips Jodi rang the doorbell.

Carmen opened the door and stood speechless; staring at the young rain-soaked girl on her doorstep with a sleeping baby drooped over her shoulder.

"Hello," Jodi said, smiling tentatively. "I'm Jodi. I had to come to Harrison on some business and I wanted so much for you to see our baby."

"Oh dear," said Carmen, as her hand flew to her mouth and her eyes grew misty. "You know this is very awkward for me."

"Yes, I'm sure it is," Jodi replied, "and I'm sorry." Because of the rain, she had draped her jacket over Christopher so his face could not be seen. Only one little hand hung down. Carmen's eyes flicked with curiosity to the covered bundle on Jodi's back and she longed to lift the coat and look upon her son's child.

With a sigh, she opened the door, and said, "Come in. He must be heavy."

"Thanks," Jodi said gratefully. She stepped in and swung the baby carrier to the floor. She bent and untied her running shoes and kicked them off. Only then did she take the jacket off the baby, lifting him gently out of the carrier.

"Come and sit down," invited Carmen. Jodi sank onto the comfortable couch while Christopher curled up against her chest. He really wasn't awake yet. Jodi talked to him softly, while removing his little blue coat and hat.

Carmen sat beside Jodi, facing her, and took the baby's clothing as Jodi removed it. She caught her breath as Christopher's jumbled golden curls emerged from under his bonnet and his huge blue eyes opened and regarded her solemnly.

"Oh!" she breathed. "He's adorable! He looks just like Brett did at that age. He was such a beautiful baby."

"He still is," smiled Jodi. "But he's grown up an awful lot in the last two years."

"Yes...you two have been through a lot, haven't you? I'm sorry we haven't been a help to you at all. My husband is very much against it, as you know."

"Yes, I know. It's why I came today. Brett and I want to talk to him, and you, about our plans to get married." Carmen gave her a worried look.

"Oh, I don't think that's a good idea. I think you should probably go before he gets home. There could be a terrible scene. He has a bad temper and he's dead set against Brett getting married. They don't even talk to each other."Carmen's voice quavered, and her blue eyes filled with tears. Jodi bravely put her hand on Carmen's.

"I know all that," she said, looking right into her eyes. "It's time for healing, love, and forgiveness. Brett and I need you both. We believe that Christopher can help make the transition from hate to love. Who could resist this little cherub as a matchmaker?"

Carmen rose and dabbed her eyes with a tissue from her apron pocket. "I'm going to make some tea. Would you like some?"

Jodi nodded and set Christopher down on the floor where he immediately crawled off to investigate his surroundings. As Carmen made the tea and set out cups and cookies, she felt a sense of shame in her own weakness that she hadn't gone to see Jodi and her grandson long before this. She had glimpsed an inner strength in the younger woman that she herself didn't possess, or didn't dare to express.

Christopher crawled into the kitchen to watch her. With a smile Carmen squatted down beside him and opened the cupboard where the Tupperware was kept. "Do you want to play with this?" she asked, pulling some out. "My kids loved playing here." Christopher was definitely interested and proceeded to pull everything out. Carmen went down the hall and came back with two photo albums, which she gave to Jodi. "These are pictures of Brett and Bev's baby years. You might find them interesting."

The two women were sitting at the dining room table with their tea, looking through the pictures, when Brett arrived home.

Jodi stood up as he bounded up the three stairs and entered the dining room, feigning surprise. "Jodi!" he exclaimed. She took two steps and melted into his arms in a big bear hug. Emotion overcame her and tears slid down her cheeks.

"Shhh....don't cry," he said, as he stroked her still damp hair. "Everything will be all right." Then as Christopher crawled over, excitedly repeating "Dada, dada" Brett bent and scooped him up into his arms too.

They all sat down at the dining room table drinking tea, eating cookies, and looking at the old photo albums. Christopher climbed onto Carmen's lap in order to see the pictures better. He pointed and said, "Baby", and was praised for his smartness.

A moment later Christopher pointed to Carmen and said, "Whazzat?"

Jodi chimed in, "He means, who are you?" To Christopher, she said, "That's your Grandma, Honey."

"Nana would be easier for him," suggested Carmen.

"No," said Jodi. "He thinks nanas are bananas."

"Oh," Carmen laughed. " Grandma it is then." Jodi repeated it several times for him, and with a cookie-covered face, Christopher tried to say it. The word came out something like 'Kemma.'

After tea, Carmen busied herself making supper. Brett went down to the basement and brought up the old family highchair and a box of old toys for Christopher to play with. Then he sat quietly in the living room with Jodi, holding hands, waiting for 'Papa Bear' to come home.

A little after six p.m., Bruce drove up outside. Jodi's stomach lurched, but she tried to calm herself with deep breathing. Brett squeezed her hand and let it go as Bruce and Bev came in shaking the raindrops off their coats.

Bev, who had been at basketball practice, came over first. "Hi, Jodi!" she exclaimed, as she gave her a hug. "It's good to see you. And is this Christopher?" She hunkered down close to the child, and said, "Ooh, he's *so* cute!" And to the little boy, she said, "Can you show me your big truck?"

As Christopher overcame his initial shyness to show her the toy, Brett said to Bruce, "Dad, I'd like you to meet Jodi and Christopher."

With scarcely a flicker of emotion or recognition, Bruce said tersely, "I *know* who they are. What I want to know is what are they doing here?"

Brett flushed with anger at the rude remark, but Jodi stood up, smiled sweetly, and said, "I came because I wanted you to see your grandson. He's going through such a cute stage right now, learning to walk and talk. I just wanted to share him with you because he's so special. And I hoped that you could find room in your heart for a dear little boy who doesn't have a family, except me, and Brett when he can come. My parents are dead, and my sisters live in Vancouver." She took a deep breath, and went on. "I feel...that is...Brett and I feel that Christopher needs to get to know his Grandma and Grandpa and his Auntie Bev. He needs an extended family, and....well, I just hoped that once you saw him, you might accept him into your family."

Christopher had come to her while she was talking and wanted up. Jodi picked him up and gave him a kiss on the cheek. "I see he has his grandpa's golden curls," she said, flashing Bruce another smile.

Jodi's brave answer and the beautiful wide-eyed golden-haired child she held on her hip momentarily stunned Bruce. At a loss for words, he turned away, embarrassed, and called to Carmen as he disappeared down to his bedroom.

As soon as he had gone, Brett hugged Jodi joyfully. "Wow, round one! You scored, kid!" He gazed at her with admiration. "That was a great speech. It knocked the wind out of him. He didn't know what to say."

"Yeah," said Bev. " He really didn't expect you to stand up to him, and you did it so nicely."

Down in their bedroom, as Bruce changed from his office clothes into casuals, he questioned Carmen as to her part in this. Carmen convinced him she had nothing to do with it. Jodi had simply appeared on the doorstep in the rain with the baby and she had invited them in. She told Bruce that Jodi was staying for supper, and possibly overnight. She said that she had a lot of admiration for Jodi, and that if Bruce would just give her a chance, he would come to like and accept her. And wasn't Christopher a darling? And their son was obviously so much in love with Jodi. It was nonsense to be so hostile about it when all they wanted was to be together.

Brett had asked his mom to make Shake and Bake Chicken; his favourite, and had hinted that they hadn't had a chocolate cake for a long time. Now Carmen understood why Brett had wanted a nice supper.

The meal went well, with most of the attention focused on Christopher. He dropped some peas off his highchair onto the floor and said, "Oh-oh." He got such a great response with smiles and laughter, that he did it twice more before Jodi put a stop to it.

Bruce forced himself to be pleasant. He asked Jodi a lot of questions and was secretly impressed by her ability to cope so well alone with running a home, caring for a child and animals, and keeping up with her music and schoolwork. She was also pretty, but not in a voluptuous way, as he had imagined her. She was a decent, hard-working, God-fearing girl from a nice family that had just been through some very tough things in life. Despite himself, he began to like her.

After supper, Bruce retired to the living room to watch the news. Carmen and Bev did the dishes, while Jodi put Christopher into the tub to wash off the remains of his meal. He had chocolate cake in his hair, and grease all over his face from gnawing on a chicken drumstick. Brett helped get him dried off and into his diaper and pyjamas.

Then they all gathered in the living room for the confrontation. Bruce flicked off the TV and turned towards them. He ran his hands through his curly hair, and sighed. "Okay, let's talk. What is it you want?"

Brett cleared his throat. "I want you and Mom to accept Christopher and Jodi into our family. I want them to be treated with respect and consideration. I want them to be welcome in our home. I want to be free to go and visit them without feeling guilty. And I think we've proved that we're determined to be together." He took Jodi's hand, and looked into her eyes. With emotion threatening to break his voice, he said, "We love each other and our son very much, and we want to get married this summer. We'd like your blessing, and your help."

Carmen had tears in her eyes. She couldn't trust herself to speak. Bruce was very moved too. He tried to hide his feelings by getting up to pace. "But you're so young. You don't even have a decent job! You're going to school and getting a minimum wage as an apprentice. How are you going to support a family?" Brett stood up too. The fight was on.

" It wouldn't cost us much to live in Jodi's house," Brett said, his voice pleading. It's paid for, and she has a big garden, and tons of fruit, and she has goats and chickens for milk, eggs, and meat. I can drive back and forth for work and school. If the roads get too bad, I could stay here, and go up on the weekends."

Bruce continued to pace, as he considered this idea. "So, you intend to continue with this electrical career? I wanted you to come into the business with me. I could use a Jr. Partner."

Brett heaved a big sigh and shoved his hands into his pockets. "Dad, I'm sorry. I don't want an office job right now. I'm a physical kind of guy. I want to use my body to work, at least right now, while I'm strong and fit. Maybe when you want to retire, I could look at that option, but not now."

"But I need someone now," Bruce persisted. "There are a lot of new people moving into the area, and the business is growing."

"Train Bev then. She'd be a great Jr. Partner."

Bev looked up in surprise. "Would you Dad? I'd like that. I could work part-time now and then join you as a partner when I graduate."

Clearly, it was a possibility that had not occurred to Bruce. His children were proving to be a mystery to him. He stroked his chin and sat down again, looking at Bev speculatively. "I think we could work something out."

Christopher, sensing an easing of tension in the room, slipped off of Jodi's knee where he had been cuddling and reached into the box of toys. Extracting an old Tonka backhoe, he crawled over to Bruce's legs and pulled himself up. "Whazzat?" he demanded, holding up the toy. Bruce bent and picked up the child and the toy. He set Christopher on his knee and began to show him how the contraption worked, complete with sound effects.

Jodi breathed a prayer of thanks. *Her little boy was working his magic!* She said to the family, "You know, I think you should be very proud of Brett. He made a promise to me as soon as he knew I was pregnant, that he would stick by me and help me all he could. It's been very difficult for him to keep that promise, but not once has he ever let me down. When he couldn't come up, he'd phone or write. He's helped me financially; he pays my phone bill because we talk a lot. He's gone along with my crazy schemes such as coming back to Kelso from Vancouver, and running away to the cabin to have the baby. He buys things I need for Christopher. He's tried hard to take responsibility for his actions. He's kind and gentle, and fun, and he's a heck of a good kisser and lover!"

Brett hid his face in his hands. "Stop it, Jodi. You're embarrassing me!"

"Well, I don't care" she replied. Her eyes flashed and her jaw set in a stubborn line. "It's all true."

There was a shocked silence and then Carmen began to laugh. Bruce joined in too, then Bev, then Brett and Jodi. So much gloom and tension had prevailed in the house over the past year and a half. It was a wonderful release to hear laughter again.

Bruce set Christopher on the floor and motioned to Carmen. "I'd like to talk to your mother in private for a moment. Excuse us."

As Bruce and Carmen disappeared down the hall, Brett grabbed Jodi and smothered her with kisses. "It's working! They're coming around. You're fantastic!"

"Get off me, you big oaf," Jodi admonished, half-heartedly. We're not in the clear yet."

Down in their bedroom, Bruce sat down in the rocking chair, while Carmen perched on the edge of the bed beside it. Bruce reached out and took her hand. "I've been such a jerk, Carmen." He had a pained expression on his face. "I've done them a great disservice. Neither one of those kids deserved the treatment I've dished out for the past year and a half. I've made it hard for you too, and Bev. I'm sorry." Bruce was quiet for a moment.

Carmen slid off the bed onto the carpeted floor by Bruce's feet and laid her head on his knees. He stroked her hair, lovingly. "I've torn up this family with my anger, and none of it was justified. Jodi is nothing like I imagined. I thought she must be a rough little tramp, probably into booze and drugs along with teen sex. Brett tried to tell me otherwise, but I wouldn't listen. I've abused him physically, verbally, and mentally. No wonder he hates me."

Carmen took his hands, and squeezed them. "Jodi said when she came this afternoon that it was time for healing and forgiveness. She has a lot of wisdom and understanding for such a young girl."

"Yeah, she's something special." agreed Bruce. "Let's go out there, and give them our blessing, and see what we can do to help."

Christopher was getting sleepy. He crawled up on the couch with the little backhoe in his hand. Bev got some milk for his bottle, and he lay back, his eyes heavy with fatigue. He was soon asleep.

Carmen and Bruce entered the room hand in hand. Standing solid and resolute, determined to make amends, Bruce said softly, "Son, come here." Brett stood and approached him.

"I owe you an apology for the way I've treated you over this thing. I was wrong, and I hope you can forgive me." He held out his hand. Brett grasped it; a huge smile spreading over his face. Then his father pulled him into his embrace and hugged him, patting him on the shoulder. Bruce's eyes met Jodi's. He released his son, and said, " Jodi, I misjudged you completely. I apologize to you as well." As she rose and came towards him, he added, "We'd be proud to have you join our family as Brett's wife". As he hugged her, he said, "You have our blessing."

Jodi managed to squeak out a thank-you between her clenched teeth and her tears. Then everyone was hugging each other. Brett turned to Jodi and hoisted her up high. She grabbed him around the neck and hung on as he spun her around, head thrown back, joy and relief written all over his handsome features. Then he let her slide slowly down his body, and when they were face to face, kissed her ardently.

There was excited chatter for the next half hour as the family discussed dates and plans for a wedding. Jodi suggested Saturday, July 18th, Brett's birthday. "That way," she laughed, "you'll never forget our anniversary."

Brett grinned, "I couldn't think of a better gift, than to have you for keeps on my birthday. Let's do it!"

The date decided, they talked of guests, attendants, food, and other arrangements until late. Then, with a huge yawn, Bev asked, "What are the sleeping arrangements, Mom?"

Brett slipped his arm around Jodi and pulled her close. "Jodi and Christopher can sleep with me down in the basement."

Carmen looked up. "Hold on, I don't think so. You're not married yet". Looking at Brett, she said, "Jodi and Christopher can have the guest room. You two sleep in your own beds.

"But Mom!" protested Brett. "That's not fair! Whether you like it or not, we're a sexually active couple. To be in the same house and not be allowed to sleep together is ridiculous. It's torture for us! Dad, don't you agree?"

Bruce held up his hands. "Your mother is the boss of the household. Leave me out of it." He stood up and stretched.

Jodi gripped Brett's hand, warning him to keep his anger under control. "Let it go," she said. "We're all tired tonight, and I don't want to get into an argument now, when we've accomplished so much."

Brett sighed and laid his head back on the couch, closing his eyes. "Okay, but I still don't like it. Goodnight Mom, Dad...'night Bev. Thanks for everything. We'll just sit here for a little while longer. We've got things to talk about." As his mother shot him a questioning glance, he said, "We'll behave...I promise."

After they had gone, Brett slid off the couch onto the soft pile rug, and held out his arms to Jodi. She dropped down and fitted her body against his, soothing away his anger and disappointment with soft kisses. They held each other for a long time and then went reluctantly to their separate beds, happy with the success of the day.

The next day as she and Brett were preparing to leave for Kelso, Jodi invited the family to come too. She assured them she had plenty of room, and they could have a visit with the Taylors as well. Carmen accepted with pleasure. Many months had passed since they had all gone to Kelso.

Bruce and Carmen were pleasantly surprised and impressed to see how organized and competent Jodi was. Her house was tidy, her garden was full of vegetables, shrubs, and flowers, and her animals were well cared for.

As she showed Bruce, Carmen and Bev to their rooms upstairs, Jodi looked pointedly at Carmen, saying, " When we're at your house, we'll go by your rules. Here, we'll go by mine. Brett sleeps with me, downstairs." Carmen blushed slightly and then nodded in agreement.

Since they were all together and Christopher's first birthday fell in the middle of the following week, Jodi suggested they have a birthday party for him. Everyone got in the party mood. While Brett and his dad chopped wood and mowed the lawn, Jodi, Carmen, and Bev baked a cake and went shopping for dinner supplies and a few gifts. They invited the Taylors over and it was a noisy, fun, wonderful evening for everyone. It was the beginning of new ties and new friendships, some of which were long overdue.

As Jodi lay with Brett later that night she was filled with relief that the long struggle was finally over. With Brett's strong arms around her and the love and support of his family and hers, she felt she could face anything.

Little did she know that in a few short years her world would be turned upside down and she would be facing the loss of everything and everyone she loved, including her own life.

CHAPTER THIRTY-ONE

Jodi Marie McCallum and Brett David Randall were united in marriage just after four o'clock on July 18, 1975 in the Kelso United Church. Their hand-written invitations read:

Jodi and Brett would like to invite you to come; gather with us in celebration of a new covenant; of water to wine.
Leave behind misgivings of tired roles.
Come with vision and fresh ties.
Leave behind fancy attire.
Come with picnic clothes.
Our material needs are small; We need your gifts of wisdom, of counsel, of your love.
Come celebrate with us our marriage at Kelso United Church, 4 P.M. Saturday, July 18, 1975, and our wedding picnic/potluck supper at the McCallum house, 'B' Ave. next to the park.

A wedding in Kelso was always a big social event and in this case, folks were happy to see things put right in regards to a union which had already produced a child. The church was filled to over-flowing and extra chairs had to be brought in from the hall. Nobody had very much money but the whole community pitched in and helped, sharing what he or she had.

The bridesmaids, Linda and Beverly, re-modeled their best dresses. Jodi received an offer of a wedding dress from a friend's mother and gratefully accepted.

The woman was divorced and didn't want the dress back so Jodi took it across to her neighbour Pat, who picked the seams apart and remade an outfit that was simple, yet elegant. The neckline of the dress was suitably modest, curving gently, and the sleeves were long, ending in lacy cuffs at the wrists. The bodice fitted closely over her slender waist and then billowed out in a cloud of satin and lace, falling just below her knees. Jodi wanted neither a veil nor a train to get in her way.

Carol did Jodi's hair for her, sweeping it up on top of her head, twisting the strands into a knot from which several tendrils fell to frame her face.

Jodi picked her bouquet herself from gardens, fields, and ditches, to reflect the thistles as well as wheat and daisies in a relationship.

Brides are supposed to look lovely on their wedding day and Jodi certainly did. Her face was flushed and her blue eyes sparkled with anticipation as she slowly walked down the aisle following her two bridesmaids to join the nervous knot of young men waiting at the front of the church.

Brett looked devilishly handsome in a charcoal grey suit that he had rented. His usually unruly hair was neatly combed and slicked into order with some kind of gel. Rick Taylor, and Brett's best friend from school, Earl Horvath, stood up with him. As Jodi reached his side, and took his arm, their eyes met, and they exchanged gentle smiles.

The time-honoured and beautiful ceremony commenced and went according to plan except when Christopher, seated with the Delaney family called out 'Hi Mommy!' during the exchange of vows. Jodi gave him a little wave and he was quickly shushed up with a candy.

The happy couple was showered with rice and confetti as they came down the church steps arm in arm and climbed into the back seat of the Pontiac. The car was decorated with blue and white streamers, a 'Just Married' sign, and the inevitable cluster of tin cans. Rick and Linda rode in front; Bev and Earl followed in his car. The wedding party drove all over town, honking and waving, but just about everyone was at the church or heading down to Jodi's, so they didn't have much of an audience.

Pictures of the wedding party and family were taken in the garden while some of the local women prepared the supper. Jodi's family provided a turkey, a ham, and roast beef. As was the usual practice in these small close knit communities, every family that came brought food, so that soon the tables were laden with potato salads, casseroles, buns, home-made pickles and relishes, lemon and apple pies, chocolate cake, and bread pudding.

Although alcohol was not served openly, there were coolers stashed here and there under the trees outside and the men folk wandered out now and then to smoke and have a drink or two. People took their supper on a paper plate and found a seat wherever they could - on the stairs, out on the washstand, at the picnic tables set up on the lawn, or on a chair if they could find one.

After the sumptuous supper, the dining room was cleared for dancing, and the party began in earnest.

The two little cousins - Christopher, just fourteen months old, and Jake - two years old, were the darlings of the party. Lori and Lisa were kept busy trying to keep tabs on them. To the Randall family the two toddlers, one blond, one dark, but both possessing those huge blue eyes, were like a re-incarnation of Brett and Rick as little ones.

As the evening wore on and darkness descended, the party continued inside and out. Brett was outgoing and chivalrous, asking all the girls, young and old, to dance. He cooled off between sessions visiting with his friends out in the yard. He was careful not to drink too much. He knew Jodi would not be happy with him, and he didn't want to be drunk when he took her to bed.

Although she loved the music, Jodi did not care for dancing very much, unless it was a slow one with Brett. When she had a chance, she slipped away, un-noticed, and went out to Blossom's paddock. She kicked off her shoes and stood in the cool grass in her nylons, leaning on the fence.

Blossom snorted at the white apparition standing there. Then as Jodi talked softly to her, the pony came over and nuzzled her hair, tickling Jodi with her big whiskers and inquisitive, rubbery lips.

Jodi stroked the pony's velvety nose absently as her thoughts turned to her mother and father and all the events that had taken place since their death, just over two years ago. The pain of their loss wasn't as deep, now that she had a child of her own and a wonderful husband to share her life with.

Her thoughts were interrupted by a step behind her. She looked over her shoulder to see Brett approaching in the dark; his jacket and tie discarded somewhere, his shirt open at the neck, and his hair out of place.

"Hey, Jo, are you all right?" He leaned on the fence beside her.

"Yes, I'm fine. I just needed to get away and be alone for a while."

"Are you missing your mom and dad?" he asked gently.

"Yeah, I was thinking of them. I wish they could be here."

Brett slipped an arm around her, pulling her close. "I'm not surprised to find you out here, talking to the animals and communing with the angels."

She laughed lightly. "You're getting to know me pretty well. Remember our first night together? It was a night just like this...warm and beautiful, with a million stars shining overhead...a magical night."

He murmured softly. "Yeah, I'll never forget it. The way you came on to me so strong. You knocked me for a loop." He moved closer and took her in his arms.

Jodi answered with a smile in her voice. "It was very shameful of me but I was desperately in love with you already and that has never changed. It really was love at first sight."

"Just like in a fairytale, hey Princess?" he answered, kissing her on the lips. "I haven't told you how beautiful you look tonight."

"Thank-you. And I haven't had a chance to wish you a Happy Birthday yet."

"I'll settle for another one of those kisses," he whispered against her ear.

Jodi turned her face towards him and put her arms around his neck, as his circled her back and held her close. Their kiss was long and sweet. They hadn't seen each other for two weeks and Jodi could feel the heat and desire rising between them. She slid her hands from around Brett's neck, down over his broad shoulders, along the length of his arms, and took his hands as she backed up a step.

"Let's save it for later," she said. "We'd better get back to our guests."

At ten o'clock, a light supper was served, with a birthday cake and gifts from the family for Brett. Shortly after, they both made a little speech, thanking friends and family for all the great food, music, gifts, and money that was so freely given. Jodi threw her bouquet over her shoulder and if Len hadn't caught it, it would have hit him in the face. He had come alone to the wedding but spent most of the evening dancing and talking with Carol.

Bruce and Carmen rented a cabin for the honeymooners out at Twin Bays Resort. Some of the ladies went out earlier in the day to stock the little fridge with food and a bottle of champagne. As an added touch, they left a basket of fruit and an arrangement of flowers on the table. The honeymooners could only stay one night, as Brett had to join his crew Sunday evening.

With the well wishers surging out to the car and a rattle of the still-attached tin cans, the happy couple made their escape. Brett stopped a few blocks away at the bridge and cut the cans off, throwing them into the trunk. Then they drove slowly - for he was a wee bit inebriated - out the lonely lake road to their little hide-a-way.

Their cabin was the only one with a porch light on so they found it easily. They were still in their wedding clothes. Both had packed a small overnight bag with toiletries, jeans, T-shirts, and sneakers. Brett carried the bags up the three steps, unlocked the door, then turned and swept his bride into his arms and carried her through the open door. Jodi planted a kiss on his cheek as he set her on her feet inside the door.

"Thank-you, Prince Charming." she laughed. They kicked off their shoes and walked through the neat little A-frame cabin to the sliding glass doors that opened onto a small deck overlooking the lake.

There was no moon to be seen but the sky was ablaze with a multitude of stars. Frogs chirruped from a wood side pond and the scent of pine and wood smoke lingered on the soft summer breeze.

Intoxicated by the beautiful night, the lovely girl beside him, and that last bottle of beer, Brett pulled Jodi to him, and kissed her hard, bending her back slightly. She was somewhat taken by surprise at his unusually abrupt and forceful manner and she pushed against him in protest. She broke away and saying nothing, but feeling hurt, she went into the bathroom, removed her wedding dress, and hung it up. She washed, and brushed her teeth.

When Jodi came out in her slip and nylons, Brett was sitting on the big double bed. He had been immediately sorry for kissing her like that, and as she disappeared into the bathroom he gripped the wooden deck railing, shook his head to clear it, and took several deep breaths. He told himself to slow down and take it easy. He didn't want to spoil their wedding night by rushing this part of it. He wished he hadn't had that last drink. The alcohol was making him stupid. He patted the space beside him, and said quietly, "Come here, Doll."

Jodi looked at him sideways as she took the pins out of her hair, letting it fall around her shoulders. Then she came over and sat gingerly on the edge of the bed.

Brett circled her waist with one arm and brushed her cheek lightly with his lips. "I'm sorry I kissed you like that. I'm a little bit drunk and I'm just *so* excited!" He lay down on his side, across the bed, propping his head with his elbow. He pulled Jodi down beside him and draped his right arm loosely across her hips. "Just think, Princess. We actually did it. We're married!"

"Hey, Dream Boy," she smiled back. "We are sure enough married, and nothing's going to separate us; neither death, nor life, neither angels or other heavenly rulers, or powers, neither the present nor the future, neither the world above nor the world below - there is nothing in all creation that will ever be able to separate us."

"There you go," he said, looking at her with amusement. "One of your little sermons?"

"It is. There are so many wonderful promises in the Bible. That passage is from Romans, where Paul is talking about our relationship with God. It's beautiful."

"So are you," Brett replied, letting his hand wander down from her hip to thigh, to calf. "You know what I find really sexy?"

"No, what?"

"That swishy sound your nylons make when your legs rub together." He took hold of her foot in his hand and slowly pushed her leg up against her other one, making the sound he liked. "Will you dress up for me sometimes, and put your hair up like it was?"

"Sure, if you'll take me out on a date sometimes."

"It's a deal." He kissed her lips, gently.

She relaxed now, trusting him again, and rested her palm against his cheek. "You look great in your suit too." She smiled. "I almost hate for you to take it off."

Brett chuckled, "I'm going to have a hard time making love to you with my clothes on." He pulled her against his body and kissed the hollow at the base of her neck. He ran his tongue around it, then kissed it again, before moving across to kiss her bare shoulder. His voice was husky and tender with desire as he suggested, "Why don't you just slip out of this slip, and I'll just slip into the bathroom and brush my teeth, and then we'll slip right into bed, okay?"

The toothpaste disguised the beer smell somewhat, but Jodi didn't really care. She was as hungry for him as he was for her, and when he climbed under the covers beside her, fully aroused, she was naked and ready for him. Their passion was like a runaway horse; unbridled and unstoppable until it had run its course and finished in shuddering sighs of pleasure.

Then a night of love began that was somehow different from all the other times they had made love. They consummated their marriage well and truly, dozing off wrapped in each other's arms between the sweet frantic joining of their bodies. Once again in the early dawn, Jodi half-awoke to find him moving on her in a dream-like state. Neither spoke but words were not needed for the kind of communication they were sharing. Finally, exhausted, they slept late into the morning.

Jodi stirred first and attempted to sneak out of bed without waking her golden-haired Prince but he caught her around the waist, mumbling sleepily, "Don't go, I've got something for you."

"No way, " she answered, I'm hungry. I'm going to check out the fridge."

"Humph" came the reply, as he let her go.

Checking out the tiny kitchenette, Jodi came back with two large glasses of orange juice. Brett was now awake, his deep blue eyes following her naked lithe body as she propped up the pillows for him, and then seated herself cross-legged on the bottom of the jumbled bed.

"I'm going to have a bath," she said, sipping the cold, tangy drink, " and then I'll make us some breakfast."

"May I join you?" Brett asked, looking mischievous. "I need one too, and it conserves water, you know".

Jodi laughed and collected his empty glass. "That's a good excuse, but sure."

She went and began to run the hot water into the large, old fashioned, claw-footed tub, pouring a liberal measure of strawberry scented bubble bath under the tap. As she was pinning her hair up out of the way, Brett came in with a chair, which he set beside the tub. Jodi's raised eyebrows and question got no answer, just a little smile. Brett disappeared again as Jodi blissfully sank into the hot, soothing water.

In a moment he was back again carrying a bowl of segmented oranges, a bunch of grapes, two wine glasses, and the bottle of champagne. Setting the fruit and glasses on the chair, he took a white hand towel off the rack and draped it over his arm. "Would Madame care for some wine?" he asked, in his best French accent.

"Mais oui, Garcon," Jodi giggled. "Ooh, I just love these bare naked, cute waiters they have here!" Her eyes matched the sparkle in the wine as he filled up both glasses with a flourish. Then Brett stepped into the tub, lowering himself gingerly into the hot scented water. Jodi made a space for him between her legs and he leaned against her with a sigh of contentment. They raised their glasses to each other and drank the sweet, bubbly liquid. They fed each other orange pieces and grapes between light affectionate kisses.

    Jodi's thoughts kept straying to Christopher. She had never been away from her child overnight before. She missed him, and couldn't get over the feeling that she should be listening for him. On the other hand, she had never done anything as wild and crazy like eating, drinking, and cuddling in a bath and she was enjoying herself immensely.

    Finally, reluctantly, Jodi and Brett emerged with faces flushed from the wine and the hot water. Brett dried himself off and wrapped the large towel around his waist, like a skirt. He offered a steadying hand to Jodi, who was feeling a little dizzy and towelled her dry, gently kissing her body in a myriad of places as he did so

    The whoosh of cool air from the outer room was a welcome relief. Brett lifted his pack onto the bed and began to search in it for his clothes. Whether it was the champagne, or the kisses, or a combination of both that turned her on, Jodi didn't know. She came up behind Brett, unhooked the towel and dropped it to the floor. He turned in surprise as she pressed her body to his. Recognizing immediately the desire in her eyes, he kissed her. After the long kiss, he asked breathlessly, "Hey, hey Princess, what's this? Didn't you get enough last night?"

Jodi didn't answer as they collapsed in a heap on the rumpled bed. She stroked Brett's damp hair, his shoulders, his back; cradling him like a baby as he melted into her once again. She knew it could never get any better than this, and she told him so.

When Brett's heart stopped hammering and his breathing slowed, he said, "Oh Princess, I think I've just died and gone to heaven. That was great," He raised himself on one elbow, looking down at her with admiration. "You know," he smiled, pushing a tendril of hair off her face, "You never cease to amaze me."

"Hmm?" she mumbled, starting to doze off.

"You know...you seem so quiet, but underneath that shy exterior, you have this wicked sense of adventure and you can be extremely bold". He lay down again, and pulled her close. "I love you" he sighed.

"I love you too," she whispered back. "I am sooo.. happy."

The newlyweds drifted off to sleep, to awake sometime in the afternoon, ravenously hungry. They dressed, and then made a meal from the food in the fridge. Jodi tidied up the bed and the bathroom;

they had a walk on the beach, and then it was time to go home. The honeymoon was over. It had been short, but certainly unforgettable.

At home Scamp greeted them joyously and then as they came in, Christopher flung himself at Jodi for hugs and kisses. As soon as he wiggled down, Brett scooped him up and carried him around on his shoulders as he and Jodi went out again to close in the animals for the night.

    All too soon a truck arrived for Brett, full of noisy young men sitting on wooden benches in the back. There were stock racks on the sides. The center was piled with work boots, hard hats, and backpacks. Brett threw his gear onto the pile then turned and swept Jodi into a tight embrace. The rest of the family were also gathered around to say goodbye. They would be leaving for Vancouver before he returned next weekend.

    The boys hooted, cheered, whistled, clapped and stamped their booted feet as Jodi and Brett kissed long and intimately. They let go of each other reluctantly. Brett gave Carol and Marnie a hug and thanked them for coming and for looking after Christopher. He shook Rob's hand warmly, and then took Christopher from Carol, hugged him gently, and put him into Jodi's arms. With a farewell kiss on his wife's cheek, Brett stepped up into the truck. Someone banged on the cab roof as a signal to go and the truck ground into gear, moving off with a lurch.

Good-byes were always emotional for Jodi. She hated them. Tears slid down her cheeks as she turned to go in. Her two sisters slipped their arms around her for moral support and suggested a cup of tea. Jodi was grateful for their company and bright chatter. Soon she would be alone.

It wasn't going to be any different than before. Brett was going to be away a lot and they would just have to accept that. At least now they had the satisfaction of knowing that they belonged together legally, as well as in body and soul.

CHAPTER THIRTY-TWO

After the summer, Brett commuted between Kelso and Harrison as often as he could while he went to school and learned his trade. But for long stretches in the winter when the roads were treacherous for travel, Jodi insisted he stay in Harrison rather than risk an accident coming home. They missed each other terribly at these times and the realization slowly dawned on them that maybe they should sell the Kelso house and move to Harrison.

Jodi completed her high school by correspondence and was thinking about taking a two year Veterinary Assistant Course. A move closer to Harrison would put them nearer the college for their studies. Brett's family would be able to help with childcare and he would be close to his work. As much as Jodi hated the thought of leaving her home in Kelso, she knew she could not stand another year of repeated separations from her loved one and she determined to do whatever it took to be with him.

As it turned out, things resolved themselves quite nicely. Shortly after he had caught Jodi's bouquet at the wedding, Len met and fell in love with a girl who had come up from Montana to work with Fish and Wildlife on a study of the bear population north of Kelso at the head of the lake. Susan Baird was a Biologist on the team. Len was hired to guide the researchers into the remote areas in which they wished to study the habitat and movements of the grizzlies. Susan and Len hit it off immediately. She was petite, olive skinned, and pretty, with sparkling brown eyes and a vivacious smile. Susan loved the outdoors, sharing Len's love of camping, hiking, fishing and to a lesser degree, hunting. Within weeks Len and Susan were engaged and by the following summer Susan had taken out Canadian citizenship and had become Len's wife.

When Len and Jodi had a chance to talk at his wedding dance and he found out that Jodi wanted to move to Harrison, he jumped at the chance to rent the house from her. That suited Jodi fine; she wasn't ready to part with it for good and she knew Len would take good care of the property for her.

Jodi and Brett had been watching the Real Estate News closely for a small house to rent in Harrison. Once again, she was going to have to part with Blossom and the goats. Christopher was crazy about the pony. Now, at two years old he could sit on Blossom by himself, clutching her mane tightly while Jodi led him around.

One day in early June as she took cookies out of the oven and put them to cool on last week's newspaper spread out on the counter, Jodi happened to notice an ad she had missed completely. It was not in the property for sale or rent column, but was in the want ads.

WANTED: FAMILY TO RUN SMALL ORCHARD AND FARM. OWNER RETIRING. 15 ACRES WITH HOUSE, BARN, OTHER OUTBUILDINGS. LARGE GARDEN. NEAR HARRISON. PHONE LUDLOW 3238.

Hardly able to contain her excitement, Jodi called Brett in Harrison to tell him about the ad as soon as he got home from work. Brett was as enthusiastic as she was. Jodi waited by the phone while he called the number and talked to a pleasant elderly lady. He made an appointment to see the place on Friday evening, after supper, and then he called Jodi back to tell her to come down to Harrison.

On Friday, instead of Brett coming home, Jodi and Christopher went down on the bus with Stuey. They were all excited at the prospects of the farm, and anxious to see it.

When Brett steered the Pontiac up the hill and parked in the yard beside the old white clapboard farmhouse, Jodi knew in her heart she wanted the place. It felt like coming home. Careful to hide her eagerness, she stood a moment gazing at the tranquil setting. She noted the large hip-roofed barn with the cleared land sloping gently up behind it, dotted with fruit trees and disappearing into the forested hillside above. She looked with pleasure upon the summer garden; ablaze with red peonies, roses, rhododendrons and a multitude of other blooms; the honeysuckle, sweet on the summer breeze, wildly out of control on the veranda lattice, and the lake down below, reflecting perfectly the pink- tinged dark mountains on its placid surface. "Oh, my God!" she exclaimed, meeting Brett's eyes as he straightened up from lifting Christopher out of his car seat. "Why would anyone want to sell this?"

Brett just smiled at her as a white- haired slender lady with twinkling cornflower- blue eyes met them. "Come in, my dears, come in" she said brightly. "I'm Edna Bates. Come in and meet Frank, and have some tea."

Jodi introduced themselves and then said, "If you don't mind, Mrs. Bates, we'd like to look at the land and outbuildings before it gets dark. Would it be all right if we walked up to the orchard?"

The old woman's pale blue eyes registered surprise, then her mouth crinkled into a genuine smile. "You go right ahead, and look around. We'll have tea when you get back." Then, looking at Christopher, she said, "What a lovely boy. Would he like to stay with me while you go off exploring? I have some little kittens here in a box on the veranda." Brett set Christopher down as Edna held out her hand to him. Surprisingly, he took it and showed no hesitation in going with the older lady.

First, Jodi and Brett investigated the barn with its huge hayloft, old dairy cow stanchions, and pens for smaller animals such as sheep or pigs. In a roomy stall at one end they were greeted by a low 'moo....ooooo' and a pair of soft velvety brown eyes. The tan coloured Jersey milk cow pushed her head against them, inviting attention.

Coming outside again, Jodi and Brett watched with amusement as chickens, ducks, and geese scratched and waddled past, heading for their shelters for the night. An old Collie dog ambled after them on their walk up the hill.

The orchard contained about thirty trees, laden with various kinds of fruit; apples, cherries, plums, and apricots. Several hazelnut and walnut trees were well on their way to producing an abundant crop.

They didn't speak as they walked hand-in-hand through the orchard. Jodi knew it would be a lot of hard work, caring for the trees. There would be pruning, spraying, grafting, and then the work of harvesting and selling the produce. Brett had never done that kind of work, and he was away so much. *Could she do it alone? Would he even be interested in fruit farming?* Jodi's thoughts whirled as she pictured them working side by side with their children over the years; selling fruit, vegetables, nuts, flowers, and homemade jams at their own roadside stand, or at the Farmer's Market in Harrison.

Her eyes roamed up to the dark forest beyond the fence line. She could just imagine exploring the miles of old logging roads on their new horses; for here, there was room not only for Blossom, but also for several more horses. In a few years, Christopher would be able to handle the pony on his own, and Jodi was going to need a bigger and more challenging horse for herself.

Back at the house, in the big old farm kitchen, Jodi sat in a daze drinking tea as Christopher played with the kittens and some old trucks, and Frank Bates told them the history of the farm.

"Back in October 1890, my father, Reginald Frank Bates, stood on the beach way down below us here, where the sternwheeler had dropped him off." Giving Brett a nod, he said, "He was just about your age, son. Reg looked up in apprehension at the forty acres of wilderness he had just purchased. Fresh out of Agricultural School in Ontario, he had seen ads promoting the opportunities for fruit growing in this area. Many a young man would have despaired at the formidable task that faced him, but, being of tough British stock, he took the challenge and built a one-roomed cabin with the help of a neighbour. With hand tools, he felled the huge timber, and blasted the stumps out with dynamite.

Then he bought a roan ox named Billy. Well, Billy was eccentric, but powerful, and with him my dad plowed the land, picking out roots and rocks as he went. Then he planted fruit trees. Later, his brothers came out from Ontario and helped him build a small house. It still stands, down by the lake."

Frank Bates leaned back in the old kitchen chair, and hooked his thumbs under his red suspenders. His bushy, greyish-white eyebrows almost came together over his creased weather-beaten brow as he searched for words to continue the story.

"I was born in that old house, and two sisters too. One of the girls died as a baby, but my sister Ida still lives in Vernon." Frank sipped his tea, reminiscing.

"When the road went through here my dad helped to build it with Billy, his plow, stone boat, and logging chain. The work was horrendous, and he got thirty-five cents an hour for a thirteen-hour day. Dad also worked at the smelter in Castle River and at sawmills around Harrison. Fruit farming wasn't very rewarding in those days. Pretty tough to raise a family." Frank laughed ruefully. "The pioneers in this area had a hard struggle to survive."

Jodi and Brett nodded respectfully. They would never travel that stretch of road again without thinking of Reg Bates toiling through the rocks and mud with Billy, his big, roan ox.

Frank took another fresh home-baked scone off the plate and continued, "My mother was never very strong. She never got over the loss of my little sister. She passed away when I was thirteen. Dad sold the land below the road shortly after that. We lived up here in a little shack for years, before I built this house."

Edna broke in with a smile. "He built it for me, when we got married." Jodi was relieved that neither one of them had said anything disparaging about the house. "We built the barn too, and ran a dairy farm for quite a few years. Old Dolly there in the barn is a granddaughter of one of our first Jerseys.

"She's a sweetheart," Jodi smiled.

"Yep" the old man mused, "Mother and I celebrated our 50th wedding anniversary in April. We've worked hard on this land, cleared it bit by bit. Worked it with oxen and later on, horses. Never did own a tractor. Never liked them noisy things."

Edna chimed in, " We raised five kids in this house - three boys and two girls. They're all married now with little ones of their own. We've got eleven grandchildren," she added with pride.

They chatted on, visiting like old friends, until it grew dark outside and Christopher began to get cranky with tiredness. Jodi insisted they must be going.

As the little family drove slowly out to the main road, Edna turned to Frank as they stood on the veranda waving goodbye, and said simply, "They're going to buy it. I'm glad."

Frank scoffed. "We didn't even discuss the price. How can you be so sure they're the ones? They're just kids. They don't have any money!"

"Because," his wife said knowingly, "They're the only ones who have really cared about the land first, and the house second. She even asked me what perennials were in the garden. They didn't point out all the things that need to be fixed in the house. They love the land, and that's all that matters. They'll do all right here.

Back at the Randall's, after Jodi had put the sleeping toddler to bed in Brett's old room, and they had told Carmen and Bruce all about the farm, Brett slipped his arms around her and nuzzled her neck. "C'mon, let's go to bed."

Down in their basement room Jodi tried to find out how Brett felt about the place, and what the chances of getting it were. However, he had other things on his mind and kept evading her questions with a kiss, a touch, and a nibble, that soon shifted her focus from buying land to making love.

Afterwards, as she lay cuddled up in his embrace, she whispered, "Don't you dare go to sleep! I want to know if you like the place as much as I do."

He sighed deeply. "Sure I do, Honey. I like it a lot. But don't get your hopes up, because you know we don't have much money saved up yet."

"I know that," she replied, turning to face him in the dark. "But if I sold the Kelso house it would give us the cash for a down payment."

There was a moment of silence. Then from out of the dark, Brett asked tentatively, "Would you be willing to do that? I mean...I know what that place means to you."

"Well...Carol owns half of it, but if she's agreeable, I would part with it. We need to be closer to Harrison, and I don't want to endure any more long separations. It would be so nice if you could come home every night instead of just on weekends."

"Yeah, that's for sure." Brett agreed. "I've been driving that twisty road for three years now, and I'm sick of it." He kissed her lightly. "I must say though, that it's kept our love life interesting." Jodi laughed in agreement.

As Jodi and Brett talked, they discovered that both of them had felt a special attraction to the farm. Jodi knew right away she would love the place, but she was afraid that Brett would balk at the workload in caring for all the trees in addition to his job, and that the house was too old and awkward. She was amazed when his answer was, "You and I can fix up that old house, but that piece of land is like heaven on a hillside. Let's go for it!"

The next morning, Jodi phoned Len first to see if he and Susan would be interested in buying the house. They were - definitely! Then Jodi phoned Carol down in Vancouver, and quickly got permission to sell it. Carol loved the city and had no desire to return to Kelso. She was pleased for Len that he had found someone more in tune with his interests than she had been, and was secretly relieved to be rid of him and that old house too. Jodi had always wanted a farm and it would be so much easier for them to be near Brett's work and Christopher's grandparents. The move would be good for all of them.
    Bruce and Carmen accompanied the young couple as they drove out to the farm again and made an offer which was immediately accepted. Edna's eyes sparkled as she told them over tea and cake. "I just knew these young'uns were right for the place when I saw them go up that hill, hand in hand."

The young Randalls celebrated their first wedding anniversary and Brett's twentieth birthday in a frenzy of packing, sorting, cleaning, and moving to their new home.

It was an exhausting time, but they were filled with a sense of adventure and the prospects of being together at last on their very own piece of land.

CHAPTER THIRTY-THREE

A year passed quickly, and another. Brett, Jodi and Christopher were content with each other, and the new farm. They worked hard and the land prospered, making the family almost self-sufficient with a bounty of fresh fruit and vegetables.

They bought Dolly, the Jersey cow from the Bates' when the elderly couple moved to White Rock to be close to their daughter, and Jodi still had a few goats. With the extra milk, she raised half a dozen piglets each year, so along with a calf from Dolly, they had plenty of meat too. With Brett's parents, they exchanged farm produce for baby-sitting; an arrangement that seemed to be working well.

Jodi had just received her Diploma as an Animal Health Technician, and was working three days a week as a Veterinary Assistant at the St. Francis Clinic in Harrison.

Christopher was four now, a handsome, sturdily built little boy with blond curly hair and a dazzling smile which lit up his big, blue eyes whenever he laughed. He was a happy child, with an avid interest in animals, bugs, books, and trucks. He had started Playschool two days a week, and loved it so much that he wanted to go every day. Jodi felt he was lonely sometimes, and now that they were getting ahead financially, and with all but one college course behind them, her thoughts turned often to having another child.

Brett still had another year to fulfill on his Apprenticeship Program, but he was a fairly knowledgeable electrician now. He was still employed by, and under contract to West Kokanee Power, but he did quite a bit of extra work on the side for cash. He was a very thorough and hard worker. He had re-wired most of their old house, and together they had painted, papered, and re-done all of the rooms so that their home reflected the love, care, and attention of those that lived there.

Last February, for her twenty-first birthday, Brett and Christopher took Jodi by the hand and led her, blindfolded, out to the barn. A whisper of falling snow was in the air as tiny flakes drifted down from a thin cloud of white mist. Their faces tingled with the cold as they crunched through the snowy yard and entered the comforting warmth and familiar animal smells of the big barn.

Jodi was led to the box stall beside Blossom's. She knew there was a horse in it before the blindfold was removed. She heard the restless stamping of feet and the nervous breathing of a young animal that had been recently removed from it's own familiar surroundings.

When her men folk removed the bandage with a great flourish, she was suddenly looking into the large, dark, prominent eyes of a beautiful young chestnut mare. The mare's mane and forelock were extremely long and heavy. They were a beautiful silvery blond colour, which contrasted sharply with the golden-red of her body. A large star right in the center of her broad forehead graced her slightly dished short face. Her tiny ears pricked forward with interest as she blew gently on Jodi with her large nostrils.

"Oh!" Jodi exclaimed. "She's absolutely drop-dead gorgeous!" Her eyes roamed approvingly over the mare's wide chest, pretty arched neck, the short back and well-sprung ribs, and strong, beautifully rounded rump and hindquarters. The horse's thick, silvery tail almost dragged on the ground. The legs were fine, but with good bone; the dark hoofs were round and dense, and extremely strong looking. Jodi's first thought was that she was an Arab, but something about the stocky, compact build wasn't quite right. She stood still in the corner of the stall, letting the filly come to her.

After she had checked Jodi out with an inquisitive sniff, the horse took two soft steps toward Jodi and laid her pretty head over her shoulder. Jodi's arms went around the mare's neck and they literally hugged each other. Immediately, love and acceptance flowed between them, forming a bond that would last for many, many years.

Brett and Christopher joined her in the stall, and Jodi turned from hugging the mare to hugging her husband and son. "She's so beautiful! I just *love* her! Thank-you, thank-you, thank-you!" she mumbled with tears in her eyes and a tremor in her voice. "What breed is she anyways? I've never seen such a beautiful horse!"

Brett produced a rolled up certificate from his inside coat pocket, and put it into her hands. "Here," he smiled, "it's her pedigree."

Jodi unrolled it, and her eyes grew wide as she saw the name at the top of the papers. *American Morgan Horse Association.* "Wow!" she breathed. "A Morgan! I knew she was something rare and special."

Her eyes scanned the neatly typed pedigree, and she read out loud, "Hylee's Torchfire, by Hylee's Top Brass, out of Hylee's Torchsong. Bred by Mr. and Mrs. Robert Behling, Hylee Farms, Cambria, Wisconsin. Imported by Jeanne Connolly, Crestbrook, B.C. Canada." Jodi couldn't believe it! She was familiar with, and had a great interest in the Morgan breed, but she had never seen one in the flesh. And now she owned this beautiful two-year-old filly!

Names on the piece of paper jumped out at her like history coming to life in her hand. *Flyhawk* was there, that great black ranch-bred stallion who became a legend in his own time. Jodi recalled the strange, but true story of his son *Shadowhawk*, who spent most of his life as a ranch and stock horse on the Canadian prairies before changing hands several times, ending up in obscurity in Alberta somewhere. After the death of Flyhawk, his breeders in Illinois sought out and tracked down the old ranch horse and took him back to the states where he was re-trained and shown as a Park horse. His foals were much in demand and a very important line was saved for the perpetuation of the breed.

Jubillee King was on the bottom, or mare's side of the ancestors, and Jodi recognized immediately that her filly had probably inherited her beautiful colour and kind temperament from this famous stallion.

She had read that many Morgan horses had been absorbed into the Quarter Horse breed from the huge Sellman Ranch in Texas, as well as from the Roland Hill Ranch in California. She knew too that the American Saddlebred, the Standardbred, and Tennessee Walking Horse all traced back to Morgan blood. Her thoughts flew to other Morgans she had read about - the celebrated *Blackhawk* - trotting champion of the world back in the 1800's, and the famous First Vermont Cavalry in the American Civil War; one thousand Green Mountain boys, all mounted on tough little Morgans. She thought of General Philip Sheridan, who made the famous ride from

Winchester to Cedar Creek, a twenty-mile gallop, on *Rienzi*, his faithful and tireless Morgan gelding. When the retreating and demoralized troops saw the mighty black charging into battle, they rallied and restored their broken ranks, and turned the tide in their favour that day. Jodi could remember parts of the poem she had learned in grade eight. Most of all, Jodi thought of *Figure,* or *Justin Morgan,* the foundation stallion of the breed, who although being a small, compact horse of only fourteen hands, was able to out-walk, out-trot, and out-pull any horse of his day. Although the Morgans were the 'Pride and Product of America', and part of their history, there were still very few in Canada. Jodi felt a thrill of pride to own this lovely creature with such an interesting breed history.

    Blossom was now eighteen years old, and as much as Jodi loved her old pony, she wasn't much of a challenge to ride. Besides, Christopher was able to ride alone now, and the pony was now his.

    Jodi was ready for a new horse and she set to work slowly and carefully in the corral, training the young mare to carry the saddle and bridle; to walk, trot, canter, and whoa on voice command, and finally to accept her rider.

    In a month, she was riding her new horse out on the trails, and by the summer, Jodi and Torchy were a team, wandering the orchard, trails, and beaches in perfect harmony. Christopher now rode with her too, and so that Brett could join them, Jodi reciprocated his gesture, and bought him a horse for his birthday in July.

    Old Pete wasn't a pedigreed animal like Torchy. He was just an old Appaloosa gelding with leopard spots and a bit of a sway back, but he was kind and gentle and very trustworthy as a trail horse. Brett had ridden Blossom from time to time, but had never had time or inclination for a horse of his own. He was happy to join his family on their little jaunts. He was a natural rider, being so athletic, and he could soon gallop and jump and ride as fast as his wife and son could.

Their lives were full. The fruit and vegetables ripened and were harvested, as autumn crept up with it's clear, still days and sparkling, frosty nights. It was Jodi's favourite season. She loved the fall with the spectacular yellows, oranges, and reds of the maple and chestnut trees contrasted so sharply against the deep green of the pines and spruces. She loved the smells of decaying leaves, and their crunch under her horse's hooves as she rode down the woodsy trails under brilliant blue skies, which soon she knew, would be overcast with their burden of snow.

CHAPTER THIRTY-FOUR

For some time now a pain in her left leg had bothered Jodi, but she had been far too busy all summer to pay much attention to it. Once in a while she would rub some deep heat cream into the hollow behind her knee. That seemed to be where the pain was, although there was nothing to be seen. She didn't mention it to Brett and never thought much about it.

One night in November exactly a month before Christmas, Jodi was lying in bed, cosily contented after lovemaking, with Brett snuggled against her back. An icy sleet drummed relentlessly on the roof, and a cold wind rattled the bare bones of the apple tree outside their bedroom window. Brett's free arm was draped lazily over Jodi's hip, and at random intervals in their conversation he ran his hand down her thigh and over her lower leg. They were talking about having another baby. Now that the hard work was all done for the year, Jodi wanted to get pregnant. Christopher would be going to Kindergarten next fall. If she got pregnant right away, she explained, she would have the baby next August, just before Christopher started school.

Brett wasn't saying 'no'. In fact, he was ready and eager to do his part. He was just about to say so, when his hand stopped on Jodi's calf, and he asked, puzzled, "Hey, Jo, what's this?"

"What's what?" she asked.

"This bump, on your leg. It's big." His fingers traced around the edge of the egg-shaped lump. Jodi's fingers joined his, and she felt a stab of fear as she felt the size of the mass. She reached over and turned on the bedside lamp and they both re-examined her leg, squinting as their eyes adjusted to the light.

"I don't know. I must have bumped it," she said softly, turning out the light again, and snuggling down beside him. "I'll go get it checked, okay?"

"Yeah, I think you should." They kissed and said 'goodnight' but Jodi lay for a long time, listening to Brett's even breathing and the icy rain drumming on the roof. Somehow, instinctively, she knew the lump was the cause of the increasing pain behind her left knee, and she also knew that it was a serious problem. As she drifted off into a fitful sleep, she prayed for strength to face whatever life threatening obstacles were being thrown into her path.

The next afternoon, Jodi left the Vet Clinic early for her appointment with Dr. Sarah Houston. The nurse had booked Jodi in right away when she heard that she was concerned about a large lump in her leg. Dr. Houston had not been out of Medical School very long. She had done her practicum at the small Harrison Hospital, and then had accepted employment there as a family doctor about a year ago. She was very young looking and Jodi felt comfortable with her. She chatted brightly about the horses, her work, and Christopher, while Sarah examined her leg.

    She was sent down the hall for x-rays of her left leg, and surprisingly, her lungs as well. When Jodi asked the technician why, she was answered with a shrug, and a terse "doctor's orders." She was instructed to wait in a cubicle until the x-rays were developed, and as she waited, Jodi overheard Dr. Houston telling the nurse to cancel the rest of her appointments as she had an emergency to deal with. Jodi felt a deep sense of foreboding, as she wondered, *is she talking about me?*

    In a little while, a young Volunteer knocked on the cubicle door and popped her head in. "Hi, Mrs. Randall. Could you come with me, please? Dr. Houston would like to speak with you." The young girl showed Jodi into a room with a long table, some chairs, and a blackboard. "Please wait in here," the girl said. "The doctor will be here in a few minutes." She handed Jodi some movie magazines, and disappeared. Jodi looked at her watch with exasperation. She was late already. She should be picking Christopher up from his grandma's and getting on home to do chores and make supper. She flipped through the glitzy magazines impatiently, and wondered what was going on.

Meanwhile, Brett was on the lakeshore side of Harrison, reading utility meters at the wealthy homes situated around the bay. He liked this part of his job. The work was easy and it was kind of neat having an excuse to drive into private property and look at the lavish homes that were secluded by thick hedges, tall trees, and long driveways.

He was just climbing back into the company truck when he heard the radio dispatcher call him. "Base to Randall, come in." The light was fast disappearing. The air was getting nippy, and with his thoughts on home and food and his family, Brett slid into the seat, slammed the door, and grabbed the handset. "Randall to Base." He started the truck and turned the heater on as the radio crackled to life.

"Yeah...there's a message here...Dr. Houston would like you to come to the hospital immediately. Something about a conference with you and your wife." With a shock, Brett remembered the lump on Jodi's leg, and realized she must be at the hospital, and that it must have caused the doctor some concern. Feeling numb, he spoke into the radio, "I'm on my way. Thanks."

At the reception area, still in work boots and coveralls, Brett was shown into the room where Jodi waited. She looked up in surprise.

"What are you doing here?" she asked, as he bent to kiss her cheek.

"Dr. Houston called our office and they radioed me to get over here. What's up?"

Jodi answered quietly. "I don't know yet, but if they called you, it must be serious."

Brett sat beside her, and took her hand, just as Dr. Houston, a nurse, and an older grey-haired distinguished looking man came into the room. Dr. Houston's smile looked like it was pasted on, and she tried to exude confidence as she brightly apologized for keeping them waiting. Jodi was used to interpreting the body language of horses and other animals. Humans weren't that much different. She knew right away that the young doctor was nervous, shaken, and trying hard to preserve her professionalism.

The older doctor had a very serious look on his face as he wearily dropped Jodi's file and x-rays on the table and extended his hand. "I'm Dr. Ian Murdock." He came right to the point. "We need to talk." Brett and Jodi sat wordless, as if they were frozen in time, as the doctor continued.

"I'm sorry, but we have reason to believe that there may be a cancerous tumour in your left leg, Jodi, and that it could be dangerous to your life." Jodi swallowed, and nodded, while Brett gripped her hand tightly. She had expected bad news.

Dr. Murdock continued, "We would like to send you to Vancouver for a biopsy as soon as possible. Then we'll know exactly what we're dealing with, and the Oncology specialists will decide on a course of action."

"What does treatment involve?" Brett asked, grim-faced.

"Usually amputation, and a course of chemotherapy to make sure it hasn't spread to any other part of the body, Dr. Murdock said. " So far, there's no sign of it in the lungs, and that's a good thing. It doesn't appear to have spread."

Jodi now understood the reason for the chest x-rays, but she still could not trust herself to speak. Her mind reeled with the shock of it. Cancer! The big C! She inwardly groaned. *Oh God! Not that! Anything but that!*

Dr. Murdock was speaking again. He asked gently, "Is there any chance that you might be pregnant, Jodi?"

She flashed a quick look at Brett and then looked at the doctor. "No....but we were hoping to have another baby very soon. We were just talking about it last night.... (she blushed)...when we discovered this lump."

The doctor smiled, in understanding. "Okay, whatever you do, don't get pregnant right now. You may have to take some pretty strong drugs and they would probably kill or damage a fetus."

Dr. Houston showed them the x-rays and explained how, as the tumour grew, it began to press on nerves and ligaments causing the pain Jodi felt behind her knee. She told them it had probably been there for a long time, but was also probably growing, as evidenced by the increasing pain.

The rest of the interview concerned the choice of hospital in Vancouver and the necessity of booking a flight immediately. The doctors were pleased that Jodi had family in the city. "That's going to make things a whole lot easier for you". Dr. Murdock smiled weakly.

Arrangements were quickly made for Jodi to fly to Vancouver in two days time, and have the biopsy and tests done at the Lion's Gate Hospital. She would stay with Marnie and family until the results were known. In a hurried consultation, Jodi and Brett agreed that he would stay to look after the animals and to be with Christopher in the evenings. It was going to be tough on the little guy to have his mommy gone and as much as they wanted to be together, they both felt that Brett should be at home for their son.

At last, Jodi and Brett were free to go. They walked in numb silence out to Brett's truck. Darkness had descended, and the night was crispy cold. Light snowflakes swirled through the air.

Sounds were muffled as a cold, late November wind moved in off the lake.

Brett helped Jodi in on the passenger side, moving his lunchbox, thermos, and various electrical parts out of the way for her. He went around to his side and gripped the steering wheel hard, fighting off tears. "Do you want to go to Mom and Dad's and get Christopher?" he asked.

Jodi answered, almost in a whisper. "No, not right now. I need some time alone. Let's go home. Maybe they could bring him later, and pick up the car too." She reached into her coat pocket and produced the car keys. Brett went out into the frosty night again and quickly tucked the keys under the seat of the old green Pontiac. No one was around.

Back home, both moved automatically to the jobs that had to be done. Brett fed the hungry animals while Jodi got the fires going. She felt like she was someone else – a stranger watching from a distance as the crisis of her life unfolded. She knew it was real - she had cancer - but the reality hadn't sunk in yet.

Feeling exhausted and cold, Jodi sank onto the comfortable old couch in front of the fire that was just beginning to throw off some heat. She stared into the flames, trying not to think, but visions of herself as bald and leg-less flooded her mind, and her whole being recoiled against the ugly harshness of the disease and the dreaded hospital stays it would involve.

When Brett came in he found Jodi cradling herself, moaning and crying. He sat beside her and drew her into his arms, murmuring, "I'm so sorry, Honey, so sorry." He'd been crying too, out in the barn. Fresh tears rolled down his cheeks, as he kissed Jodi and held her tight.

She spoke through her tears with clenched teeth. "I'm going to lose my leg, and maybe even my life. Things will never be the same for us again. The whole picture has changed, and I'm really, really scared!"

Brett was so choked up with emotion and tears he couldn't answer, but Jodi knew he was just as scared as she was. This disease wasn't going to be easy on him either.

"Brett?" Jodi asked, sniffing and getting her tears under control. "If I don't ...if I don't make it...through this ordeal..."

He stopped what she was going to say by putting a finger against her lips. "Shhh....don't talk that way! You *have* to make it! I wouldn't want this place without you. Hell, I wouldn't even want to live!"

Jodi took his hands in hers and looked into his teary, blue eyes. "For God's sake!" she said. "We're not Romeo and Juliet. We have a son to think of. He'll need you to be strong."

Brett held her tight as he said, "Christopher's my right arm, but you're my heart and soul, Jo. I could never love anyone else."

She smiled a little then at him, and said softly," You could, in time. You'd still be very young...and handsome." Her eyes, clear now, but full of pain, regarded him steadily. "Promise me you won't neglect Christopher if I die."

Brett's arms went around her again, and as Jodi laid her head against his shoulder, he whispered, "Of course I won't. He'll be surrounded with love from me, Mom and Dad, and Bev, and your family too. He'll be all right."

The phone rang, jarring their thoughts, and Brett went into the kitchen to answer it. Jodi knew it would be Carmen, wondering what was going on, and she wondered how Brett was going to break the news to her. She knew she had to call her family too and tell them she'd be arriving in Vancouver on Saturday, and that she needed to be taken to the hospital first thing on Monday morning for tests. More than anything, she just wanted to go to bed and sleep, and wake up in the morning to find it had all been a bad dream.

In a few minutes, Brett came back with two cups of hot instant coffee. As the aroma assailed her senses, Jodi realized they had not eaten since noon and she was suddenly hungry. She accepted it gratefully and as she took a sip of the hot liquid, she tasted their favourite liqueur,

Bailey's Irish Cream. They only used it for special occasions like their birthdays, or anniversary. Right now, they both needed a shot of courage.

As Brett sat down beside her again, he said, "That was Mom. They're on their way out. They'll pick up the car at the hospital." He put his arm around Jodi and she leaned into him, drawing strength from his solid, warm body.

Once she finished her coffee, Jodi forced herself to move. "I'm going to call my sisters before your folks get here." Brett nodded and let her go. They had to start dealing with this.

It was very hard, talking to Marnie. More tears were shed as the devastating news hit home. All felt shock, horror, and disbelief, as the events of the day were related. Marnie promised to be at the airport to meet Jodi, and to do everything they could to make the suffering easier for her. Marnie wanted her to bring Christopher too. She would gladly look after him, but Jodi felt it best to disrupt his schedule as little as possible, at least until they knew what they were facing.

As she hung up the phone, two sets of headlights swept across the yard, and soon Carmen, Bruce, Bev, and Christopher were surrounding her with hugs, kisses, and tears. They brought fried chicken with them, which they made Jodi and Brett eat. It was a relief to let Carmen take charge. While Jodi took Christopher up to bed,

Carmen made all the necessary phone calls that would have been so hard for Jodi to make. She called Jodi's minister at the little church where Christopher went to Sunday School, and Jodi helped with the music for worship; she called Dr. Higgins, Jodi's boss at the Vet Clinic, and she let Brett's boss know he wouldn't be at work the next day, and why.

Upstairs, Jodi lay with Christopher in his little bed and explained that she had a bad 'owie' in her leg and that she had to go away to the big hospital in Vancouver to get it fixed. She told him she needed him to stay and help Daddy with the animals and that his grandma would look after him in the daytime and take him to school. They talked for a while about the sore leg, and Jodi was amazed at Christopher's understanding and simple faith. "God will take care of everything, Mommy." he said. "Don't you worry."

Jodi sighed as she kissed him goodnight. If only it could be that easy.

She went downstairs to find the Rev. Jim Forsythe and his wife Pat there. Carmen had made tea and filled them in on Jodi's condition. The family gathered in the living room for prayer, and Jim encouraged the young couple to hold on to faith - even when they felt like letting go. He read some marked passages from a book he left with Jodi. "Through faith the weak are made strong; therefore the trials of our faith are made precious. The crisises of life reveal that faith."

Soon everybody left. Brett and Jodi were left alone with their pain and exhaustion. Jodi's head throbbed, and once again tears soaked her pillow as she stared at the black ceiling, unable to sleep. Brett was restless too, and cried out several times as he woke from a fitful sleep. About three a.m. Jodi got up and found some travel sickness pills in the bathroom cupboard. She took one and brought one to Brett with a drink of water. The drug calmed their nerves and made them drowsy, for finally they slept.

CHAPTER THIRTY-FIVE

A whimpering cry like an animal in distress awoke Jodi early the next morning. She opened one eye and caught sight of Christopher standing by the bed, tears running down his face, and clutching himself. She forced a little smile, and whispered to him, "You go to the bathroom, and then you can come back for cuddles."

He turned and padded into the bathroom, then was back quickly, climbing under the covers and snuggling under Jodi's chin. As she put her arm around his little body, Brett stirred, turned over, and snuggled into her back. He reached over her with his arm and rested his hand on Christopher's curly, blond head. "What's the matter?" he mumbled.

Christopher's small, quavery voice came out of the blankets, "I thought Mommy had gone away, and I was sad."

Jodi stroked his back. "I don't have to go until tomorrow, and you don't have to be sad. Daddy will be here with you, and Grandma, and Poppa, and Auntie Bev"

For a few more moments, the three of them lay together in their safe, warm, little world. No one wanted the closeness to end, but each knew that change was coming, and that those changes were going to disrupt their lives drastically.

Christopher, never one to keep still for long once he was awake, crawled over

Jodi and wiggled against Brett's chest. "Dad, will you do 'Row Your Boat' with me?"

Brett groaned and sighed, realizing his peace was at an end. "I guess so," he said, as he rolled over onto his back and pulled his knees up. He lifted the small boy up, and holding his hands, began to make a rowing action while Christopher sang the words.

Samantha, who had been sleeping on the end of the bed, jumped down with a disdainful look, and shook herself daintily, as if to say, *of all the nerve! Imagine them disturbing my rest like that!*

Jodi slipped out of bed too, dressed quickly, and picked up the indignant cat as she headed downstairs to make breakfast. From the bedroom came chortles of glee from Christopher as his daddy invariably made the boat sink, capsize, or ram into the wharf, spilling its occupant into the bedclothes.

The smell of coffee, bacon and pancakes brought the game to an end fairly quickly. Brett donned his coat, and with the old black spaniel at his heels, went out into the frosty November morning to feed the horses and goats. Fortunately, the cow was dry right now, and wouldn't need milking while Jodi was gone.

Before they had finished breakfast, the phone started ringing - people from the church offering sympathy, help with the animals, offering prayer, wanting to look after Christopher. Other friends called with offers of money, rides to the airport, bone marrow and blood donations. Jodi was overwhelmed with the out-pouring of love and support from the community of Kelso and their own little neighbourhood as well.

The phone continued to ring as Jodi tried to do housework, bake, and get the bills paid. Brett took a lot of the calls, and tried to spare her from having to tell yet another well-meaning person about her condition, but just about everyone she knew wanted to 'just have a few words' with Jodi.

Finally, she'd had enough. She couldn't face talking to anyone else. Having to tell it over and over again just made the reality of having cancer sink in, and Jodi felt she had to get away; scream, cry, anything!

"I'm going riding!" she announced, as the phone rang yet again. Brett went to answer it as she pulled on her heavy sweat pants, winter coat, toque, and mitts.

The sun was shining, but it was clear and cold as Jodi swung up on Torchy's back. Her leg hurt, but she ignored it. The filly arched her neck and snorted rollers through her nose in excitement as she pranced across the yard, lifting her feet in graceful arcs above the snow, and snapping them down like pistons. Jodi felt as if she were sitting on a keg of dynamite.

So much power, energy, and joy radiated out from the young horse and into Jodi that she felt her spirits lift immediately.

Brett came out to tell her that Linda phoned and was coming out after work to see her. She was now working as a hairdresser in Harrison. Jodi felt a twinge of guilt for not calling Linda herself. She was sorry her friend had to get the news second-hand. After all, the girls had been friends for years, not as close as they used to be of course, but still, good friends.

Christopher came running out too, and called "Mommy, can I ride too?"

Brett put his arm around his son, and gently admonished him, "Not now Chris, Mom's going to ride real fast today". Then, catching Torchy by the bridle rein, he held her back while placing his other hand on Jodi's leg. "Don't do anything stupid and dangerous, okay?"

Jodi nodded her assent, and as Brett released the rein, the mare sprang into a joyful gallop, showering the two on the ground with clods of churned up snow. Jodi bent low over her neck as Torchy dashed uphill, through the orchard, and slid to a stop by the gate that led out to the woods beyond. Jodi side-passed the mare up to the gate, leaned over, opened the latch, guided her through, and applying pressure on the opposite side with leg and rein, moved the mare over to shut it again. "Good girl, Torchy," Jodi praised. "Well done, you smart little horse."

Torchy snorted with impatience as Jodi held her there for a moment, then as she released the reins, the mare moved off at a fast trot.

The ride did much to rejuvenate and refresh Jodi. Her cheeks tingled with the cold, but her body had never felt so alive as she moved in rhythm to the Morgan's fast high-stepping trot. Her exhilaration was tinged with sadness as she realized that this would be her last ride for a long time.

A few miles along, the old logging trail branched off and Torchy stopped, unsure of which way to go. Thinking immediately of Robert Frost's poem, Jodi mused out loud, "Torchy, I'm going to take the road less traveled by. It will be a hard and dangerous journey. I'll be hurt, and I'll fall down and cry, but by God, I'm going to get to the end." She nudged the mare forward, onto the unfamiliar trail. "And you'll be waiting when I get back, and even if I only have one leg, you'll teach me to ride again, and we'll travel these trails together for years and years."

Torchy's gorgeous blond mane lifted and fell on her glistening neck as she strode forward boldly through the snow, picking her way carefully over deadfall on the trail. Ears pricked, head up, and eyes never missing a thing, she was perfectly obedient to Jodi's rein and leg pressure, even though she really didn't want to be on this strange road, heading away from home and the other horses.

Finally, too many snow-laden branches and a tangle of fallen trees halted their progress over the path. Turning for home, Jodi resolved to accept with courage and dignity whatever it was she had to endure. Like her horse, she would go forward obediently, trusting in her master - her God - to guide her safely on the rough trail ahead.

Jodi had just finished feeding the animals when Linda arrived, terribly upset. As she made tea, Jodi managed to convey to her some of the calmness, strength, and faith that she had mustered on her ride.

Linda smiled through her tears as she sipped her tea. "Oh Jodi, you were always the steady one; the sensible one. I just know you're going to be all right, but I don't want you to have to go through with it! I'm sorry."

Linda brought a hundred dollars in cash donated from the girls in the beauty shop. She pressed it into Jodi's hand as the two friends hugged goodbye with renewed tears and promises to keep in touch. Brett came down from upstairs and hugged Linda too, thanking her for coming. Linda's heart ached for him as well. She secretly loved Brett, although she would never do anything to come between he and Jodi. Linda wondered suddenly if Brett could ever be interested in her, if Jodi didn't survive. Then, feeling guilty, she shoved that thought out of her mind, and drove away.

Later on, Brett insisted on taking Jodi out to a nice restaurant in Harrison for dinner. They dropped Christopher off at Bruce and Carmen's for the night, and then spent a large portion of Linda's hundred dollars for a lavish meal and expensive wine.

Back at home, Brett built up a roaring blaze in the fireplace. He brought down two big quilts and the pillows from their bed. Then he pulled Jodi down gently and began to remove her clothing piece by piece, kissing each area of bare skin as it emerged. Slowly, with infinite tenderness, and without a word, he made love to her.

Jodi opened herself to his gift of love, accepting it with a mixture of bittersweet joy and sorrow. They pulled the quilts around them, and fell asleep, entwined in each other's arms.

CHAPTER THIRTY-SIX

The two-hour trip to Castle River was grim. The roads were in fair winter condition, but a heavy wet snow beat relentlessly on the windshield, making the squeaky wipers necessary, yet irritating.

Jodi found it terribly difficult to say goodbye to Christopher. She tried to be brave and cheerful as she hugged him goodbye and told him to be good for his Auntie Bev, but as soon as she was in the car, she dissolved into tears. Brett was not able to comfort her. They sat in the back, holding hands, while Bruce drove, and Carmen tried to keep some semblance of conversation going.

At the airport, as Jodi prepared to go through the gate, Bruce broke down in tears as he held Jodi in his large embrace. His early rejection and dislike had long been transformed into a love and respect for her that rivalled how he felt for his own daughter. Carmen also had trouble with her emotions and composure. Tears flowed freely as she hugged Jodi and told her, "Don't worry about Christopher or anything here. We'll make sure everything is looked after."

Jodi nodded her thanks and turned her eyes towards her handsome husband. Her heart ached for him, and for herself. They had endured separations many times already in their relationship, but none as painful or as frightening as this. Since they had bought the farm, they hadn't been apart for even one night.

Brett took Jodi by the hand, and led her a little distance away from his parents. Bruce and Carmen discretely turned away, not wanting to watch this painful goodbye process.

Swinging Jodi around to face him, Brett placed her two hands on his chest, and covered them with his own. He looked deep into her misty eyes, took a breath, and spoke haltingly. "You know I would do this for you if I could...I'd trade places with you in a heartbeat."

Jodi nodded, unable to speak, and they drew close together, standing cheek to cheek, holding each other gently. "Thanks" she managed to whisper. "And thanks for last night. That was really special." They kissed lightly, then Jodi stepped back, squared her shoulders, turned, and walked resolutely through the gate without looking back.

On Monday morning, Jodi stepped through the doors of Lions Gate Hospital into the busy Outpatients area. As Marnie helped her through the seemingly endless paperwork of family history and questions, Jodi felt she was being imprisoned. *Hell,* she thought bitterly, *they may as well take my fingerprints too.* She contemplated the fact that she had deliberately avoided having her baby here, and now she was back - with something far more serious. In the waiting room, Jodi's voice rose in frustration as she complained to her sister about the unfairness of it all. "Is this my punishment for running away with my sweetheart, five years ago?" she asked Marnie. "Do you think God is mad at me for doing that, and has given me this terrible disease to put me in my place? Why am I here?"

Marnie was deeply saddened by the events that had brought her little sister here and she sympathized with her. "I don't think God is punishing you, but he might be testing you. The Bible says that evil falls on the just and the un-just, so you're probably not singled out to suffer. Bad things happen to good people all the time. Jesus never promised us that our lives here on earth would be easy".

Jodi grumbled, "I thought I'd been tested enough. We've been through a lot, already. I don't want to be tested anymore."

Marnie smiled weakly and continued her line of reasoning. "Maybe God is making you face up to your fear of hospitals. There's got to be a purpose in all of this, and it will be revealed, in time." She quoted, "God works in mysterious ways, his wonders to perform." She took Jodi's hand and gave it a squeeze. "Just try to have faith that good will come out of it, and put your trust in God - that's all we can do."

After the routine blood and urine samples were taken, Jodi was led away - *like a lamb to slaughter* - she thought, for a Cat Scan, Bone Scan, and M.R.I. tests. Then the sisters waited some more as the results were viewed and written up by the technicians. Jodi was very scared during the tests, but they were actually painless, and the staff was very nice. They tried hard to put Jodi at ease, explaining how the machines worked, and asking her questions about herself.

Jodi and Marnie tried to eat something as they waited for the test results, but they were both tired and teary. It was hard waiting.

Finally they were called into a little conference room and Jodi was introduced to the Oncology Team that would be working with her throughout her illness. Dr. Jansen was to be Jodi's personal doctor, and was the head of the team. He was Dutch, over six feet tall, with a beaky nose and a sandy brush-cut. His assistant was a young female resident, Dr. Kirkland. Dr. Wong, was the surgeon who would be doing the biopsy.

The diagnosis was confirmed. It *was* bone cancer, but they wouldn't know what kind until a biopsy was taken, and a sample sent away to several labs for testing. Consequently, because of the urgency of the situation, the surgery had been scheduled for the next day. Jodi listened; numb with fear and growing apprehension as Dr. Jansen explained how they would slice into her leg and take a sample of the tumour. Then Dr. Wong talked to her about inserting a broviac line while she was under the anaesthetic. This was a rubber tube inserted through a cut they would make in her neck. It was lodged in the large vein that ran across the chest into the heart. Through the capped end, blood samples could be taken and the chemotherapy medication could be administered.

    All three doctors tried to convince Jodi that it was the best way to go; it avoided the necessity of having many needles. Although Jodi hated the idea of being cut into and her body invaded by foreign objects, she agreed to the biopsy and the broviac. She signed the consent forms.

    Jean, Dr. Jansen's nurse, then took her to a room in the Women's wing on the second floor. Exhausted and weepy, Jodi put on a hospital gown and climbed into the strange, hard bed.

    Marnie had been a tremendous support all day, but now she had to get home to her family. With a hug, and a 'God Bless!' she was gone and Jodi was left alone with her fears and her sorrow. She closed her eyes and repeated the 23rd Psalm over and over again, until she felt a sense of calm.

    That evening, Carol and a girlfriend visited with Jodi. After they left, Jodi called

Brett; related the events of the day, and told him of the operation that was to take place tomorrow. She was quite calm now; remembering her earlier resolve on her ride with Torchy that she would face whatever was thrown at her with as much courage as she could muster. She was the one who comforted Brett, who was feeling guilty for not being there with his wife. They hadn't known she would have surgery so soon - in fact, they didn't know what to expect at all. There wasn't much to say - a few words to Christopher, and then their good-byes and promises of love.

Jodi was relieved to have the semi-private room to herself so far, but later that evening a young woman about her own age was brought in. Even though visiting hours were over, the room filled with crying relatives, a young sad-looking man Jodi assumed to be the woman's husband, and many bouquets of flowers, balloons, and gifts.

After the visitors had all gone and the room was in darkness, Jodi lay, unable to sleep, trying not to think of her own surgery tomorrow. The curtains were drawn around her roommate's bed, but she could hear the young woman crying softly.

Slipping out of bed, and forcing her natural shyness aside, Jodi sat on the end of the stranger's bed and said quietly, "Hi...I'm Jodi Randall. Can I help?"

There was no answer, but Jodi heard the girl swallow, trying to control her crying with little sniffs. Jodi plunged ahead, not really knowing how to start. "I'm feeling pretty lost and upset too. I'm from Harrison, up in the interior. My husband and little boy are back home. I've just been diagnosed with bone cancer. I had a bunch of tests today, and tomorrow I'm having a broviac line inserted in my chest, and a biopsy of my tumour. I'm probably going to lose my leg, and have up to a year of chemo." She laughed scornfully, "I wonder what my husband will think of having a one-legged, bald wife for the next year...if I even live that long." She sighed. "What happened to you?"

Instead of an answer, a question came out of the dark. "How old are you?"

"I'm twenty-one," Jodi answered.

"So am I," came the choked up voice. "I gave birth to a baby girl this morning, but she died about seven o'clock tonight. She was premature. Her little lungs wouldn't function properly. Her intestines weren't fully developed either. The doctors tried hard, but they couldn't save her."

Jodi reached for the girl's hand, and held it tight. "Oh...how awful for you...I'm so sorry." Tears filled her eyes and spilled over. She couldn't help but feel the agony of this young mother who had suffered such a loss. The girl sat up and wiggled down the bed, wrapping her arms around Jodi. They hugged each other and cried for several minutes, sharing their grief.

"My name is Sharon," the young woman said through her tears. "And our daughter's name was Sylvia. I'll be going home tomorrow. The funeral is on Thursday." There was a pause as they tried to compose themselves, passing the tissue box back and forth. Then Sharon said, "I'm really sorry about your leg too. You must be really scared, eh?"

"Yes, I am," Jodi replied truthfully. I've always hated hospitals, and the thought of being carved up on the operating table is not pleasant." The two continued talking far into the night; sharing their sorrow, their hopes, fears, and dreams. They talked about their husbands and families. Jodi told her new friend all about the farm, the animals and her passion for horses. The sharing did them both good, and finally Jodi returned to her bed and was able to sleep.

At noon the next day, Jodi bravely waved goodbye to Sharon, Marnie, and Carol as the Porter wheeled her to the elevator and up to the operating room. She caught a last look at their distraught faces as she was whisked through the doors.

At 3:30 p.m. Dr. Wong came down and told the waiting sisters that everything went well, but the diagnosis was now confirmed. They didn't really expect to hear anything different. In another hour, Jodi was down from O.R. feeling very groggy and nauseated. Her eyes couldn't focus. Her lips were dry and chapped. She had tubes and bandages in her neck, back, chest, hip, and leg. The morphine was controlling the pain, but making her sick. A student nurse fussed around her, taking notes, and measuring vital signs.

Brett called the nursing station and was told that Jodi was fine, although she wasn't able to talk to him yet. Frustrated, he called the hospital gift shop and ordered a dozen red roses and a cuddly teddy bear to be delivered to her room. The nurse put the roses where Jodi could see them when she woke up, and tucked the teddy bear under her arm.

At 6:30, Dr's. Jansen and Kirkland met with Jodi's sisters and pretty well repeated what Dr. Wong had told them. The sample would be analyzed and sent to various clinics including the Mayo for evaluation. They were told that the leg would have to be amputated, but until the exact nature of the tumour was identified, Jodi could go home as soon as she was feeling better.

When she had recovered enough to hear the news, Jodi was excited. She felt her leg might be saved if she could get to her little church for 'hands on healing prayer' as described in the Book of James. She was grateful for the respite, however short. Things were moving too fast. If she could just get home for a few days, she could gather the strength for the next big ordeal.

Two days later, Jodi was back on the plane, heading home and into Brett's waiting arms. She was very sore from the surgery, and the tube in her chest felt weird. She had to learn how to flush the broviac line before the nurses would let her go home. With syringes full of water, she practiced on 'Chester' a plastic model. On herself, she used Heparin, a substance that prevented clots from forming in the line.

On Sunday, at the church were she and Christopher were so much a part of the worship team, a small group gathered after the service for the anointing with oil and laying on of hands. Brett didn't often attend church and was somewhat sceptical that prayer and some kind of oil could dissolve things such as the tumour lodged in Jodi's leg. However, he didn't want to discourage her, so he came along up to the front while a group of five or six laid hands on her leg, and prayed.

Jodi got up and told everyone what had happened over the past week. She looked peaceful and happy. She said she could see order in the chaos and she gave thanks for her situation. She talked about Sharon, who lost her new baby, and of other suffering she had already seen at the hospital, and related that her condition was certainly not the worst.

However, as she and Brett arrived at the doors of the hospital the next afternoon, they were both dreading what lay ahead. Jodi turned to Brett. "Remember when I was scared to come here to have a baby? And now I have to get my leg cut off. If I had a choice now, having a baby would seem so easy!"

Brett gripped her hand, interlacing her fingers with his. He gave her hand a squeeze. "I want you to know, that no matter what happens, I would have done everything the same way. I have no regrets about anything we've done together."

"Yeah," she smiled. "Me too. But I feel sort of betrayed that God didn't heal my leg yesterday. The lump is still there. I was really hoping and praying I wouldn't have to go through with this."

"I'm sorry you got your hopes up, Jo. It wasn't realistic I guess."

At 5:00 p.m. the doctors met with the young couple and gave them the bad news gently. The biopsy was back from Mayo and somewhere else in the states. It looked very serious - a very rare form of bone cancer called 'Fibrosarcoma'. There wasn't much information other than this type of bone cancer was characterized by a fast-growing invasive tumour. The doctors advised surgery right away. An opening was available in O.R. the next day - Tuesday, or the day after tomorrow. They needed a decision.

After only a moment's hesitation, Jodi chose Tuesday. She felt there was no use putting it off, and with Christmas only three weeks away, every extra day that her leg had to heal would be an advantage.

The amputation was scheduled for 2 p.m. Tuesday, December 7th. It was a long day of waiting. Jodi couldn't have anything to eat or drink, and as the day progressed, her thirst increased by the hour. Surgery was postponed until three-thirty, then four, then five p.m. The stress of waiting was terrible. Carol and Marnie were there most of the day, trying to give moral support to Brett, and pouring out their love and concern for their brave little sister. Jodi was calm. She did not cry or show any fear about the approaching operation, and waved serenely when she was finally wheeled away to O.R.

Brett, Carol, and Marnie went to the cafeteria and tried to eat something, but no one had an appetite. The knives in their hands were grim reminders that the one they all loved so much was under the knife right now, having her leg sawed off above the knee.

Several hours later, the family was notified that the operation went well. Relief flooded over them. They stayed until Jodi was wheeled back into her room. She was heavily sedated and the nurses were busy with her vital signs. There was nothing the family could do tonight. They went home, exhausted.

CHAPTER THIRTY-SEVEN

Jodi's first day as an amputee was tough on all of them. Marnie and Carol hung back; curious, yet reluctant to look upon the space where Jodi's leg once was. As Brett bent to kiss her, Jodi tried to be brave, but as she reached for him and put her arms around his neck, the tears came immediately. Her throat hurt, and the pain from the wound was terrible, despite being 'frozen' from the hip down.

The Pain Team was called in to boost the dosage, making things more comfortable for her. She slept on and off, while the family was shown how to change the dressing, and wrap the stump with a tensor bandage. They practiced on a cylindrical piece of foam. They were also kept busy with phone calls and visitors. The room filled with flowers and gifts from friends and family. By late afternoon, Jodi was able to eat some soup and make jokes about the nifty diet she had just gone on. "Yes," she quipped, " I lost fifteen pounds in just two hours."

Four days later, all the tubes were removed, and Jodi could slide onto a wheelchair to tour around the hospital. She had lots of phantom pain and itching, but she did her best to ignore it as she went with the family to the cafeteria, to the games room, or by herself to the little chapel.

By the sixth day, Jodi was doing so well, the doctors said she could go home - first to the Delaney's for a few days, and then if she continued to improve and have no problems, she could go home to the farm for Christmas.

Her happiness was somewhat subdued by the Oncology doctors, who dropped in to see the family just as Jodi got back from Physio and her crutch walking session. A treatment program was being set up. They had to give her a little time to get over the massive surgery she had just undergone, but the Oncologists were afraid to wait too long. They felt there was an eighty percent chance that other cancer cells were in the body. Dr. Jansen looked serious when he said, "Once they show up, it's usually too late. We'll be hitting you pretty hard with heavy doses of three drugs."

Jodi felt numb and sad as Dr. Jansen outlined the course of chemotherapy treatments and indicated what the side effects might be. He said, "I'm sorry about your long hair. It usually starts to fall out after the first treatment". Then he cracked a smile. "But you'll look really cute with short hair when it starts to come back in. It might even be curly." Brett looked shocked, and Jodi wasn't amused at Dr. Jansen's attempts to be light-hearted. They had tried not to think about this part of the treatment, but now it was looming over them like a dark cloud.

After lunch, a nurse from the cancer ward came to visit Jodi, bringing her a booklet of information on the procedures she would be going through in Clinic, and finally, when she had gone, the long process of discharge began.

Comfortably ensconced on the couch at her sister's home that evening, Jodi was surrounded by love and attention from everyone. The girls and Jake all wanted to help their Auntie Jodi as much as possible by arranging her pillows, or bringing her a drink, or more pain killing pills. There was a lot of excitement about Christmas, and all three in turn brought the Wish Book to show Jodi what they hoped Santa would bring. The Delaney family all wanted Jodi and Brett, and Christopher too of course, to be with them for what might be Jodi's last Christmas. Jodi knew that thought was in the minds of her dear sisters, but she felt a fierce love and loyalty to her own home, and if it was to be her last, she wanted to spend it on her own beloved farm.
On day ten after the operation, Jodi returned to the hospital to have the eighteen stitches removed and undergo a heart-stress test. The young, smiling nurse explained, "We need to see what your heart looks like normally now, before your chemo starts. The Adriamycin you'll be receiving sometimes causes the heart

muscle to enlarge, so we'll need to monitor any changes that take place."

At the Outpatient's Department, Jodi and Brett were able to borrow a collapsible wheelchair, and the two set off bravely into downtown Vancouver to do their Christmas shopping. As Brett pushed her chair through the maze of aisles packed with busy shoppers, he muttered grimly, "This isn't exactly what I had in mind, when I promised to bring you back to the big city for a holiday."

Jodi, sensing the exasperation in his voice, shrugged and gave him a thin smile. "Yeah, things sure didn't turn out as we planned. But let's try to have fun, okay? Once I start chemo, outings like this will be few and far between."

They arrived back at the big house, laden with parcels and exhausted from the long day. It had been too much for Jodi. That night, while negotiating the two steps down to the bathroom, she fell - her crutches clattering noisily on the tile floor. Brett leaped up and was at her side immediately, cradling her in his arms, alternately soothing her with soft words, and cussing the unfairness of it all. She was not hurt, but the pain from the severed leg, the itching, and the tiredness caused them both to toss and turn; sleepless for the rest of the night.

When Brett tried to put his arm around her or touch her, Jodi pushed him away, complaining that she was too fidgety to be held. She knew she had hurt his feelings, and that he was only trying to comfort her, but she couldn't help it.

The next evening, the family held a small Christmas celebration. They exchanged gifts, played games, sang the beloved carols around the piano, and ate too much rich food. Carol came, bringing Tony, a photographer whom she was dating. He wanted Carol to come to his family's home on Saltspring Island for Christmas, and Jodi could see that her sister was pulled in two directions. She was relieved and happy when Carol told her she'd be coming home with them to the farm. Carol knew in her heart that if it was meant to be, other opportunities with Tony would arise, but Jodi needed her more just now.

Jodi worried needlessly about Christmas preparations, for when the three of them arrived home, they found Carmen busy in the kitchen baking pies. Trays of fresh buns were cooling on the counter, and a delicious aroma of roasting meat wafted to their senses. There was a huge evergreen wreath on the door, and as they moved from welcoming hugs and kisses in the kitchen to the living room where a cheery fire blazed, Jodi was delighted to find a huge pine tree in place, all decorated, with many brightly wrapped gifts underneath.

Christopher's big, blue eyes registered shock and surprise when he first saw his mom on crutches and with her left leg missing. Then, hesitating only a moment, he ran to her side, hugging her around the hips. He looked up at her with his angelic smile. "Oh Mommy! You are so brave! Does it hurt lots?" Without waiting for an answer, he babbled on, " I been saying my prayers every night for you! Do you like the tree? Poppa and Grandma and I did it. And look at all the presents! And Santa hasn't even been here yet!" After a quick hug for his daddy, and his Auntie Carol, he was off on the run to help bring in the boxes and bags from the car.

Over the next few days, and right up until Christmas, Jodi was swamped with visitors and phone calls. Friends and neighbours all wanted to offer sympathy and support. The farmhouse filled up with beautiful red poinsettias, boxes of oranges, tins full of shortbread, Christmas cakes, hams, sides of bacon, and roasts of beef. The church ladies came for tea, bringing with them a sizable cheque. Many Christmas cards held cash or cheques along with the good wishes. An executive from the airline in Castle River phoned to tell her that they had been made aware of her condition, and that they would be donating free air travel for herself, Brett, and Christopher anytime they needed it, for as long as her treatment lasted. Jodi was overwhelmed with the outpouring of generosity shown by so many friends and strangers alike.

Christmas passed in a blur of activity. The Taylor family came from Kelso. Rick was home from his oilfield job out in Alberta. He had left West Kokanee Power after a year, looking for change, adventure, and big money. He found all three, plus plenty of good-looking women to keep him company through the long winter nights.

He and Brett were like school kids again; teasing, roughhousing, and bantering nonsense back and forth. Bev had come, bringing her fiancée Chad Williams, a quiet, serious young man with sandy hair and a golden voice. He sang and harmonized with Jodi as she played her guitar, with everyone joining in on the choruses.

Bev now managed the insurance business that her father had started, and hoped that his son would carry on. She worked well with her dad - something Brett never could have done - and had brought new ideas and innovations into the office that kept the business competitive and growing.

Bruce was proud of her, and of Brett too, and all they were accomplishing. It was a terrible thing to have their young lives marred by Jodi's illness, and he hoped fervently that his precious daughter-in-law would not be lost to them.

In the afternoon, while the turkey was slowly roasting to perfection, everyone trooped outside into the snow and dazzling sunshine for a walk. Janet, Ronnie and Christopher wanted to ride the horses, so Brett caught Old Pete and Blossom and put the saddles on. Jodi stood in the snow on her crutches, watching Torchy gallop the length of the corral, slide to a stop, spin, and gallop back to the gate again, flinging her long, blond mane wildly as she whinnied her distress at being left alone. She was *so* beautiful! Jodi longed to ride her.

She knew Brett would be upset with her, but she hobbled over to where he was adjusting the stirrups for Ronnie, and said, "Honey, will you get Torchy for me? I want to go too."

He looked at her in disbelief. "You can't ride her! She's like a time bomb ready to go off! I don't want you to get dumped off and hurt." Seeing the disappointment in her eyes, he added in a softer tone, " I don't think you should try to ride yet."

"How about if you and Rick lead her? She'll be happy to follow the others, and you two could work up an appetite for supper."

Brett still looked sceptical, but Rick chimed in, "Sure, I'll lead her for you. If you do fall off, the snow is soft. You won't hurt yourself." Flashing him a grateful smile, Jodi told him where to find the halter.

So Torchy was brought out too. She settled down and stood quietly as soon as she was tied alongside her pasture pals. Brett saddled her while Jodi stood at her head, stroking her velvety nose and talking to her. She leaned her crutches against the fence as Ronnie and Jan mounted. Brett lifted Christopher up behind Jan on Old Pete, and Rick scooped Jodi up in his arms and lifted her onto Torchy. Jodi settled her right leg into the stirrup, and grasped the saddle horn. She had never had to 'grab leather' before, but as Torchy pranced behind the other horses, led by Rick and Brett, Jodi felt out of balance, and somewhat precarious without her left leg.

Torchy seldom walked, especially at the beginning of a ride; she had so much pent up energy. Jodi could feel her mare's legs snapping up under her, as if she were on coiled springs. She closed her eyes and willed her body to find its center of balance and move with the rhythm of the horse. She found it a challenge and was grateful for the two young, strong men at her side; one to control the spirited mare, and the other to grab her if she started to fall. She relaxed then, and began to enjoy the ride, listening happily to the easy chatter between the cousins. Someone, (she couldn't remember who) had told her down at the hospital, to 'take one day at a time', and to 'find joy in small pleasures'. She knew this whole thing would be easier if she didn't look too far ahead, worrying about the future.

In less than an hour, the horses and riders arrived back at the barn. Jodi swung her good leg over Torchy's neck, and slid down into Brett's waiting arms. Her cheeks were rosy from the cold, and her eyes sparked with life and excitement. Brett felt a jolt of desire for her as he held her tight.

She kissed him, lightly and quickly on the lips, whispering "Thank-you", and then she turned and took the crutches Rick was holding out to her, and slipped them under her arms. The spell broken, Brett turned to un-saddling the horses and putting them away.

Much later that night, after the excellent turkey dinner had been consumed, the carols sung, the new toys, books, and games enjoyed, and the guests either gone to the Sr. Randall's to sleep or bedded down on the couch and in the extra bedroom, Jodi and Brett prepared for sleep too. She flushed her broviac line, took some more Tylenol with Codeine, and let Brett wrap her stump in a fresh bandage.

As Brett gently folded the length of elastic around, over, and under what was left of Jodi's leg, the same feeling came over him that he had experienced earlier in the day when he had held her in his arms. He raised his deep blue eyes to hers, and she saw the question there - saw the need, the longing, the wish that things could just be normal between them.

Jodi took his face between her hands and pulled him gently towards her, leaning back against the pillows on the bed. Their eyes held each other until their closeness made everything blurry, and then they closed as their lips opened to each other in delicious, intimate, kisses. Brett's hands roamed over her body, and he sighed in pleasure as Jodi massaged the muscles of his bare, broad, shoulders and back.

He couldn't believe it then, when Jodi pushed him away a little, placing her hands against his chest. Again her eyes held his as she said softly, "I know what you want, and what you need...but it just isn't possible. I'm sorry."

"What do you mean, not possible?" Brett stammered, looking shocked. "I'll be very, very, gentle. I promise...please, I won't hurt you."

He looked so adorable, and so hurt, that Jodi's heart almost broke, looking at him. But she steeled herself and turned away, lying down on her side with her back to him. "We can't," she said simply. "We just can't. I'm off the pill now, and I just can't take a chance on getting pregnant."

Brett didn't answer. He couldn't believe that she was turning him away after the way she had kissed him, and let him touch her; let him believe that they were going to make love. He lay on his back; frustration, anger and disillusionment washing over him.

Jodi reached over and turned off the bedside lamp. She wiggled under the covers. Still Brett lay on top; not moving, not speaking. She turned over and laid her cheek against his shoulder. It felt cold. She slipped her arm around him and squeezed. He ignored her.

"Sweetie," she began. "I love you so much...you don't know how much it breaks my heart to do this to you."

"Then, don't!" came the terse reply out the darkness.

"Come on, get under the covers. You're freezing!"

"That's okay. ...I have to cool off. Maybe I should go take a cold shower too."

He still sounded hurt, and angry.

Jodi tried again. "Honey, when I start chemo, I'm going to be sick for a long time. My hair will be gone, and I'll be susceptible to infections. I'll bleed easily. I'll be weak and scrawny, and ugly." She paused, searching for words. "Somehow, I have to put away my personal desires and concentrate my energies on getting through those awful treatments. There won't be any place for sex in our lives for a long time." She added with a touch of a smile, "Haven't you heard that abstinence makes the heart grow fonder?"

"That's *absence*, you ninny!" he answered, thawing a little. Jeez! He *was* getting cold! He pulled back the heavy quilt and gratefully snuggled under its warmth, reaching for her again.

"I know all that's coming, " Brett said huskily, "and I try not to think about it...but, what about now, why not tonight?"

"Because...I still have a lot of pain, both real and phantom...like right now, I feel like there's a red hot nail in my foot - the one that's not there. Because...as I said before, I'm not on the pill, and I know you don't have any condoms. And because...well...I want to hold on to the memory of the last time we made love - in front of the blazing fire when I still had *both* of my legs, and I didn't have this stupid tube hanging out of my chest that we have to be so careful of..."

Her voice broke, and Brett heard her sniff a few times, trying to hold back the tears. He held her tenderly; kissed her cheek. "It's all right; I'm not mad anymore. It's just that - well, how am I supposed to cope with this? "

"I don't know. I'm sorry. It's always been a highlight of our relationship, but it has to change now. It won't ever be the same. You have to learn to deal with it."

"It's not fair," he grumbled.

"I know that," Jodi said patiently. "It's not fair to you, but more than that, the whole thing is not fair to me. I've accepted that. You'll have to come to terms with it too."

Suddenly, Brett realized he'd been thinking only of his own physical needs; needs that were nothing compared to what she had faced, and was still to endure. He felt very small, very insecure, and very weak. He knew she was right. They were silent for a while, still holding on to each other, but more in a comforting embrace now, than in a lover's tangle.

The codeine was starting to make Jodi drowsy now. She kissed him on the lips, not in a passionate way, but as a mother would kiss her child. "Goodnight, my love," she whispered. "Thanks for a wonderful Christmas. I'm so glad I could be here with all of you. "We're so lucky to have such a great family."

"Yeah, we are. Goodnight, Princess. I love you."

Jodi turned over again, away from him. He snuggled against her back, his arm over her protectively, his hand holding one of hers. They slept.

CHAPTER THIRTY-EIGHT

"Wow, this is weird!" exclaimed Jodi, as she awkwardly crutched her way down the narrow aisle to a vacant double seat half way down the bus. "Almost exactly five years ago, you and I were leaving on a bus like this, for Vancouver." She plopped into the seat, and handed her crutches to Carol, who put them up on the overhead rack. She got a few overt stares from people who were probably wondering how she lost her leg, but she ignored them.

Carol slid into the seat beside her. Jodi sighed deeply, and laid her head back, closing her eyes. "Sure was hard to leave Brett then," she said softly, "and it isn't any easier now. Now, I have even more to lose - my son, my horses, my home." She promised herself she wouldn't cry, but tears glistened for a moment on her eyelashes, then spilled over and ran down her cheeks. She wiped them away, impatiently, and tried to smile. "At least this time, we only have to ride this bus to Castle River. I hate that long drive to Vancouver."

"Me too," agreed Carol. "The flight is so quick, and its great that your fare is paid for now. You'll be home again in a week or ten days. It's not like you'll be leaving everything behind forever."

"Yeah, I know... it's just that I hate good-byes, and it seems like I have to deal with them over and over again."

Jodi and Brett had talked it over, and decided that since Carol was going back to Vancouver, she could accompany Jodi this time. They had to be realistic. Brett had already taken three weeks off to be with Jodi during her surgery and for Christmas. The mortgage and other bills had to be paid. Brett could not afford to be away from his job any longer, and he still had a course to complete at college. As much as Jodi wanted him to be with her, she knew he needed to stay home and keep things under control there. Anyway, her sisters were much better than he was at handling the tedious waiting and boredom of being confined to hospital.

Carol's friend Tony met them at the airport, and drove them to the hospital, waiting while Jodi checked in to the dreaded Cancer Ward, and had a short meeting with her doctors. Then Carol and Tony took Jodi out for a wonderful steak dinner. They drank wine, and laughed, and tried not to think of the tribulation Jodi must face alone tomorrow.

Jodi began her chemo at eleven the next morning with good tolerance of Vincristine and Cyclophosphamide. The third drug, Adriamycin, was started at three-thirty in the afternoon.

That evening, she told Marnie, Carol, and the girls who had come to visit, "I don't feel too bad. I think I can handle it okay." But by bedtime Jodi was restless.

She was having hot and cold spells, a headache, and a stomach ache. She felt awful, and was suddenly very lonely, scared, and unhappy.

The New Year dawned while Jodi lay in her hospital bed, barely able to function because of the pain in her jaw, mouth, and neck. Her leg hurt too.

"It's the Vincristine," her young nurse, Diana, explained. "The symptoms usually occur about three days after you get it."

Jodi replied, with a raspy voice from her sore throat, but with an attempt at a smile, "it says somewhere in the Bible that you should give thanks in all situations. I'm just thankful that my husband doesn't have to see me like this. When he phoned last night, I didn't sound this bad." Diana smiled in sympathy, and gave her some Ondansetron for her nausea, and some Codeine for her pain. Soon, she slept.

Jodi endured another day of nausea, vomiting, and pain, while the Adriamycin dripped slowly through her broviac lines.

Much to her disappointment, she learned that even though the chemo was finished at three-thirty, she still had to stay hooked up to the pump for another night to be hydrated. She hated the tubes, and longed to be free of them, but she devised a way to get away from the crushing boredom of her room and the TV with its mindless programs. She could slide into her wheelchair, and by hooking the stand of her I.V. unit into the space where her left foot would have rested, she could push the pump in front of her and go exploring.

That night, after her visitors left, Jodi wheeled down to the Children's Ward at the end of the hall. Missing Christopher as much as she did, she was curious to see the little ones, and wondered if she could possibly help by reading stories or keeping a lonesome child company.

In the Family Room she saw a very young mother trying to shush a fussy baby while she warmed a bottle for him in the microwave. Jodi wheeled on over. "Could I hold him for you while you heat that up?" she offered. The girl looked questioningly at Jodi, then smiled and passed her the baby. She seemed relieved. "What's his name?" asked Jodi, as she put the little squirming body up to her shoulder and patted his back.

"Christopher", came the answer.

"Christopher?" repeated Jodi, as she looked up sharply. "That's *my* little boy's name too! He's four years old, and he's got blond, curly hair, and big blue eyes just like his daddy's." Then she held out her hand. "I'm Jodi Randall, from Harrison. I've just finished my first chemo. I had a tumour in my leg."

The young girl smiled, and held out her hand. "Cindy Shumi. We live in Richmond. That's my husband Tom over there. Jodi glanced over to where a young, bearded, Japanese man sat watching TV. Cindy looked to be about Jodi's age. She had short, straight, light brown hair, and her face was dotted with freckles. She looked tired and worried. Her soft brown eyes filled with tears as she took the fussy baby back from Jodi, offering him the warm milk from the bottle.

Cindy spoke sadly, "Christopher is five months old. He has a tumour on his optic nerve, right between his eyes. He's already had surgery, as you can see from this great big scar on his head. He's supposed to start chemo tomorrow, if he's well enough."

Jodi said, "I'm sorry, Cindy. That's so sad." She stayed and talked with her for a while. Tom came over and chatted too. They'd been married for two years. Christopher was their first baby.

Jodi wheeled back to her own room, and crawled up into bed for the night. She waited for her medication, but it didn't help much. She couldn't sleep for thinking about that baby, and the distress his young parents were going through. Tears slid down her cheeks, as she prayed for that little Christopher, and for her own. She was thankful tonight that it was she, and not her child that had to suffer through this terrible illness.

Jodi was able to go home with Marnie the next day. She wanted desperately to go to her own home, but the doctors thought she should stay close by in case problems developed from the chemo. After three days of lying around, regaining her strength and her appetite, Jodi phoned Dr. Jansen and convinced him to let her go home. She told him how knowledgeable and conscientious her own family doctor in Harrison was, and suggested that the team in Vancouver keep in touch with Dr. Houston. Jodi's doctor relented, called and talked to Dr. Houston, and got back to Jodi.

"You were right," he chuckled. "I'm very impressed with your doctor up there. She's right up to date on your case, and understands it completely. She's been doing her homework."

"Does this mean I can go home between treatments, then"? asked Jodi enthusiastically.

"Yes, I'd say so." Dr. Jansen agreed. "Your doctor in Harrison will be a part of our team. If anything out of the ordinary happens - a rash, a fever, a bump on your big toe - anything - you let her know, and she'll phone me, and we'll be on top of any problem immediately, okay?"

"Okay! That's great!" enthused Jodi. "See you on the 24th then."

Next, she had to convince her family that she could manage just fine by herself at the airport. She carried her luggage in a small rucksack on her back and she was very adept at using her crutches. The flight was only an hour, and the bus ride to Harrison another hour and a half. Reluctantly, the sisters waved goodbye at the airport, as Jodi disappeared into a sea of faces.

Brett, Christopher, and Scamp met her in Harrison several hours later. Brett thought she looked tired, as they drove to his mom and dad's for supper, but he could detect no real difference in her appearance. He could not imagine what Jodi had just been through.

Although Jodi loved being home, she found the days long and frustrating. There was so much she could not do.

Since their car was a standard, Jodi could not drive Christopher to Playschool, so Brett continued to take him in the morning. Carmen picked him up and took him to her house, until Brett came for him after work. That was only two days a week, but Jodi found those days long and lonely without the little guy around. She could go out and visit with the horses, but she could not climb the ladder into the loft to get their hay, nor could she carry the bales, or even flakes of hay, let alone a bucket of feed. She found she could scatter wheat for the chickens and collect the eggs, but trying to carry water to them was a frustrating, futile task. No matter how smooth she tried to be on the crutches, the bucket bumped against them, spilling the water down her good leg where it instantly froze.

Inside, Jodi could not accomplish much either. She could make a meal by hopping on one foot around the kitchen, or by standing at the stove leaning on the crutches for support. She was slow and awkward; she tired easily; she dropped things, and she even fell a few times when she tried to move too fast.

In the evenings, Brett worked on his electrical course at the kitchen table while Jodi read to Christopher and helped him with his bath before bed. She usually went to bed early too. She guessed it was the after-effects of the chemo, causing her to feel so tired. Brett wandered around the house at night - restless and at loose ends. He'd make a snack and stay up to watch the evening news, then slip silently into bed beside his wife.

They were married, yet could not be as man and wife. "Damn this cancer!" he cursed to himself as he forced himself not to touch Jodi in the ways he used to do. The first night she had been home, he had held her in his arms as she related in detail how it felt to have chemo - the fear and repulsion of having strong chemicals coursing through your body; the nausea, the vomiting, the aching teeth; the headaches and stomach aches that accompanied the treatment.

Brett felt sick with fear and remorse as she related her experience in hospital. And the horror of it was that she had to go back and do it again, and again, and again.

In a voice choking with emotion, he promised her, "I won't make any demands on your body. I understand what you're going through, and I know you can't deal with my needs too. It's okay."

But it wasn't okay, really. Brett felt lonely, sexually frustrated, and angry. He didn't know how to handle it. He felt that he and Jodi were drifting apart; living in different worlds almost, and he knew it was only going to get worse.

Jodi was still bothered by the pain in her stump; in fact, it wasn't getting any better. She had seen enough wounds and injuries at the Vet Clinic to know that her incision wasn't healing properly.

To make matters worse, when Jodi awoke on her last Saturday at home before returning to the hospital, her pillow was covered in clumps of long hair. Hopping to the bathroom, she looked with horror at her rapidly thinning hair. Although she had expected it, she could see her own shock registered in her wide eyes reflecting back at her in the mirror. She brushed her hair carefully, only to have much more come away on the brush.

Christopher came in, and sat on the edge of the tub. He regarded Jodi with his huge, solemn blue eyes. "Mommy, why is your hair coming out like that?"

She forced a smile, realizing that she should have prepared him for this, as she had for the amputation. "Oh, it's just the strong medicine they gave me in the hospital. It makes *all* your hair fall out. Pretty soon I won't have any eyebrows or lashes either. But don't worry, Honey. It will all grow back when I finish my treatment," She dared not tell him how long that treatment would last.

"You mean, you're going to be bald? Like Mr. Clean?" Christopher's baby-blue eyes sparkled and his little serious face lit up in glee as his hands flew to his open mouth to suppress a giggle. "You're going to look real funny, Mom!"

"Yeah. Thanks kid." Jodi gave him a playful poke in the ribs with the brush. As he shrieked and dived to get away, she heard the kitchen door slam downstairs as Brett came in from doing the chores.

"Quick Chris, run down and ask Daddy to bring in the horse clippers, okay? Hurry, before he takes his boots off."

"Okay!" Holding his arms out as if he were an airplane, the little boy roared off complete with sound effects to deliver the message.

Shaky from standing on one leg for so long, and upset at her appearance, Jodi sat down on the closed lid of the toilet seat. She choked back tears. "It's nothing to cry about," she told herself fiercely. "I knew it would happen. I just wasn't expecting it so soon."

When Brett came back with the clippers, he wasn't sure what to expect. Christopher had told him excitedly, "Mom's hair is coming out by the handfuls!"

Brett was shocked to see how thin it had suddenly become, and as he bent to kiss her cheek, he saw Jodi tighten her jaw as she clenched her teeth against the tears that threatened to come. He knew she didn't want sentiment, or sympathy now.

He plugged the clippers in and draped a towel around her neck. "Crew-cut, or buzz-cut?" he asked with an infectious grin. Then, with a wink at Christopher who had resumed his seat on the tub, he added, "Mom's gonna look like a boy!"

Jodi closed her eyes and sighed. "Just shave it all off. It's all falling out anyway."

It hurt both of them to see what was left of Jodi's beautiful hair fall to the floor and be swept up and into the garbage. Her long, dark, silky tresses had been one of the first things Brett had noticed and liked about her. He always loved to touch it, and he loved the way it cascaded around and over them when they made love. Now, both of those things were gone.

Later at breakfast, Christopher asked, "Mom, are you going to come and watch me skate today?" Jodi groaned inwardly, wincing at the thought of going out in public with no hair. She felt naked; vulnerable.

"Umm..." she hesitated, casting a desperate glance at Brett. "I...don't think so."

"Aww...why not?" The little boy's face registered disappointment, and Jodi immediately felt guilty. Brett looked at her sharply.

"Jo, we want you to come. You should see how good he's getting. I hardly have to hold him up anymore." Then, as he rose from the table with his empty plate in one hand, Brett dropped his other hand onto her shoulder as he passed by and said, "Honey, you can't stay home and hide just because your hair is gone. You might as well get used to it. Put a toque and a smile on, and make the best of it. We really want you to be with us as much as possible."

Jodi nodded, looking sad. She knew he was right. It wasn't fair to take it out on their son, just because she was feeling sorry for herself. She knew she had to take each opportunity to be together and treasure it, because there might not be much time left for them as a family. Forcing a smile, she said, "You're right. Of course I'll come."

Christopher was happy again. "Yay!" he yelled. He launched into an elaborate description of how he was learning the snowplow, the stop, the T-start, and the spin.

So Jodi went, and was glad she did. It was fun to watch her men on the ice -

one so small and clumsy, but trying so hard to be like his dad; Brett so fast and lithe, and graceful. His feet crossed over so effortlessly, his spins were impressive, and his stops sudden, but always under control. He had always been so athletic.

Jodi loved following his graceful body around and around; his unruly blond hair flying out and around his fine-looking face.

Brett held hands with some teenage girls and they formed a 'whip' around the arena, shrieking with mock fear as they swooped around the corners at breakneck speed. He broke off from the girls, and skated up to where Jodi leaned over the boards watching, and stopped so fast he sent a shower of ice crystals over her face. Then, laughing, he was off again, this time to take his son by the hand and help him around at a slower pace.

Jodi had to laugh too. It reminded her of the times before they were married, when he would flirt with the girls, then come to her and kiss her, just to let her know that he loved her and that his actions were just frivolous, harmless nonsense.

After skating, Brett took them for burgers and ice cream. Then they stopped in for a visit with Carmen and Bruce before returning home.

In two days, Jodi would be back in hospital facing a New Year of what? Hope?

Despair? Anger? Frustration? She wasn't sure, but holding on to happy memories like today was going to help her cope with whatever came her way.

CHAPTER THIRTY-NINE

Back in hospital, Jodi waited to see Dr. Jansen in the Oncology Clinic. One by one, the patients were called for their blood work and other tests. She didn't feel too conspicuous without her hair. Over half of the people waiting were bald from the effects of chemo.

Jodi drank coffee and read magazines, feeling too depressed to talk to anybody. She was last. The nurse brought her the 'roadmap' or protocol treatment schedule for the nine months of chemo. It looked strange and wrong, but Jodi couldn't think why, as the doctor talked to her about her three weeks at home and checked her over.

Afterwards, Jodi had a chance to read the schedule and realized with a shock that she would be called in after this and each chemo every *two* weeks, not *three!* Also, a lot of tests had been scheduled throughout the treatment - meaning she would have to come in *between* chemos! This was awful! She also had not realized that each chemo was in two parts - 'A' being the four-day she had already had, and 'B' being a five-day treatment with two different drugs, Ifosphamide, and VP 16. So that meant she would endure chemo eighteen times, not nine!

Jodi was already homesick and lonesome. The shock was too much;

realizing that sometimes she wouldn't be able to return to the farm. Jodi tried to read a magazine, but found it impossible. Tears were blurring her vision.

When the nurse came to get Jodi and found her crying, she tried in vain to comfort her. Looking at the schedule, she affirmed what Jodi had such trouble accepting. "Yes," Jean said, "You'll be here for two weeks out of every month. The specialists feel that this is a very serious form of cancer, and they have to attack it as aggressively as they can."

Double the time here? No way! Jodi raged inwardly as the tears continued to roll down her face.

Her chemo was started in Clinic, as the cancer cluster was full. Jean kept up a steady chatter as she took notes, monitored blood pressure and pulse. Quite a while later, Jodi was moved to a bed in the ward. She was still crying and scarcely noticed her roommate, a lady of about forty, who was watching a movie.

Dorothy, the cluster nurse, tried to talk to her, but Jodi wasn't able to tell her why she was crying. It was just so many things! She felt devastated. Her head ached and she felt dizzy, and sick. In a little while, Sandy, the Social Worker, was called in. The two women got Jodi into a wheelchair and took her down to the conference room - the same one where Jodi had got the bad news about her biopsy results. Sandy talked with her for forty-five minutes or so. Jodi had been crying for five hours! *Where did all the tears come from?* Jodi wondered. She was drained, hungry, and exhausted, but she was grateful to Sandy for her kind and sympathetic understanding

The next day, Sandy returned with Dr. Jansen to see how Jodi was. "Better," she smiled bravely, although she still felt weepy and shaky. Dr. Jansen expressed how sorry he was, but they were trying to do the best they could for her.

"You see," he said, measuring his words carefully, "we have to make this year miserable for you, in order for you to live the rest of your life cancer free. If we don't use drastic measures now, it will kill you."

Jodi nodded her understanding. "I know. I understand. But it still doesn't make it any easier." They visited and chatted a bit more, and Jodi expressed concern over the increased pain and sensitivity at the end of her stump. The shape had changed from flat across to a definite 'pointy' end, and all agreed that the bone was growing again. It was the body's desperate attempt to heal itself. The muscle had shrunk and was stuck to the bone in one spot, causing pain. The doctor suggested that it might have to be trimmed back again. Meanwhile, the nurses were to massage it with cream. That hurt!

Jodi didn't have time to think about possible surgery due to the stream of visitors that came by all afternoon and evening. Jo-Anne, from Physio, came by with Steffen, the Prosthetist who was to make an artificial leg for her. Her roommate, Maureen, (who Jodi found out had breast cancer) had friends and family drop in, and they talked to Jodi too. Luigi, the Psychologist, came in for a chat, and later, Marnie, Robert, Lori, Lisa and Jake all crowded into the room. Jodi was tired, but happy to see them all.

"That was great timing," she said, beaming. "I just threw up a few minutes ago. Let's go down to the coffee shop for a snack. I just lost everything I ate today, and that wasn't much." She told her family, "These two drugs I get on this part of the chemo only run for an hour each morning. I get nauseous in the afternoon and early evening, but then it's not too bad."

When all the visitors had left, Jodi wheeled herself down to the Children's Cluster. It was late, but she wanted to see if Tom and Cindy were there. She had been thinking a lot about little Christopher. As soon as she pushed open the door, she heard the plaintiff wail of the baby. Tom was walking the floor with him, looking exasperated. As Jodi approached, he looked at her quizzically. "Jodi?"

"Yeah, it's me." She smiled. "My hair's gone now too. How's he doing?"

"Not good," Tom said sadly. Jodi reached for the baby, and Tom passed him into her arms.

"Why don't we go for a walk?" suggested Jodi. "If you could push me, I could hold him. The motion might stop the crying. It used to work for my baby."

Relieved to try anything, Tom agreed, and they set off down the hall, catching up on the events that had happened to both of them over the past three weeks.

Christopher's cries lessened to a whimper as Tom pushed Jodi's chair up and down the quiet corridors. Jodi learned that Cindy had gone home for a few days to get some rest. The baby cried almost continuously, and the nurses just didn't have time to hold him constantly. Tom came in the evenings after work and stayed until ten or eleven at night. The gruelling regime was pretty rough on him and his wife. The doctors had told the couple that there was no hope, but Cindy and Tom refused to believe that.

When they got back to the Cluster, Tom thanked Jodi for her help as he took the sleeping baby from her. "He won't stay asleep for very long," he said, but the night nurses will be on soon and they're very good with him."

Jodi said, "Yep, the staff is very kind here. They try to make it easier for us, and that's a tough job." She wheeled her chair around. "Good night Tom. Say hello to Cindy for me."

"Sure will. Good -night. You take care now!"

Jodi had hoped to go back to the Children's Ward the next morning, but found she was scheduled for x-rays of her chest and stump.

Dr. Jansen came by later when she was having her chemo and told her matter -of- factly. " The x-rays show that the bone is growing, but we can't do anything about it until the growth stops." He added apologetically, "This will likely delay getting an artificial leg built for you, and it will get more painful as the bone pushes against the skin."

Shortly after receiving this unpleasant news, Jodi was sick; then her afternoon flew by with more visits from doctors. It seemed there was quite a lot of concern about her leg - concern that there might be a breakthrough, and then infection. Two Surgeons and an Infection Specialist came to check her out. They weren't sure if they should let her go home.

That night, as she tried to sleep amidst the noise of I.V. units beeping for attention, the regular checks the nurses had to do, and the lights from the nurses' station and the hallway, Jodi turned to memorized scriptures for peace. Over and over she repeated the 23rd Psalm, *The*

Lord is my Shepherd... and when she tired of repeating that one, she recited Psalm 121; *I will lift up mine eyes unto the hills...* Finally exhausted, but no longer worrying about the outcome of the doctor's concerns, she slept.

The next morning, the specialists were back again to see her. Jodi told them, "As much as I hate the idea of more surgery, maybe it would be better to deal with it now, instead of having to come back next week with a problem".

The Infection Specialist chuckled, "Those are brave words, but I think it will be okay for a while. Just be careful at home, and try not to fall or bump it on anything."

Jodi spent the rest of that morning down at the Children's Ward. She had to be back in her room at eleven for her Ifosphamide, but in the meantime, she wanted to see if she could volunteer to help with the kids. Her nurse phoned the Child Life Activity Staff, who welcomed her and introduced her to the children who were well enough to take part in games, crafts, and activities.

First Jodi met Robin, an eleven year old who was on his last treatment for ALLS - 'acute lymphphocytic leukemia'. He had been in and out of hospital for a year on various strong chemo doses, had endured bone marrow aspirations, lumbar punctures, x-rays, scans, ultra-sounds, and finally a bone marrow transplant. Robin's happy face, made round and pudgy by the Prednisone he was taking, smiled at Jodi as she wheeled her chair in and manoeuvred her I.V. unit up to the table.

"Think you could beat me at Chinese Checkers?" Robin grinned. "I'm the Champ around here!"

"I'll give it my best shot." Jodi grinned back. Sitting across the table from Robin was a very pale little girl of about eight.

"This is Sherri," Robin indicated, with a jerk of his head.

Jodi smiled and said, "Hi, I'm Jodi. Will you play with us too?" A slight nod of the head was the only indication that the child had heard. Her eyes looked huge in her small, thin, face, and her movements were slow and deliberate, as if each took a great deal of thought and effort. She had a Wilm's tumour in her left kidney and it was not responding to treatment. Sherri was dying.

Over in the corner, sprawled on beanbag chairs, Jodi caught sight of a little boy about her Christopher's age, and a very tired looking mom. She noticed right away that part of the boy's right leg was missing. All of the kids were bald. A few wore hats, as Jodi did, but most of them didn't seem to care. They were all alike - all fighting a vicious disease. Some were going to be victorious, and some were destined to lose the fight. Jodi found it hard to concentrate on the game. She was strangely moved to watch these little ones coping with their illness.

After Robin beat her twice at Chinese Checkers, Jodi gave him the palms up victory slaps, then excused herself to go over and talk to the little boy in the corner. He had moved from the beanbag chair to a mat on the floor where he lay, with a tangle of lines and tubes protruding from under his Bat Man shirt, connecting him to his I.V.pump. He was listening to a story, but his mom was yawning so much, she could hardly read.

Jodi wheeled her chair and pushed her own I.V. unit across the playroom somewhat awkwardly. The little boy watched her progress and the woman put down the book as she approached. Jodi smiled and held out her hand. "Hello, I'm Jodi. I'm in for my second chemo. I have Osteogenic Sarcoma". The woman, about ten years older than Jodi, shook her hand with a smile.

"Pamela White...pleased to meet you. This is Parker," she said, her eyes resting on the little body with so much love and pain, that Jodi felt tears spring to her eyes. "He has Ewing's Sarcoma. He had a tumour in the marrow of his shinbone. He's just started chemo too."

Parker regarded Jodi with his large, grey eyes, taking in her stump, which was even shorter than his own, her tubes and

I.V. pump; her lack of hair. "Are you a mommy too?" he asked.

"Yes," she smiled. I have a little boy just about your age. He's four and a half now. How old are you?"

Without moving his body, or smiling, Parker held up four fingers. Jodi reached down and grasped them, shaking his hand. "I thought so. You're four. Just like my Christopher!" They chatted a bit, exchanging information, and then Jodi offered to continue reading to Parker so Pamela could go to the Parents Room for a rest. It was exhausting, living by a child's bedside at the hospital, trying to sleep in a strange, noisy environment, and cope with the shock of having a loved one diagnosed with a dreaded life-threatening disease. Pamela looked relieved and grateful as she accepted Jodi's offer. She promised to be back in time for Jodi to return to her ward for her own chemo.

Jodi was sick all afternoon and early evening after the Ifosphamide and VP16 ran through the lines. Sharon, the young woman who had lost her baby back in December, came in to visit but Jodi had a hard time even talking to her between bouts of vomiting. Sharon just held her hand and passed her a tissue and a cold cloth each time she threw up. Sharon felt guilty that she was still grieving for her baby. She was young and healthy and her husband loved her. They could have another child, but Jodi might not live long enough to see her own son grow up.

"Jodi, this is awful", she sympathized. "I'm so sorry you have to go through all of this. What I had to deal with is nothing compared to what you go through every day with this thing."

Jodi laughed. "No, you're wrong, Sharon. This will pass, and I'll forget how awful it was, but you will never forget that pain of losing your first child. You'll put it behind you, and you'll have other children, but no one will ever take the place of baby Sylvie. No, your sorrow is worse than mine, I think."

The two friends hugged, not knowing what else to say, and Sharon made her departure as the doctors came in on rounds.

"Well young lady," Dr. Jansen smiled, "I have good news for you. We've decided to leave you alone for now and just let you go home. Watch it carefully for any changes, and try not to bump it on anything. We'll see how it is when you get back in two weeks."

Jodi was happy and relieved to be going home again. She called Brett that night and told him when to expect her, leaving out the details of a possible revision in the not too distant future. *One day at a time,* she said to herself. *One day at a time!*

CHAPTER FORTY

Jodi's two weeks at home seemed to fly by too fast. It took a few days of rest and quiet before she re-gained her appetite and some degree of strength; but then her once busy mind and body grew restless with the lack of activity.

One afternoon when Carmen picked her and Christopher up to go grocery shopping, Jodi asked her to drive up to the College. She put a touch of lipstick on and adjusted her toque over her ears. Then, while Christopher and Carmen waited in the car, Jodi bravely went in and asked to see a Counsellor. Half an hour later, she came out with a heavy looking canvas bag over her shoulder, which bumped against her side as she crutched to the car.

Carmen knew better than to get out and help her. Jodi liked to manage on her own. She opened the car door, swung the bag of books to the floor, flopped into the seat, pulled her crutches in after her, and slammed the door.

"Well," Jodi said, sounding pleased. "I just enrolled in an English Appreciation course. I need something to work on at home and in hospital. I can't stand the dumb TV shows down there, and I have too much time to think about my illness. I'm hoping this course will help me focus on other things besides cancer."

Carmen gave her a wink and a grin as she pulled out of the parking lot.

"Good for you. I think that's wonderful. Brett will be so proud of you. In fact, we're all terribly proud of you; of the way you're handling all of this."

Jodi shrugged off the compliment. She sighed audibly and deeply. Turning towards Carmen, she said, " I've had some awful times already, trying to deal with it. I've cried a lot, and I've been very depressed and angry. But the way I'm starting to see it now, is that we have a choice. We can be miserable and give in to it, or we can fight it and carry on normally as much as possible, and make the best of things. I've decided to fight."

Later on that week as Jodi took a break from her study of Chaucer to go out for some fresh air, she naturally ended up at the pasture fence, talking to the horses. The snow was deep, soft and powdery; the day sunny and fairly mild. The cats had come with her for a walk, and the old dog, Scamp, sat patiently at her feet waiting for her next move. "Should we go riding Scamp?" she asked. The little black dog wagged his stumpy tail vigorously, and grinned up at her. He hadn't heard those words for a long time.

Not really sure how she was going to manage it, but determined to try, Jodi got Blossom's bridle from the barn and entered the corral. The three horses crowded around her, sniffing her head, and checking her coat pockets for treats.

Jodi gave Torchy a kiss on her velvety chestnut nose. "I'd love to ride you girl, but I'm not ready for your antics yet." Turning to Old Pete, she said fondly, "And you - you great big lug - you're just too darn tall for me to get on!" Slipping the warmed up bit into Blossom's mouth, Jodi said to her, "So it's back to you, little one. You're going to have to teach me to ride again."

Leading the pony out of the corral, Jodi's eyes searched for something she could use to get up on Blossom's back. "Aha! the car." she exclaimed to herself, the dog, and the horse. She managed to push and pull the pony into a position beside the front bumper. Commanding her to 'stand!' Jodi struggled up onto the bumper, where she balanced precariously on one leg, supported by one crutch. Then, laying the crutch aside carefully, she leaned forward, grabbing a handful of Blossom's thick shaggy mane as she swung her 'little leg' as she called it, over her back. Blossom stood resolutely still, bored with the proceedings already, and in no hurry to get going.

"Good girl," cried Jodi - half to herself for making it, and to the pony who had co-operated by not moving. Picking up the reins and squeezing with her one good leg, Jodi steered Blossom up towards the orchard. She hadn't been on a horse since Christmas, when Rick and Brett led her around on Torchy. It felt wonderful to be riding again, even if it was her old gentle pony, and not her fiery high-stepping Morgan.

That night, when supper was finished, and Christopher had been excused to play Lego for a while before bed, Brett and Jodi lingered at the kitchen table, drinking tea.

"I went riding today," she said nonchalantly, watching overtly for his reaction. She certainly got one.

"You what?" Brett's eyes grew wide in alarm and his jaw clenched as he bit back his fear. "You weren't on Torchy, were you?"

Jodi shook her head. She laughed as she rose from the table and hopped over to the counter for the tin of cookies. She placed them on the table and then slipped her arms around Brett's shoulders. She kissed him lightly on the cheek before letting go and moving towards her own chair again.

Brett caught her wrist and pulled her back, setting her on his knee as he swung his chair out from the table. "What have you been up to, young lady?" he asked sternly, but with a hint of a smile at the corners of his sensuous mouth.

His blue eyes looked right into hers, and Jodi felt herself blush as she stammered, "I...I rode Blossom today. I was really careful and I just went slowly. I don't have very good balance." She tried to move away, but Brett held her tight, still looking into her blue eyes that were flecked with green and gold. His own eyes became soft as he visibly relaxed and gazed at her fondly.

"Well I guess that's okay. Just don't get on that high falutin' filly by yourself."

"I won't. Not yet, anyway", Jodi grinned. "Hey, my tea's getting cold. Let me go!"

"Yeah, and I'm getting hot. Give me a kiss first."

"I just did, a minute ago."

"You never kiss me anymore - just a little peck on the cheek once in a while. I want a real kiss; a long, yummy, sexy, hot kiss."

Brett's dreamy blue eyes closed, and his dark, golden lashes lay as delicate as a butterfly's wing against his flushed cheeks. God! He was beautiful! Jodi's heart thumped as she moved her hands around his neck and buried her fingers in his silky hair. She bent to his upturned face, closed her eyes, and pressed her lips to his. Her body came alive with delicious sensations as his hands moved over her hips.

Brett moaned softly as he covered her face with little kisses. "Let's go upstairs," he whispered against her cheek.

Jodi sighed deeply and slid off his knee and onto her own chair. She looked at him sadly, almost regretfully. "I don't think so," she said softly. "We had a deal, remember?"

Brett shifted in his seat and leaned forward, arms on the table. He looked puzzled. "Yeah...but can that be negotiated?"

Jodi covered her face with her hands. She spoke so softly he could hardly hear her. "*That's* why I don't kiss you like that. I'm afraid of where it will lead."

"Afraid?" he burst out. "What the hell are you afraid of?" Jodi didn't answer.

"Oh, I know you're afraid of getting pregnant, but there's more than one way to give and take pleasure."

Jodi tried to explain. She was near tears, and her voice came out high pitched and strained. "I just feel so damned unattractive. I'm in constant pain with this leg bone growing, and....and....I'm bald...and these tubes in my chest are such a nuisance..."

Brett broke in, "I *know* you're still attracted to me. I can tell by the way you look at me, and the way you just kissed me. Do I *look* like you turn me off? Look at the boner you've given me!" Jodi had to smile a little at that.

Brett continued, "I've been your lover for five years. I *still* want to be your lover! Nothing's changed.

"Yes, it has," Jodi said quietly. "Everything's changed. I'm sorry."

Brett was incredulous. He couldn't believe she was turning him down again. He pushed his chair back from the table angrily. "Okay, fine! If that's the way you want it!" He strode towards the stairs, and then turned in the doorway for a parting shot. "If you're well enough to ride a horse, you're well enough to make love with me!" He stomped up the stairs, and in a few minutes Jodi heard the shower running.

She laid her head on her arms and let the hot tears flow. She felt incredibly sad that the situation had turned ugly.

They avoided each other for the rest of the evening, and in the morning, Brett fed the animals and left for work before Jodi got up. Christopher didn't have to go to school today, so there was really no need for her to be up early. Jodi felt sad and depressed all day. Tomorrow she had to go back to Vancouver, and the day after, which was Valentine's Day, she had to start her second round of Chemo A.

That night when Brett came in from doing the evening chores, Jodi met him at the door as he stamped the snow off his boots and hung his coat on a wooden peg. Jodi leaned on her crutches and said simply, "I'm sorry about last night."

He turned and put his arms around her, crutches and all, just holding her for a long moment. "I'm sorry too, Honey. Let's just forget it for now, okay? " He gave her a little hug, but did not kiss her. "What's for supper? It smells delicious."

"Beef stew," she said, smiling and relieved that they were friends again. "I made cloud biscuits too".

The next day at the bus depot as Brett helped Jodi out of his work truck, he tucked a little gift-wrapped parcel into her backpack. "Make sure you're alone when you open this, okay?" She didn't have time to question him as the bus was ready to go, and besides, she could tell by the smug look on this face, that it was for him to know and for her to find out.

Jodi flung her arms around him and hugged him tight. "There's something for you under my pillow at home," she whispered. "See you in about a week. Bye!"

Jodi spent the remainder of the day with Marnie and Rob, watching a movie on TV and just enjoying the company of the family as well as Marnie's wonderful cooking.

Later that night, when she climbed into her old bed in the basement room, Jodi remembered the gift that Brett had sent with her. Overcome with curiosity, she got up and retrieved it from her bag.

Sitting on the edge of the bed, she unwrapped the package to find a box within a box - a small, pink heart-shaped box of chocolates. Opening the lid, Jodi's hand flew to her mouth to stifle a giggle as she realized why Brett had warned her not to open it in the presence of others. Two chocolates were missing, and in their empty spaces, lay two condoms, each neatly packaged. Jodi removed them, read the directions, then hopped over to her pack again, and placed them on the bottom under some clothes.

She selected a chocolate, popping it into her mouth as she lay back in bed, thinking of her husband and lover. *Gotta give him an 'A' for trying,* she mused to herself. *He sure is telling me that he loves me, and wants me.*

Smiling to herself, Jodi resolved to do something about their love life when she got home. As she drifted off to sleep, she thought, *He's right...I can make love with him, and I'd better, if I want to keep him!*

CHAPTER FORTY-ONE

Marnie took Jodi to the hospital in the morning, and stayed while she went through the routine blood work and check-up by Dr. Jansen. The leg was much the same. Jodi went for x-rays of her stump and chest, and then was scheduled for a bone-scan at one thirty. As this was a lengthy process of being injected with a dye, and then waiting for an hour to have a series of pictures taken, Marnie left to be back when the girls got home from school.

Jodi could see her own skeleton on the technician's video monitors, and was overwhelmed with sadness because it looked like a dead body. She prayed continually that no new spots would turn up.

She knew now what to expect from the Adriamycin and Vincristine. Jodi expected to be sick, and she was. She expected pain, discomfort, nausea, restlessness, sore throat, aching teeth, and headaches. She had them all. At no time over the next four days was she able to visit the children or spend any time reading or studying. The days passed in a blur of sickness and sleeping. Jodi was exhausted when the chemo was over, and she could once again go home.

Again, Jodi was thankful for Marnie's help and hospitality for a few days, as she re-covered her strength enough to manage the flight and the bus trip home.

Jodi arrived home in a snowstorm on the afternoon of February 21st. She was vastly relieved to be able to curl up on the couch in a blanket beside the crackling fire with Christopher cuddled up on one side of her and Samantha on the other. Scamp lay at her feet, occasionally rising to lay his head on her remaining knee and gaze at Jodi with devotion. Being home was wonderful, and it was gratifying to know that her family and animals had missed her so much.

Brett treated her with kindness and love, yet he kept his distance physically from her. She thanked him for the chocolates, but made no mention of the contraceptives. He had made himself clear; now it was up to her to make the next move.

Brett was making supper - spaghetti and salad - and at intervals he came in to the little circle of love and warmth to ask a question, or to see if Jodi needed anything. At supper, he asked her, "Jo, what would you like to do for your birthday next weekend?"

"Oh," she said, "I don't know; just a family dinner here would be nice."

"There's a new steakhouse in town," Brett said, twirling his fork in the spaghetti. "What do you think about going out on a date; you know, a nice dinner, a bottle of wine, and maybe a show. Mom would look after Chris."

Jodi was quiet for a moment. Inwardly, she cringed. It made her nervous to have to enter a public place on crutches with only one leg, and although she wore a hat, it didn't completely conceal the fact that she had no hair. On the other hand, Brett did not seem embarrassed to be seen with her like that. She bit her lip, and then smiled at him across the table, looking into the depths of his blue eyes. "That would be real nice, Sweetie. Thanks."

He laughed, looking pleased. "It's a date then. I'll make reservations for Saturday."

When the day came, Jodi tried to get excited about going out, but she had to put on an act. She really would rather stay home, but she didn't want to disappoint Brett. He seemed flushed and excited, and eager to go out. He sang and whistled as he showered and shaved, and gave Jodi a couple of playful tickles as she balanced on one leg, trying to get dressed in her long, grey cotton skirt and white sweater.

Carmen and Bruce arrived to baby-sit. Jodi thought it was a little strange that although they hugged her and wished her a Happy Birthday, they did not have a gift for her, and Carmen had not offered to make a cake.

"You two have fun." Carmen called after them. "And don't drink too much!"

"Yes Mom," Brett laughed. "We'll try to behave ourselves."

As they pulled into the restaurant parking lot and found an empty space, Brett cursed softly. He shifted his weight onto his left hip and felt in his back pocket. "Oh dammit!" he said, annoyed. "I forgot my wallet! How could I be so stupid? I left it in my other pants, when I got changed. I'm sorry, Honey. We'll have to go back - unless you brought your purse."

"No, I never bring it anymore. I don't need my license since I can't drive, and I just assumed you had money for tonight." It wasn't a big deal, but Jodi felt mildly annoyed at him. "Well, let's go back." she said. "It won't take long. You can call the restaurant from home, and tell them we'll be a bit late."

"I guess we'll have to. I'm sorry." They didn't say much on the ride home. Jodi waited in the car while Brett went into the house.

"Hi Mom," he said. "Is everything ready?" Carmen was bustling around the kitchen, setting the table with plates and wine glasses.

"Yes," she beamed. "You can bring her in."

In a few minutes, Brett came out to Jodi's side of the car and opened her door. "I got my wallet, and I phoned the steak house. It's okay, they'll hold our reservation."

Jodi forced a smile. "That's good," she said."Um…" Brett hesitated. "Christopher fell and hurt his knee, and he wants you to come and kiss it better. Would you mind?"

"Oh for heaven's sake! Maybe we should just stay home!" Jodi felt exasperated, then immediately sorry. "Of course I'll come."

Brett assisted her with her crutches as she got out of the car and up onto her one good leg. "I know it's a nuisance, and we're in a hurry, but he needs his mommy for a few minutes. We have to remember that this whole ordeal isn't easy on him either."

Brett pushed open the kitchen door, and let Jodi go in first. Christopher, Carmen, and Bruce were standing by the table holding up a huge paper banner that read, HAPPY BIRTHDAY JODI! In unison, they yelled,"SURPRISE! The table had been pulled out to its full size, and was set with a white linen tablecloth and the good silver and wine glasses. A vase of fresh flowers graced the center. Blue and white streamers stretched from the four corners of the room, ending over the middle of the table in a cluster of colourful balloons.

Delicious aromas emanated from the oven and on the counter was a large cake decorated with sugar horses and blue candles.

Brett closed the door behind them, and helped Jodi off with her coat.

Christopher hurled himself at her, hugging her around the hips and looking up at her with sparkling eyes and a mischievous grin. "I'm all right, Mommy! It was just a trick to get you in!" He was hugely pleased with himself, and his part in the deception, and excited at the prospects of a party.

Jodi scarcely had time to recover from her surprise. Cars began to arrive outside, and soon the house was filled with people. The Taylor family arrived, minus Rick, who was out of town. Linda came, and of course Bev and Chad. After supper, many friends and neighbours dropped in with their good wishes. Brett's boss and crew from West Kokanee Power came, Jodi's co-workers from the Vet Clinic, the minister and his wife, and several friends from the church. Jodi was touched by all the love and generosity shown to her by these people.

Several times over the course of the evening, Jodi caught Brett's eye as he was busy entertaining, and she flashed him a smile of gratitude and love. Once he winked at her, and later, he blew a kiss across the room. He could still make her fair skin blush, and cause her heart to beat rapidly when he looked at her with those gorgeous blue eyes. Jodi felt a stirring deep within herself. She wanted more of him than just a wink and an imaginary kiss.

The party moved to the living room where a cheery fire gave off a cozy warmth and glow. Jodi sat on the couch to open her gifts. There was a new T-shirt with a happy face on it, bath beads and special soap, hand and body lotion, and some pretty nighties. She left Brett's gift till last. It was a large box inside a black, plastic garbage bag. A red bow held the neck of the bag closed.

Brett grinned as he brought it over to her. "I didn't wrap it, 'cause I thought you'd give me heck for wasting so much paper."

"You're right," she smiled back. "It would be a waste. This way, we can re-use the bag *and* the box. I don't have Scotch blood in me for nothing."

She reached in and opened the flaps of the box. Immediately the pleasing smell of leather and saddle soap met her senses. Everyone watched in happy anticipation as she pulled out a black bridle with blinkers and a snaffle bit. Attached to the bit were reins about ten feet long. Jodi looked a little puzzled, but as she pulled the next piece out - a wide breast collar with long traces - realization dawned on her what it was.

"Oh wow! A driving harness! How wonderful!"

Brett came and sat next to her. He pulled the last and largest piece out of the box. "This is the back pad, girth, and britching," he said, proudly. "I had old Mr. Olafson, down at the Rusty Buckle Harness Shop make it for Torchy." He leaned back on the couch and turned towards Jodi. "I thought that when you get your new leg, I could help you to train her to drive. She already ground-drives, so she just needs to learn to carry the crupper under her tail and get used to pulling something instead of carrying weight. She's so smart, I'm sure she'll be easy to train. With that airy trot of hers, she'll make a beautiful driving horse."

Jodi hugged him in joy, and gave him a kiss. Her eyes shone as she imagined the picture Brett was painting in their minds. "Thank you Sweetie. It's a wonderful gift! I'd love to train her to drive."

Brett took the pieces of leather, and dropped them back into the box. "I'll be watching out for a suitable cart," he said, "and Mr. Olafson knows a guy who builds them, if we can't find one.

When the party came to an end, Jodi stood leaning on her crutches by the door, saying her thank-yous and goodnights while Brett helped the guests into their coats. When the last one had gone, she turned to him with a smile. "That was *so* much fun. Much better than going out to dinner."

Brett gave her a hug, crutches and all, and then realizing that she couldn't hug him back, he took the crutches and leaned them against the wall. "You don't need these," he smiled. "You can lean on me."

Thankfully, Jodi wrapped her arms around him, and laid her head on his chest. They just stood there for a moment, enjoying the closeness of the embrace. Brett held her lightly, hopeful of where this might lead, but not wanting to initiate anything that would spoil the mood or the evening. He did not want to risk the pain of rejection again, and yet - she seemed to want to be close to him tonight. Brett sighed and looked down into her face. "Would you like to sit by the fire for a while, before bed?" he asked.

"Yeah...that'd be nice. I'm too wound up to go to bed yet." Jodi turned to reach for her crutches, but Brett slid his arms down her body and picked her up in his arms.

"I'll carry you," he offered, throwing his yellow hair back out of his eyes. His lips were parted a little, showing his even, white teeth and his pink tongue.

"I guess I don't have a choice," she laughed, as she put her arms around his neck to hold on. "Let's go!"

Brett set her gently on the couch and bent to put a couple of cedar logs on the fire. Christopher had fallen asleep in the big armchair with the old cat Samantha curled up against his legs. She loved a warm body to snuggle up with.

Jodi lay back against the cushions at one end of the couch, stretching her leg out. She lifted her foot as Brett turned to sit on the couch. He took it in his hand

and lowered it to rest across his thighs. His fingers rested lightly on the top of her calf, curving gently around the muscle, where they moved absently, sending little shivers along Jodi's body.

   He turned from staring dreamily into the flames to look at her. Jodi had been enjoying watching his finely chiselled features; his deep blue, half-closed eyes, his hair, looking somewhat like a patch of straw. "Are you tired out?" he asked with a little smile.

   Jodi smiled back at him as their eyes met. "Yes, I'm tired, but it's a good kind of tired; a happy tiredness, if that's possible." She drew back her foot and pushed it behind his back. She held out her hands to him. "Come and cuddle with me," she invited.

   Brett took her hands, looking somewhat puzzled as she drew him down to her. She slipped her arms around his neck, hugging him quickly, as he bent to kiss her. She held his face in her hands, gazing into his smoky blue eyes, and asked him, "Don't you find me unattractive with no hair?"

   He smiled, and then grew serious again. "Honey, when I close my eyes and kiss you, it's not your hair I'm thinking of."

   Jodi giggled then, enjoying the moment, and her lips were parted in a smile as he kissed her again, longer and more insistent. She ran her hands down his back, and tugged his denim shirt out of his brown cords. She slid her hands under his shirt and rubbed her fingers gently along the ridges of muscle on both sides of his spine, and then over the little bumps of vertebrae in the hollow of his broad muscular back. Brett raised himself up on his elbows and looked at her. "You know what you're doing to me, don't you?" he asked.

""Uh-huh...." she replied. "And I'm not going to run away this time."

"Well well," he grinned. "That's the best news I've had in a long time! Why the change of heart?"

"Because," Jodi smiled, her eyes soft with love for him, "You were right, and I was wrong." She fiddled with his hair as she spoke, "You said if I can ride a horse, I can make love with you. And after I got your little gift for Valentines, and I got to thinking about it, I realized that as long as I'm well enough, and we're careful, there's no reason why we can't". He kissed her again, and held her tight. She whispered against his ear. "I guess I just needed some time to adjust to my own appearance, and to realize that you still wanted me. I just didn't think you'd be interested in making love to a cripple."

"Jodi! Don't talk like that"! Brett raised his head and looked at her sharply. "I told you a month ago, I still wanted to be your lover, and that nothing has changed for me. I know everything's changed, but my love for you hasn't. *That's* what I meant!"

"I know that now," she said softly. "I'm so lucky to have you. I love you too."

Brett rolled off her, onto the floor, and then stood up pulling her to a sitting position. "C'mon," he urged. "Let's go up."

"Aw...I hate to leave this beautiful fire", Jodi said. "Why don't you go up and get my little Valentine's presents? They're in my make-up case on the bathroom counter."

Brett still had a hold of her hand, and he pulled on it persuasively. "No, come on up. The couch was fine when we were young and foolish. Our bed will be a lot more comfortable. Besides, there'll be a fire there too before long." He let go of her hand and backed up a step. "I'll go get your crutches, and then I'll carry Christopher up to bed. I'll meet you upstairs, okay?"

He bent and kissed her on the mouth. It was an order; not a request. Jodi sighed and gave him a mock salute.

"I'll be there," she smiled.

CHAPTER FORTY-TWO

The next day was Sunday. Jodi was surprised when Brett offered to accompany her and Christopher to church. Despite the three months of abstinence, he had been gentle; even tender with her last night. Jodi was amused that such a simple act had restored harmony between them so easily. He couldn't do enough for her this morning, such was his gratitude.

The day was sunny and mild, and again to Jodi's surprise, Brett suggested they go riding after lunch. Brett whistled a tune as he saddled up the three horses. He lunged Torchy in the corral for twenty minutes first to take the snuff and nonsense out of her before lifting Jodi up onto her back, and he insisted on keeping the spirited mare on a lead line in case she acted up. But Torchy was well behaved. She seemed to realize that Jodi's balance wasn't right, and she followed along beside Old Pete obediently.

Up in the woodsy trails above the orchard, the snow was up to the horses' knees, and they had to work hard to break trail through it. Torchy was tireless at this task. Brett threw the lead rope over her neck as she surged ahead, lifting her feet with snappy animation. "She's not going to run away with you," he laughed. "She loves having a job to do." The Morgan strength and stamina was legendary and Jodi felt an immense surge of pride and happiness that she actually owned one of these intelligent and spirited animals.

It was a good day - a happy day. But by evening, Jodi didn't feel well. Despite sitting by the fire with a blanket around her, she couldn't seem to get warm. Chills ran down her spine periodically and she felt a general aching in her bones and joints. Her face was flushed, even though she felt cold.

With a feeling of apprehension, she asked Brett to bring her the thermometer. He sat beside her, looking worried as she stuck it under her tongue and waited. After a minute, she took it out and handed it to him to read. "Damn!" Brett said, running a hand through his hair in concern. "It's 101 F; 38.7C. I'll phone Dr. Houston."

Jodi just nodded, feeling depressed already. *Now what?* she thought miserably, as Brett went into the kitchen to call the hospital. They both knew the importance of reporting anything abnormal immediately.

A few minutes later, Brett came back into the room looking sad, yet resigned. "Sarah phoned Dr. Jansen in Vancouver and he said that you're to get into hospital here so they can get you on antibiotics right away."

Brett sat beside Jodi again, and took her hand. "I called Mom too. She'll be here in about twenty minutes to stay with Christopher. I'm sure sorry, Honey."

"Yeah, me too." Jodi touched his cheek with the back of her hand. "The fun didn't last very long, did it?" Brett didn't answer, and she didn't expect one. "I'll go up and pack my bag. Will you please warm up the car? I'm freezing."

At the hospital, Jodi was rushed right into a private room. Blood was drawn from the broviac line and then the tube was attached to an I.V. unit containing a broad-spectrum antibiotic. Her condition was monitored closely all though the night, but by morning there was no improvement. Her temperature was up to 39.2C. They ruled out the flu' or a cold, as Jodi didn't have the symptoms that usually accompanied those ailments. The doctors were fairly certain it was an infection of some kind, but they didn't know where it was in her body.
There were only two flights a week from Castle River to Vancouver, and Dr. Jansen wanted Jodi on the next one available. He did not want to play around with this. An infection could be deadly serious.

On Wednesday morning, Jodi was transported to the small airport by ambulance. Brett rode with her. He had taken a week off work so he could go to Vancouver with her. He was almost sick with fear and dread that he was going to lose her this time. Jodi's condition was getting worse.

By the time they arrived at the Lion's Gate Hospital, Jodi was vomiting. Her temperature had risen to 40.6 C. and she had severe neck pains and a bad headache.

Teams of doctors swarmed around her bed, asking questions, checking her over, taking more blood. A change of antibiotics was suggested, but as it ran through the lines, Jodi experienced an allergic reaction to one of the drugs. Her chest, scalp, back, groin, and arms became severely itchy, almost driving her crazy. She groaned and cried for two hours while Brett and Kathy, the sympathetic nurse, bathed her with cool cloths and rubbed her itches. Finally, exhausted, she slept.

Brett, exhausted himself, kept a vigilant watch beside her bed as Dr. Jansen and two specialists from Infectious Diseases held a conference at the workstation. He tried to eavesdrop, but could only hear snatches of the conversation, and Jodi's name.

The doctor came back some time later to check on Jodi and to talk with them. He sat down heavily on a visitor's chair. He seemed tired, but he looked at the young couple kindly. "Even though you have an open sore on your stump now, the infection is not coming from there. We think it may be in the broviac line." Then, looking directly at Jodi, he continued, "We'll keep you on antibiotics for a couple of weeks to get rid of the bugs. If things don't improve, we may have to pull the line. Then once the infection is gone, we'll put in another line and resume the chemo. It's a dirty, rotten thing to happen. I'm sorry."

After he left, Jodi turned on her side and cried softly into her pillow. Brett just sat beside her quietly, handing her a Kleenex once in a while. He sighed. "Maybe this is our punishment for trying to have a little fun."

She stopped crying, sniffed, and cracked a weak smile. "Are you referring to the riding or the love-making?" she asked.

"Uh...the latter, I guess. I've been feeling terribly guilty that maybe I gave you the infection." He looked at Jodi, his eyes two blue pools of remorse.

She lifted her head, propping it on one elbow, and stared at him incredulously. "Is that what you think? That *you* gave me this infection? Because we were intimate?"

Brett squirmed in his chair, looking uncomfortable. "Yeah...well...I thought maybe I could have...I should have told the doctors, but I was too embarrassed."

Jodi hadn't realized that he had been torturing himself about this. "Come here, you big lug," she said softly.

He rose and bent towards her as she reached out and put her arms around his neck, pulling him into an awkward embrace. The I.V. unit and all the tubes were in the way, making close contact difficult.

"Don't you dare tell the doctors our secrets," she said. "And stop worrying about it. Our lovemaking didn't have anything to do with this stupid problem. I'll bet the bugs were already there when I came home. They just needed to incubate for a little while and then they erupted."

Brett breathed a sigh of relief. He wished he could just crawl into bed with Jodi and continue to hold her in his arms, but their tender moment was interrupted by a knock on the door and a voice calling "Hello!"

It was Marnie. Jodi was glad to see her and relieved that she hadn't brought the children. She still felt quite ill, and wasn't able to talk much, but just having her sister there was a tremendous relief. Brett felt he could leave for a while, and went for a much-needed break down to the coffee shop. He had slept - or tried to sleep - on the chair beside her bed last night. It was terribly uncomfortable, and with the lights and night activities going on, he had only dozed off for little naps between interruptions. He now understood why Jodi was so tired when she got home. This place was a zoo.

By midnight, her fever was down, and Jodi was out of danger. However, the news still wasn't very good. Although the central line could stay in place, she had to stay in hospital for two more weeks on antibiotics. Then she would have two days off, and then resume her five-day chemo. It was turning into a long, tedious stretch of hospital time. Brett felt he'd better go home and tend to his job, the farm, and their son. Jodi hated to see him go, but knew he was bored and restless at the hospital. His energies were better spent at home, taking care of things.

Once she felt better, Jodi was able to get into her wheelchair and go visiting. Down at the Children's Ward, she found that little Christopher had just had further surgery to have a shunt inserted in his head. He was blind now, and constantly sick and crying from the chemotherapy. Jodi knew he was going to die. It was only a matter of time.

A little native boy, Jesse Cardinal, who was three years old, had recently passed away. Jodi remembered seeing his crib heavily padded, and the little boy's hands bandaged so he couldn't scratch himself and start his bruised and fragile body bleeding.

As she wheeled over to the Playroom, propelling her I.V. unit ahead of her, Jodi pondered, *this disease is so twisted and savage. Am I going to be another of its victims?* It was not a pleasant thought, and she tried to push it away, as she joined the children.

　　She learned that Robin had finished his treatment and had gone home. Sherri was too sick to come to the Playroom. Her counts were very low, and she was in an isolated room to guard her from infection. Parker wasn't there today either. He was between chemos, spending some time at home. The Child Life Staff Coordinator introduced Jodi to Ruth, a young teenager, and a couple of other new kids. She watched T.V. and chatted with them, till lunchtime.

　　That afternoon, Jodi's I.V. lines were disconnected. She was informed that she could go out on day passes for the next ten days as long as she was back at four p.m. for her meds. The only stipulation was that she had to avoid malls or other crowded places, and people with colds. This was great news! The sense of freedom she felt was euphoric! She wished Brett were still here so they could go out together, but she knew they could not afford to have him come down again.

　　Marnie and Carol came as often as their busy schedules allowed, pushing her wheelchair along the sea wall and through Stanley Park. They went to movies in the afternoons and ate out at various places. It was a joy to have a change from hospital food and get away from the hospital scene.

A week passed in which Jodi was relatively happy. The hospital no longer held the fear and dread it used to for her. It was almost her second home, so familiar was she with its smells, sights, and sounds. She had her favourite nurses, but there were none that she didn't like. Jodi knew the receptionists in Admissions, the pharmacist, most of the doctors, the cleaning staff, the cafeteria workers, and most of the cancer patients that came and went for treatments.

On Jodi's last afternoon of freedom before she began her five-day chemo, she had just got settled into her room and was waiting for the supper trays to arrive. Her roommate was an older lady named Esther. She had cancer of the lymph nodes. She and Jodi were just getting aquatinted when Dr. Jansen and his nurse came in. They chatted pleasantly for a few moments. Then the doctor dropped the bomb.

"We'd like to talk to you down in the Conference Room" he said.

Oh-oh, the Conference Room. I always get bad news there, thought Jodi as she obediently hopped onto her wheelchair and allowed Jill to push her along. With a feeling of dread, Jodi steeled herself for the news. Dr. Jansen came right out with it.

"Four Radiologists have been studying your latest chest x-rays, and there may be a spot to be concerned about. They can't say for sure it's cancer, but it's something that wasn't there before."

Jodi asked, outwardly calm. "Where, exactly?"

"Right lung - at the back. We'll have to re-do the x-rays and do a C.T. scan to make sure, but we may have to look at surgery as a possibility in the near future. It might be a good time to schedule a revision of your stump too - take care of both problems at once."

Jodi knew that the bone on her amputated leg was growing, causing the skin to erupt in an open sore, and she was prepared to have it dealt with, but to have her chest opened and her lung cut? Horrors! She felt sick with revulsion at the thought, and paralysed with fear that the cancer had probably spread to her lungs.

Jodi held herself together as they went back to her room. The supper trays had arrived, but she had lost her appetite. She wanted to weep and wail, but with Esther watching T.V. in the adjoining bed; she couldn't make a big scene. Jodi turned on her side and cried silently, so hard that the bed shook. She was glad that Esther didn't seem to notice.

She phoned Brett at ten, and after listening to the news from home, she told him what the doctor had said. There was a stunned silence, then a whispered, "Oh God! This nightmare just seems to get worse." Brett took it hard, and Jodi knew he was crying when they said their good-byes and hung up.

A hard week followed. It was emotionally and physically exhausting as Jodi endured her chemo with all it's nasty side effects, as well as a heart stress test, ultrasound, x-rays and a CT scan. Then there was more waiting and worrying as the Tumour Board and the Radiologists met to discuss her test results.

In the meantime she was allowed to go home. Carol took time off from her window-dressing job at The Bay, to accompany Jodi right onto the plane, and Brett met her at Castle River. He did not want her riding the bus after what she had just gone through, and for once, she agreed.

Two days later, Jill phoned from Dr. Jansen's office to tell Jodi that double surgery was booked for March 31st. The surgeons would cut the bone back on her leg and refold the skin over it again, and they would remove the growths on her right lung. There was nothing they could do but wait, and try not to think about the impending operation.

CHAPTER FORTY-THREE

The night before Jodi and Brett left for the mid-week flight to Vancouver, Reverend Forsythe and a group that called themselves 'The Sharers,' came over to the house. They formed a circle and prayed for healing for Jodi. Carmen and Christopher were part of the circle too, and as Brett hung back, unsure of whether he should be a part of this, little Christopher held out his hand and called to him, "Come *on* Daddy! We need you to help too!"

With a shrug, Brett took the small hand offered to him, and bowed his head in prayer. He was not handling this well. He was nervous, jumpy, and depressed. He didn't feel like talking to anyone. His responses to attempted conversations were curt, almost rude in their brevity. He did not want to have to think. His mind was so overwhelmed with the reality of what his beloved Jodi was going to go through on Thursday.

Brett's dark mood continued as he and Jodi arrived at the hospital the next day, and went through Admissions, Clinic, and a meeting with the O.R. Staff to discuss the operation and anaesthetic procedures.

Jodi called her sisters to let them know she had arrived and had been 'processed' as she called it. It was now late afternoon and Jodi was allowed out on a pass. Marnie offered to send Robert over to pick them up, but Jodi declined with thanks. "I think we'll just spend a quiet evening together," she said. "We're going to walk over to Lonsdale; just window-shop, go out for dinner, and see a movie. We're going to see 'Song of Norway'. It's that new film about Edward Grieg, the composer." She and Marnie chatted about the movie for a bit, then since neither sister could be there with Jodi in the morning when she went up for her surgery, there were some tears and talk about the operation.

Being very adept on her crutches, but still un-used to the stares invoked when she entered a public place, Jodi tried her best to ignore the looks she got as they entered the restaurant and were seated at a quiet table near the back.

Technically, the operation was called 'stump re-vision and thoracotomy', but once they had ordered, Jodi put her hand over Brett's and squeezed it lightly. "Lighten up, will you?" she said with a smile. "I'm just going up for a little 'slicing' and 'dicing'."

Brett had to laugh then, admiring her spirit, and at least made an attempt to have fun for her sake.

That night, after Brett had gone, leaving kisses and promises to be there in the morning, Jodi prayed not for herself, but for her beloved husband. She was not afraid for herself. If she didn't make it, she knew it was always harder for those left behind to cope. For herself, she would know nothing more of this earthly struggle. She would be free. Free from her disease-ridden, clumsy, one-legged body. Free, she believed, to let her spirit soar with the birds and animals and angels of heaven, free to mingle with the departed souls of her mom and dad, and others that had passed on to another dimension. No, she was not afraid of death. Her only concern was for her child, and for Brett, her only true love.

Jodi's surgery was scheduled for one p.m. but luckily she was rescheduled for a twelve p.m. time slot. Just time for a bath and away she went. She had slept well, despite all the nightly interruptions, and when Brett arrived looking pale and tired, she chatted brightly to him, and showed him what she'd done to her leg. On a piece of masking tape, she had printed 'operating instructions: 'do not cut above this line' and taped it around her stump. "I want to make sure that Dr. Wong doesn't take too much off," she kidded.

    Jodi got a tiny bit upset at the O.R. doors when Brett had to let her hand go. He almost fainted as she was wheeled away through the doors, and the nurse that had come up with them asked, "Are you going to be all right?" Pulling himself together, he nodded, and stepped into the elevator with her.

"I'm okay, thanks. I just wish I had her faith. She's amazing."

"Yes," the nurse agreed. "We often get inspiration from our patients. Jodi is one that we all enjoy looking after and talking to. She has such a positive attitude and a wry sense of humour. I'm sure she'll come through this just fine."

They parted on the ground floor, and Brett stood, hesitant for a moment, wondering where to go. He wanted to be alone; to cry, to rage, to torment himself over the unfairness of it all. The cafeteria wouldn't do. *Too many people,* he thought. *Ah! The chapel! It would be quiet there.* He knew Jodi went there sometimes. It was a place he could feel close to her as she was being prepared to go 'under the knife'.

Brett entered the room quietly and looked around. Great. No one there. He made his way to a soft padded chair, and sat heavily, head in hands. He willed the tears to come, but nothing happened. He felt fine; totally supported and surrounded by...something! He wasn't sure what. He felt an inner peace... a presence. Suddenly, he *knew* Jodi was going to be all right.

Feeling happier than he'd been for days, he stood up and stretched. He felt the tension drain out of him. A shaft of sunlight streamed in the stain glass window on the side of the chapel that faced the street. Brett moved closer to see the picture and to read the scripture that was printed in gothic style beneath it. The scene was of Jesus standing in flowing robes, with hand outstretched, blessing a crowd of people. The caption read, 'Come to me all ye who are weary and heavy laden, and I will give you rest.'

Suddenly, Brett got a strong urge to go shopping. What was this? He hated shopping, especially in the crowded malls of the city. To his amazement, he found himself whistling a tune as he walked out of the hospital into the spring sunshine and caught a bus for downtown. It wasn't that he forgot about Jodi. He kept on supporting her and the doctors in his mind - he supposed it was prayer - but he remained happy as he enjoyed a plate of Chinese food at the Ginger Beef Kiosk, bought expensive Easter chocolates, and tried on new jeans. He bought a pair for himself, for Christopher, and Jodi.

Back at the Flower Shop in the hospital, he bought six red roses in an arrangement of Baby's Breath and green ferns, and went up to her room to wait.

Jodi came back at four thirty p.m. heavily sedated, and Brett spent an anxious hour while two nurses did her vital signs, checked her dressings, the drainage tubes, and the machines. She was on oxygen, and a P.C.A. (Patient Control Analgesia) machine. She could push a button for more pain control when needed.

At last Dr. Wong came in and gave Brett some great news. "Well Mr. Randall," he said with a big smile. "The spots on the lung are not cancerous!"

Brett almost blurted out; *I know - God told me not to worry!* Instead, he grabbed the surgeon's hand and shook it, hard. With tears of relief in his eyes, he simply said, "Thank-you."

The doctor continued, "I removed two tiny growths; one on the bottom lobe and one on the middle lobe, but they don't appear to be anything of concern. They just kind of crumbled away to nothing when I touched them." Dr. Wong looked a little puzzled, and then shook his head. "Pathology will study the tissues anyway, and we'll have a full report in a day or two."

Brett nodded, relief showing all over his face. "How did the revision go?" he asked.

"Just fine," replied the doctor. "Should be no more problems there. Dr. Keeland did that part of the surgery. He took off about an inch of bone, and got a good fold of skin around it. It looks good." He looked over at Jodi. "She'll have a lot of pain and discomfort for a while, but hopefully, the worst is over."

"Brett ran a hand through his untidy blond locks. His shoulders sagged with relief. He hadn't realized how tense he had been. "Thanks again, Doctor" he said with a smile.

As Dr. Wong left the room, Brett asked Angela, the attending nurse, "Do you think she heard? Is she conscious?"

"I'm not sure," came the reply, "Why don't you talk to her? I'll leave you alone now."

Brett took Jodi's hands in his and leaned close to her, his lips against her cheek. "Hey Jo," he whispered, "Did you hear the great news? That God of yours is awesome! He made those spots go 'poof' right under the surgeons' hand. They're nothing to worry about!" He kissed her cheek lightly. "And your leg's all fixed up too."

Jodi was dimly aware of his presence through the fog of painkillers and the remnants of anaesthetic. She understood the message, but felt no emotion either way as yet. She managed a groan to let him know she'd heard, and a tiny squeeze of her hand in acknowledgment. Then she slipped into oblivion again.

While she slept, Brett went to phone their families who were anxiously awaiting the news. Of course everyone was relieved that Jodi had come through another big surgery all right, and that the news was so good.

The next day was Good Friday, and as far as Jodi was aware, there wasn't anything good about it. She had terrible pain and discomfort. The Physio crew came in mid-morning and again in the afternoon to try to get her lungs functioning. Her chest was very sore. She had a seven-inch incision from front to back between her 4th and 5th ribs on her right side where the surgeon had spread the ribs apart to get at the lung. It was pure torture having to sit up and blow into a little device to make some little plastic balls jump around.

Carol, Marnie, and Brett took turns at her bedside all day and into the evening. They held her sick tray, helped her to the bathroom, and fed her ice chips and bathed her with cold cloths.

In the Cancer Ward, the nurses encouraged families to come and stay and to take part in the care of the individual. In many cases, it was the last thing they could do for their loved ones. Therefore, there were no set visiting hours.

There was a Cluster available for out-of-town family caregivers to stay in. Brett slept there last night, but after many hours at the bedside, he was tired out. He was going home with Marnie to get a good nights' rest. The hospital was the worst place to try to get any sleep.

Recovery was slow, and very painful. Jodi almost passed out with the pain of trying to use her crutches to get to the adjoining bathroom. Hopping was even worse. Brett carried her the first few times; after that she gave up and asked for a bedpan.

When the drainage tube was taken out of Jodi's side on Easter Sunday, she cried out with pain as a lot of brownish fluid squished out and soaked her bed. Brett lifted her gently out of her bed so the nurses could change it. He sat in the big comfortable recliner chair with Jodi cuddled up in his arms. She laid her head on his chest and cried quietly as he rubbed her back and shoulders.

Angela, the young nurse on duty asked as she and Karla finished tucking in the fresh bedclothes, "Do you want to get back into bed now?" Brett answered for her.

"Just put a blanket over her please, and we'll sit here for a while. I can put her back into bed."

"Okay, just ring the bell if you need anything," smiled Angela. Their eyes met, and Angela blushed as she tucked the blanket around Jodi. Then the two young nurses left the room.

Back at their station, the nurses sat down to write up their reports, as their twelve-hour shifts were almost at an end.

"He's heartbreakingly handsome, isn't he?" sighed Karla, her eyes flicking to the room where Brett sat with Jodi in his arms.

"Down girl!" laughed Angela. "Eat your heart out. He's married!"

"He might not be for long, if she doesn't make it." Karla said very quietly.

Angela shot her a warning look. "Come on, you know that's unethical talk."

Karla shrugged. "I saw the way he looked at you when you bent over to tuck that blanket around her. He was looking at your breasts."

"Sh....write your report, and be quiet." Angela bent her head, writing furiously.

"I'll bet he hasn't had any nooky for a long time." Karla persisted.

"Karla! It's none of our business."

The younger girl sighed, "Yeah, I know. But I can dream. He's *so* gorgeous!"

Angela rested her chin in her hands. "She was real pretty too before she got cancer. She showed me her photo album. They have a little farm up in Harrison. They have horses, and they grow fruit and stuff. They have a little boy, almost five years old. He's really cute too."

"Oh yeah?" Karla said, looking very interested. "Do they make their living off the farm?"

"No, not entirely. Jodi was an Animal Health Technician before she got sick, and he works as an Electrician."

A wicked grin lit up Karla's young, pretty face. "Well, I'd sure like to be plugged in and turned on by him!"

The night nurses were arriving, and quickly the girls finished up their reports, leaving their gossip for another time.

Jodi was discharged at noon on Tuesday, April 5th. She and Brett waited anxiously in the lobby for Marnie to pick them up. Jodi's personal belongings were piled on her lap in the wheelchair. She and Brett were arguing.

"Look," Brett was saying, somewhat exasperated. "I don't think you should come back with me tomorrow. You're still too sore. And you'll just have to come right back again on Saturday, so you can be here in time for your chemo on Monday. You'd only be home for three days, and all that traveling would be really hard on you. It's best if you just stay at Rosedale this time.

"I *know* it makes sense to stay here," Jodi grumbled. "But I'm just *so* homesick. It seems I've hardly been home since my birthday. I want to see Christopher. I missed Easter with him. I want to see the horses, and Dolly's new calf, and see what flowers are coming up in the garden. Oh hell! I just want to see springtime on my farm!"

Just then, Marnie arrived and they left the issue unresolved until later that evening when everyone else had gone to bed. Jodi's bed had been made on the couch in the living room so she wouldn't have to negotiate any stairs. Brett made them some hot milk and when he had finished his, he came over and kneeled in front of Jodi, nestling his head under her breasts, his arms around her waist. Jodi put her cup down and rested her hands on his shoulders.

"I *have* to go home tomorrow," he said, sadly. I *have* to get back to work. We're so busy on that strip mall site, and I've got to write my exam in June. I've got homework to do every night. And on the weekend, I need Dad to come and help me get the trees pruned. There's so much work to do. I won't have time to drive you to Castle River on Saturday. And you still need lots of nursing care. I know Mom's good, but I just can't be there all the time for you."

"I know. It's okay," Jodi sighed. "I'll stay. ...You're right. It would be too hectic, and I need the rest. I'm still not feeling very strong."

A great silence and sadness stretched between them. They held each other for a long time, until they were both almost falling asleep. Then Brett tucked her in and kissed her tenderly, before going down to Jodi's old room in the basement.

CHAPTER FORTY-FOUR

April 11-15th. Chemo 'A'. The nasty one. The five day one, where Jodi was trapped by the lines and tubes supplying a slow but steady drip of poisonous, nauseating, chemicals into her body.

She was almost frantic to get home. She needed to smell the earth coming to life again with the re-birth of spring; to watch the snow melt under the increased heat of the sun; to see the new life in the buds on the cherry, apple, plum, and apricot trees; to see the horses roll in the mud, flailing their legs in the air, trying to rid themselves of their long, itchy winter coats; to see the little shoots in the garden, poking their heads out to see if it was safe to come out and grow into beautiful roses, peonies, daffodils, crocuses and tulips.

As they drove home from Castle River, Christopher cuddled against Jodi and said, "Mommy, I'm not going to school while you're home, okay? I just want to be with you." His little jaw was set in a stubborn line, much like Jodi's did when she wanted her own way. Brett looked over his son's little blond head and met Jodi's eyes. She caught the look; floated in those blue depths, and wondered what was behind all this.

Brett spoke softly, "I'm not the only one having a tough time without you, Jo. He's been coming into my bed at night, upset and crying. He has nightmares. He wets the bed sometimes. He's very clingy right now."

Jodi choked back tears, nodding that she understood. She gave Christopher a hug. "You can stay home, Sweetie. We'll have lots of fun while I'm home."

"Do you have to go back again Mom? Aren't you better yet?" His little face looked at her so seriously.

Jodi wished with all her heart she could tell him it was over, but it wouldn't be fair to lie to him. She forced a smile. "You know, I'm almost half-way through the treatment now. And, as soon as Playschool is finished, you can come with me to Vancouver and stay at Auntie Marnie's house. You can go to the beach with Jake and the girls and you can come and see me in the hospital."

That got Christopher's interest and attention, and he pestered them all the way home with questions about riding on the airplane, what they would find at the beach, what toys Jake had, and what it was like in the hospital.

The two weeks seemed to pass by far too quickly. Brett went about his work in a quiet and determined manner. He spent long days on the job, and after supper he was always out repairing a fence, cleaning out a pen in the barn, trimming the horses' or the goats' feet, tending to the orchard, or fixing some appliance or giving something a coat of paint. A few evenings Jodi crutched out to the corrals to watch him ground-drive Torchy with her new harness on. It was frustrating for Jodi. She wanted so much to be the one holding the reins, but even moving around the barnyard was a challenge. The rubber tips on her crutches got stuck in the mud, and several times she fell, jarring her ribs that were still sore from surgery.

In May, Jodi had chemo twice, once at the beginning of the month, and again at the end. In between she was home for Christopher's fifth birthday. He was thrilled with his inflatable alligator beach toy, and was full of excitement as he proudly accompanied Jodi back to Vancouver on the plane.

The day before she was discharged, Jodi learned that little Christopher Shumi had died. Cindy told her, and both young mothers held hands and cried. Later on that evening, Jodi learned that the doctors had stopped treating Sherri too. They were just trying to get her counts up, so she could go home to die. *So, So, sad,* Jodi thought. She cried for the sweet little girl, and the baby boy, and the anguish the parents were facing.

Once again, Jodi experienced a setback that prevented her from returning home. On the Wednesday following her discharge, the day she and Christopher were to fly home, Jodi woke up with a sore throat. With a temperature of 38.5C, Jodi knew she was hospital bound again, and sure enough, she was back in on a course of I.V. antibiotics for nine days. Then it was back for rest and recuperation on the patio at Rosedale before returning to hospital for her June chemo.

The only thing she could think of to give thanks for at night when she said her prayers was that Christopher was with her. His curiosity and concern had been alleviated since he had been to the hospital many times now, and knew and understood why his mom had to spend so much time there. He was having a great time with his cousins, especially Jake. The two little boys were so close in age they became good pals, playing trucks, lego, or hide and seek. Their favourite game was re-enacting episodes from 'Star Trek' in which Jake, being a year and two months older, always got to be Captain Kirk. Christopher was usually willing and happy to be Spock or one or the other characters on the spacecraft.

While in the hospital, Jodi had her first fitting for an artificial leg, or 'prosthesis' as she learned to call it. She had trouble even pronouncing it at first. Now, words like Oncology, Adriamycin, Doxirubicin, Cyclofosphamide, Thoracotomy, and AGE (absolute granulucyte counts) rolled off her tongue easily. She had learned a whole new vocabulary now.

Jodi's fitting did not go well. She had to stand against the wall with her stump in a metal holder while Steffan, her Prosthetist, applied a plaster cast. Apart from the embarrassment of standing there in her underwear having a man other than her husband touch her hips and thigh, she felt faint, and had to sit down for a while. On the second attempt, she just had to throw up. Luckily, Carol was with her and held a bucket for her, and wiped her face with a wet towel. She had to stay where she was or the cast would have to be all redone.

In a couple of days, Jodi was taken down to Physio to get the new leg. She was so tired, and so adept on her crutches by this time, that she did not feel very excited or even interested in having two legs to stand on again.

The new leg looked quite ugly. Jodi had to put on a long stump sock, which was open at both ends. Then her stump fitted inside a plastic mould at the top of the leg. There was a little round hole with a screw-in cap located just above the artificial knee joint. The end of the sock had to be pulled down and out this hole, thereby pulling the skin down into the socket where it was supposed to fit snugly. Below the knee joint, the 'leg' was composed of a metal alloy; light and strong, and only about an inch and a half in diameter.

Later on, Steffan would build it up with foam and plastic to look like a real leg. The metal was imbedded into a solid moulded plastic foot. There was no ankle joint as yet. That too, would come later.

Jodi tried her best to walk, supported by the parallel bars, but the hard plastic hurt her groin and the point of her bottom. Tired and frustrated, she returned to her room for her chemo. Learning to walk again was going to be a huge challenge, and it would entail many fittings and adjustments before the prosthesis became comfortable and familiar to wear.

In July, Jodi had her last round of Chemo 'A'. The remaining four treatments were to be a daily dose of Iphosphamide and Etoposide, along with Mesna and an injection of G-CSF that helped to boost the blood count. The injections hurt like a bee sting, but Jodi learned to accept them stoically as part of the necessary torture to get her well. She almost looked forward to the 'B' chemos. The drugs were run through the I.V. over an hour instead of continuously, and although she always threw up, for the rest of the day Jodi didn't feel too sick. She could enjoy visitors, go visiting herself - usually down to the Children's Ward, read, and study her course material, or go down to the cafeteria for a snack. Just to be able to do these things were small victories.

Back home at the farm again in mid-July, Jodi walked somewhat unsteadily on her new leg around the garden one evening, just enjoying the scents on the soft summer breeze, and the sounds of the frogs and the birds chirping as they settled down for the night. Scamp never left her side when she was home, even though his old body was stiff and sore from rheumatism and his eyesight was poor. Samantha followed Jodi too, pretending to be intent on catching bugs, but she was really just supervising Jodi. Several other cats lived in the barn now, but none was as dear to Jodi as the old white matriarch that had been her dad's special pet.

It was after ten now, but it still was not completely dark. Jodi sat down in the garden swing and rocked herself gently. Sam jumped up on her knee, and Scamp lay down with a sigh beside her. She closed her eyes, listening to the night sounds around her.

The swing seat creaked and moved as Brett joined her, sitting down with a weary sigh. He had been working in the large vegetable garden, hoeing weeds between rows of corn, while Christopher played trucks in the dirt nearby. He smelled earthy - dried sweat mingled with good, black soil, and a faint aroma of something spicy - was it marigolds or tomatoes? Jodi leaned against him as he draped an arm around her shoulders. Christopher lay on his back on the still-warm grass, watching the first stars appear. It was one of those perfect moments when they could just about believe that they were happy and content, without a care in the world.

Jodi asked, "What would you like to do for your birthday and our anniversary next week?"

"I don't know - maybe go out for a nice dinner somewhere, or we could have a BBQ here... invite all our friends and family. What do you think?"

"Yeah...that would be nice, but I have another idea...want to hear it?"

"Well sure," he chuckled, "but some of your ideas are pretty far out. What have you got cooked up this time?"

"Nothing yet," she laughed. Then, becoming serious, she continued, "I'd like to go up to Kelso, see the old house, and have a visit with Len and Susan, and your cousins. I haven't even seen the twins since Christmas, and they'll be almost a year old now. I bet they're really cute."

"Yeah, double the trouble; double the fun." Brett agreed. "I'm glad we only have one."

Last August, Susan had given birth to twin girls they named Kari and Katie. When their proud parents stopped in last Christmas, the four-month-old babies had identical masses of dark hair and lively dark brown eyes, like Len's. *It would be fun to see them walking and talking now,* thought Jodi.

She continued, "Remember that Len told us he bought the cabin up on Lake Leviation from Paul? I'd love to spend a few days up there; show Christopher where he was born - just go away for a little family holiday. I never seem to see you, even at home. You're always so busy."

"Well, there's a lot to do around here. The place doesn't look after itself."

"I know, I'm not blaming you. I'm proud of how hard you work, and how nice you keep everything. I just wish I could help you more. I'm kind of useless as far as the yard work goes." Jodi dropped a hand onto Brett's thigh, patting him affectionately. "So what do you think? Should I phone Len and ask him if we can use the cabin?"

Brett felt a sense of foreboding at the idea. This sounded like 'last request stuff' and he replied, "You're not giving up on me, are you Jo? Is there something about your condition you haven't told me?"

"No! Nothing like that. I'm okay, as far as I know. I just have a hankering to see the old haunts, that's all."

"Well, you know I worry about you getting sick when we're so far away from hospital."

She argued back, "It's not so far away, really. We could be down and across the lake to Kelso in an hour, and back here in two, if we had to be. I doubt that I would die in that time frame."

Brett knew it was useless to argue with Jodi; she had a way of persuading him to see things her way. He wasn't a weak man at all, or a pushover. He could be very determined in his own right, but he bent to Jodi's will to please her, because he loved her and wanted her to have some happiness in the gruelling ordeal she was living with.

So that's what they did. Jodi packed the cooler with steaks, and brought along a bottle of wine and candles to celebrate their wedding anniversary. She baked a chocolate cake and kept it frozen, decorated for Brett's birthday.

Up at the cabin, she and Christopher presented Brett with his gifts - a T-shirt with 'World's Best Dad' printed on the front, and from Jodi, a new pair of leather hiking boots. Brett's old ones were ready for the scrap heap.

"Great!" he grinned. "Should I chuck these old ones into the lake for the fish to nibble on?"

Christopher piped up, "Let's keep them for my new puppy when we get one. They'd be just perfect for a puppy to chew on." And so the old boots were packed up and taken home.

"What's this about a new puppy?" Brett asked Jodi later on, when Christopher was out of earshot. I hadn't heard about it." Jodi smiled at him.

"Oh, he's been asking for a dog of his own, and I know we'll have to think about losing Scamp before too long. I don't think he'll make it through another winter."

The cabin, and the fact that he was born there, fascinated Christopher. He was full of questions. He knew about the birth process, having seen kittens, goats, pigs, and cows have their young, but he knew human babies were born in hospitals, and he wondered why he wasn't.

Jodi just hugged him and said, "We wanted you to be born in the most beautiful place we could think of, and this was it." She told him how lovely it was the morning he was born, and how the deer had come down to drink at the lake while they stood out on the porch, and how she and Brett had held him up to the sun and the mountains and showed him to God and all the angels and asked for a blessing on him. Christopher's blue eyes were wide with interest as he took all this information in. From then on, it was 'his' cabin, and 'his' lake. It was 'his' special place.

He was excited about sleeping in a top bunk for the first time. As soon as it was dark, he wanted to get into his sleeping bag, so Jodi lay down on the bottom bunk to be near him.

Brett sat out on the porch in the dark, just listening to the night sounds, and thinking about the birth of his son, and all the events that had happened since then. *Five years!* he thought. *I wonder what the next five will bring?*

Brett was feeling guilty. For the first time in a long time, he really didn't want to make love to Jodi. She was so thin, and so tired all the time. She bruised easily and had frequent nosebleeds. She was like a fragile flower, in danger of being crushed. The smell of her skin and hair used to remind him of honeysuckle and orange blossoms. But now, she didn't smell good the way she used to. Her skin gave off an acrid smell; Brett supposed it was all the chemicals she had in her body. And try as he might, he could not get used to her having no hair. These were subtle things, but they put him off, and he felt badly about it since he had been the one to make a fuss about keeping their love life going in spite of everything.

In fact, there had been so few opportunities for love making, over the past seven months with Jodi's treatments, surgeries, and time spent in hospital with infections that it was hardly worth bothering about at all.

Brett had passed his Journeyman's Electrician exam in June, and was released from the Apprenticeship Program. He received an offer to stay on with the company, along with a substantial pay raise. Jodi advised him to take it and stay put for now. What Brett really wanted to do was to go into business for himself. There was lots of work out there, and he knew how to go after it. But as he sat there in the dark, he realized Jodi was right. There was no point in adding any stress to the family at this time. *Get through this year,* he thought, *and then we'll see.*

After three days of fishing, hiking, swimming, and lazing around, they were ready to go back to the farm and plunge into all the work it demanded. Jodi returned to hospital for yet another round of chemo.

CHAPTER FORTY-FIVE

On Monday, in the third week of July, Brett was driving home to the farm having picked up Christopher at his parents' house. The afternoon was blistering hot. Heat waves shimmered on the pavement and Brett warned Christopher not to touch the metal sides of the truck, lest he get burned. His thoughts were on a cold beer and a cold shower. Then he'd think about getting some supper for himself and the boy. Jodi had left the day before, and wasn't due back for another week.

"Oh Christ!" Brett cursed, as he caught up to a line of vehicles stopped ahead of him. "What the hell is going on here?"

Christopher shot him a furtive glance. "You shouldn't swear, Dad. Mom doesn't like it." The little boy wiggled to the edge of his seat and looked down the line of cars. "It looks like road construction," he said matter-of-factly. "I can see a big bulldozer and some dump trucks up there."

Brett sighed with exasperation. "Oh yeah, *now* I remember reading in the Lakeside News that they were blasting out the cliffs near Cherry Creek and widening the road. I forgot it was today."

Christopher sat up, wide eyed. "They're blasting? With dynamite?"

"Yeah, I guess."

"Boy, I wish I could see that! Can we go up there, Dad?"

Brett grinned at his son and tousled his damp curls. His anger vanished, leaving only a frustrated tiredness. "No, I think not. Here comes a traffic person. She's talking to everyone, probably explaining about the delay."

Brett watched with growing interest as the flag-person came down the line, stopping to chat with the drivers. As she approached the truck, Brett felt his heartbeat quicken and was aware that his hands gripping the steering wheel were perspiring. *Jeez! What a sight for a tired body! She was a knockout!*

The girl walked up to the open window with a jaunty stride. A wide smile showed strong, white teeth. A red sweatband held back a wild tangle of curly, dark hair framing a pretty face with lively dark, brown eyes. As she stopped beside him, Brett's gaze was eye-level with her ample bosom that was barely contained in a skimpy, blue -denim tank top. Over this she wore an orange traffic safety vest. Below her cut-off jeans, her long, tanned, muscular legs disappeared into men's work socks and scuffed leather boots.

As Brett's eyes met the stranger's, sparks practically flew between them, and it wasn't all due to the temperature outside! She was as delighted as he was, to happen upon a gorgeous hunk on what had been her first long, hot, tiring day with this particular crew on this section of road construction.

"Hello." she smiled, leaning over to look into the truck. "Sorry for the delay. They're just about ready to blast up ahead, and then it'll take about fifteen minutes to clear the rocks off the road so you can get by."

"That's okay," Brett grinned. It had just become very interesting, waiting around.

The girl moved on to the three cars that had pulled into the lineup and then she came back, stopping conveniently beside Brett to chat.

"Do you live around here?" she asked.

Brett answered with one of his fabulous smiles, "Yes, we have a little farm just up the road a few miles."

Christopher interrupted, "Dad, can I get out to watch? He looked at Brett hopefully.

"Sure, I guess you can. Come on out this side". The little boy climbed over the electrical junk on the seat. Brett lifted him out and stood him up on the hood of the truck. He said to the girl standing nearby. "Will we be able to see anything, do you think?"

She moved closer. "You might see a dust cloud, and you'll hear it for sure."

"All right"! Christopher clapped his hands together, then shaded his eyes from the glare of the hot sun with both small hands. He stared up the road, trying to see what was going on.

The girl looked at Christopher, then at Brett. "Cute kid," she said, "Sure looks like you. Is he yours?"

Brett did not miss the compliment, or the way her eyes flicked over his body with undisguised interest.

"Yeah, he's mine." he grinned. Despite the heat, Brett felt a shiver go down his spine. His skin began to tingle across his belly, his groin, and down his legs.

The girl moved away a few paces and spoke into the two-way radio she held in her hand. To Christopher she said, "It's ready to go. You watch that cliff up there, and you'll see it fly apart."

In a few seconds, there was a tremendous 'BOOM'! Rocks, dirt, and small trees catapulted into the air, then fell with a muffled sigh into a pile of rubble that was immediately attacked by the bulldozer, loaders, and dump trucks.

Brett made small talk with the girl while they waited. He found out her name was Ursula; that she was from Peace River, Alberta, and that she was a student at Athabasca University. She worked for construction camps all over B.C. and Alberta in the summers to pay for her studies in Geology.

Brett asked her, almost shyly, "What do you do for fun and excitement when you're not working?"

"Well," she answered, "I just got here on the weekend, so I don't know my way around yet. The crew usually goes for beer on Friday nights, and we party in the motel or we go out and see what the nightlife in the town is like."

Brett nodded. She was starting to move away, back up to the blast site. Without thinking, he blurted out, "Ursula...would you...I mean...." he looked down at his feet, embarrassed, then looked up into those deep brown eyes. "Could I show you around? Maybe take you for a drive, or something?"

She walked back and stood squarely in front of him, staring intently into his face; then with a toss of her curly head and a mischievous grin which lit up her whole face, she replied, "Sure, I'd like that. Tomorrow night? Around seven? Siesta Motel, number nine. See ya!"

Brett smiled and nodded. "Sure. Great! Guess I'll see you here on the road tomorrow too!"

"Yep! I'll be here, but I won't be stopping you. We'll be open to one-lane traffic tomorrow. I just have to hold the silly sign up to tell you to go slow." She rolled her pretty eyes heavenward. "It's boring, but it's good money. I gotta go. See you tomorrow." She took a step back and turned away.

It seemed to Brett that her trim buttocks and shapely legs were winking at him as she walked up the line of parked cars. He watched, intently, until she had disappeared, then with a sigh he lifted Christopher down from the truck and set him on the seat where he scrambled over to his own side. The child was talking excitedly about all the big machinery that they were going to see working at close range up ahead, but Brett wasn't listening. His thoughts were on Ursula. He knew what he was getting into, and he was scared, yet strangely exhilarated. He had no intention of backing out now.

The next morning, when Brett dropped Christopher off at Carmen's house he said, "Mom, I'm going to play ball after work with some of the guys, and we'll probably go out for a few drinks afterward. We'll be out late, so could I leave Christopher here for the night?"

"Sure" said Carmen. "You know we love having our grandson stay with us, and I'm happy to see you go out for a change. Have fun!"

At exactly seven p.m. Brett was knocking on the door of #9 at the Siesta Motel on Water Street. Ursula opened the door, looking lovely and fresh, and very feminine in a short, pale yellow dress with a full-length zipper down the front. Her thick dark hair was freshly washed and still damp. Her long, tanned legs were bare, and on her feet she wore white sandals.

"Hi!" Ursula smiled. "I don't know about you, but a long, hot day standing on the road has sure given me a thirst. Could we go somewhere for a beer?"

Brett was a little surprised. He had envisioned a nice, quiet drive along the lakeshore, but he smiled back and said, "Sure, whatever." He wasn't in the habit of going out to drinking establishments. Jodi didn't drink, except for the occasional glass of wine, and they seldom went anyplace where liquor was served. However, every week in their local paper, there were ads for 'Tiny's Tomb', a nightclub located in the basement of a warehouse downtown. Brett decided he would take her there. It should be fairly quiet during the week, and there might be some entertainment.

When Brett and Ursula arrived, they found there was only live entertainment on the weekends, but the jukebox was in constant use by the small crowd there and several couples were out on the dance floor.

As soon as they got their drinks, Ursula downed half of hers in one go, and grabbed Brett's hand. "Let's dance!" she said. It was intoxicating feeling Ursula's warm, lively body against his. Dancing close in the semi-dark sent shivers up and down Brett's spine. He was somewhat surprised at Ursula's capacity for beer. His head whirled as he tried to keep up to her, both at the table and on the dance floor.

In a couple of hours, the place got pretty noisy and crowded. Brett was hot and dizzy, and the smoke in the air was making his nose itch. He put his lips close to Ursula's ear and suggested, "What do you say we get out of here, and go for a walk on the beach to cool off?"

She nodded agreement, emptied her glass, and said, "Let's go."

Brett picked up a six-pack as he paid the bill, and grasping Ursula's hand, they headed rather unsteadily to the car. He drove to a beach a few miles out of town, and parked the car. Getting out, he kicked off his sneakers and socks and threw them into the back seat. As Ursula slid over to get out his side too, Brett picked her up and set her up on the front fender of the Pontiac. "What are you doing?" she giggled.

He took first one foot and then the other in his hands, removing her sandals gently. He tossed them into the back seat after his own shoes. Then, he ran both hands up her bare legs, letting his fingers rest lightly on her warm thighs as he leaned forward to kiss her. Ursula was eager to participate; his touch on her legs kindled a fire that had been smouldering for hours. As he kissed her, she opened her legs and wrapped them around his hips, holding him tight. All his instincts and desires were focused on taking her right there, right then, but she put her hands on his chest, holding him away.

"Wait," she laughed, tossing back her dark curls. "I can't do this right now. I have to go pee."

Brett sighed in exasperation, thinking, *why in hell didn't she go at the bar?* He released his hold on her. Ursula slid off the car and disappeared behind some scanty willow bushes. Brett got a beer out of the carton, popped the cap, and took a sip as he leaned on the car. He knew he should go home now, before things got out of control. It was hard to think clearly, but he knew he didn't want to leave. Ursula re-appeared beside him, and he took her hand. "Let's go for a walk," he suggested.

The sand felt cold on their bare feet, bringing them to their senses a little bit, and the water felt even icier as it lapped at their toes. Brett hadn't felt so happy or relaxed for a long time. All his senses felt alive! He draped an arm over Ursula's shoulder, and she walked hip to hip with him, her arm around his waist. They talked; they sang bits of songs; they laughed a lot, sharing the beer as they tried to dodge the gentle waves that rolled in.

By the time Brett drove her back to the motel, he had resolved to just drop Ursula off and go on home. However, when he stopped the car, she immediately put both hands on his face and pulled him down to kiss him long and passionately. She whispered to him, "You are such a sweet guy. I *really* like you, and I *really* want to make love with you."

All Brett's resolve melted then as he buried his face in her luxuriant hair, kissing her neck, and opening the zipper on her dress to kiss the tops of her breasts. Ursula broke away, reached behind the seat for another beer; then, taking his hand, she said, "C'mon."

Obediently, he followed, stripping off his T-shirt as soon as they got in the door. Brett reached for her, slid that zipper all the way down, and Ursula stepped neatly out of the skimpy yellow dress. They fell on the bed together, rolling over and over; wrestling, laughing, kissing, and touching each other everywhere. She was like a slinky cat, arching her back and clawing at him, biting him on the shoulders and neck. She pretended to crawl away from him, and he dragged her back by the ankles, pinning her down with one arm, while he kissed her belly, moved on up to her breasts, then her tantalizing mouth.

Brett surprised himself by having the presence of mind to ask if she needed protection before they went all the way. Ursula told him not to worry; she was on the pill. Brett insisted that she show him. He definitely did not want to father a child with this wildcat! Ursula got up reluctantly and brought the little plastic disk to him. A week's worth of pills were missing. There was nothing left then, but to carry out what they both wanted so badly. They came together easily, and afterwards, Ursula held Brett tight, whispering that he did everything right, and that he could come to her bed anytime.

As they lay, drowsy and spent after their wild passion had died, Ursula's curiosity about Brett grew stronger. She had slept with married men before, and usually they unloaded all their marital problems on her in the bar, or long before they got to this stage. This guy hadn't said a word about his private life. He seemed like such a nice young man, and he was *so* good looking. She wondered what kind of problem he had to cause him to look for female company outside his marriage. She decided to find out. She took his hand, and rubbed a finger lightly over his gold wedding band.

"So," she said, looking at him with her soft, brown eyes, "How long have you been married?" Brett returned her long look, and then disengaged her hand. He turned on his side, away from her. He didn't answer.

"I'm sorry," she said. Ursula kissed him on his shoulder. She had glimpsed the hurt in his eyes before he had looked away and turned over. "It's none of my business," she added.

He let out a big sigh. "It's okay. We just celebrated our fourth anniversary. Our son was born a year before we got married. I've never had anyone else. I've always loved Jodi."

Ursula couldn't believe her ears. *A guy this good looking had never slept around? Incredible!* She moved close, and put her arm around him gently. "Mmm... what's wrong then?"

Brett looked straight ahead, at the wall. "She's sick. Cancer. Had her leg amputated last Christmas. She's going through nine months of chemotherapy down in Vancouver."

Ursula was shocked. "Oh God! That's horrible! Does she get home sometimes?"

"Oh yeah, she's home between treatments, but she's struggling to walk with a new prosthesis. She hasn't got much energy, and her hair is gone of course. It used to be down to her bum. She's just not my beautiful Jodi anymore." Brett's voice faltered, and two tears rolled down his face. Ursula laid her cheek against his shoulder.

"I'm sorry," she whispered. "It must be really hard on all of you."

Brett sniffed. "Yeah, the past year has been a real nightmare." He was silent for a moment, and then he said softly, "I shouldn't be here. She's down there in hospital, coping with nausea, and pain, and boredom, and homesickness, and I'm just having a wonderful time drinking and going to bed with a gorgeous chick." Now that the deed was done, he was feeling remorseful and angry with himself. He slid off the bed, reaching for his clothes. "I've gotta get going. "It's late, and we've both got work in the morning."

"Brett, wait!" Ursula implored. She stood and put her arms around him, tight, preventing him from leaving. "Listen!" she said. "Sit down a minute."

He sat on the edge of the bed, and she sat beside him. She rubbed his shoulders lightly and stroked his hair.

"Please don't be so hard on yourself for this. You *needed* it! Just accept that, and go with it. I'm not going to make any long-term demands on you. I'm only here for the summer. I don't want to break up your marriage, or cause you any hurt. You're an attractive guy, and you're really nice, and well, I just want to have fun...I'd like to see you again. I like being with you."

Brett turned to her with sorrowful eyes. "But it's *wrong*, Ursula. I can't do this again."

"Sure you can. It's good for you! You need to get out and have a little fun; blow off steam...get rid of your frustrations." She added in a softer tone, "Jodi doesn't ever need to know about this. It doesn't have anything to do with loving her."

Brett held his head up with his hands, elbows resting on his knees. "I don't know. I'm just mixed up about things right now." He stood up to leave.

Ursula stood too. She hugged him, and raised her face for a parting kiss. Brett obliged.

"Thanks for a really fun night," she said with a seductive laugh. "See you around, okay?"

"Yeah, see you on the road tomorrow. Goodnight."

The feel of Ursula's naked, luscious body stayed with Brett on the drive home and long after he was in bed. He felt so good - peaceful and content, even happy, yet so guilty. He moaned to himself, "Oh God! Why does it have to be wrong? Please don't let it be wrong!" Then he drifted off to sleep.

CHAPTER FORTY-SIX

Brett was making supper for himself and Christopher the next night, when a strange truck drove into the yard. He had seen and talked to Ursula briefly on the road twice already today, so he was surprised to see her emerge from the vehicle. She was alone. He met her on the porch with a quick kiss and a hug.

"Well, hi," he smiled. "This is a surprise! What's up?"

"I left my sandals in your car last night" she grinned, "and besides, I miss you already. I hope you don't mind me coming over."

"No, not at all. How did you know where I live?"

"Oh, I just asked around. Everyone knows you."

"Hmm....I see... have you had supper?"

"I had a snack at the motel, but I can always eat. What are you making? Smells good."

"Just burgers; nothing fancy. Come on in. Want a beer?"

"Sure! That's a hot and dusty job I have - gives me a terrible thirst."

After supper, Brett showed her the animals and the orchard with the apples ripening on the trees. He was careful not to touch her with Christopher around, but he longed to lay her down on the soft scented earth, and make love to her under the fruit trees.

Later, he left Ursula in the kitchen making tea, while he took Christopher up to bed. The little boy had some pressing questions. "Dad, why is she here? Is she your girlfriend?"

Brett tried to word his answer carefully. "No," he lied; she's just a friend. She doesn't know anybody around here, and she's lonely. So, is it okay with you if she comes over for a visit once in a while?"

"Yeah, I guess so...but I don't like her." Brett could detect a little pout in the dark.

"Why not?" he asked gently.

"Cause she doesn't talk to me. She could tell me all about those neat trucks and stuff she works with, but she only wants to talk to you."

Brett laughed. The kid was sensitive and observant all right. What he said was true; Ursula didn't have much patience or liking for children, even one as cute as Christopher.

"Don't worry about her," Brett reassured him. She won't be here very often."

"When's Mommy coming home? Christopher asked. "I sure miss her."

"Me too. She'll be home next week. Don't forget to say a prayer for her, okay? Night-night." He kissed the soft little cheek and was rewarded with a tight hug around his neck.

"Night Daddy!"

Jeez! He'd have to be very careful about having Ursula come around too often. He'd have to talk to her about it, and also about the bruises and bite marks on his neck and shoulders. If they were going to carry on this affair, it had to be very discreet. He just couldn't take a chance on his parents, Jodi, or Christopher knowing what was going on.

As they sipped their tea out on the veranda, Brett explained his predicament and asked for Ursula's cooperation.

"I'm sorry," she said. "I shouldn't have come."

Brett reached out and took her hand, pulling her over to him and onto his knee.

"I'm glad you did; I wanted to see you again too." He murmured against her throat, "Just don't make a habit of it." They kissed then, arousing each other with their intimate touches and nibbles.

Brett stood up and set her on her feet; then took her by the hand and led her through the darkened quiet house to the guest bedroom off the living room. There was no way he would take her up to his and Jodi's bed. It wouldn't seem right, and besides, Christopher just might come and crawl in with them.

Their lovemaking was passionate and wild, as before, and Brett knew he couldn't resist her. When it was over, despite his better judgment, he knew he would do this again and again, as long as Ursula was willing and available.

And so began a period where Brett led a double life of subterfuge, excuses, and lies. When Jodi came home the first part of August, Brett told her he was working on a big construction project and that he would have to work late a couple of nights a week.
At these times, Brett parked his truck several blocks away and went to Ursula's motel room. They would shower together and share pizza, chicken, or Chinese food from the take-out restaurant across the street. Then they would make love, watch TV, and make love again, before Brett would reluctantly leave to go home.
When Jodi left again, Brett was a little freer to meet with Ursula, but he still had to keep his guard up where Christopher was concerned.

    Once, the three of them went on a picnic, and another time they went riding. The lovers tried to be nonchalant with each other, but their eyes and their actions betrayed them. Brett wasn't quite careful enough. Christopher caught them kissing once, and he couldn't help noticing that their hands, arms, feet, and other body parts touched at times. Like the time Ursula was up the ladder, picking apples, and she came down frontwards right into Brett's arms while he was holding the ladder. Ursula had playfully ducked under

Brett's arms, but the little boy could see by their lively eyes and laughter that they were playing a game. He felt angry and left out.

The closeness between Ursula and his dad bothered Christopher, but he didn't know how to express his annoyance at having her come around. To make matters worse, Brett had asked him to keep Ursula's presence a secret. He had made it sound as if Ursula was 'their' special friend, and nobody should know about her, especially Mom and Grandma.

Brett said to Christopher, "Women are always jealous of a man having a lady friend, so let's not tell anyone about our friend, okay?" He felt like a traitor, swearing the little guy to secrecy, but he was desperate, and he had to take desperate measures.

It was a heavy burden for one so young to bear. One night, the three of them had gone out to a show, and Christopher had fallen asleep in the back seat on the way home. Ursula had been there for supper, and so had left her truck out at the farm. Christopher woke up, and watched in shocked silence as his daddy and Ursula kissed over and over again in the front seat. They made moaning noises that scared him, and their hands moved all over each other's bodies. He was very surprised to see the places they touched each other, because that year in Playschool, he had been taught to never let a stranger touch you between your legs, and if you were a girl, on your breasts.

After watching them necking and petting for a while, he was gratified to see them spring apart when he blurted out, "That's enough Dad. Let's go in."

Another time, when Ursula was there in the evening, Christopher had awakened from his sleep. He felt lonely and scared, so he padded silently down to his parents' room to crawl in with his daddy. Only Daddy wasn't there!

Clutching his old, brown teddy, the little boy sat at the top of the stairs, listening. A light was on in the living room, and he could here faint noises down there. Slowly, slowly, he slid down a stair at a time on his behind, making no sound. At the third stair from the bottom, he could peer around into the living room. The sight he witnessed shocked him to his marrow. There was his dad - naked - lying on top of Ursula! She had her legs wrapped around him, and they were kissing and moving up and down. Christopher had seen the farm animals mating, and he knew right away that his dad and Ursula were making babies. He watched, fascinated, but when they started making loud whimpering noises, he got scared, and skedaddled quickly up to bed. He didn't know what to make of the scene he had witnessed. It was all a mix-up with his mommy gone so often. He missed her so much! Christopher hugged his teddy tightly, and cried himself to sleep.

When Jodi came home the third week of August after Chemo B, she found Christopher angry and sullen with his father, and more clingy than ever to herself. Instead of being excited about going to the Early Childhood Services program (ECS), at school, he was refusing to go. He didn't want Brett to bath him, or read him stories, or tuck him in at night. He demanded and got Jodi's undivided attention. Jodi was worried. She had a feeling that something other than her absences and illness was bothering him, but when she questioned him or her husband, she got no answers.

Carmen and Jodi took Christopher to the school to meet his Kindergarten teacher, Miss Colleen Shergold. Colleen took Christopher by the hand and showed him all the interesting things in the room - the shelves of books, the big wooden blocks, the puzzles, the rest area, the water station with its funnels and waterwheel, the painting easels, and the cubicles where the kids could put their lunch boxes. Jodi could see by her son's expressive eyes that he was definitely interested, but he hung back shyly, not saying a word.

Then Colleen asked him if he'd like to paint a picture before he left. Christopher nodded, 'Yes.' Colleen put the little red plastic apron on him, gave him a cup of water, and put a fresh sheet of paper on the easel. The three ladies sat on the tiny chairs at the little tables talking quietly while Christopher painted.

Jodi was saying, "I know he's ready for ECS. He speaks very well, and has a lot of knowledge about many things. We've read to him since he was a baby, and he loves books. He can recognize a lot of words, and he can print his own name, and mine, and his dad's." She sighed in frustration as Carmen added, "There's nothing wrong with his mind; he's a very bright child."

Jodi continued, "I know he's fine physically too. He can ride his pony by himself and a little two-wheeler with training wheels. He builds amazing Lego creations, and his drawings are good too. I just don't know what's wrong. There's something eating at him."

"Let me talk to him," suggested Colleen. She went over to where Christopher was finishing up his painting. "Nice job!" she praised. "I see some very large trucks, and a bulldozer. I like their bright yellow colours. Can you tell me what is happening?"

Christopher put down his brush and regarded her evenly. Then, looking back at his picture, he began to tell her about it. "These cars parked here have to wait, because there's going to be a big 'splosion. The construction guys are blowing up the cliff here, so they can make the road wider." Pointing to two stick figures, he told her, "That's me and my dad, right there."

"I see," said Colleen, looking very interested. "And who is this person, up near the rocks?"

Christopher scowled, "Oh, that's Ursula. She's the flag lady. She tells you if you have to stop and when it's okay to go." Then surprisingly, he added, "She's going to get hit by all the flying rocks, when the dynamite goes off!"

"Oh no," Colleen said, looking horrified. "That's really awful!"

"No, that's *good!*" Christopher said, adamantly. "She's a *very* bad person!"

Colleen noticed right away how his little body had tensed up. "Why is she bad?" the teacher asked gently.

Christopher took off the apron before he answered. "I can't tell you," he said, not looking at her, "but she just is!"

"Would you like to take the picture home, Christopher?" Colleen asked. He nodded, still looking serious.

As they prepared to leave, Colleen whispered to Jodi to stay a minute; then she waved cheerfully to Christopher as Carmen took him back to the car. "See you next week." she called. "Thank-you for coming to visit me!"

Clutching his picture, Christopher waved goodbye too. Miss Shergold was really nice. *Maybe I will go to school,* he thought.

When they were out of earshot, Colleen turned to Jodi. "He seems to be very hostile about a person named 'Ursula'. Do you know her?"

Jodi shook her head. "No, it's a mystery to me."

"Maybe you can get him to tell you about the picture he painted." Colleen suggested. "She's the one holding the STOP sign."

"Okay," agreed Jodi. "Thanks a lot for seeing us. I hope we can convince him to come next week."

"So do I. Bye."

They put Christopher's painting up on the fridge at home, but apart from telling Jodi about the blast and the big trucks, he would say nothing more.

Jodi forgot about it until the next week when she was doing laundry the night before leaving again for Vancouver. She was absent-mindedly going through the pockets of jeans and shirts, removing bits of tissue, coins, and nails. She despaired of ever teaching her men to empty their pockets before tossing their clothes in the laundry basket. In a work shirt of Brett's, she removed a folded piece of paper from a front pocket. It read, 'Ursula Scherrer' followed by an address in Peace River, Alberta. Jodi sat on the bed, holding the scrap of paper in her hand. *Ursula,* she said to herself. *Where have I heard that name before?* Suddenly, it dawned on her. Christopher's picture! The flag-girl! *What was the connection? Why does Brett know her, and why is Christopher so angry with her?* It seemed like a puzzle to Jodi. *I wish Brett didn't have to work late tonight,* she sighed. *I miss him!*

Jodi would have been devastated if she could have seen her husband right now. Ursula was also leaving the next day, driving back to Alberta to resume her studies. She and Brett were saying goodbye in the motel room with a last desperate joining of their bodies, kisses that would live in their memories forever, and for him, sadness mixed with relief that the affair was over.

Jodi was in bed, but not asleep when Brett came in near midnight. He removed his clothes quietly, so as not to disturb her and eased under the covers slowly. Jodi stirred, turned over, and slipped an arm around his waist. "You're late," she said, sleepily.

"Yeah, I had a few beers with the guys. Sorry...how are you?"

"Lonesome...it seems I've hardly seen you this time around." Jodi's fingers moved in a small circle on his back, and then she let her hand slide down over his hip and thigh. Gently she cupped his knee, and then started back up on the inside of his leg. Brett's hand closed over hers and took it away.

"No!" he said emphatically. "Don't!" He moved away.

Jodi was surprised and hurt. She swallowed hard, fighting back tears. "What is it?" she asked. "You haven't touched me for months. What's wrong? I thought we were okay with this?"

Brett lay on his back, hating himself for what he'd done. Jodi deserved an answer, but he couldn't give her the true one. He exhaled audibly, and reached in the darkness for her hand.

"I don't know what's wrong...it's a lot of things. It's hot. I'm tired. It's so hectic working overtime and trying to get the fruit picked too. And I'm afraid...it seems every time we make love you end up in hospital for weeks at a time. I just think we should wait until your treatments are over. It's only another month. It's hard to believe the end is in sight. I just don't want to do anything to jeopardize you getting through this. I love you...you know that, don't you?"

Jodi didn't answer. Lately, she wasn't so sure about that.

Brett moved close to her again and put his arm around her, kissing her on the cheek. "I do, you know."

"Leave me alone," she mumbled, still puzzled and hurt. "You smell like beer."

CHAPTER FORTY-SEVEN

The Iphosphamide always gave Jodi a bad taste in her mouth as soon as it started though her I.V. line. She had tried various things to disguise the taste - gum, cinnamon candies, peppermints, lifesavers, fudgicles, popsicles, and revels. Today, she gagged on the lifesavers, and threw up immediately. It was almost predictable now.

This Labour Day Monday marked the fifty-third time she had endured chemo. After this week, only four more days to go! The end was near!

Jodi was given her follow-up procedure protocol - tests all day on October 4th; results and removal of broviac line on November 1st; check-up in February, and every three months for the first year.

Throughout her week in hospital, Jodi continued her Literature studies and helped out in the Children's Cluster. She watched movies with the kids, played Monopoly and Bingo, read to the little ones, and talked to the kids and their distraught parents about ways to cope with cancer. Jodi called it 'counselling each other' as there was always something to be learned from another patient.

A new patient had arrived; a sullen, angry and depressed fifteen year old named Jeff Livingstone. He had just come back from a summer on his grandpa's farm in Saskatchewan to find that he had cancer, and would have his leg amputated. Jeff would not be returning to school with his friends. He would be facing what Jodi had just gone through over the past year.

The doctors had asked Jodi to talk to Jeff and his family, and she did her best, telling them about her horses, the farm, her husband and son, and what it was like to be an amputee. Always she talked about faith, and encouraged the family to trust in God for all their needs. She said, "There are many angels working in this place. Some are real humans, and others are spiritual beings. Try to open yourself to them for healing help. Try not to be bitter and sad, but to find something good about each day - and take it one day at a time. Don't look too far ahead."

These people Jodi saw and shared so much with daily were almost like family to her. It was always hard to leave them in hospital while she went home, but home was always her focus and her goal. Her life and her loves revolved around her own husband and child, her animals, and her deep-rooted love of the land.

The apple harvest was in full swing when Jodi arrived home on the bus the next Saturday. She was already waiting at the depot when Brett arrived dishevelled and dirty in his grub clothes. He had been out in the orchard as soon as the dew was off the leaves, picking and packing the golden-red fruit. He apologized for the dirt and sweat as he hugged her, but to Jodi it was ambrosia - real earth smells - after the sterility of the hospital.

Brett thought that Jodi looked cute in her denim overalls and black leather 'John Lennon' cap. She was walking much better now on her prosthesis. She had been for many adjustments until Steffan had got it fitting right, and she had practiced with determination to walk with as small a limp as possible. She seemed bright and happy with some colour in her usually pale cheeks. There was re-newed hope in her eyes and fresh enthusiasm and confidence in her bearing, now that she knew the torture was almost over.

Carmen, Bruce, Bev, and Chad were all hard at work when Jodi came out to the orchard to help. She and Christopher set to work picking up the windfalls off the ground and putting them into sacks to be stored under piles of straw in the barn for the pigs and horses over the winter.

Jodi also helped with picking as much as her energy would allow, but mostly she was in charge of driving Blossom back and forth from the orchard to the yard, where the crates of apples were unloaded from the stone boat onto the waiting truck. Through Brett's old contacts at I.G.A. he was able to sell their entire crop to the grocery chain.

For two weeks, Jodi and Carmen worked with apples. They made apple pies by the dozens, and froze them; they made jars of applesauce, apple butter, and apple juice. They ate apples until they were sick of them. All the other garden produce had to be picked and processed too, so the women spent long days in the garden and in the kitchen, making pickles and blanching vegetables.

The purchase of a large freezer that summer had been a godsend. It cut down on the need for so much time- consuming canning, but still their days were busy and full. Jodi was indebted to all the family for their help, but without Carmen's help and support, Jodi could never have accomplished alone what they did together.

Christopher had reluctantly agreed to go to school, but he had made a big fuss on the first day, wanting his grandma to stay with him. He seemed happier now, but Jodi sensed there was still something bothering him.

She didn't have time to dwell on it much. Both she and Brett fell into bed exhausted every night, and were immediately asleep as their heads hit the pillows.

Jodi almost looked forward to going back to hospital at the end of September for her last chemo. She was going alone, but Brett and Christopher were going to come down when it was really over, celebrate with her, and bring her home.

The fall colours were beautiful as Jodi rode the bus to Castle River. She felt that she should feel excited that only one chemo treatment remained, but new fears raised ugly thoughts. *Is it really the end of a year of weeklong stays in the hospital, or will the cancer return?*

The last few days in hospital passed quickly with many people stopping in with good wishes and good-byes. On Friday, a bunch of nurses and doctors came in and sang 'For She's a Jolly Good Patient'. They presented Jodi with a beautiful cake; dark chocolate with whipped cream, all decorated with orange happy faces. Jodi was astounded to learn that they were thanking *her* for her volunteer help with the children, while suffering herself with so much adversity. Jodi felt gratitude and love for these people who had given so much of themselves to help her cope with cancer.

Jodi had her last chemo from ten to eleven on Saturday morning. Brett and Christopher arrived in the afternoon, and unfortunately, Jodi was quite sick - probably from the rich cake the day before and all the excitement. She didn't care; she was laughing and joking between bouts of throwing up. Brett had never seen her acting so bizarre, and Christopher was doubled up with laughter from her antics. His mom could be really funny! None of them knew where the sense of humour was coming from. It was so unlike Jodi, but it was contagious, and great fun. By making jokes about it, Jodi was able to lighten up an otherwise miserable situation.

That night in the Family Room, there was a chemo completion party for Jodi. Marnie, Carol, and Brett had put up thirty or forty balloons, and ordered in Chinese food and pizza. The weekend staff, parents and children, some of Jodi's roommates over the past nine months, the Delaney family, and Carol and Tony were all there. It was a very noisy and happy time. Christopher had the most fun, popping all of the balloons after the party.

Jodi was discharged at ten a.m. Sunday morning, October 2nd. She walked out of the hospital, holding Christopher by the hand, while Brett brought the Delaney's car around to pick her up. "I'm free!" she yelled, to no one and everyone. She was feeling good - so good she asked to be taken out for brunch.

Then came a quiet few days at Rosedale with Rob, Marnie, and the family. The weather was cold and rainy, and the house was quiet with Rob and the kids all at school, but Brett and Jodi were content to sit by the fire and read, or play games and watch TV with Christopher.

On Tuesday, Jodi had to return to hospital for blood work, CAT scan, bone-scan, echocardiogram, and MRI. Then it really was all over. She was free to go home, and it was a happy trio that arrived back in Harrison the next day.

Just in case they hadn't had enough partying, Carmen arranged a homecoming bash for Jodi that weekend. Since the weather was still good with clear sunny days and mild temperatures, they decided to have a BBQ and corn roast out in the yard.

Bales of straw were set in a circle around the fire-pit along with all the available lawn chairs. Long planks were laid between two sawhorses for tables, their roughness covered with clean, white bed-sheets.

For hours, a huge haunch of farm-raised pork had been tantalizing tastebuds with a delicious aroma as it slowly roasted on an iron grate above the fire. Bruce and Brett doused it with beer occasionally when the dripping fat caused the coals to flare up and threaten to burn it to a crisp.

Out of the freezer came apple pies and applesauce; potato and green salads were made from the produce of the garden, and the golden corn was shucked and ready for the cauldron.

Many friends and neighbours came to welcome Jodi home and to wish her health and happiness.

After the feast, Reverend Jim Forsythe stood up called for quiet. He took Jodi's hand and drew her into the ring of firelight.

"Everybody," he began, "I would like you to join me in a toast to this wonderful, courageous, young woman. Jodi Randall has endured nauseating chemotherapy sixty times; she's had more than one hundred injections of a stinging substance to boost her white cell count; she's had major surgery three times in a six month period, and she's come through two serious bacterial infections."

Only the crackling of the fire could be heard. There was silence from the listeners as the Rev continued, " She had to overcome her fear of hospitals; she's had to endure pain, and loneliness, and fear, and homesickness, and long separations from her husband and son."

Jim had everyone's attention, and he spoke like he was giving a sermon. "Through it all, she reached out to others; especially the children with cancer down at the hospital, and gave many hours of her time counselling them and their parents. She also had the determination to complete a college level course in English Literature. Jodi has had to re-learn to walk, and is still faced with the difficulty of learning to drive a gearshift and to ride her horse."

Jim paused for effect, as he picked up a glass and raised it toward Jodi. "She has grown in wisdom, and in faith, and obedience to God. Let us all continue to support her and her family in our thoughts and prayers that this battle will be victorious!"

There was a burst of applause and some 'Amen's' heard around the fire. Jim let go of Jodi's hand as Brett came up and wrapped his arms around her. His were not the only eyes that were wet with tears. Jodi turned in his arms and locked her hands around his neck, raising her face with closed eyes for a kiss. Brett had not kissed her like that for a long time. It was like a wedding kiss; long and full of promise and love; not the kind of deep, erotic kiss that would cause embarrassment to the watchers. The guests clapped and cheered as glasses were clinked with their neighbours and raised towards Jodi with shouts of 'Cheers!' 'All the best!' and 'Bravo!'.

CHAPTER FORTY-EIGHT

Later on in the evening, Jodi sat beside Christopher on a bale of straw and put her arm around his little shoulders, hugging him to her. "Are you happy now?" she asked, looking dreamily into the dying fire.

His handsome little face looked up at her adoringly. "I'm happy that you'll be home now, and I'm *especially* happy that that *damn* woman won't be coming back!" Christopher spoke so forcefully that Jodi drew back in surprise.

"What woman?" she asked quietly, ignoring the curse that had just come out of his mouth.

Christopher looked down at his black gumboots while his little legs drummed a tattoo on the straw bale. "That Ursula. Dad said she was *our* special friend, but she wasn't *my* friend, only his."

Jodi felt her heart thud in her chest. A hot flush swept over her face, followed by a shiver down her spine. She struggled to remain calm as the dreadful truth dawned on her.

The guests were starting to leave. Jodi got up from the bale to find her whole body shaking. She forced herself to walk with her friends out to their cars, bidding them goodnight, and thanking them for coming. Then she took Christopher by the hand and led him up to bed. She left Brett and his family putting the food away and tending to the fire.

Jodi was cold now; her limbs felt heavy and weak. She lay down beside Christopher and pulled a quilt over herself as he snuggled down under his covers. "Would you like to tell me about Ursula?" she asked. Jodi dreaded knowing, but she *had* to know. She *needed* to know the reason for Christopher's fears about her, and she *had* to confirm her own suspicions that her husband had cheated on her.

Christopher's small voice came out of the dark, questioning. "Is it all right to tell you, Mommy...now that she's gone? Daddy didn't want you to know about her so I kept it a secret."

Jodi felt her anger rising. *That bastard!* she thought. *Swearing a little kid to secrecy to cover up his own wrongdoing! Coward!* She forced herself to breath deeply before she answered. She was too angry right now for tears.

"You can tell me, Honey," she whispered. "I might get really mad and upset about it, but none of it is your fault. Just remember that. You won't be in any kind of trouble if you want to talk to me about it, okay?"

"Okay Mom." Christopher was quiet for a moment, thinking. Then, bit-by-bit, the story came out, of how he and Brett had met Ursula at the blast site that hot day in July when the road was being widened at Cherry Creek. He told how she came to the farm after that, and how the three of them went riding, and swimming, and out to the show once.

"But I never had any fun, Mom! They were always kissing and holding hands, and they hardly ever talked to me when I was with them. And then...one night...I got really scared. I came downstairs, and they were making babies on the couch."

Jodi covered her face with her hands, and curled up in a tight ball in an effort to stifle sobs of shock and rage that were threatening to erupt and spill over. She willed herself not to re-act violently for the sake of her child. He put his arms around her neck and squeezed. "Mommy, I was so worried that you wouldn't come back and that Ursula would be my mom, and I just didn't want that to happen."

Jodi hugged him back, kissing his cheek and running her hand over his hair and his back.

Jodi sighed. "You go to sleep now, and don't worry any more. I'll always be your mommy, nobody else. Night-night, and God Bless. I love you."

"Night Mommy, I love you too." Christopher said. Then as she rose to go, he asked, "Will you be very mad at Daddy for this?" Jodi could hear the concern in his voice, and she sat again on the edge of the bed.

"What Daddy did with Ursula was wrong," she said with a sigh, "and yes, I will be *very angry* with him. We'll just have to work it out."

She stood again, and left the room, closing the door quietly. That was just precisely what Jodi didn't want to do. She did not feel like 'working it out' tonight. But on the other hand, she could not go to her own bed and wait for Brett to come up, perhaps with the idea of carrying on where they had left off with that wonderful, loving kiss by the firelight. No, she had to confront him now.

With fear and dread making her whole body feel like something alien, Jodi came into the kitchen where her husband was still tidying up from the party. Everyone else had gone home. She sank into a kitchen chair, thankful for the heat of the old kitchen range, and watched Brett with a detached sort of disgust as he wiped the counters and put dirty dishes into the sink.

"That was a great party, eh?" Brett said as he flashed a smile over his shoulder. "It's *so* nice to have you home. Would you like some tea?" Jodi shook her head, 'no'. He chatted on, washing dishes, apparently misconstruing her quietness for tiredness. "That was a nice tribute Jim gave you. You sure deserve it. I'm proud of you Jo."

Brett turned from the sink then to look at her, and noticed how still, how pale, and how devastated she looked. He grabbed a towel and dried his hands quickly. He was immediately concerned.

"Jo!" he said. "Honey, what is it? You

look like you've just seen a ghost." He started towards her, hands outstretched.

Jodi held up a hand to stop him, locking her eyes with his, and spat out, "Don't *Honey* me! And don't *touch* me! I thought I knew you, but I guess I don't!" She sat back with her arms crossed, regarding him icily.

Brett leaned back against the kitchen counter, towel clutched in both hands, looking puzzled. "What's this all about? Why are you so mad?"

"It's about betrayal! It's about trust!" Jodi yelled.

Brett's face blanched and he moved slowly over to the opposite end of the kitchen table, where he sat, head in hands. He could not look at Jodi. A piece of wood collapsed with a sigh in the woodstove behind her, as the fire consumed it. The kitchen clock ticked off the seconds as the silence hung between them.

Then in a voice so soft she could hardly hear, Brett said, "I had a brief affair, but it's over. I'm sorry. I never wanted to hurt you."

"Oh yeah?" she sneered. "Then why were you screwing some dame from the road crew while I was toughing it out at the hospital? You think that doesn't hurt? How could you *possibly* think you could keep it a secret?"

"How did you find out?" he asked. There was pain in his eyes as he lowered his hands and faced her across the table.

Jodi sighed. "There were clues; pieces of a puzzle that didn't fit together, until tonight. I just innocently asked Christopher if he was happy now that I was home, and he told me what really made him happy was that Ursula was gone. Suddenly it just hit me, and I mean hit! I feel like I've just been run over by a truck!"

Fighting back tears, Jodi rose and threw another chunk of wood into the stove. Then, too agitated to sit again, she turned and faced him. "You bastard!" she shouted. "You double-crossing son-of-a-bitch! How could you do this to me...and to Christopher? Do you have *any* idea how nervous and upset he's been, thinking that I wasn't coming back, and that...that...dame would be his *mother*?"

Brett looked genuinely shocked. "He thought *that*? Where did he get that idea? I never, ever mentioned that there was anything lasting about it."

Jodi dropped her hands to her sides in exasperation; her fingers made fists that she ached to pound him with. She was shaking with rage. "Did you even *know* that your own little boy *saw* you humping her on the couch? Do you know how scared and confused he was?"

Brett blushed a deep shade of scarlet. Jodi could see that he hadn't known their union was being watched that night.

Brett stood up too, and banged his fists on the table. "Look!" he said, getting angry too. "So I made a mistake. I was lonely, and weak, and scared to death of losing you." He sat again, and in a quieter tone continued, "She was there, and she came on to me, and I was attracted to her, and I simply screwed her...that's all. No more, no less. That's all it was."

He met Jodi's angry blue-green eyes with his own deep pools of blue. "I've *always* made love to you. Do you understand the difference?" He looked at her pleadingly.

Jodi didn't answer. She folded her arms again, setting her jaw in a stubborn line to hold back the tears.

"I love you, and I love Christopher," Brett continued. "I'm really sorry I've caused you so much heartache. I'd like to make it up to you both if you'll let me." He held out his hands to her.

Jodi wasn't buying it. Not yet, anyway. Her feelings were too raw; her shock and dismay too fresh to want to make up so easily. Serious damage had been done and the repair job wasn't going to be easy, if it even could be fixed. Jodi shook her head and turned away as Brett rose and came towards her.

"Jo, please..."

"Don't *touch* me!" she hissed at him, stopping him in his tracks. "I want you to go away. I need to be alone for a while. I need time to think."

Brett dropped his hands, looking incredulous. "You want me to go away? Tonight? Now?"

"Yes," she said. "I can't stand being in the same house with you. I want you to leave - go to your mom and dad's for a while, or something. Just go!" She stared at him, grim-faced and pale.

He wanted so much to just take her in his arms and kiss away all the hurts and disillusionments, but he knew Jodi was deadly serious. He turned and went upstairs to pack his things.

Jodi sat again at the table, and let her arms cushion her head. She felt so tired; so sad. After all she'd been through, she could not believe that this was happening.

Only after Brett had closed the door quietly and she heard his truck pull out of the yard, did she let the tears come. And they came in volumes. Great racking sobs shook her body as she moaned and cried, and cursed for almost an hour. Then, exhausted, she stumbled up the stairs and climbed into their bed, alone.

CHAPTER FORTY-NINE

Bruce and Carmen had just gone to bed when they heard a truck pull up outside and the front door quietly open. The door was never locked. Brett was hoping that nobody would be up, and he cursed softly as the hall light came on and Bruce appeared in his bathrobe, followed by Carmen. Bev was still out with Chad somewhere.

"Hello, son," Bruce said. "What are *you* doing here? Is something wrong?" His eyes took in the packsack that Brett had set on the floor, and he watched with concern as Brett slowly hung up his coat, then kicked off his un-laced boots, and flung them into the closet.

Carmen came forward and took his arms, making him look at her. "Brett," she asked, worry lining her face, "What's wrong? What's happened?"

"Jodi kicked me out. Can I stay here for a while?" Brett's shoulders sagged, and he looked haggard.

Disbelief registered on Carmen's face as she said, "Well, of course, but what's going on? I thought you two were the happiest couple in the Kootenays tonight."

Brett moved away from his mother's embrace. "We should be," he said grimly, "but I messed it all up. It's all my fault."

To his dad he said, "Have you got anything to drink? I need something strong."

Bruce raised his eyebrows in surprise. "No, I don't think I have. I think we had enough beer tonight, already. How about some hot chocolate?" He put his arm around Brett's shoulders. "Come on, let's go in the kitchen and talk about this. Tell us what happened."

Bruce and Carmen were shocked and saddened as Brett haltingly and with great shame related the story of his involvement with Ursula. They could understand the reasons for the affair and found it hard to blame Brett, but they loved Jodi and Christopher too, and knew that their lives had been seriously damaged by their son's actions.

Carmen phoned Jodi in the morning to see how she was, and to say how sorry she was about the whole thing. Jodi said she was okay. She and Christopher were going riding, and then they were going to make a play dough dinosaur village. She didn't feel like going to church today, despite the Rev's glowing tribute to her last night. Christopher talked to his daddy briefly, but Jodi did not want to speak to him.

A large part of Jodi's pain was for Christopher, and the further trauma this separation would cause him. More than anything, she wanted their fragmented lives to come together in peace and harmony, and they had been so close to that. Why, oh why did Brett have to go and spoil it for all of them?

The rest of October went by, and still Jodi refused to have Brett come home. The poplar leaves dropped like golden pennies as the nights got colder and the winds of approaching winter forced the trees to give up their coverings of gold, red, and brown.

Jodi's days were busy. She began by milking the cow and feeding the horses, pigs, chickens, and goats. 'Chuck', Dolly's adopted beef calf from last year, was being fattened with grain for butchering in November. There were four nice big hogs almost ready for market too.

Jodi was managing everything herself. She declined politely any offers of help from Brett. Re-learning to drive the car was a tough challenge, but eventually she mastered the clutch with her heavy prosthesis, and was able to take Christopher to and from school twice a week. She spent a lot of time with her son; playing games, reading and doing crafts with him, and in return, he helped her with feeding the animals, cleaning pens, and carrying wood.

The physical work felt good after long months of inactivity. Jodi's health was good and she gained weight despite all the hard work.

She planned to go back to work at the Vet Clinic after Christmas. Christmas!

It was something Jodi didn't want to think about yet. She supposed they would have some kind of a family celebration for Christopher's sake, but she still felt hostile towards Brett.

As the days passed and Jodi coped better and better with the running of the farm, she felt she could live without Brett. The nights were lonely but Christopher often slept with her, so there was a comforting presence in the bed; someone dear to hold and cuddle.

Jodi had asked Dr. Higgins at the Vet Clinic to let her know when any stray dogs came in for adoption, and one afternoon he called.

"Hey, Jodi!" he said. "I think we've got a great dog for you. Can you come and see him?"

"Sure, Christopher has school tomorrow, so I'll drop in. What's it like?"

"Well, he's a young dog, maybe seven or eight months, and he's big. He's a Yellow Lab-Golden Retriever cross. He's gentle, and very smart. You'll like him, and your son will adore him." Dr. Higgins went on to tell her that a young couple that worked, and had no time for him owned the dog. He was left alone all day, and was starting to wander and follow the kids on the block to school, so they felt they should get rid of him. He'd be happy out on a farm.

"He sounds perfect for us. See you tomorrow. Thanks." Jodi said happily.

She didn't tell Christopher, until they stopped in to see the dog after school the next day. Christopher was used to Jodi stopping at the Clinic to visit with the people she used to work with.

When the big friendly, yellow dog was let out of his crate, he headed straight for Christopher. With tail wagging furiously, he licked the little boy's face with a huge, pink tongue. Then he sat, barked twice, and offered a paw to shake. Christopher grabbed it, and then threw his arms around the dog's neck, burying his face in the golden ruff. "Oh Mom!" he said, looking up at Jodi. "I wish *we* could have a dog like this! What's his name?"

Dr. Higgins and the staff were all standing around, smiling happily. Jodi gave the Vet the 'thumbs up' sign, and to Christopher she said, "Anything you want to call him. He's yours!"

From the moment the two of them jumped into the back seat together, the boy and dog were inseparable. Christopher named him 'Rowdy' and for the first time in a long time, Jodi didn't have to try to answer the question, 'When's Daddy coming home?'

The last hospital visit was fast approaching. Jodi had not heard any results after her last round of tests, so she assumed that 'no news is good news'. She was looking forward to having the broviac removed on November 1st. It was a constant nuisance, and still required flushing every other day. She would be glad to be rid of it.

Jodi booked her flight for Saturday, October 30th with a return on the 3rd of November. She stopped in at the Randall's house after dropping Christopher off at school to make arrangements for the care of the farm while she was away. She was surprised and somewhat flustered, when Brett opened the door. His truck must have been around the back - she hadn't seen it.

"Uh...hi...I thought you'd be at work," she stammered. She was shocked at his appearance. Brett was thin and unkempt looking. He looked like he hadn't shaved for days, and his usually silky blond hair was dark and greasy.

"Come on in," he offered, opening the door wide and standing back. "Dad's down at the office, and Mom is out somewhere. Want a coffee?"

"Okay," Jodi said, removing her coat and boots. "How've you been?"

"Not good," he shrugged, heading for the kitchen.

They didn't know what to say to each other as Brett made two cups of instant coffee, fixing Jodi's just the way she liked it with honey and cream. He slid it across the table to her.

"How's the new puppy working out?" he asked.

"Just great!" she smiled. Here was common ground they could talk about. Jodi told him all about the dog, and how much Christopher was enjoying him, and how responsible he was with Rowdy's care and feeding.

Then, that subject exhausted, Jodi told him, "You look terrible! Are you eating? Sleeping okay?"

Brett sniffed, and shrugged his shoulders. "I'm doing okay, I guess." His eyes looked longingly across the space between them. "I miss you."

Jodi nodded, sipping her coffee in silence. She felt sorry for him; felt her anger dissolving into pity for his rough appearance and sad demeanour. But still she held out against him. Somewhere in her inner being there was a knot of resistance that would not accept what he was trying to ask.

Brett screwed up his courage, took a deep breath, and plunged in. "So, what about us, Jo? Where do I stand with you? Are you going to stay mad forever and keep me dangling here like a puppet? I'm so damn nervous I don't know which way to jump."

He ran a hand through his hair, making it stand on end. Jodi almost laughed at his comical appearance. "We can't go on like this," he was saying. "I know from Mom and Christopher that you're doing a great job out there on your own, but it's the quiet season, and you know you can't run things all year round without help. You have to decide if you want to give up the farm, because if you want out of our marriage, I can't keep supporting it. I don't want to lose it, and I don't want to lose you, and everything we worked so hard for. I want to come home, and be a husband to you, and a father to Christopher. This has been a hell of a tough year for all of us. I want to put it all behind us and start fresh."

Jodi was moved by his speech. He must have been saving this up for a long time. Jodi couldn't look him in the eye, and she couldn't think of an answer. She fought back a fierce desire to cry.

The coffee cups were empty. Jodi pushed back her chair, taking them to the sink. "I have to go now," she said softly. "So, you'll come and look after things while I'm away in Vancouver"? She stood at the sink, still with her back to Brett.

"Yeah, I'll be there. Can I take you to the airport on Saturday?"

"No thanks, it's okay. I'll ride the bus. I've done it lots of times before. I'll leave the car at the I.G.A. parking lot. You can use the spare keys if you need it. I'll be back on the 3rd, usual time."

Brett walked with her to the door, and stood awkwardly as she put on her coat, toque, and boots.

"See you Saturday, then. I'll be out in the morning, before you go."

"Okay, thanks. Bye."

"Jodi!" Brett called, as she started down the three cement steps to the sidewalk. "Think about what I've said. It's up to you."

CHAPTER FIFTY

Brett arrived at the farm about an hour before Jodi had to leave. Again, he offered to drive her to the airport, or at least to the bus depot in town. Jodi refused politely, preferring to go alone, and they avoided each other for the time remaining.

Christopher was anxious to show his dad how good Rowdy was at fetching a ball or stick. He thought *his* dog was *way* smarter than Scamp, who'd never shown an interest in bringing anything back. They were outside, playing, when Jodi tossed her bag into the Pontiac and started the engine to warm it up.

Christopher came running over, and threw himself at Jodi. "Mommy, please, please promise you'll be back soon," he cried.

Jodi held him tight. "I promise. I'll be back in five days." She held up one hand, fingers spread out. "This many, okay? You have a good time 'trick-or-treating' tomorrow night. Daddy's going to take you to town for that. Your clown costume is hanging up in your closet." She hugged him again. "Don't eat too much candy. Bye... you and Dad have fun!"

Brett was standing there awkwardly. "Do I get a goodbye hug too?" he asked. Without waiting for an answer, he pulled Jodi into a quick embrace, kissing her on the cheek. "Good luck, and good riddance to that thing," he said, releasing her quickly, before she had time to protest.

Getting the broviac out was a simple procedure. In clinic, after Jodi and Marnie had been given the good news that all her tests had been normal, Jodi was given some kind of mind-altering drug through the line. She was fully conscious, but felt extremely giddy and vacuous. She had not one intelligent thought or feeling in her body as Dr. Wong placed a wad of gauze soaked in alcohol against the tube where it entered her skin above her left breast, and pulled it out gently. That was it! She was done; finished completely, and free to go until her first check-up in February.

As Jodi entered the terminal at Castle River on her way home, and headed for the bus stop outside, she was surprised to find Carmen waiting for her. They hugged, genuinely happy to see each other; and Jodi inquired as to how everything had gone in her absence. Then, she filled Carmen in on all the doings of the family in Vancouver; how she'd been wined and dined at fancy restaurants with Carol and Tony who now lived together in a luxurious penthouse overlooking the ocean, and about going swimming for the first time in over a year at an indoor pool with Lori, Lisa, Jake, and Marnie.
    It had snowed while Jodi was gone; a deep, soft, powdery snow that blanketed

the trees and surrounding hills like mounds of soft cotton. They drove for a while, and then Carmen revealed her reason for coming to get Jodi.

"I need to talk to you about Brett," she said, a worried frown creasing her brow. "Bruce and I have tried to talk to him about getting off his butt and doing something to get your lives back on track, but he's totally despondent." Carmen glanced at Jodi, and then quickly turned her eyes back to the challenging road. "I don't know how he's been out at the farm, but at our place he just sits in front of the TV night after night. He drinks a lot. Did you know?"

Jodi shook her head, and sighed. *That's probably why he wasn't at work that day I dropped in. He was hung-over.*

Carmen spoke again, her concern for them both showing in her serious mien.

"Brett says he tried to talk to you about coming home, but you wouldn't give him an answer. This can't go on forever, Jodi. It's tearing him apart. He tortures himself every day for what he did to you. He hardly eats enough to stay alive. He works himself to a frazzle, just trying to get tired enough to sleep. Then, he goes to the booze to help get rid of the pain."

Tears trickled down Jodi's face as she stared out the window at the wintry landscape flashing by. The words came out in a sob, haltingly.

"How can I ever trust him again? How do I know he won't do this again?" She turned and looked at Carmen. "Whatever my faults and my physical limitations were, I did *not* deserve to be treated like that! Not by him."

Carmen shrugged. "I know. It was unfair. But so was having cancer. You didn't deserve that either. And you learned to live with it." She smiled at Jodi; a warm, reassuring smile. "Remember that shy little girl that appeared on our doorstep with a baby on her back about five years ago?"

Jodi smiled through her tears. "Yeah. I was scared to death of you people then."

Carmen nodded. "Exactly. You were scared, but you reached out in faith and brought an end to the rift that was tearing our family apart. Do you remember that you said it was time for healing and forgiveness?"

Jodi sniffed, and wiped her nose. "Yeah, something like that."

"Well," Carmen said, "Try a little of your own advice again. Take a chance. If you don't give Brett an opportunity to try, you'll drive him away forever. He's still very attractive to women. It wouldn't take much for some other girl to latch on to him once they know he's available."

Jodi knew this was true and she didn't want to lose him again. Brett had made his wishes clear. It was up to her to make the next move.

She had been thinking about making amends over the past few days, realizing in her heart that she still loved her husband and wanted him back. Hearing about how sad and depressed Brett was, and with a possible drinking problem, Jodi felt the last of her resentment and bitterness dissolve. She was ready to negotiate.

"I'll talk to him," she promised Carmen. "I think there's a chance we can patch things up. Thanks for the sermon!"

That night, Jodi phoned Brett to thank him for looking after Christopher and the animals while she was gone. She still felt strange, talking to him, but she asked him to come for supper on Friday night. " I've sorted things out in my mind," she said, "and I'm ready to talk."

Brett came, bearing fresh- cut flowers from the Chinese grocer. He still looked thin, but his hair and clothes were neat and clean. He and Jodi were polite, yet distant with each other throughout the meal and afterwards as they did the dishes together. Then it was off to the living room to watch 'Bonanza'.

Christopher cuddled up to Brett on the couch. He seemed to have forgiven his father. Jodi considered sitting on Brett's other side, but instead, picked up the sleeping cat from the easy chair in the corner and slid into the space Samantha had occupied. She re-settled the cat on her chest.

"Ya know what, Dad?" Christopher said as the four horsemen galloped up the TV screen to the Bonanza theme.

"What?" Brett asked.

"Mom's in love with Little Joe."

Brett looked over at Jodi and flashed her a grin. "No kidding!" he laughed.

Jodi grinned back. "I am *not!* Little Joe *is* kind of cute, but I like his horse better. It's such a gorgeous pinto. I've always loved pintos, ever since I got Blossom."

Brett laughed again. It was good to hear laughter and see his face light up. *Little Joe may be cute,* Jodi thought, *but he looks like a turnip compared to you.* She found herself staring at the profile of Brett's handsome face. She had a fierce desire to go over and kiss him. *He's my Adonis, she* thought.

The little family watched Hoss, Adam, Little Joe and Ben Cartwright sort out a problem between neighbouring ranchers about water rights to the Ponderosa Ranch. It was a good show with lots of chasing around the country on beautiful, well-trained horses. Jodi loved to watch it, just for the horses.

When it was over, Christopher begged Brett to come up and read him a story and tuck him in. He was making the most of his father's visit. Brett raised his eyebrows at Jodi to ask if it was all right, as if he needed permission to put his own child to bed.

Jodi laughed. "Go ahead!" She was happy to see harmony restored between her 'boys'. Brett must have really worked at his relationship with Christopher while she was in Vancouver. *Now, she thought, if we can only find happiness with each other, everything will be all right.*

With an air of detachment, Jodi watched the news, which came on the TV next. *How should she approach the touchy subject of her relationship with Brett?* She was restless. She got up and switched off the TV.

Rowdy had gone upstairs with Christopher, but Jodi put Scamp out for a few minutes before she too went up to bed. She brushed her teeth, and took off her prosthesis. There was no sound or light coming out of Christopher's room. *Must be asleep,* she thought.

Jodi put on a pair of Brett's striped, flannelette pyjamas that he had got for Christmas one year from a well-meaning relative. Since he always slept naked, Jodi wore them herself in winter.

She opened her book and tried to read. It was no use. She couldn't concentrate. Her heart was doing 'flip-flops' and she was excited that Brett was in the house, even if he had dozed off. *What should I say to him?* she asked herself. Then, out loud, she said, "Mom, I need help!"

Jodi put down the book and picked up her Bible from the bedside table. She flipped it open at random. It opened at 1 Corinthians, Chapter 13. These words leapt out at her: *Love is patient and kind; it is not jealous or conceited, or proud. Love is not ill mannered, or selfish, or irritable; love does not keep a record of wrongs; love is not happy with evil, but is happy with the truth. Love never gives up, and its faith, hope and patience never fail. Love endures forever.*

Jodi closed her eyes, and breathed deeply. "Thanks, Mom." she whispered. As Jodi closed the Bible, she heard Brett go into the bathroom and in a few moments he appeared at the bedroom door.

Brett slouched against the doorjamb, his hair and clothes rumpled from sleep. He hung back, not wanting to make a wrong move; still afraid of Jodi and her anger. He looked lean and lanky; sultry and sexy, for all the world like a tawny-haired version of James Dean. Jodi felt her body responding to his male magnetism.

"Hi," he said with a shy grin. "Guess I fell asleep. Do you still want to talk, or should I go now?"

Jodi smiled and patted the space beside her on the bed. "You could stay," she said softly. "I want to read you something."

Brett came, tentatively at first, then with more confidence as Jodi continued to look at him in a more than friendly manner. As he curled up close beside her, she opened the Bible again. Slowly, and with great feeling, she re-read the beautiful passage out loud. Both had tears in their eyes when she closed the book and turned to him.

"Does this mean you forgive me?" Brett asked.

"Yes. 'Forgive us our trespasses, as we forgive those who trespass against us.'" Jodi quoted.

Brett's shoulders dropped as he sighed deeply, relieved of his burden. He laid his head on Jodi's shoulder, and she could feel his hot tears soaking into the soft flannelette. "I was so scared," he said. "I thought that when you wanted to talk to me, you were going to ask for a divorce."

Jodi wiped away his tears with her thumbs and raised his head to kiss him. "I could have died from the cancer, but no one dies of this; not you, not me. We're survivors."

Brett's gorgeous blue eyes were soft and misty from crying; Jodi's looked at him with intense joy. She ran her fingers through his hair lovingly. A dark fuzz covered her own head. Her hair was coming back in; her features returning with eyebrows and eyelashes.

Brett sat up and rubbed his lips lightly against her head. "Tickles," he laughed. It feels like the down on a duckling."

"An ugly duckling?" she smiled.

"Mmmm....maybe on the outside, but your inner beauty has always shown through". He quickly added, "You'll soon be beautiful again."

Brett's touch on her head was causing erotic shivers to run up and down Jodi's body. His hand moved down over her shoulder, her breasts, then moved the covers aside, and continued over her thigh. Jodi leaned into him, and sighed, "I want you. I want to make love with you."

She un-did the buttons on her pyjama top, and his eyes followed her fingers as she slid the garment off. He kissed the scar where the broviac had been and laid his head between her bare breasts. Jodi had always kept the broviac pinned to a T-shirt, so he'd had precious few opportunities to see or touch them over the past year. Brett welcomed each of his old friends with a kiss.

He kissed Jodi's forehead, her cheeks, and then her lips with tender, sensuous kisses. There was none of the wild passion he had shared with Ursula. This was fragile and beautiful, and Brett was thankful for the difference.

Jodi said dreamily, "Doesn't this feel like deja vu? On a beach? About six years ago? It feels like the first time with you; magical, mystical, and very, very, special."

"Yeah, kind of," Brett laughed. "Oh-oh... what if you get pregnant?"

"So what?" Jodi kissed him again. "We're married, aren't we? And we wanted another baby anyway."

"Yeah, let's just pick up where we left off a year ago, and carry on."

As Brett removed his jeans and shirt, and crawled under the blankets, taking her in his arms, Jodi mused, "That first time... I don't think we had a choice... there was some kind of an inner voice telling me that we belonged together. I've heard that voice lots of times now, and I've learned to listen to it and rely on it. I think I have a spirit guide or a guardian angel around me. Sometimes I think it's my mom, and at other times I feel it's some other kind of presence."

Jodi put her finger against Brett's lips to slow him down. He was fast losing interest in talking. "Brett...wait... just before you came in; I was led to that passage in the Bible. I had no idea what I was going to say to you, and now look at us. That particular scripture was just the perfect thing to bring us back together! I just want you to know, it wasn't me. There's something... an outside force working around and through us."

"I know...I've felt it too." Brett said. "I never told you this, but when you went up for your double surgery, I had a mystical experience too. Remember how down and depressed I was then? Well, something just lifted me up by the bootstraps and set me free from worry. I just knew you were going to be all right. I think God spoke to me that day. I think he was trying to get my attention, and I'm going to listen to Him a lot more now. He gave you back to me, *twice*. That's something I'll always be thankful for."

Jodi hugged him tight, tears of joy threatening to spill over. She whispered against his throat, "I get the feeling now that even though time changes us and takes a toll on our lives, we'll still be together for a lifetime. This house will be here for our children and our grandchildren. We're going to grow old together. As long as we keep on walking with the angels, we'll be all right."

"Till death do us part," Brett said, nuzzling her neck. "Isn't that what we promised?"

"Yes", Jodi answered with a kiss. "For richer, for poorer, in sickness and in health; now and forever. Right?"

"Right!"

Jodi and Brett knew now that enduring, unconditional love was possible. Good years and times of trouble would lie ahead, but they knew their love was strong enough to survive separation, hardship, and illness. Strong enough to last a lifetime.

THE END

ISBN 141203103-6